Praise for Kelly McCullough

# SPELLCRASH

"Simple and elegant . . . McCullough is the true demigod of Web magic. Brilliant!"                         —*Huntress Book Reviews*

"The book is filled with action and suspense. The world-building is awesome, the plot intense, and there is plenty of pathos and humor."                         —*Three Crow Press*

"Entertaining and rapid-fire."          —*San Francisco Book Review*

# MYTHOS

"A smooth, flowing tale that entices the imagination."
                              —*Huntress Book Reviews* (4½ stars)

# CODESPELL

"A hint of cyberpunk, a dollop of Greek mythology, and a sprinkle of techno-magic bake up into an airy genre mashup. Lots of fast-paced action and romantic angst up the ante as Ravirn faces down his formidable foes."                         —*Publishers Weekly*

"One long adrenaline rush, with a few small pauses for Ravirn to heal from his near-fatal brushes with the movers and shakers of the universe, all while trying to figure out how to survive the next inevitable encounter."                         —*SFRevu*

"Imaginative, fascinating, with a lot of adventure thrown in . . . Mr. McCullough has followed his first two books with a worthy sequel. *CodeSpell* will keep the reader on edge."
                                                            —*Fresh Fiction*

"This third book featuring hacker extraordinaire Ravirn is every bit [as much] of a fast-paced energetic page-turner as its predecessors. Ravirn continues to be a fascinating protagonist, and the chaotic twists of the plot carry the reader through to the end."
                                                            —*RT Book Reviews*

*continued . . .*

# CYBERMANCY

"McCullough has true world-building skills, a great sense of Greek mythology, and the eye of a thriller writer. The blend of technology and magic is absolutely amazing, and I'm surprised no one has thought to do it quite like this before." —Blogcritics.org

"This is the second book in McCullough's series that fuses hacking culture with ancient gods, and it's every bit as charming, clever, and readable as its predecessor." —*RT Book Reviews*

"It's smoothly readable, vivid, and fun . . . highly recommended." —MyShelf.com

"McCullough has the most remarkable writing talent I have ever read . . . Not satisfied to write a single genre or to use a subgenre already made, he has created a new template that others will build stories upon in later years. But know this: McCullough is the original and unparalleled." —*Huntress Book Reviews*

# WEBMAGE

"The most enjoyable science fantasy book I've read in the last four years . . . Its blending of magic and coding is inspired . . . *WebMage* has all the qualities I look for in a book—a wonderfully subdued sense of humor, nonstop action, and romantic relief. It's a wonderful debut novel."
    —Christopher Stasheff, author of *Saint Vidicon to the Rescue*

"Inventive, irreverent, and fast-paced, strong on both action and humor." —*The Green Man Review*

"[An] original and outstanding debut . . . McCullough handles his plot with unfailing invention, orchestrating a mixture of humor, philosophy, and programming insights that give new meaning to terms as commonplace as 'spell-checker' and [as] esoteric as 'programming in hex.'" —*Publishers Weekly* (starred review)

"A unique first novel, this has a charming, fresh combination of mythological, magical, and computer elements . . . that will enchant many types of readers." —*KLIATT*

*Ace Books by Kelly McCullough*

*The WebMage Series*

**WEBMAGE**
**CYBERMANCY**
**CODESPELL**
**MYTHOS**
**SPELLCRASH**

*The Fallen Blade Series*

**BROKEN BLADE**
**BARED BLADE**
**CROSSED BLADES**

# BARED BLADE

## Kelly McCullough

ACE BOOKS, NEW YORK

**THE BERKLEY PUBLISHING GROUP**
Published by the Penguin Group
**Penguin Group (USA) Inc.**
**375 Hudson Street, New York, New York 10014, USA**
Penguin Group (Canada), 90 Eglinton Avenue East, Suite 700, Toronto, Ontario M4P 2Y3, Canada
(a division of Pearson Penguin Canada Inc.) • Penguin Books Ltd., 80 Strand, London WC2R 0RL,
England • Penguin Group Ireland, 25 St. Stephen's Green, Dublin 2, Ireland (a division of Penguin
Books Ltd.) • Penguin Group (Australia), 250 Camberwell Road, Camberwell, Victoria 3124, Australia
(a division of Pearson Australia Group Pty. Ltd.) • Penguin Books India Pvt. Ltd., 11 Community
Centre, Panchsheel Park, New Delhi—110 017, India • Penguin Group (NZ), 67 Apollo Drive,
Rosedale, Auckland 0632, New Zealand (a division of Pearson New Zealand Ltd.) • Penguin Books
(South Africa) (Pty.) Ltd., 24 Sturdee Avenue, Rosebank, Johannesburg 2196, South Africa

Penguin Books Ltd., Registered Offices: 80 Strand, London WC2R 0RL, England

This is a work of fiction. Names, characters, places, and incidents either are the product of the author's
imagination or are used fictitiously, and any resemblance to actual persons, living or dead, business
establishments, events, or locales is entirely coincidental. The publisher does not have any control over
and does not assume any responsibility for author or third-party websites or their content.

BARED BLADE

An Ace Book / published by arrangement with the author

PUBLISHING HISTORY
Ace mass-market edition / July 2012

ISBN: 978-1-937007-67-6

ACE
Ace Books are published by The Berkley Publishing Group,
a division of Penguin Group (USA) Inc.,
375 Hudson Street, New York, New York 10014.
ACE and the "A" design are trademarks of Penguin Group (USA) Inc.

PRINTED IN THE UNITED STATES OF AMERICA

10   9   8   7   6   5   4   3   2

ALWAYS LEARNING                                                    PEARSON

For Laura,
the bright star at the center of my universe

# Acknowledgments

———◄•►———

First and foremost I want to thank Laura McCullough; Jack Byrne; Anne Sowards; my mapmaker, Matt Kuchta; Neil Gaiman for the loan of the dogs; cover artist John Jude Palencar; and cover designer Judith Lagerman.

I also owe many thanks to the active Wyrdsmiths: Lyda, Doug, Naomi, Eleanor, and Sean. My Web guru, Ben. Beta readers: Steph, Ben, Dave, Sari, Karl, Angie, Sean, Laura R., Matt, Mandy, Becky, April, Mike, Jason, Jonna, and Benjamin. My family: Carol, Paul and Jane, Lockwood and Darlene, Judy, Lee C., Kat, Jean, Lee P., and all the rest. Lorraine, because she's fabulous. My extended support structure: Bill and Nancy, Sara, James, Tom, Ann, Mike, Sandy, Mandy, and so many more. Also, a hearty woof for Cabal and Lola.

I'd also like to thank the many people at Penguin who do so much to make me look good: Kat Sherbo, Anne Sowards's fabulous assistant; production editor Michelle Kasper; assistant production editor Andromeda Macri; interior text designer Laura K. Corless; publicist Brady McReynolds, and my copy editor, Mary Pell.

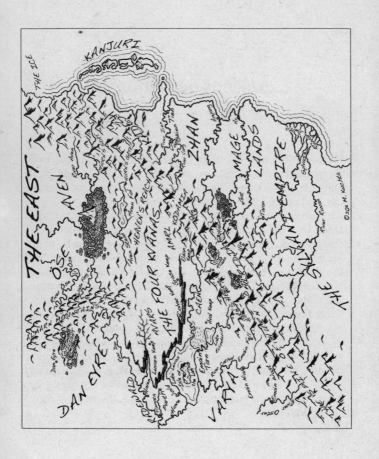

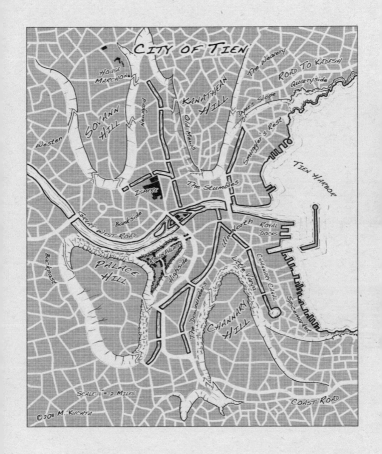

CITY OF TIEN

HOUSE MARCHON

SOVANN HILL

KANATHEAN HILL

The Weavery

ROAD TO KADESHI

Quarryside

Westen

Neugard

Old Mews

Dyer's Slope

Smuggler's Rest

TIEN HARBOR

Ismere

The Stumbles

Great West Road

Bankside

Ulm North

Royal Docks

Backpost

STONE PALACE

Highside

Little Vorda

Channary Canal

PALACE HILL

The Downunders

CHANNARY HILL

Splane Market

SCALE 1" = 2 MILES

©2011 M. KLICHTA

COAST ROAD

# 1

---

Every story has to start someplace, though it's rarely at the beginning. I came into this one when it came into my office. I had two sips of good Aveni whiskey left in my glass when the woman walked into the taproom at the Gryphon's Head. Women, really . . . or, well, it's complicated. I believed there were two of them at the time, so we'll go with that for now—two women walk into a tavern. My tavern.

The place I work out of is named after the skull the owner nailed up behind the bar. Jerik used to hunt monsters for a living. Poach monsters, really, but it's not the kind of poaching that gets you arrested, because the royal game wardens don't want the damned things around either. He retired when the one behind the bar nearly bit off his head. What the Gryphon lacks in elegance it more than makes up in character, every one of them dangerous and most of them wanted by the Crown. My silent partner and I fit right in, though no one ever sees him.

They call me Aral these days, or shadow jack. The one is my name, though not quite as it appears on all the warrants and wanted posters. The other is my new job. I've become a jack of the shadow trades, a fixer of problems that you'd rather not bring to the attention of the law.

Anyone who knew me in the old days would call it a huge step down. But only if they missed the place in the middle where my world shattered. I may be nowhere near the man I used to be, but I'm infinitely more than the wreck I was a year ago. Someday I might even figure out how to bridge that gulf and get back in touch with the old me. There are some pieces that I'd like to collect for future use.

In the meantime, I work out of the Gryphon because it's the kind of tavern that attracts people with shadowside problems. Well, that, and because my partner, Triss, likes the ambiance—it's always dark in the Gryphon and he lives in the shadows. Quite literally.

He's a Shade, a creature of living darkness and a legacy of the days before my fall. Triss is my partner, my friend, my familiar. Yeah, I was a sorcerer once upon a time. A sorcerer and what some would call an assassin, though I don't much like that word. I never killed anyone for money.

But back to the women. I was trying hard to make sure my second drink didn't turn into a third—I'd followed that road all the way to the bottom. The eighth hour bells had just rung when the first of the pair stepped into the Gryphon, briefly occluding the red gold light of the westering sun. The doors and windows were all open to help with the heat of high summer, which put me in a chair next to the empty hearth. It was the only windowless wall and it offered me a perch where I could keep an eye on front and back doors while staying as much in shadow as possible.

The first one came in fast and immediately stepped to one side, getting out of the light and putting her back to the wall while she waited for her eyes to adjust to the tavern's gloom. Add in the way the woman moved—smooth and quiet, balanced on the balls of her feet amidst the dirty straw on the floor—and I marked her down as some sort of trained killer. Though whether that meant hunter, mercenary, black jack, or something more exotic, I couldn't say without the closer study I proceeded to give her.

She was tall and broad shouldered, built like a farm girl or a soldier. Wide hipped and busty, she had thick muscle showing on her bare arms along with a number of interesting, if minor, scars. She had black hair and dark eyes, which was common enough in Tien, and golden brown skin almost as pale as mine, which wasn't.

Her clothes were foreign, too, tight green breeches and knee-high brown walking boots below, with a short sleeveless cotton tunic the color of rust above. Over that she wore a heavy leather vest that hung to midthigh—too warm for this weather and closer to armor than clothing, though not as close to armor as she would have liked, if I was any judge. Her stance wanted chain mail or possibly plate. She had a pair of short iron-tipped rods hanging where another might have carried daggers, an interesting choice.

The woman who followed her in a few moments later was short and lean with almost no breasts or hips to speak of and the whipcord muscles of a dancer or acrobat. Her outfit matched the larger woman's in style, though she wore blues and grays instead of greens and browns. She headed straight across the bar to a little table right in the center of the room, moving fast and without any of the hesitancy you'd expect of someone suddenly crossing from light into darkness. She even managed to avoid stumbling over a stray chair that had been left between tables, deftly stepping around it without actually appearing to see it.

When she got to the table, she took a seat facing back toward the front door and started idly tapping her foot. Between the dancer's build and the nervous energy she reminded me of my fellow assassin and onetime fiancée, Jax. A lot. That would have been enough to focus my attention even without the sudden pressure Triss exerted on my back as he slid up to peer at the two of them over my right shoulder. A surprise, since he's normally not that interested in strangers. Once she was in her chair, the larger woman headed across the bar to join her.

Like her companion, the little dancer type wore her black hair short—cut just above the collar on the sides and back with bangs in front. Her skin was darker than the taller woman's, though still light for Tien, and her eyes were a shockingly pale blue. Really, she looked nothing like Jax, and yet there was something about her bearing that made me think back to soft lips and whispered words of . . . I shook my head. Those days were gone. Focus on the now and the woman in front of me. From the way she kept rolling her shoulders and neck I didn't think she liked the heavy leather vest any more than the bigger woman did, though for reasons I guessed to be pretty much the opposite of her friend.

Or, should I say bodyguard? Because that's what I made them initially—some foreign noble and her minder. Which meant I could safely ignore them. And I tried, really I did. But Triss kept peering over my shoulder, and somehow I found I couldn't take my eyes off them either. Oh, I didn't make it obvious—the priests who raised me had taught me better than that. But I did watch them as close as I'd have watched one of my goddess-assigned targets back in the old days.

A lot of that was Triss, of course. What he cares about, I care about. He's all I've got left of the old me and these days he has to spend the vast majority of his time hiding in my shadow and pretending he doesn't exist. When the Emperor of Heaven murders your goddess, orders his head priest to burn your temple to the ground, and then declares your entire order anathema, it kind of puts a cramp in your social life.

It didn't help that the goddess Namara had made herself and her followers deeply unpopular with the world's secular authorities. Seeing to it that justice applies to kings as well as to commoners is not a recipe for making those kings love you. Quite the contrary. But that was my life once upon a time: a Blade of Namara, bringing the Unblinking Eye of Justice to those too powerful to find it in the courts.

Torture the innocent? Foment wars of aggression? Murder your way to the throne? Namara would send me or one of my fellows to have a few words with you. Usually "rest in peace." Occasionally "burn in hell." In either case, we arranged an immediate interview with the lords of judgment and a chance to ride the wheel of rebirth. For that, some lumped us in with paid assassins, mostly the sort of people with guilty consciences and high titles attached to their names—king, general, Son of Heaven. . . .

But those days were gone, destroyed with the temple, or buried with the goddess, or simply hiding in the shadows like me and Triss. Hiding or lost. It's hard for me to tell the difference between those two things these days. Once I was a Blade of Namara and I knew my purpose, believed in it absolutely.

Now? I'm not sure. I think I can be more than just a jack, or I hope so at least. But is it even possible to be a Blade without the goddess? To serve Justice when its avatar has left the scene? Those were the questions I'd been asking of late. But with Namara gone there was no one to answer me but me. And who could trust the word of a shadow jack? I sighed and once again tried to focus on the moment.

The Gryphon is full of dim corners and mysterious smells and even on summer days when the sunlight spilled in at doors and windows, it seemed to hold onto more of the night. That affinity for shadow allowed Triss considerable extra freedom of movement. He used it now as he studied the two women from his resting place on the wall behind me.

After the big woman stopped at the bar to place their orders, she'd taken a seat at a right angle to her fidgety companion, which meant that neither of them could see both doors. Overconfident or foolish—it was hard to tell the difference. They split a bottle of wine, with the taller one doing the opening and pouring while they waited for our host Jerik to send someone over with the specialty of the house—fried bits of anonymous meat and lightly bruised vegetables served on a bed of brown rice.

They weren't doing anything but eating and drinking in the most casual fashion but there was something about them that kept drawing my eye, and it wasn't just the way that the smaller one reminded me of Jax. There was something off about their body language and I couldn't figure out what. That was irritating enough, but I might have been able to drop it if Triss hadn't been equally fascinated.

The only obviously strange thing about them was how quiet they were. They spoke only rarely and then barely moved their lips, speaking so softly I hadn't been able to hear a word from where I sat despite the relative emptiness of the tavern when they arrived. They also moved with a sort of intermittent dance-like grace, though I hadn't yet figured out the pattern. For a while I'd thought they might be a couple, but they didn't have the right sort of interactions, so I went back to my original guess.

By the time they'd finished eating, the sun had well and truly gone to bed, which meant the Gryphon started to wake up as the night crowd rolled in. I ordered another Kyle's somewhere in there, just to give me a reason to stay in the bar and keep an eye on the women. I could feel Triss's disapproval, but I watered the whiskey heavily, so it hardly should have counted.

It wasn't long after sunset that the trouble started. Boquin, a young shadow lieutenant—about third in the hierarchy of the gang that claimed the Gryphon as part of its turf— swaggered in the door and almost immediately headed for the table with the two women.

"How much?" he demanded.

"For what?" replied the taller of the pair, speaking loudly enough for me to hear her for the first time.

Her voice was low and sweet, gentler than I'd have expected from her appearance, and carrying only the faintest trace of some foreign accent—Kvanas maybe, though I couldn't place it firmly. Her companion froze. It was the first time I'd seen the smaller woman hold still all evening.

"The two of you together in one of the rooms upstairs," replied Boquin. "I like the look of you. How much?"

I don't know whether he was serious or just messing with them, but it didn't really matter. Either way, things looked like they were escalating. The tall one dropped her hands down to rest on her fighting rods, while the short one slipped a hand inside her vest then went still again. Perilously so. That air of precisely focused danger *really* reminded me of Jax. What was going on with these women?

"Why don't you go away before you get hurt," said the tall one.

It was a challenge, and Boquin took it as such, flipping back his light jacket to expose the hilt of a short heavy sword. He didn't yet put his hand on the blade, but the implication was there.

Normally at that point, my impulse would have been to slip back even deeper into the shadows while I waited to see what happened next. I didn't have a stake here. Somebody else's problem, and all that. Not to mention that the action to come might well serve to reveal whatever it was about the women that kept hitting my sense of something off.

But I still hadn't so much as moved my chair back when Triss's voice whispered in my ear, "Help them."

Since he was incredibly careful about not breaking cover under anything but emergency circumstances, I'd already popped to my feet and crossed half the distance to the women's table before I had time for second thoughts or even first ones. By then, of course, it was too late. Boquin had spotted my move-in—his eye likely attracted by the suddenness of my actions.

He turned and gave me an appraising look. "These two with you, Jack?"

I nodded, but made no other move, and it hung there for a moment. I could almost hear Boquin weighing up my reputation against the possible loss of face from backing down. I didn't have a hard name, not as Aral the jack anyway—no major notches on my sword hilts, no history of playing the enforcer, but not a single lost fight or turn-tail moment either. My reputation was all about getting things done on the quiet and without costing large. It was close, I could see that from his eyes, but in the end he made the right choice.

He shrugged and let the jacket cover his sword. "Well, keep 'em on a shorter leash in the future."

I nodded again and snagged a nearby chair, sliding it over to the women's table. It put my back to the bar and to the door into the kitchens, which made my bones itch, but I didn't have a lot of choice.

"I don't recall inviting you to sit down," said the tall one, and again I wondered about her accent.

Her companion remained still and quiet, though she had removed her hand from her vest. The change in the character of her actions didn't fit with my original assessment of noble and bodyguard, but so far I hadn't come up with anything I liked better, and she wasn't giving me any more clues.

"I'm only planning on staying long enough to convince Boquin I wasn't just twisting his dick for the fun of it." I spoke as quietly as they had earlier because I didn't want Boquin or any of his friends to overhear me. "Name's Aral."

"Stel," the tall one said grudgingly after a long thoughtful pause, though she too spoke quietly. "And we didn't need your help with this little problem." Her companion ignored me, or pretended to.

"Actually, you did." There was something about the way she said that they didn't need help with *this* problem that made my business ears prick up, but I decided to come back to it in a bit. "Boquin's a lieutenant in the Cobble-runners, and several kinds of bad news."

"What's that, some Tienese gutter gang?" She shook her head. "We could have handled him."

"Physically, probably—you look like someone who knows how to use those Kanjurese fighting rods you're carrying. But you wouldn't have been able to do it without seriously injuring or killing him. That would have bought you a world of hurt when you tried to get out of the Gryphon. His Cobble-runner buddies would have been all over you before you got fifty feet."

"We can deal with gutter slime easily enough." There was a sneer in her voice now, like she'd taken my measure and found it wanting. "Even in numbers."

"Can you deal with a crossbow quarrel in the back of the neck? Because that's how they'd do it if they saw you take down Boquin too easily. They're mean bastards, not stupid. You wouldn't do your boss much good then."

"My boss?" She looked puzzled.

I glanced at the shorter woman for emphasis, wondering why she hadn't added anything to the conversation, but she continued to look past me as if barely aware of my presence.

"You think I'm working for Vala—" But whatever she was about to say, she never finished the sentence.

Instead she leaped to her feet, drawing the rods from her belt and spinning toward the door. In almost the same instant a big man in the uniform of a lieutenant of the Elite came striding in with his huge stone dog behind him. Preset spells wrapped them round in a network of multicolored light like dew-hung spider webs catching the reflections of a shattered rainbow—beautiful and deadly for those with the eyes to see it. Mage's eyes.

The shorter woman, Vala, kicked her chair over backward and somehow turned the motion into a back handspring. I twisted up and out of my chair with vague intentions of heading out through the kitchen, but even as I turned that way, a Crown Guardsman came in—one of perhaps a dozen entering through various doors and windows.

I had one of those brief moments of clarity then, the kind you sometimes get in the midst of incipient chaos. I realized that I could turn my lunge out of the chair into a drunken-seeming fall and hope that the Guard was there for someone else—Stel and Vala most likely, though Boquin or a score of other possible offenders of one degree or another offered other options. That seemed likely enough given the numbers, only a dozen guards and one Elite. If they'd come for me they'd have come much better armed.

If I played the drunk and they were here for someone else, there was an excellent chance I'd get lightly roughed up and then thrown back as a small fish. After all, the wanted posters with my name on them didn't yet come with a picture—a leftover gift from the goddess, if you will. Of course, if I was wrong, and they *were* here for me, they'd have my head nailed up over the traitor's gate by this time next week.

Though I have to admit Vala's resemblance to Jax weighed on my decision, it was Triss's "help them" that made the difference. I still didn't know why my best friend had taken such an interest in the women, but it was enough for me that he had. I reversed course then, moving away from the bar and back toward the lieutenant and his stone dog. I was lightly armed, daggers only, but there was no other possible choice. The Elite mage-officer, with his stone dog familiar and his network of powerful spells, was a greater threat than the rest of the soldiers combined.

He shrugged his right arm now, sending a golden loop of spell stuff sliding down off his shoulder into his hand— some sort of entrapment magic by the look of it and one of his presets. With a snap of his wrist he lashed the golden line at Stel. Good. Tying her up might keep him distracted long enough for me to get in close and—*blood of the goddess!*

Instead of being caught by the line, Stel dropped under the ensnaring spell while simultaneously lunging toward the Elite lieutenant in a fencer's extension with her right-hand rod. Far more startling was the way she brought her left-hand rod up and back, using it to snag the spell-line. Looping it quickly around the tip a half dozen times, she brought it down and around behind her back, jerking the lieutenant off balance and into her other rod. The iron tip caught him in the floating ribs with an audible crack of breaking bone.

His stone dog lunged forward then, and would probably have bitten her arm in half if a blast of raw magical force hadn't caught him squarely in the chest, spinning him half around. A second blast hit him in the shoulder and threw his thousand-plus-pound bulk into the wall just to the left of the door frame, scattering stone chips in his wake. The wall came apart in a cloud of shattered boards and plaster and I turned a quick eye toward the source of the blast. Vala.

She held a pair of short wooden wands, hilted like

fighting daggers and likewise positioned. Both glowed with an intense green light in my magesight and I wondered what had gone into their making. But I didn't let that distract me from my main goal—the lieutenant was still alive and that meant he was still a threat.

For about two more seconds. Stel let the spell-line she'd caught fall across her shoulders. Then she pivoted, using her own body as a sort of spool to take up the line and pull the lieutenant in closer before she crushed his throat with her right-hand rod. She was terrifyingly fast, completing the whole maneuver before the Elite had time to even begin the process of unweaving his spell. Somewhere outside the stone dog thrashed and gurgled as its own life boiled away in sympathy with its dying master's.

Suddenly, Stel dropped to the floor. I had an instant to wonder why before a beam of bright blue light passed through the space she'd just been occupying. About as thick around as my thigh, it came from the door behind her and punched a hole through the dust and debris from the broken wall. It likewise punched a hole through Boquin, the post he was leaning against, the guy across the table from him, an unknown drinker near the fireplace, and the fireplace itself.

A moment later, a second stone dog charged into the room through the wreckage left by the first, and a third came in through the front door. Panic ensued as everyone, including several of the Crown Guards tried to find someplace else to be. One particularly clever shadowsider took a moment to throw his shirt over the mage-light chandelier, plunging the already dimly lit room into near blackness. I left the second Elite by the back door to Vala and her friend and headed toward the one coming in through the front.

I went by way of rolling under the nearest empty table, picking up the gods-alone-know what kind of vermin from the filthy straw in the process. An odd choice perhaps, but one that came out of a lifetime of hiding what I am. In the dark and the chaos, the table provided plenty of cover as I called on Triss to cover me with his darkness. In a world where spells shine bright in magesight, there's no such thing as true invisibility, at least not from your fellow mages. Triss and his Shade cousins can, however, provide a very effective substitute.

Triss is both a part of my personal shadow and apart from it, a creature of elemental darkness. With the table and the madness around it hiding us from most eyes, he flowed up from the floor to encase me in a thin layer of condensed darkness like a second skin made of icy silk. But the sensation only lasted for a moment before he expanded outward into a cloud of enshrouding night.

It was a bit like being wreathed in thick smoke. No one could see me and I couldn't see anyone else. But that's less of a handicap than it might seem. The priests that raised me as a weapon for the hand of a goddess now dead, had trained me from earliest childhood to operate comfortably in complete darkness. Moreover, while I can't see in the conventional manner when I'm shrouded, I *can* borrow the senses of my familiar.

Triss possesses a sort of 360-degree unsight, focused much more on texture and differences in light and dark than on the shapes and colors that dominate human vision. It's a very different way of seeing, and it took me years of practice to be able to make sense of it at all, much less use it effectively.

As I slipped out from under the table, the unsight provided a sort of confused view of turbulent motion as Crown Guards tried to hold the exits against the mass outpouring of panicked shadowsiders. I narrowed my attention to the slice of the taproom near the front door, where I'd last seen the third stone dog. It wasn't hard to spot, not with the giant circle of completely empty space around it. People stayed away from it even in the dark and half mad with fear. Who could blame them?

Stone dogs are flat terrifying. Imagine one of those guardian statues that sits out in front of the bigger temples. You know the ones; size of a small horse, deep chest, broad shoulders, a head more like a lion than a dog. Now imagine that one of them's come to life and is sizing you up as its next meal. Figure in that it can swim through earth and stone like a fish through water, and then add in whatever protective magic its sorcerer-companion has wrapped around it, and . . . brrr. Just brrr.

This one was moving fast, charging toward Vala and Stel. I let it go past and headed back the way it had come, looking for its master. I didn't have a lot of choice. None of the weapons I had on me would do much more than irritate the stone dog, and I'm only a middling good spell caster at my best. If I revealed myself, it'd tear me to pieces before I cracked its protections. No, the only chance I had of removing the dog from the equation was to take down its master.

A captain of the Elite, he was just coming through the front door then. Drawing a long knife from the sheath at my belt, I moved toward him as quickly as I could manage without making any significant noise. In the dark tavern, I was effectively invisible, and he didn't know to watch out for me or my kind, not if they were there for Stel and Vala at any rate. But the Elite were very, very good and I would only get one free shot. I had to make it count. I was coming in from the front, because that was faster, and just about on top of him when the captain raised his right hand and pointed at the darkened chandelier, calling out a spell of illumination.

The room practically exploded with light as the old and faded magelights Jerik had bought secondhand suddenly kindled into eye-tearing brightness. The captain's gaze flicked across the darkness surrounding me, flicked back, froze. He knew I was there.

Somewhere behind me, Stel screamed.

# 2

---

Shade invisibility has its strengths and weaknesses. Biggest strength? In the dark you are essentially invisible. Biggest weakness? The blind spot. In a brightly lit space—like the Gryphon's taproom had just become—the Shade's dark shroud registers as a sort of large moving hole in your vision. A lacuna, or void.

Most people will barely register it if it goes away quickly enough or, if they do take notice, they will dismiss it as a symptom of too much drink or incipient headache. But for people who have been trained to look for Shades and their companion Blades, people like the Elite captain I was trying to kill, it's a clear sign that one of my kind is close at hand. In this case, too close.

The captain was good and he was fast, flicking a bundled coil of deep purple magic loose of his wrist and lashing out with it in the very instant he noticed me. But I was already inside his guard. I drove my knife up and in, under his ribs and into his heart, twisting as I pulled the blade free. Hot blood followed it, contrasting sharply with the cold ice that wrapped my spine when the captain's already dissipating spell lashed across my back.

Triss shrieked in pain and the lower half of my body effectively went away, as I lost all feeling below the waist and collapsed. I caught a boot in the ribs—someone tripping over me while bolting toward the momentarily unguarded door. I rolled away, hoping to get clear before they had time to think about what had just happened. That's when I noticed that I'd lost my shadow, or rather that it had returned to being no more than a dark outline on the floor.

I didn't know what the spell had done to Triss, only that he was still alive or I wouldn't be. As much as his absence scared me, I didn't have time to do anything about it if I wanted us both to survive the next few minutes. I was half-paralyzed, exposed and vulnerable and that was after taking only the dying aftereffects of the Elite's spell. What would the full treatment have done? I shuddered and pushed the thought aside. I needed to get under cover. I started dragging myself toward the closest refuge—the dark space under a nearby table—sweating ice water all the way.

Up close, the filthy straw on the floor was more noisome and foul than ever, lousy with centipedes and nipperkins. Not that this was the first time I'd ended up crawling around on the Gryphon's floor, just the first time I'd ever done it sober. I'd just about made it under the table, when the feeling started coming back in my lower body. I had to clench my jaws to keep from swearing aloud, because I didn't think I'd be able to quit if I got started. It felt like ten thousand tiny imps had decided to use me for target practice with their tiny bows, every one of them shooting fire-tipped arrows. If you've ever been jabbed with hot needles, you know the sensation. Yes, I have. No, I don't want to talk about it.

But with the pain came the ability to move, and as much as I just wanted to lie there until the hurting stopped, I had things to do, starting with checking on my familiar.

"Triss!" I hissed, forcing myself to hands and knees. "Are you all right?"

My shadow shifted beneath me until it looked as though it belonged to a small dragon—Triss's preferred form. The dragon nodded his head briefly, though he didn't speak, then collapsed back into my own outline a moment later. That really worried me—he's normally much more circumspect, and this was a case where words would have spoken more quietly—but he *had* nodded and I still couldn't afford to stop moving.

I had to find out what had happened to Vala and Stel, help them if they were among the living, and make my escape if they weren't. Grabbing the edge of a table, I pulled myself upright and scanned the room. Compared to the chaos of a few minutes before, the Gryphon seemed positively peaceful. Three dead Elite and two stone dogs lay on the filthy floor along with a dozen other mixed casualties. The Crown was going to be profoundly unhappy—it took years to make an Elite and their numbers were few.

Stel was down and out, though presumably not dead, judging by the light of healing magic Vala was applying to her fallen companion. Most everyone else on both sides of the conflict had fled. As I staggered toward the women I noticed an unspilled drink sitting at the edge of a table—a short glass filled with something clear and no doubt brutally alcoholic. Rice-white or one of its cousins.

I thought about it, I really did. I'm not sure if that makes it better or worse that I picked it up and lifted it to my lips, and at that moment I really didn't care. The effort of getting to my feet had left me shaking and sweating. I *needed* that drink.

It was harsh and warm, the cheapest stuff imaginable, and it went down like a shot of liquid silk—sleek and soft and oh-so-soothing. Not as effective as a hot cup of efik, or even a few of the fresh roasted beans that wonder brew came from, but I'd turned my back on the Blade's drug of choice long ago. Almost against my will, I thought about all the bottles sitting behind the bar, even half turned that way. But I knew what following the impulse would make me, and I forced myself to head for the women instead.

Vala was sitting cross-legged on the floor, facing away

from me, with Stel's head cradled in her lap. She was doing some sort of intricate spellwork, healing magic well beyond my meager training in that direction. The details of the spell were far less interesting than the fact that she was doing it without a familiar anywhere in sight. I'd been watching her and her companion rather closely all night, and I'd never seen even the hint of a familiar. Nor did I now. The obvious answer to that puzzle was that she'd partnered an air spirit like a qamasiin, or some other invisible creature, but I was beginning to suspect a very different solution.

I took another silent step closer just as Stel's eyes flickered open, meeting mine. Though Stel didn't move her lips or even twitch, I saw Vala go suddenly still, and I froze. She couldn't know I was there, and yet, she did. Moving carefully and deliberately, I opened my hands and extended them out to the sides, palms toward the two women to show that they were empty. If I was right, I was on very dangerous ground. If I was wrong, the worst that would happen is that I'd make myself look the fool.

"I'm not your enemy," I said quietly. "There's no need to start up the bloodletting again."

Though she kept looking in the other direction, Vala half turned toward me, lifting her right arm away from her body. Revealed in the gap between elbow and ribs was the tip of one of her battle wands. She was pointing it squarely at my chest with her hidden hand. Stel's eyes never left mine.

"Can you give me a good reason not to use this?" asked Vala, still looking away. Her voice sounded tight and clipped.

"I killed that third Elite, the captain. If I hadn't, your pairmate would be dead now, and so would you . . . Dyad."

Vala nodded. "So you know what I am."

"I do." Though I hadn't been sure until that moment.

"All the more reason to kill you." This time the voice came from Stel's lips.

But it was the same entity speaking, the Dyad. Two bodies, two brains, one creature. A single being with three distinct minds and personalities. Stel, Vala, the motes, and their

Meld, the master entity formed from their conjoined souls—together, a Dyad, and about as far away from the familiar partnership Triss and I had as you could get. On a personal level the thought of Dyads had always struck me as a little creepy, and I found myself wondering how I could have compared one of them to Jax. On the other hand, there were the fallen Elite to consider. I couldn't argue with their deadliness, and right at the moment, with Triss incommunicado, I almost envied their ability to read each other's thoughts.

"Aren't you going to bolt, or at least try to convince me not to kill you?" the Vala half of the Dyad asked after the silence had stretched out between us.

"No," I replied. "I don't need to. If you were going to make the attempt out of hand you'd already have attacked. Since you haven't . . ." I bowed my head lightly, indicating it was still her move.

The Dyad made a little growling noise in the back of both her throats, but nodded the Vala head. "Stel took a solid hit from one of the stone dogs. It broke a half dozen ribs and she's barely up to walking. Under the circumstances, I'd rather not start a fight with anyone who can kill an Elite. Not if I don't have to. You're still talking to me instead of running for the hills. That suggests that it was skill rather than luck that did in the Elite. Also, that you're interested in some sort of alliance. What's your proposal?"

"That is the question, isn't it?" I only wished I knew what the answer was—this was Triss's gambit, not mine, and he wasn't talking. "But it's one I think would better be discussed somewhere else, don't you? Somewhere safer."

It was mainly a play for time, but that didn't make it any less true. The Crown Guards had very sensibly scattered when their Elite officers fell, but they were good soldiers and would be back with reinforcements as soon as possible. I made a quick mental calculation of the round trip time from the Stumbles to the customs house at the docks, the nearest place likely to have an Elite or two on hand—over half an hour but not by much. If they wanted to come in force, we might get an hour and a half—the time it'd take those Elite to send a message to the palace and summon more troops—but no more than that.

"Did you have a place in mind?" asked Vala. "Is it close? I don't think Stel's up to a long trip." There was something different about the tone of the second question and its follow-up, something more normally human, and I suspected it came from Vala rather than her Meld.

"I'll do whatever I have to," Stel spoke firmly, but I could tell she was having trouble breathing.

"I've a fallback not far from here," I said. Several actually, which made the thought of exposing any one of them less worrisome. After the events of the previous spring had reignited my interest in life, I'd started to rebuild old habits of caution and contingency planning. "We should be safe there, for a while at least."

"Take me there," said Vala, speaking in the clipped tones of the Meld.

Before I could move to offer Stel a hand, the Dyad flowed to its feet. Using the two bodies in perfect cooperation, it made the difficult task of getting the injured woman upright look like a carefully choreographed bit of dance. I realized then what it was about the women's behavior earlier in the evening that had made it so hard to ignore them: the inhuman coordination.

Any time the two had interacted directly, handing a wine glass across the table say, they'd done so with none of the wasted movements or minor corrections that normal people made under similar circumstances. That told me that they'd never learned to pass for standard-issue human. And, that in turn, meant this pair was almost certainly operating beyond the range of their normal duties and training.

I hadn't had much direct interaction with the Dyads; none of the Blades had within my memory. Kodamia was a much better and more humanely run enterprise than any of the surrounding countries, which meant it mostly avoided the attention of my goddess. I *had* encountered a few of them over the years, mostly while working undercover in various of the courts of the east; Kadesh, the Kvanas, Zhan. . . .

The Dyads I'd seen under those circumstances—mostly spies, eavesmen in diplomatic drag—had appeared perfectly normal except when they deliberately chose to emphasize their alien nature. Vala and Stel had pretty clearly not gone to whatever spy school those others had. An interesting detail that. So was their comparative youth—not much more than twenty-five, either of them—which was a good decade younger than the other Dyads I'd met. I wondered what it meant, finding them so far from home.

"Come on," I said, nodding toward the back door. "We're less likely to be seen going out this way and I've a brief stop I need to make on the way."

"For what?" Vala asked suspiciously.

"My gear. I rent a room over the stable . . . or I did up till today." I started walking. Either they would trust me and follow along or not. Whichever happened, I needed to grab my stuff and get out of there before the guard returned in force. "The whole place is burned now. After this I'm not going to be able to come back here for quite a while, if ever. Not with three dead Elite and reports of a rogue Dyad heating the neighborhood up. Too many people saw me with you."

I'd been too busy staying alive and in one piece to think ahead, so that hadn't occurred to me until that very moment, but it was true and it actually hurt me a little to realize it now. The Gryphon's Head was the worst sort of dive and it lay in the heart of one of Tien's most miserable slums. None of which changed the fact that it had been my home for more than six years—longer than any place other than the temple of Namara itself. I was going to miss it.

I glanced around sadly as I ducked out the back door. In the earlier panicked stampede for the exits someone had knocked over one of the cheap oil lamps that normally lit the yard. It had landed in a filthy pile of used straw from the stable, and now the flames provided a bright if fitful light that made my shadow dance wildly on the wall behind me. I spared a surreptitious glance at the spectacle, hoping to see some visual evidence that Triss was back with me. I didn't get that, but I did get a brief reassuring squeeze on my shoulder, and it sure wasn't from Vala or Stel.

The Dyad was trailing along at a safe distance behind me. They had arranged themselves so that the Stel mote could lean heavily on her smaller counterpart. She'd put away her rods but now held one of Vala's battle wands in her right hand while Vala held the other in her left. Both had reversed the short wands so that they lay mostly concealed against their wrists, but as I turned toward the stables, Vala flipped hers around again, pointing it loosely in my direction.

"I don't think I like the idea of letting you out of our sight," she said.

·"Well, it's that or use that thing," I said over my shoulder as I kept walking. "My gear is in the hay loft and I'm going to go get it now."

"I could come with you. . . ."

"But Stel couldn't, not up the ladder. Besides, I don't want you to. There are certain protections I have to disarm and I don't want you watching." More importantly, I wanted to talk to Triss, and for that I needed privacy.

"But I don't know what you are!" This time the voice came out of both throats and the second wand slid around to point at me. "You killed an Elite and that's no mere jack's work. You're a mage at the least and much more than you seem. It makes you a serious potential threat."

"Or a potential ally. It's your choice which you want to make me. But if you're not going to try to kill me, *stay here.* I'll be right back."

Since no blast of magic followed me through the door of the stable, I had to assume they'd opted to continue our protoalliance. I dashed to the ladder and hurried up the rungs—time was getting ever more precious, and I had things to do.

"Triss?" I said as I got to the door to my little room.

"Here." In the darkness I couldn't see my shadow-companion, but something about the tone of his voice told me he'd reassumed dragon shape.

"What's the plan with the Dyad?" I asked.

"There isn't one." Triss sounded a little abashed.

I groaned. "Why am I not surprised? Did you at least know what they were when you asked me to help them?"

"No, only that they didn't move like anything human and that they were in trouble. They were foreign and alone in Tien, as we were when we came here after the death of the goddess. They needed help. What more did I need to know?"

I gently smacked my forehead against the door.

Triss said, "You have said that Namara is dead and you are a man without a people or purpose, no longer a true Blade. But also that you hope you can still do some good in this world. Here was an opportunity to do just that."

"Well, yes, but—"

"But nothing. You told me that was the path you wanted to walk going forward, *and* that I should help you stay on it. Consider this helping."

Somehow I was losing an argument with my own shadow. Again. "Later, you and I are going to have a long talk about exactly what helping me means."

"But there is no time now," said Triss, and rather smugly in my opinion.

"No there isn't, so if you'll just . . ." But I could already feel him flowing up my legs to encase me in a second skin of cool shadow.

A moment later, he released his will to me. Using the part of myself that was temporarily Triss, I touched the lock on the door and extended a tendril of shadow-stuff into the keyhole. From the outside the lock looked simple enough, the sort of crude iron mechanism you might expect to find in the stable of a run-down inn, but it was more than it seemed. Much more.

The inner workings were of Durkoth make, though not their best, nor even the best they sold to humans. I couldn't begin to afford the finest the Other smiths had to offer. What I could and had done was add spells devised by the priests of Namara to reinforce and enhance the Durkoth workings. It would have been far easier for an intruder to break down the thick oak door than to pick the lock.

Shaping and hardening the shadow-stuff into a key—the original, I had long since destroyed—I sent a pulse of magic through the lock and twisted. The door opened inward. The room beyond hardly seemed worth the effort, tiny and tucked into the wedge where the roof met the wall of the stable. It barely had space enough for the pallet and low table that were my only real furniture—a small trunk provided a rough bench as well as storage for my more precious possessions.

I closed and latched the door behind me before I reached for the shaded magelight fixed to its lintel. Closing up wasted time, but not much, and it was hard to push aside the cautious habits of a lifetime. With a touch I moved aside the shade, filling the room with an intense and expensive white light. A mosaic of threadbare rugs would prevent it shining through to the stable below and I'd chinked all the cracks in the walls long ago.

I released Triss then and he dropped to the floor, briefly providing me with a normal sort of shadow before shifting to dragon form and extending himself across the room. While I applied the tip of a knife to the socket holding the magelight, Triss cracked the spelled lock on my trunk and popped the lid. I was going to miss the trunk, but it was too bulky to move quickly.

I tipped the trunk up on end, dumping its contents across the rug, then grabbed my sword rig off the top of the resulting pile. The arrangement of leather straps and steel rings held two short straight swords in a matched set of hip-draw back-sheaths as well as several smaller sheaths for knives and other tools of the Blade's trade.

Fixing a heavyweight canvas pack to several of the rings was the work of a few moments, as was filling it. I tossed in the best of my clothing, a few durable items of food, a tucker bottle of Aveni whiskey—Kyle's fifteen—and finally the magelight, plunging the room into darkness once more. Put that on my back, add my much worn trick bag, and the pouch that held what little money I currently possessed and I was ready to go. Figure five minutes total, and back out to the ladder.

I didn't bother to lock the door behind me. It wouldn't have slowed down the sort of searchers I expected to come once some witness connected me with the Dyad. There was also the slim possibility that if no one had to deal with the lock, no one would look at it closely enough to see that it was more than it ought to be. There were clues there as to what I was for those with magesight and the training to see them, so that would be for the best.

I was almost disappointed to find the Dyad waiting for me in the courtyard. Since they didn't look very happy to see me, I guess that made us even. Vala in particular looked as though she'd bitten into a rotting pastry, as she stood there angrily tapping one toe. That they hadn't bolted while I was out of sight told me that whatever else the pair might be, they were pretty desperate. They *needed* me. And that, more than anything else, was why I was going to help them, because Triss was right. My goddess might be gone, but I was ever and always her Blade, and even if I didn't entirely know what that meant in her absence, part of it had to be helping those who really needed me.

"Where to?" grunted Stel.

"Follow me." I headed for the little gate that led from the courtyard out onto the streets.

"Not till you tell us more about yourself," said Vala.

"How about this then?" I asked without slowing down. "I'm leaving. And I'm leaving right now, because the fucking Elite and their Crown Guard minions are going to be crawling all over this place in something between ten minutes and half an hour. If you want to stay and meet them, that's your lookout. But if you want my help, you'll be coming with me. It's your choice."

Vala said something in a gutter Kodamian that I didn't understand, but it sounded rude. Then they fell in behind me.

"We're not used to being treated so high-handedly," said Stel.

I didn't answer and I didn't stop moving. I've never held any sort of noble in all that high of esteem, and I wasn't about to make an exception for Dyads just because they did a better job than most of a bad lot.

In the ruling houses of Kodamia the mage gift and familiar gift ran in different bloodlines, and a mage with no familiar was no mage at all. The lack of proper mages to defend them could easily have led to the ruination of the city-state.

Instead it had become one of Kodamia's greatest assets. As it turned out, it wasn't having a familiar that was the important thing, it was having a *familiar bond*, a pairmate of some sort who could act as a lens to focus your magic. So the children of Kodamia's mage-gift-bearing sorcerer caste became the bond-companions of the children of the warrior caste who carried the familiar gift.

Because both halves of the pairing were human, the bonding was the tightest of any mage/familiar coupling in the whole of our world. Too tight by my standards. The two literally became one. But that, along with intense training, allowed them to accomplish things no other school of magery could even hope to manage.

The streets of the Stumbles were quiet and unnaturally empty and dark. Normally at this time of night, you couldn't have gone ten feet without fending off a couple of half-a-riel-a-lay whores, three caras snufflers, and a slit-purse pretending to be a sleepwalker, most of them carrying their own lights. But even the beggars and other gutterside players had vanished. News like three dead Elite traveled fast in a place like the Stumbles.

Windows were closed and doors barred on houses and taverns alike, and everywhere lights were out. The only illumination came from the stars and the half-full moon, but that didn't make me feel one jot less exposed. I could feel eyes looking out from the cracks between shutters and various other peepholes. Not to mention the fact that the lack of light would make an ideal hunting environment for the restless dead. They were rare in the city proper, but this sort of deep darkness would draw them out of their lurking places if there were any around.

Taking the Dyad back to one of my fallbacks instead of simply vanishing into a cloud of shadow seemed ever more dumb. For perhaps the dozenth time I glanced over at the laboring Stel and considered how much simpler my life would be if I just walked away right now. If it weren't for the part where I knew I'd have to look at myself in the mirror to shave, I might even have tried it. I sighed.

"What is it?" asked Vala, sounding suspicious. "Why do you keep looking at us that way?"

"It's this—" I waved an arm to take in the whole neighborhood. "There's no one around, which means we can't pull a decent fadeout. Not on the streets anyway."

"What would you do if you didn't have me to carry?" demanded Stel.

I couldn't tell her I'd vanish into shadow, not without admitting what I was, so I offered my second choice. "I'd head up onto the chimney road." I pointed toward the rooftops. "There's never much of a crowd up there to begin with, and we pretty much all agree not to see each other when we do meet. But there's no way you're going to make it up there, so we need to think of something—"

A sudden brief blast of light and sound cut me off. What the . . .

"Stel, you idiot!" It was Vala, who was glaring up toward the nearest low rooftop—a tannery. "That hurts, *and* you could have killed yourself, us . . ." She trailed off into a string of obscenity as she started up the wall after her pairmate.

It was only then that I realized what Stel must have done. She'd aimed the battle wand at the ground, triggered it, and ridden the resulting shockwave up onto the rooftops. I was just about to follow the Dyad roofward when I heard a shout from somewhere behind me.

"Look there's one of them now, by the tannery! Get him!"

# 3

————◆————

**L**ater, if we lived through the next couple of hours, I was going to strangle Triss for getting us involved in this.

"Go," I called up to the Dyad. "Head north until you run up against a big street with square stone cobbles and actual lights. Then find someplace to hole up for a bit. I'll draw them off and catch up to you there."

That was when the first crossbow quarrel stuck itself in the wall a few feet from my head. There was a slender gap between the tannery and its nearest neighbor, providing a narrow breezeway. I ducked into it and started to feel my way into the pitch-black depths.

Another quarrel followed me in, but the angle was too steep and it didn't come anywhere close to me by the sound of it. The lack of any hostile magic thrown after it suggested that I was going to be spared further Elite attention at least for a little while. That greatly increased my chances of pulling pursuit away from the others without getting myself killed in the process.

Every cautious step I took involved the sorts of crunching and squishing sounds that make you happy you can't see what you're stepping on and depressed that you can smell it. Mostly rotten food and dead rats, if I had to guess. I'd gone less than ten feet when I felt the familiar sensation of Triss wrapping me in a skin of shadow, like that moment of welcome transition when you step from the hot street into a cool tavern on a sunny summer day.

"Shroud up?" he asked.

"Not yet, we have to give the guard something to follow. I will need your eyes, though."

"Done."

With that Triss put himself into the dreamlike state that allowed me to use his senses as my own, expanding my "view" of the immediate surroundings to a full 360 degrees of Shade-style unvision.

That let me pick up the pace to a fast jog and reach the alley at the end of the breezeway just as the pursuing guards got the necessary angle to send more quarrels my way. They were still effectively shooting blind, and the majority of the quarrels stuck in the walls somewhere behind me, but even a blind shot can kill you if your opponent gets lucky. There was more light in the alley proper, so I had to close my eyes as I approached it. The overlay of the two different ways of seeing becomes especially confusing in situations where my own vision moves back and forth from useless to barely helpful.

I turned right as I moved out into the alley, away from the original direction of pursuit and started really laying down boot leather. The guards weren't stupid, so I had no doubt they would already have sent runners to try to close off both ends of the little alley. That wouldn't stop me. I could always head up to the rooftops or have Triss shroud us up and fade away into shadows. But neither of those options would draw attention away from our Dyad friend, so I preferred to avoid them as long as possible.

I could hear pursuit in the alley behind me by the time I reached the street. Triss's senses picked out the bright points of the guards' magelanterns as they chased after me, but I couldn't actually see the ones carrying them. Not without turning around and using my own eyes. Triss's unvision just doesn't work that way. The lanterns washed out his view of the area immediately behind the lights.

In some ways, Triss's analog to our vision is more like touch than sight, or maybe hearing. The Blade masters at the temple taught us that bats see with their ears. They scream and listen for the echoes to come back and tell them about the world around them. Texture is important and edges, soft and hard, rough and smooth, colors not at all.

I don't know how the masters knew about the bats— probably from quizzing mages with bat familiars—but it's not really important. What is important is how that relates to the unsight of the Shades. Triss and his fellows see by reading . . . well, call them dark-echoes that they feel rather than hear, and you'll be as close as anyone can get to describing it using the human vocabulary. All you really need to know is that the darker it is the better he can perceive things, and that it never ever looks like what you or I would see through our human eyes.

Whatever the mechanism, it makes for a surreal view of the city. Doubly so since the human mind just isn't properly equipped to see equally well in every direction. You have to sort of keep your main attention focused on where you're going, while at the same time setting aside a part of your mind to constantly flick through a rotating view of the entire circle.

**I'd** lost the last of my pursuers maybe a quarter mile ago and had just turned to head back to the Dyad, when the street rose up to meet me. And not in any wind-at-your-back, traditional-blessing kind of way. No, this street was decidedly hostile. The muck-covered cobblestones under my back foot dropped away as I was about to push off, robbing my running stride of all its power. At the same time, the street in front of me rose like a low stone wave. I was already off balance when it caught me in the thighs, and I flipped over it like I'd run full tilt into a stone fence.

I landed more or less on my head, and then slammed down onto my side, driving the breath from my body. On a cleaner street I'd probably have broken a couple of ribs and maybe my neck, but the accumulated filth of years cushioned my fall. Even so, I was stunned half unconscious by the impact and lost my grip on Triss's mind and senses. Then Triss did something he almost never chooses to do.

Normally, when Triss encloses me with a shadowy second skin, it feels as though I've got a thin layer of cold silk covering my entire body. Now that skin tightened and hardened, becoming something more like chitin. Then it started to move, first rolling me over and up onto hands and knees. Picture an empty suit of plate armor moving of its own accord. Now picture a person inside that armor, moving with it, but not out of any volition. That was my situation as Triss started us scrambling toward the nearest building—a dilapidated tenement.

I was still pretty dazed and didn't know what was going on, but I knew that it had to be urgent and dangerous. Otherwise Triss would never have seized control like that. I was just about to ask him why he didn't stand us up and run if it was that bad, when the ground dropped out from under my hands and we tumbled forward. My forehead hit the cobbles hard, but Triss's rigid presence saved me from the worst of the impact. This time I was looking directly at the ground when it started moving. I felt a feather of cold touch the back of my neck when I noticed that whatever was happening, it didn't show up in magesight.

Triss quickly got me back up onto hands and knees, but by then it was too late. The cobbles beneath my hands lifted and twisted at the same time the ones under my knees dropped and parted. The street set me neatly on my feet in a knee-deep hole in the ground, while simultaneously turning me to face toward my left. Then the cobbles closed back in, gently but firmly pincering my calves, all without any visible sign of magic. To make matters even more confusing the street was empty.

"What's going on?" I asked.

"Durkoth," said Triss, his voice a bare whisper in my ear. Then he relaxed his hold over my body.

"Interesting," said a cold, perfect voice, and it was only then that I saw my first Durkoth.

I knew that a score or more lived in Tien, but they mostly dealt with the outside world through emissaries. I'd never encountered one in the flesh before, and I really didn't know much about them. Subterranean, though I didn't know if that meant they lived in caves or castles or just swam through earth like the stone dogs. Like their Sylvani and Vesh'An cousins they were inhuman and beautiful, demi-immortal creatures of a much older breed than ours.

Or that's what the legends said at any rate. I only knew of one interaction between my order and any of the Others in the last hundred years—the assignment that had earned Siri her second name of Mythkiller. That was the big stuff. Beyond that? What I didn't know about the Others would have filled books.

The Durkoth was crouched in the middle of a shallow hole in the street, his bare hands and feet pressed against the roadbed. He was utterly still in a way that no human could ever achieve, and I would have mistaken him for a statue if the earth hadn't been bringing him swiftly and steadily closer. *He* wasn't moving, but the hole in which he crouched was, with the cobbles parting around it like water around the hull of a ship, complete to filling in behind him.

At first, he was the exact color of the cobbles, skin and cloak and all, but when he finally came to a stop a few feet away, it all began to shift and lighten. By the time he stood up to face me, he had returned to his natural coloration, looking like a statue fresh hewn from white marble. Only no statue in Tien had ever been so clean, not even as it stood in the sculptor's studio. No scintilla of dust or misplaced chip of stone marred his perfection.

Zhan had a long artistic history, including the previous century's heroic school, a movement dedicated to the artistic embodiment of the human ideal. Chang Un was considered the greatest of all of Zhan's heroic sculptors. The Durkoth looked like what Un's wildest dreams might have looked like if he'd had the skill to chisel them out of stone. I couldn't help but stare.

The impression of perfection extended to every facet of the Durkoth's appearance. His face was human in layout, two eyes, two ears, one nose, one mouth, etc. But no human had ever possessed such symmetry of feature, or fineness of line. Each pale round ear perfectly mirrored the other in every detail, including an ideal flare and height that seemed intentionally designed to balance and highlight the shape and placement of his other features and his hair. He was slightly taller than the human norm and muscled and proportioned like the realized ideal of what an athlete *should* look like. A typical example of the breed if the legends spoke true.

While I studied him, he studied me. At least, I thought he did. It was hard to tell. In living under stone, the Durkoth have become like stone themselves—taking some of its stillness and hidden depths into themselves. His eyes were blank white spheres that did not appear to move. Neither did he seem to breathe, though I knew that was something of an illusion. The Durkoth do breathe, just far too slowly for the human eye to see. After a little while—a very little while by Durkoth standards—I broke the silence.

"What's interesting?"

"You are not what I expected to catch," said the Durkoth, and again I noted how cold his voice sounded. The only thing about him that moved when he spoke was his mouth, and even that looked wrong and unnatural, as though stone had decided to flow like water.

"Then perhaps, having mistaken my identity, you'll be so kind as to release me." I was in an incredibly bad position, with my legs held in a stone clamp. If I could avoid a fight I would.

"Perhaps, though not at once, I think. I can sense that you do not have the Kothmerk. And you are obviously not the Dyad. But you did run from the guards when they pursued that creature. Why?"

"Maybe because they were shooting at me?" Then, because I had no idea if Durkoth even understood sarcasm, I continued. "I feared for my life." I let my mouth run on by itself—I needed to keep the Durkoth occupied while I tried to think of some way to convince him to let me go. I was pretty sure that knowing what a Kothmerk was would help there, but it didn't ring any bells. "The guards were using crossbows. Running away from them looked like the best way to keep them from killing me."

The Durkoth didn't respond immediately. He might have been thinking about what I said, or he might have simply forgotten I existed. His expression didn't change at all, and I had no way to tell what was going on inside his head. It was maddening. Deception and misdirection are a significant part of the Blade's job. You have to be able to sneak in close to a target if you want to kill them. In many ways it's like running a successful skip or con, which involves learning to read physical and facial cues. Cues that the Durkoth simply didn't provide.

"Could we move this along a bit?" I asked, but the Durkoth held up a hand.

"Bide." It knelt and touched the ground with its fingertips again. "One comes."

The cobbles let go of my knees, but before I could do anything about it, the ground caught hold of my feet and pulled me under. For a brief moment I stood at the bottom of a hole just big enough for one. Then the cobbles closed above my head, cutting off the light and imprisoning me under a roof of stone. I reached up and started hammering on the underside of the street, and found that the stones were moving. Or rather, as I discovered a moment later, when the cobbles above gave way to the underside of a rough plank floor, that I was.

The Durkoth's voice spoke into the darkness then, saying again, "Hush. I will release you when our business is done, but the guards come now. Bide in silence if you want to remain free."

"Triss?" I whispered.

"Just a moment." I felt him flowing off my skin and up through the wide cracks in the floor above. "There, I can see now. We're just under the lip of the tenement's porch."

"Oh good." The words came out higher and tighter than I'd planned. The narrow space reeked of piss and rot.

"It's all right," whispered Triss. "These planks won't even slow us down once we decide to move."

I forced myself to breathe deeply and evenly despite the smells, as I had been taught: *Calm the body and the mind will follow.* It would have helped if I could have borrowed Triss's senses, but that trick only worked when he held me within himself.

"What's the Durkoth doing?" I asked.

"Looking at a spot on the stree—oh." His voice grew even quieter—a shadow of a whisper, audible only because he spoke directly into my ear. "A stone dog has just swum up through the cobbles . . . and here comes his master."

I froze. The stone dogs are elementals, creatures of the earth at a level even more fundamental than the Durkoth, and I didn't know what might draw its attention when I was in its element like this. I'd never felt more vulnerable.

I tried not to think about the smoky-sweet burn of a sip of the Kyle's in my pack hitting the back of my throat, or about how much better I would feel with a glass inside me. But that only turned my mind to efik, and how very nice a couple of roasted beans would go down, or better yet, an entire, properly brewed pot of the stuff. Faster than alcohol and more reliable, efik soothed the nerves at the same time it cleared the mind. I hadn't wanted it this bad in a very long time.

"Master Qethar," the Elite called—the first syllable of the Durkoth's name coming out something between "hch" and the sound of someone clearing their throat. "Have you found something?" I could hear him quite clearly through the many gaps in the battered old porch. "Graf heard you working your earth-magic and he led me here."

"It is not magic, Major Aigo," said Qethar, his voice as flat and cold as ever. "I do not compel, I persuade. I am

Durkoth. The earth and I are children of the same house. I need no conjurer's tricks to convince my sister to help me."

"Of course," said Aigo, his voice soothing, though I could hear strain under the surface. He was clearly under orders to play nice with the Durkoth. "My apologies. Graf heard you *speaking* with your sister. What did you find?"

"Nothing," said Qethar. "I thought I had found the Dyad, but I was mistaken."

"That's odd," said Aigo. "Graf told me that your . . . conversation was quite extensive. It seems a lot of effort if there was nothing to find."

"I saw someone running from your men," said Qethar. "But it was not the Dyad, so I decided that I had no need to keep him for you."

"Did you then?" I could hear anger in the Elite's voice. "We've learned that they had help at the tavern, a man named Aral. A jack, and one who works the shadowy side of the business. We think he might have been fronting for someone who wanted to buy the Kothmerk." There was that word again. "He's wanted for questioning. You're telling me you just let him go?" The Elite's voice rose with the question.

"Perhaps," replied the Durkoth, and if he noticed the Elite's anger it didn't show in his voice. "You could draw me a sketch but I have trouble telling your kind apart by faces. This one was male and alone. He did not have the Kothmerk. I couldn't tell you more than that."

"But you won't mind if Graf and I look around a bit, right?" There was a hell of a lot of tension between the two of them, the kind that required some history, and I found myself wishing I knew what that history was.

Qethar didn't answer right away, though I couldn't tell if that was from uncertainty or deliberate provocation. Finally he said, ". . . no, of course not, search all you want, though you won't find anything."

"We'll see about that. Graf, seek."

The giant dog began to sniff around. Between its hard stone feet and enormous bulk, you'd have expected the thing to make at least as much noise as a shod horse. Instead, with nothing between it and the cobbles that were a part of its native element, its footfalls were nearly silent. I could only just make out the snuffling, but that was all.

What I *could* hear was my own breathing growing steadily thinner and more ragged, despite my best efforts to keep it under control. Triss gave me a reassuring squeeze on the shoulder, but that really didn't help. As the stone dog worked its way ever closer, I felt sure it would discover me. It took a huge effort of will to keep from simply blasting away the floor above me and leaping out to face my enemies.

Of course, the stone dog would rip my head off before I could get halfway out of my hole and I knew it—which is why I stayed put. *Your mind must always rule your heart.* I couldn't even draw my swords in the available space. My only hope lay in concealment. I kept still, but it was brutally hard.

The dog got closer, and closer still. It was snuffling along the base of the little porch. I held my breath. It took one deep sniff and froze like it knew I was there. Then, miraculously, it moved off, still snuffling loudly. A few more minutes passed like hours.

"I told you that you wouldn't find anything, Major," Qethar said after a while.

"You did," replied the Elite, his voice contemptuous and angry. "But sometimes you Durkoth have different ideas about the way the world works than we humans do. I don't suppose you want to tell me which way he went?"

"Does it really matter?" asked Qethar. "He's surely beyond your reach by now. Still, if it will make you happy, I can say with some degree of confidence that he was headed toward this very tenement when last I saw him."

"Did he go inside?"

"I didn't notice it if he did," replied Qethar, and I couldn't help but wonder why the Durkoth kept handing out obvious evasions instead of smooth lies. That was bound to put a twist in the Major's tail. No one held out on the Elite. Not in Tien. Not if they had any sense.

"Well, I'd best rely on my own devices then, hadn't I?" growled Aigo. "Be sure that I'll inform my superiors of the very telling degree of your cooperation, Master Qethar. I don't think King Thauvik will be at all pleased with your performance."

Mention of the king made my ears prick up. His name wasn't something you heard very often in my normal run of affairs, and not something you wanted to hear. In fact, I generally went way the hell out of my way to avoid situations that would bring his eye anywhere near me. If he was directly interested in this business with the Dyad . . . well I didn't like to think about it.

"How very sad for His Majesty. You'll have to tell him how deeply sorry I am that I couldn't be of more help." Qethar didn't sound sorry. If anything he sounded like he thought pissing off Thauvik was something of a perk.

Triss whispered in my ear again, "The Elite and his familiar are turning and walking away now, but the Durkoth remains. He's coming this way, so I'd better go quiet again."

The porch creaked alarmingly above me and a swath of my very limited light vanished.

"Now, where were we?" the Durkoth asked.

"I'm pretty sure you were about to let me go about my business," I said without much hope.

"No, I don't think that was it. I think you were about to tell me everything you know about the Dyad so that I don't call the Major back and give you to him."

"Wouldn't that be a bit awkward?" I asked. "He'd know that you were holding out on him."

"He knows that now," said Qethar. "Nothing would change except that I would have handed over a criminal he badly wants to get hold of. You've really nothing to bargain with except information, so you would do best to make my little misdirection of the ever-loyal Graf worth it."

I filed that last bit away without remarking on it. "What if I don't have anything useful to tell you?"

"Then you really won't like the way the Elite go about asking you the same questions I want answered now. They won't take no for an answer and they won't be gentle in the way they ask, not with Thauvik taking a personal interest in the matter."

The way he said "Thauvik" made it sound like a curse word. Whatever he had against the king it was more than just business.

Qethar continued, "I'm giving you a chance to walk away unharmed. You'd do well to take it. Your own species will not be so merciful. They never are."

"All right." I needed to buy time while I figured a way out of this. "But how do I know I can I trust you?"

"You don't and you can't, but if I'd wanted to harm you I could already have done so."

The earthen walls around my little hole squeezed in for a brief instant, trapping my arms at my side and pressing the air from my lungs in a great gasp. Then they relaxed again, and I could breathe.

"Point taken." I used the sound of my own voice to cover the faint scrape as I drew a knife from the sheath at my hip. "I'll tell you everything I know."

I tipped my head back, scanning the darkened area above me, trying to decide which crack to drive my knife through for best effect if it should come to that. I didn't think I'd get more than one chance, and I was in a lousy position for delivering a killing blow, but I thought it'd make a marginally better opening move than a burst of magelightning that would mostly get soaked up by the planks. Maybe it would be better to just have Triss garrote him. . . .

"Do put the knife away," said Qethar. "It wouldn't get through my armor."

I didn't remember any armor, just a light tunic and trousers, with a cloak thrown over the top. How had I missed something as bulky as armor?

He continued, "Even if you did manage to kill me, you would only die a moment later. My sister holds you in the palm of her hand and she would crush you in revenge."

His sister? Oh, right, he claimed kinship with the earth around me. That changed things. I didn't know whether that was some sort of Durkoth mystical gobbledygook way of talking about their own special magic or if he meant it literally. If it was the former, a quick enough kill might still get me out of this in one Aral-shaped piece. But if it was the latter, I'd have a problem of the fatal variety. Not a question I wanted to settle the hard way.

I was rapidly running out of good options. I didn't want to give up what little I knew about the Dyad, and even if I did turn nose on her, my meager information was unlikely to satisfy the Durkoth. Which meant I was going to have to bluff my way out of that hole in the ground.

"It's hard to know where to start. . . ." I began.

"Start with the Kothmerk. Has the Dyad recovered it?" Qethar asked impatiently, betraying the first sign of emotion I'd yet heard from him. "Did she have it with her?"

I wished once again that I had some idea what the hell the Kothmerk was. This was going to be damned hard to pull off without that knowledge, and I couldn't be too obvious with my fishing. "Well, I didn't exactly *see* it. . . ."

Which was the truth—when you're spinning a lie it's always best to steer as close to the truth as possible where you can manage it. It's much harder to get tripped up later if you keep things simple, and nothing's simpler than the truth.

The Durkoth caught my implication. "But you do think she had it, don't you? I can tell." More impatience, and just a touch of eagerness.

So, whatever it was, a person could conceivably carry it concealed. Small enough to fit in a pouch, then. What else could I get?

"I don't know," I said. "She seemed mighty nervous. She could have left it hidden somewhere."

"No." Flat and cold. "If she's recovered it she won't have let it out of her sight. Not after her great failure earlier. Where is she now? Tell me! If you can help me catch her, you're a free man."

"If I tell you, what's to keep you from killing me?"

"Nothing at all. You have no power in this situ— Ack!

What?" he asked, his voice going suddenly harsh and tight. "How are you doing that?"

The walls suddenly pressed in sharply all around me, pushing my pack into my back and driving the air from my lungs. Spots of white light started to eat away at the edges of my vision.

"Stop it or I'll crush you!" husked the Durkoth.

I wanted to tell him that I would happily stop whatever it was if I could, but I didn't have the breath for it. I didn't have the breath for anything.

Then, faintly through the roaring in my ears, I heard Triss saying, "If he dies, you die. Back it off right now."

"I don't know what you are, familiar, but if I kill your master, you die, too, and that frees me."

"No," said Triss. "I have set my will. If you kill me, I behead you as I die. Everybody loses."

"So be it," replied the Durkoth. "My life means nothing."

# 4

"My life means nothing," repeated the Durkoth. "Not when weighed against my sacred duty to the Koth-merk . . . but I can't find it if I let you kill me."

As suddenly as it had come, the pressure around me eased, and I could breathe again. I wasn't aware that I had started moving until the night opened up around me when the earth very gently spat me out onto the street.

Qethar was sitting on the stoop of the old tenement perfectly motionless. If I hadn't known what he was, I would have taken him for a particularly bizarrely placed piece of public art. A Chang Un masterpiece sitting unguarded in one of the city's worst shitholes.

Qethar's expression was cruel and hard, making a sharp contrast with his relaxed, almost indolent, pose. He sat with his upper body leaned way back, supporting himself on his elbows as though he had settled in for a long spell of watching the street go by. He wore the loose flowing trousers and sleeveless shirt that is the summer uniform of the people of Tien—every detail seemingly rendered in impossibly clean white marble—fully visible now that he had shed his concealing cloak. That garment had fallen away to lie across the rough planks like a carven shroud. His bare feet were firmly planted in a patch of dirt that sat amidst the hard cobbles like a sunken island.

I imagined the plaque that would have gone with the apparent sculpture saying something like "the god of dark passions watches the death of the maiden," or some other equally disturbing fancy. The only thing marring the image of a statue at rest was the thin loop of utter blackness that wrapped his neck like a shadowy hangman's noose, its tail trailing down to disappear between the cracks in the porch.

It should have been invisible there in the deep dark of the empty streets. But the Durkoth was so pale that he seemed almost to glow with an inner light, and that cast the slender loop of blackness binding his throat into stark relief. The shadow looked so fragile and insubstantial against the heavy stonelike weight of the Durkoth. Even I, who knew exactly what Triss was capable of, could hardly credit the danger that dark thread represented.

"Well played," said Qethar through lips that didn't so much move as jump from one position to the next without passing through the intervening stages. It was unnerving. "You have me at a fatal disadvantage. What are your demands, Blade?"

"Start with not repeating that last word," I replied, suppressing a pinch of worry over having my identity exposed yet again. With the death of Namara I had lost so much, not least the freedom from complication. At least the street was empty. "The Blades are as dead as their goddess."

The Durkoth said nothing, but he knew he had scored a hit, and his expression shifted without actually seeming to move. One instant he looked worried and angry, as though he had always looked that way. The next, a feral smile turned up the corners of his lips, and again, it looked as though it had always been there. It made me want to slap him. Instead, I leaned in close to tap a finger against the base of his throat, just below Triss's shadowy presence.

"I don't know what your game is . . ." But I trailed off as I touched him.

I'd been expecting him to feel the way he looked—flesh like marble, cold and smooth and lifeless. Instead, his skin was feverishly hot and softer than silk. The contact jolted through me like a tiny charge of magelightning and I couldn't help imagining what it would feel like to take him in my arms and . . . I shook my head, trying to clear away the images that had arisen there seemingly of their own volition.

"Are you quite sure?" asked Qethar and I realized his voice wasn't cold and hard, but rather crystalline—pure and perfect as a finely cut diamond.

"Wha'?" My own voice sounded slow and thick, slurred, a very poor second to the beauty of the Durkoth's.

"You're shaking your head 'no,' but your eyes are saying 'yes.' And you haven't moved your hand away. Quite the contrary. Which is the real impul—gluk!" he choked mid-sentence as Triss tightened the noose.

"I . . ." Even then I found it hard to focus on anything but the place where my palm now rested against the skin of his throat and chest. "I . . ."

A sharp pain caught me across the cheek as Triss slapped me. I staggered back involuntarily, breaking the contact between me and Qethar. It felt like I'd stepped straight out of an Aveni sauna and plunged into an icy pool. The fuzz in my head burned away in the sudden fiery cold, and I recognized it for what it was.

Glamour.

But even knowing what was happening, I had a hard time keeping myself from moving forward to touch the Durkoth again. The feelings had been so intense. I much preferred women to men as bed partners, but Qethar was so very . . . This time *I* slapped myself. It hurt. That was good. It helped remind me that it wasn't me thinking those thoughts. It was the glamour. There'd have been nothing wrong with the impulse if it were mine. But it wasn't.

"I don't like it when people mess with my head," I said quietly. "Cut the glamour magic."

"It's not magic, it's just me." His voice was still cold, but edged now with bitter contempt and loss. "Your Emperor of Heaven bound our magic after the death of his predecessor in the War of the First. *None* of the First may use magic beyond the borders of the Sylvain. We had to choose between magic and our ancient home under the mountains. Is not the history of the First still taught in your schools?"

"He's not *my* Heavenly Emperor. And, yes it is." But the Others—or, as they generally called themselves, the First—were so rare here in the lands beyond the wall that it had never seemed all that important. More mythology than history.

Besides, I wasn't sure that it really mattered what you called what the Others did. No human could hope to *persuade* the earth or to cast a glamour without using magic. From my point of view the only real difference was that Other magic didn't register in magesight. If anything, that made it *more* powerful than the human variety.

I wondered then how Siri had handled the glamour when she had been tasked with executing the Sylvani demigod whose death had made her the Mythkiller. But I pushed the question aside for now. It might matter later, if I had much more to do with the Durkoth, but at the moment I needed to focus.

"That's not important right now," I said. "I don't really give a damn about First history. What I want to know is what's between you and the Dyad. That, and more about the Kothmerk. So start talk—" I stopped as Qethar burst into wild laughter that made his whole body shake.

It looked *wrong*. A statue in the grips of an earthquake. Except there was no earthquake. It made my head hurt to watch him.

"What's so funny?" I asked when the first tremors had passed.

Between aftershocks, Qethar forced out, "You say that you don't give a damn about First history, then in the very same breath demand that I tell you about the Kothmerk." He lost control again for a moment before continuing, "The Kothmerk *is* First history. The one can no more be separated from the other than the moon from the tides. At least not for the Durkoth, though others among the First might argue the point, particularly the accursed Sylvani. It is a part of the soul of my people."

"Could you give me the short version then?" I asked. "What is so important about this Kothmerk?"

"It's a magic ring," said a familiar voice from my right. Captain Kaelin Fei.

I winced. Partially that was because I'd let myself get so distracted that someone had been able to sneak up on me. But even more it had to do with *who* I'd let sneak up on me. Captain Fei was an officer of the watch and the perfect model of a corrupt cop. A sometime employer, sometime ally of mine, I'd been avoiding her for months because I owed her a really big favor. Several actually.

I sighed and turned so that I could see the captain—who emerged now from a gap between the tenement and its nearest neighbor—while still keeping an eye on the Durkoth. Fei was a big woman, broad shouldered and fit, a jindu master as well as a street fighter of ugly reputation.

You couldn't see it in this light, but pale eyes and a spray of freckles marked her out as having non-Zhani blood in her ancestral line. That was probably why she'd turned into such a good brawler; the Tienese streets were hard on those of mixed parentage. Her face was round and would have been almost too pretty for playing the strong arm if not for the deep knife scar on the left side.

She bobbed a nod at me. "The Kothmerk is a ring, carved from a single massive ruby and magically hardened to make it tougher than steel. It's priceless."

Qethar hissed at that. "It is neither carved nor was it *magically* anythinged."

"Yeah, I know." Fei rolled her eyes. "One of your supersmith gem cutter forebears "persuaded" it to assume its present form back before the dawn of history, or some such crap. Well, that's more than close enough to magic for a simple old street cop like me."

I snorted. The captain was anything but simple. If there was a significant shadowside operation anywhere in Tien that she didn't have her fingers in, I had yet to hear about it. She was as crooked as crooked could be, and somehow she'd convinced her bosses all the way up to the king himself that it was all for the best. Where most watch captains had a regular district assigned to them, Fei's beat was the whole city. Her job was peacekeeping in the sense of making sure the criminal element didn't significantly inconvenience anyone important.

"What does this Kothmerk do?" I asked. I didn't like the direction this was going. Magic rings tended to attract nine kinds of trouble.

"Nothing," said Qethar.

"It starts wars," replied Fei.

"It *does* nothing," said Qethar. "It simply *is*. The Kothmerk is nothing more nor less than the living heart of the Durkoth." Fei raised an eyebrow at Qethar, who conceded, "Though, sometimes, that is enough to start a war."

"Well, it is not going to start one here," said Fei. "From what I've been able to find out, the damned thing leaves a trail of bodies wherever it goes. The massacre at the Gryphon's Head is only the latest and gaudiest killing since the thing hit Tien. I want that fucking ring out of my city, and I want it done yesterday."

"There we are in agreement," said Qethar. "I want to find the Kothmerk as quickly as possible and return it to its rightful master."

Fei turned a hard look on me. "Which is where you come in, my jack friend. Large scale incidents of slaughter like the Gryphon's Head are *very* hard to explain to my bosses. So, I'm calling in a favor. Make the problem go away."

"You want me to find the ring for you?" I asked. This was going to complicate my dealings with the Dyad, I could just tell.

"If that's what works, great. But I really don't care how you do it. All I care about is that it stops killing people on my streets. You understand me?"

"I think so. How long do I have?"

"Like I said, I want this thing done yesterday." Fei sighed.

"But I know that shit like this takes a while. I'll give you a week."

"You expect me to wrap this up in just eight days?" I asked, and Fei nodded. "Not a lot of time. I may have to cut some corners. . . ."

"I don't care if you have to cut throats. Just get it done."

"I thought you didn't want any more bodies found in the streets," I said.

"So make sure they don't end up there, Aral. Or, are you going to try to convince me that you can't make a body or two vanish if you need to?"

"I can help you there," said Qethar. "I can make any body vanish forever."

"Why would you do that for me?" I asked.

"Because we're going to be working together, of course. We do have the same goal now, don't we, human?"

I looked a question at Fei, who shrugged. "Like I said, I don't care what happens to the damned thing as long it stops being my problem. If swapping sweat with the Others is what it takes, by all means swap away."

Qethar looked at me and raised a stony eyebrow the tiniest fraction of an inch. I shuddered.

"I think I'll pass," I said to him. "I don't trust you. I don't like you. And, I prefer to work alone."

"Funny definition you've got of alone." Qethar touched the shadow at his throat.

"Fine, then let's say that I already have a partner, and leave it at that. Either way, I'm not working with you."

"You'll never find the Kothmerk without me. Even if you did, what would you do with it? If you want the killings to stop, it has to go back to my people. It is the most precious thing we own and it should never have come anywhere near your filthy human hands. You can't get it where it must go without dealing with me or another of my kind. You need me."

I turned to Fei. "How about if I make and get rid of another body right now?" Qethar was really beginning to irritate me. "Would that be all right?"

"You'd better not," said Fei. "He's got something going

with the Elite right now. And he's well known in certain circles here in Tien. If he vanishes, it'll generate the kind of heat that would get a lot of light shone into a lot of shadows." Fei shrugged apologetically. "I might even have to remember what you look like if that happened. I wouldn't want to, of course, you're too valuable to give away if I can possibly avoid it. But business is business."

I nodded. I wasn't happy about it, but I understood. "All right, I'll let him walk away, but you can't make me work with him. Triss."

The noose slipped from Qethar's neck and my shadow resumed the appearance of a plain old shadow—all but invisible in the darkness. Qethar rose to his feet and tipped a bow my way.

"This one is yours, human, but rest assured that we *will* speak again. You do need me." He reached into a pouch at his side and pulled out a small white pebble. "When you see it my way, crush this under your heel and I will come to you."

He held out his hand with the stone on his palm. I would have preferred to simply turn and walk away at that point, but I knew he might be right. Reluctantly, I reached for the stone. As I took it my fingertips brushed the hot silk skin of his palm for the barest instant, and I had to fight to finish the original gesture instead of taking his hand between my own. Qethar raised an eyebrow at me again. Then the ground at his feet opened up and swallowed him whole. A moment later, the cobbles closed over the bare earth, erasing the last mark of where he'd stood.

"Now"—I turned a sharp eye on Fei—"tell me more about this ring." I could feel Triss's interest, though the Shade stayed hidden.

"Not much to tell. You've seen Durkoth work, intricate, beautiful, inhuman. Unmistakable. Especially when we're talking about a ring carved from a ruby as big as your eyeball."

"What about the bodies? You said this thing has killed more people than the ones at the Gryphon. Tell me about those."

"The official count is four incidents, though I'm thinking

it's really five, maybe more." Fei sniffed loudly and glanced around as though double checking that we were alone. "First, two dead Durkoth just inside Northgate, throats cut. Outsiders, you can tell by how they dressed. You'll have noticed Qethar's gone native. So have the rest of the locals. Nobody heard or saw anything, of course."

"Of course."

"Second, and this is my maybe," continued Fei. "Anonymous teenage girl, young, very well dressed, took a crossbow quarrel through the left eye right out in the middle of the square on Sanjin Island. Nobody saw the shooter. Very professional job. High-end black jack work, if not government."

"Government?" I asked. "Whose?"

"That's where it turns into a maybe, at least formally. Two off duty Elite just happened to be walking across the bridge from the palace when it happened, a captain and a lieutenant. The official report says they hurried over to see if they could help the girl but found her already dead, and then they searched her to see if she was carrying anything that could be used to establish her identity."

"Which she wasn't."

"Nope, at least nothing our good Elite friends wanted to share with the rest of the children. The watchmen who first arrived on the scene didn't want to push them on that, or anything really. I wouldn't even have their names if Sergeant Zishin hadn't happened on the scene before they could get away. Maybe wouldn't even know they'd been there."

"Ah, and what did the good sergeant find when he searched the girl?" Zishin was Fei's right hand man.

"Well, under the fancy clothes she was half starved and dirty, though her hands and arms were freshly washed. The only other thing he could find was a purse with twenty-five gold riels in it. No other possessions whatsoever."

"The Elite didn't seize the cash and write up a receipt?"

"Nope."

"Then they weren't off duty."

Twenty-five gold riels was a lot of money. Like a year's rent on a house in a decent neighborhood kind of money.

The Elite were incorruptible and that sort of money on an anonymous corpse with no obvious next of kin would normally have had them pulling rank on the watch. They'd have gone all official about the whole thing so that the money didn't vanish into the watch's pockets, which it would have. No question. Leaving it like that was tantamount to offering the watch a bribe to forget they'd ever seen the pair of Elite.

"So you think the Elite killed this girl?" I asked. "And that it was on orders from someone higher up the feeding chain?" The Elite don't do anything without orders, and those orders generally come down from the king one way or another.

"You tell me." Fei lowered her voice. "The next official death was an officer of the Elite, throat slit in his own home. The same lieutenant who found that girl's body. The captain was reassigned out of Tien about four hours after that. I never got a chance to talk to him. That makes four dead Elite now, which is going to have the Crown sounding like a kicked-over beehive very shortly."

"At the least. Now, that's three of your murder incidents. You said you had five at least. Who are the others?"

"Another foreign Durkoth," said Fei. "Dagger from behind. Between the ribs and into the heart, as neat as could be. Professional, but not in the same way as that girl. The last one that I feel sure about is a half dozen street toughs who thought that damned Dyad looked like easy meat. It's how we found out she was here. I'm inclined to think of that one as mass suicide. If the ring weren't involved I wouldn't even care."

"And the ones you aren't sure about?" I asked.

"I haven't really got anything there but a feeling. An unusual number of minor fish from the night markets have turned up dead or simply gone missing in the last week and a half, cindersweeps, banksmen, scuttles. You know the type."

"And you're thinking that dead night marketeers might have something to do with a priceless stolen Durkoth artifact. I can't imagine why."

Fei chuckled. "I guess I'm just suspicious that way." Then her face went suddenly serious. "I'm under a lot of pressure here, Aral. Someone way up the chain ordered that raid on the Gryphon, and they did it without me hearing a thing beforehand. Things are going to get really ugly. Fix it. I don't care about how. All I care about is that you do it fast and that no one finds any embarrassing bodies. Now I need to get back to the center of things before I'm too much missed."

Fei turned away then, heading back toward the gap through which she'd arrived. As she was about to step into the deeper dark, she paused.

"Oh, and Aral, while we're on the subject of embarrassing corpses . . ."

"Yes?"

"I know you're not the type to think this way, but if it ever crossed your mind to get me out of your life by making one more body vanish, well . . . just don't. I've left instructions for what should happen if I suddenly disappear. One of those things involves a wanted poster for Aral Kingslayer. It's the only one of its kind with an actual likeness of the elusive Blade on it."

"Captain," I said rather stiffly, "you know I'd never do something like that."

"I do. Your goddess trained you too well. Your mind just doesn't work that way."

"Then why set me up like that?"

"Because mine does."

Fei sniffed audibly at the entrance to the little gap, almost as though she were taking a scent. Then she was gone, too, and I was free to go about my business.

"So, now what?" I asked my shadow.

"How about we get off the street, for starters."

He had a point, but I noticed just then that the Durkoth had left behind his marble-white cloak. It lay crumpled carelessly on the planks like the carven lid of some fanciful sarcophagus. On impulse I reached to pick it up, thinking it might come in handy later. I nearly broke two fingers when it turned out that the illusion of marble was no illusion at all.

Heavy stone met my outthrust hand. Cold and motionless now, though the garment had moved and flowed like the finest wool when Qethar wore it. I poked it again, more gently. It must have weighed close to what I did, and there was no good way to move it.

Triss murmured something impatient then, so I left the stone cloak behind, though not without a couple of backward glances as I climbed the wall of the tenement. When I hit the roof, I turned in the general direction of the place I'd told the Dyad to meet me and looked around for a spot to lay up for a little while. I needed time to think about what Fei had told me and everything that had happened with Qethar.

I chose the top of a small private water tower—popular in a neighborhood where the city was slow to fix things like the aqueducts when something went wrong. The tower—cobbled together from whatever lumber the builders could beg, borrow, or steal—looked more than a little ramshackle. But it was plenty sturdy. It had to be to support the several hundred gallons of water it held when full. I settled down into the low well of the collector and eyed my shadow, barely visible now in the light of the half-full moon.

"I ask again, now what?"

The shadow shifted into the shape of a small, winged dragon. "Go after the Dyad, of course."

"Of course."

"You don't sound convinced, my friend." Triss canted his head to one side. "Given the circumstances, what else could we do?"

"Given the circumstances, I don't know, and that bothers me. We've been doing nothing but reacting since I first went over to talk to them . . . it . . . her?" I shook my head. "I'm not even sure what to call our new friend, much less how to deal with her. I don't like the way this whole thing is going. We've got no plan, and no fallback. That's a recipe for disaster."

Triss slid closer and placed his head in my lap. "I'm sorry. I didn't know it would all go so bad so fast."

"It's all right." I reached down and scratched his spinal ridge. "You were trying to do what you thought was best for me . . . for both of us. You were even right. They did need help, just not the kind it *looked* like they needed."

Triss made a happy little growling sound and wriggled to let me know I should keep scratching. Pushing my worries aside for a little while, I smiled and obliged, working my way down from the back of his head to the always itchy spot between his wings. His flesh felt warm and comforting in the cool night wind blowing in off the ocean. The eye might only see a flat lizard-shaped shadow, but my fingers brushed along soft scales and the ridge of lumps where his vertebrae pressed up against his invisible skin.

It made for a strange contrast. One that seemed stranger still knowing that when he shifted back to aping my form, he lost all texture. Master Alinthide had explained it to me once, going on for some time about elementals and how they manifested themselves in different ways under different circumstances. But even though I more or less understood the difference intellectually, it always *felt* like a mystery to my scratching fingers.

Finally, Triss sighed and went limp under my hand. "You can stop now. I feel better. Much, much better. I also know what we should do." He turned his head and looked up at me—at least, I think he did. It's hard to tell with a shadow.

"Good, tell me about it."

"We should go and find the Dyad." His voice was firm and matter-of-fact.

"I thought that was what we *had* to do, given the circumstances."

"It is, which makes it doubly nice that it's also what we *should* do."

"I'll bite. Why *should* we do it?"

Triss held up a front paw and poked out one claw. "First, because it's the only real option."

I raised an eyebrow at him, but he continued, extending another claw. "Second, Captain Fei wants us to solve the problem of the Kothmerk, and there is no doubt that the Dyad is involved. If we want to learn more about that we'll have to talk to them. And the good captain even gave us free rein to solve things however we want, which means we just might be able to make *everyone* happy."

"Conceded. The part about needing to talk to them at least. The making everyone happy bit seems much iffier to me. What else."

Another claw. "Third, they need the help. They're foreigners here, alone and hunted by the Elite, the Durkoth, and who knows who all else. They have a major problem."

"I'm not sure why that means *we* have to help them, but go on."

"Fourth, I liked them. Even if we did only spend a little time with them, they struck me as good people. I want to help them."

"That's the best reason I've heard so far."

He held up the last claw on that paw. "Fifth, I'm curious and this is fascinating. I want to know how this ends. Don't you?"

"Truth be told, yes, though not enough to risk my life over it."

"Finally"—Triss closed his paw into a fist and held it up in front of my face—"and this is the real reason we should— no, *must* go meet the Dyad. It is the *right* thing to do. The Kothmerk is dangerous. Tonight, without even making an appearance, it killed people at the Gryphon, which has been our home since we arrived here over six years ago."

He growled low and harsh, then continued, "It hurt people we know, forced us to kill an Elite, lost us our home. That's wrong and it has to stop. Namara may be dead along with most of her followers, but *you* are ever and always a Blade. A rusty one at the moment perhaps, but a Blade still, the living tool of Justice, and I am your partner. It is our duty."

A year ago I'd have laughed at a call to duty, and it would have been a bitter, broken laugh. The laugh of a man pretending he wasn't drinking himself to death, while every day he sank a little further into the bottle. Things had changed since then. My goddess was dead, yes. But Justice lived on. The ideal Namara had once personified survived beyond the death of its champion. I had felt its touch, like the benediction of a ghost. Triss was right. As long as there was still a hope of doing some good, I couldn't turn away from my duty.

# 5

---

"**Y**ou win." I hopped up into a crouch and looked out over the edge of the water tower. "We'll go after the Dyad."

"Only because I'm always right," said Triss, fanning himself with one wing.

"But Triss . . ."

"Yes."

"You do realize there's a possibility that this Dyad you like so much is the villain here, don't you? What then?"

He sighed. "The same as before, the same as always. We do our duty." Then he slid upward, enveloping me in a thin skin of shadow before expanding outward into a cloud of obscuring darkness and releasing his consciousness into my care.

This time, I had more leisure to settle myself properly into my familiar's skin. With my vision subsumed within the Shade's radically different way of perceiving the world, paying attention to my other senses becomes more important. I took a moment now to focus on each one individually. Hearing, smell, touch, taste, each has its uses.

It's a discipline the masters started teaching us on the

first day—even before we knew which of us would be chosen by the Shades—running us through lightless tests in the deeps below the temple. They would send us into mazes where all the clues and warnings were designed to force us to think with our ears or noses, or the tips of our fingers.

Once you know how to do it you can find a pit by the changing echoes of your own footsteps, or follow a scent trail marked out with dots of perfume. Your fingers can show you things hidden from the eye, subtle differences in wall surfaces that betray the presence of hidden doors or traps. Even taste can serve, if less directly, telling you things about what your targets eat or wear, things that can be used to craft the perfect poison or deliver a drug.

When I was ready, I climbed to the edge of the water tower. Then I spread wings of shadow, leaped into space, and soared. For perhaps a dozen heartbeats I glided above my city, heading west and north toward the place I'd told the Dyad to meet me. It should have been a much shorter flight, but I prolonged the sail-jump by pulling nima from the well of my soul and using it to push myself that extra bit higher on launch.

It was a dangerous choice, because it involved a brief flare of magic that would mark me out if anyone with mage-sight happened to be looking in the right direction at the right time. Doubly so, since there isn't enough of Triss to both cover me and provide me with wings.

But sometimes I just can't help myself. I love it too much, this time, where I get to break the bonds that tie me to the earth and play the bird. No matter that I must risk exposing myself to hostile eyes to do it. No matter that it uses the least of magics—the brute manipulation of forces. No matter even that it paints me for what I am, or once was—the "flight" of the Blades plays a prominent part in the stories they tell about us.

Sometimes I just need the release that only comes from dancing with the sky.

All too soon, my feet touched down on a ridgeline, divorcing me from the heavens. A story-and-a-half building, it was the sort that usually housed a little business of some kind—workshop and storefront below, tiny apartment above. Pulling shadow around me once again, I ran lightly from one end of the roof peak to the other. I hopped from there to a narrow balcony that peered out from the back of a dilapidated tenement much like the one where I'd met the Durkoth earlier. Using window frames and cornices I quickly climbed the six stories to its flat roof.

I had to slow up a little then and ghost my way across, stepping lightly to keep from waking sleepers who'd sought escape from the summer heat by laying their ragged blankets on the roof. Drop two stories to another aging tenement. Roll out of the fall and step up onto the low wall that circled a rooftop whose lack of sleepers warned of a rotten roof. On and up to the next. Avoid stepping on the human carpet once again.

Over, under, sidewise, down.

I made my way across the roofs of this twistiest of Tien's slums, heading for a rendezvous with two women who together made up something not quite human.

"I don't think he's coming," I heard Vala say from just above where I lay hidden within my concealing shadow, her voice barely more than a whisper.

The Dyad had picked a good temporary refuge, a tall slender corner tower on a much larger building. In addition to the view afforded by the extra height, it had a sloping roof that would discourage any residents from sleeping up there. Vala's position, lying flat atop the little shack that housed the stairhead, allowed her to keep a lookout while remaining hidden from most watching eyes. She had set herself up facing back toward where they'd last seen me, scanning the rooftops while idly twirling her wands in her fingers.

"Good." Stel sat propped against the little shack on the side opposite Vala's lookout and the door, to give them a complete view of the surrounds. Her voice was likewise soft. "We're better off without him."

"Don't start that again," the Meld said, speaking out of Vala's mouth. "He knows the area. He took down an Elite. He has resources we don't."

"We don't need help," growled Stel.

"Said the lady with the broken ribs." Vala glanced upward as if asking for strength. "If he hadn't pitched in when he did, there's a good chance we'd be dead now."

"I'll be fine," said Stel. But she didn't look it. She had one arm pressed against her tightly wrapped ribs, and was using the other to stay upright. "Just give me a couple of days to rest up."

"Counting the time we spent tracking the thief here to the city, we've been at this for nearly a month." The Meld again, speaking through Vala. "We don't have any time to waste. I say we're taking his help. That's final."

Stel's back stiffened briefly at that, but she shut up. It was fascinating to watch, this three-way argument between the different facets of the Dyad. It sounded more like the kind of back and forth I'd have with Triss than the perfect two-minds-one-body supersoldier of the Dyad legends. I wondered whether that meant my Dyad was unusual, or if they all talked to themselves like this when they thought no one else was around. Maybe the myth and the reality had less in common than I'd believed.

Unfortunately, the Meld's declaration seemed to have ended the out-loud portion of their conversation. After several minutes passed without another word, I decided eavesdropping wasn't going to give me anything else. That made it time to make myself known. But not without some setup first. I slipped silently back off the edge of their roof and climbed down to street level to look things over.

The streets were still eerily silent and dark, but I didn't find any guard presence within the two block circle I checked before returning to the rooftops. Nor, thankfully, given the unusual darkness and quiet, any restless dead. Once I returned aloft, I found a secluded corner and dropped my shroud before releasing my hold on Triss. Then, careful to make a little noise to draw Vala's attention, I started back in the general direction of the Dyad's hiding place. As I went, I made a show of looking for the pair.

I was on a slightly lower roof and just starting to go past their perch when Vala hissed like a cat. I stopped then and glanced up in her direction, and she waved a hand over the edge of the roof. I nodded and jumped across the gap, catching hold of a terra-cotta drainpipe that vanished into the building a few floors below—a supply for a kitchen garden in the courtyard, probably. From there it was the work of seconds to pull myself up beside Vala.

I flattened myself out a few feet away from Vala. Close enough to talk quietly, far enough away to let her know that was all I wanted to do. "Stel?"

"Behind us, against the back wall." Vala had tucked her wands away before she waved me over, but kept running her fingers through the twirling motions.

"How's she doing?"

"Grumpy as a manticore that's stung itself in the back of the neck." Her smile flashed in the darkness, and I thought of Jax again. "Which means she's practically her normal self again."

"I heard that," said Stel.

"You were supposed to," replied Vala. "Through my ears, if nothing else. Consider it a subtle hint."

"Subtle. Right, that's you all over."

I slithered around on the roof and stuck my head over the edge to look down at Stel. "Speaking of subtle. What the hell were you thinking back there when you launched yourself up onto the roof?"

She dropped her shoulders a little bit. "I wasn't and Vala chewed me up real good on that one already. I was in pain and I just wanted to get somewhere that I could collapse in a heap." Her voice dropped even lower. "This is our first real mission outside of Kodamia. I made a stupid choice. I'm sorry."

"I couldn't ask for a fairer answer than that." Well, I *could*, but not without playing the hypocrite. "It's not like I haven't done more than my share of stupid things over the years." Triss gave me a quick slap on the back that I took for hearty agreement. "So, how about we get you someplace where you *can* collapse for a bit?"

"I'm certainly all for it." Vala rubbed her own ribs, and I remembered that Dyads were supposed to be able to feel each other's pain.

Stel just nodded.

"Where is this place?" the Meld asked via Vala's lips. "How sure are you that it's safe?"

"No place in Tien is completely safe for anyone who was involved in what happened at the Gryphon tonight, but my fallback's as good as you're going to find. There's an abandoned brewery about a quarter mile from here. I sealed off one tiny section of the attics. The only way in is to go down an old ruined chimney." I had an even better fallback, but it was farther away and I wasn't willing to take a stranger there.

"What's to keep some other squatter from setting up shop?" asked the Meld.

"The chimney is capped with a ceramic pipe not much bigger around than your arm."

"So, how do you get in?"


**"There's** a catch down here," I said half an hour later as I stuck my arm into the chimney pipe.

Out of sight of the Dyad, Triss extended himself down the chimney another three feet to release the latch. Then I pulled my arm out and pivoted the chimney's top cap aside. The opening thus exposed was narrow and dark, barely big enough to fit a person, especially with a bamboo ladder eating up some of the space.

"I have some surprises set up for unwanted visitors, so I'd better go first." I slipped off my pack and used a line that I pulled from one of the side pouches to lower it into the darkness before climbing into the gap myself. "The ladder's on the fragile side and won't hold two. Wait for me to call up to you before you start down. Oh, and the ceiling's low. Be careful."

Stel came second, with Vala following after. Once they were down, I told them to wait quietly just a little bit longer. Then I had to slither my way back up to close and latch the lid. When that was done and I'd dropped a thick light-blocking curtain over the opening I'd cut into the side of the chimney, I finally started to relax.

"Half a minute more," I said while I dug in my pack for the intense little magelight.

I'd intended to bring it out slowly to give everyone time to adapt, but it tumbled out onto the floor when I moved a shirt, and the light stabbed at my eyes. Vala swore, and even Stel, who had her back pressed firmly against Vala's so she was looking away, grunted unhappily at the reflected brightness.

The room thus illuminated was long and low, no more than five feet at the midpoint that ran beneath the roof peak, and sloping down from there. It was a sort of secondary storage space above the main attic over the southern wing of the brewery. When I'd first found it, it'd been full of rotting bits of ancient brewing equipment, most of which I'd scattered on the level below. It was maybe fifty feet by fifteen at the floor level.

If you didn't mind rats and bats and slinks, the complete lack of air flow, and an ever present risk of death by fire due to the nature of the downstairs neighbors, it was actually nicer than my room at the Gryphon had been.

"Is that magelight going to draw attention?" asked a still blinking Vala.

"It shouldn't." I picked it up and wedged it into a gap in the bricks of the chimney, which gave us better light—though the chimney itself now shaded a good third of the room. "The ceiling in the room below is plastered over and doesn't leak light, and the roof is shockingly sound."

"What about noise?" After carefully helping Stel lower herself to lean against an upended half barrel, Vala started to prowl around the room. She looked into every corner and crevice.

"Noise shouldn't be a real problem as long as we keep it down to a reasonable minimum," I answered her.

I crossed to the corner where I'd left a half dozen big amphorae. Sealed properly, the clay jars make for cheap vermin-proof storage. Add a few simple spells and they'll keep food and other perishables in good condition for years. These days I generally buy mine off the back of a wagon that collects empties from local taverns. There's always some breakage, so the foreman at the firm that recycles them turns a blind eye to the pilferage as long as he gets a cut.

"Downstairs neighbors?" interjected Stel. "I presume you've got 'em in a building this sound. What are they like? Can they get up here?"

I could tell that I wasn't going to get any peace until I reassured my guests, and that "trust me" just wasn't going to do it. If our positions were reversed I'd have been the same way. Rather than play twenty questions, I decided to give them the full run down.

"Floor below us is another, much larger, attic. There used to be a ladder up to a trapdoor from there to here. I pulled the ladder—it's in the chimney now—and nailed the trap-door shut. I also plastered over the hole from beneath and aged the plaster to match the surrounding ceiling."

"How?" asked Vala from somewhere off in the dark beyond the chimney.

"Trade secret." I wasn't willing to admit to magic yet, though I knew they figured me for a mage. "Anyone who looks up from below and actually thinks about it will know there's a void up here, but a couple of factors play against them bothering or doing anything about it.

"First, the floor of the main attic below is thoroughly rotten and likely to drop anyone wandering around up there onto the main brewery floor. The fall's thirty feet and there are enough uneven surfaces on the old brewing gear to make that a fatal height. Second, the ground level of the brewery houses a caras seed-grinder. She keeps her little band of skull-crackers well and truly dusted up, which makes them paranoid, intermittently homicidal, and pretty damned slow on the uptake. It also keeps everyone but her dustmen the hell away from the building."

"Sounds like the perfect neighbors for something like this." Stel nodded approvingly, and for the first time she sounded something other than hostile and suspicious of me.

"Pretty much. As long as we don't make any more noise than can be easily explained away by the rats, bats, slinks, and nipperkins, plus the various critters that hunt them, they won't give us any trouble.

"Now, who's hungry?" I'd just finished cracking the spelled seal on two of the amphorae to expose the rations within, mostly salted pork wrapped into neat bundles in the one, and bags of rice cakes in the other. "It all tastes like the inside of an amphora, of course, but it'll keep skin and bone together in a pinch."

"Sounds . . . delightful," Vala said in a tone that suggested she was trying to convince herself. "We'd love some."

I tossed her a bag of rice cakes and slid a greasy bundle of pork over to Stel, then went on to the next amphora. It held blankets and a large bottle of Kyle's, the six year. It was drinkable but nowhere near as good as the fifteen I kept at my main fallback—a necessary economy given the state of my purse. I set the bottle aside and divided up the blankets.

"You won't really need them in this heat, but they'll give you some padding against the floor. I tried keeping a straw pallet up here for a while, but it didn't work out. Even a good strong mix of fleabane and worrymoth won't keep the rats and nipperkins away after they've gotten into the caras seed."

The next amphora held water skins, and I passed one to Vala to carry back to Stel. There were more supplies in the remaining amphorae, but I didn't want to breach the spelled seals if I didn't have to. Both for convenience's sake and to keep them preserved against future need.

Reluctantly, I left the Kyle's unbroached as well, both the six and the smaller fifteen from my pack, and grabbed myself a water skin instead. The salty pork and bone dry rice cakes needed a lot of washing down. Now, with basic amenities taken care of it was time to move on to other, more dangerous, necessities.

Moving casually, I crossed to another broken-down half barrel and took a seat. It lay midway between the magelight and Stel, and my shadow fell across the lower half of her body—a deliberate choice on my part. I might like the Dyad, but I was still a long way from trusting her, and putting Triss there made for cheap insurance.

"We need to talk," I said quietly.

Somewhere behind me, Vala stopped her inspection of the room. I half turned, so that I could look at both halves of the Dyad. Vala's farther hand was out of sight, concealed behind her hip, though I guessed that it now held one of her battle wands. I didn't blame her; casting my shadow across Stel's legs was a very similar tactic, though they didn't know it. Or, at least, I hoped they didn't.

"Yes, we do." The Meld spoke through both of her mouths. "Why don't you start."

Though in this case it was quite obvious, I'm not entirely sure how the Meld made it so clear when she was speaking instead of Vala or Stel. Something about body language as much as tone perhaps? Certainly, Vala moved less in those moments when the Meld came to the forefront, but that didn't explain the obvious differences in Stel's demeanor. It was clearly much more complicated than the stories had led me to believe.

"It's pretty clear that you have a problem," I said. "A big one, and one that puts you in opposition to Tien's charming authorities. I'm a shadow jack. My job is helping people with exactly that kind of problem. . . ."

Stel frowned and Vala sighed. Then, the Meld spoke. "Something was stolen from us. We need to recover it. How much would you charge to help us find it?"

"That depends on a couple of things. The value of the item. How dangerous the job is. How long it takes. Etc. Oh, and I don't work in the dark. You tell me everything you know or think you know about the job, and you do it up front."

"How do we know we can trust you?" asked Vala, who had resumed her pacing.

"You don't. If you had time and knew the city, you could ask around about my rep, but that's not a luxury you have, not with the amount of heat you've already generated."

"I wouldn't be so sure about that," said Stel. "We might surprise you there."

"That's certainly possible, but the impression I've gotten is that in addition to the heat coming from the guard, you're under a lot of time pressure on this thing."

"What if we tell you what you want and then you decide you don't like the odds?" asked Vala.

"Easy. If I don't like the job, I won't take it, but I also won't slink you out to the guard. That's one of the things you'd know if you'd had time to check me out."

"Actually," said Vala, "that reputation is exactly why we came looking for you at the Gryphon's Head, Jack Aral."

I blinked several times then, and Triss jerked sharply, but only a few tiny fractions of an inch. If the Dyad noticed either gesture of surprise, neither of her faces betrayed it.

"That's an interesting statement," I said after a slightly too long silence. "If you were at the Gryphon looking for me, why didn't you say so in the first place?"

"Say that we were of three minds about it," the Meld said from both sides of me, "and you will hit close enough to the mark."

"I didn't like the idea," said Stel.

"I wasn't thrilled with it either," agreed Vala, "though I thought it worth investigating."

"But I . . . felt we needed some sort of help," said the Meld.

I noted the choice of "felt" as opposed to "knew" or "believed," and could tell there was something interesting going on there, if not what. "It sounds like there's some major significance to the way you phrased that. Or am I mishearing?"

"You have a good ear," replied the Meld. "I . . . or in this case, *we* had not reached a formal decision about whether to consult with you in your professional capacity. We had hoped to spend some time observing you in your natural surrounds before doing anything more. Several days, perhaps. But circumstances got away from us and now we are come to the choice prematurely."

"I don't know. In many ways you've had a better look at what I'm capable of than most of my clients ever get. I don't normally let on that I'm up to dealing with Elite problems, if you know what I mean." Nor would I have allowed that information to get out this time, if I'd had much in the way of a choice about it. "In fact, I generally flat refuse any job that would bring me in close contact with the king's personal bonebreakers."

"That's only made the decision harder," said the Meld, speaking through Stel. "Before, we thought you no more than a common jack. Now, you are revealed to be much more than we expected. But exactly how much more and in what ways is still a dangerous mystery. So, Aral, what are you?"

"Funnily enough, that's a question I've been asking myself a lot lately."

Anger flashed in Stel's eyes and Vala stiffened. "We didn't come here to play verbal games!" said the Meld.

"No, you came here because you need me." I jumped to my feet and walked toward Stel, keeping her firmly in my shadow. "I offered you the best hope of a temporary refuge and redress for your problems. You made that choice after checking me out as much as you could from a distance and then you kept me in the dark about your intent until now. If I've got doubts about the arrangement, they're no less valid than your own, so let's not get all high-horse about things, shall we?"

Behind me I heard Vala quietly shifting to the side, presumably so that she could blast me without putting Stel at risk if she had to.

Without turning, I continued, "For starters, that means that your Vala mote stops pointing those wands at my back, Dyad, and you start trusting me at least a little bit. That or you take your best shot and only one of us walks away. Which is it going to be?"

# 6

———•———

I tried not to let my tension show in any way as I waited to find out whether I was going to have to kill the Dyad. I had no doubt that I could, even if she decided to attack first. I just might not live through the experience.

"Well, I'm going to have to vote for shooting you in the back," said Stel, her voice perfectly calm. "No offense, but there are a lot of jacks in this city. We can find another, one who doesn't present so many unknowns and risks. And, I don't see any way that we can lose the fight. Vala?"

"I'm leaning that way as well. But I am wondering why our jack friend here isn't acting all that worried about the possibility."

"Is that concern the only thing that's keeping you from attacking me from behind right now?" I asked. "Because, if it is, then we're never going to establish the kind of trust that we're going to need to make this work, and we might as well get this over with."

"No, it is not the only thing," said the Meld, speaking through Vala's mouth. "That would be me. I have chosen to overrule the thinking of my motes."

*And how did that work?* I wondered. Clearly there was more to the Meld than just the sum of its parts. There were definitely three distinct people sharing the two bodies.

"So far you've done us nothing but good turns," continued the meld. "Most recently, giving us the chance to have this conversation, instead of simply killing Stel when Vala drew on you."

"What?" Stel looked shocked. "He's empty-handed. Even if he's a mage, he hasn't so much as pointed a finger in my direction."

"Yeah, I'd have blasted him before he could even begin to get off a spell," said Vala. "What haven't you told us, Valor of Steel?" Vala sounded indignant, and I had to assume she was addressing the Meld by its formal title, a thing I'd heard rumored but never confirmed.

"He is a Blade," said the Meld, speaking through Vala's mouth. "Some would say *the* Blade, if I'm not wrong in my guess at his identity. You *are* the Aral known as Kingslayer, are you not?"

I nodded slightly, but said nothing. I don't really think of myself as the Kingslayer anymore, but this weird conversation was far too fascinating to interrupt.

"I still don't understand," said Stel. "A Blade is just another type of mage, no matter what the legends say. What makes you think he could kill me before Vala could stop him?"

"You're sitting in his *shadow*," said the Meld, and exasperation crept into her voice. "His Shade holds your life in the palm of its hand, and has since before this conversation started. Honestly, motes, I sometimes wonder how I manage to think half so clearly as I do when it's your minds I have to use to do all the work."

"Oh," said Stel, her voice gone suddenly very small, while somewhere behind me Vala swallowed audibly.

"You both know about Shades," said the Meld. "I know you do because I can see the lessons about Blades in your memories. But apparently it's never occurred to either of you to actually *think* about them. Not even when you've got one with its fingers wrapped around your throats."

The Meld's eyes looked out at me through Stel's face. "I've turned the battle wands away, Kingslayer. Now I'm going to bring Vala over here so that we're all where you can see us. At that point I'd take it as a gesture of good faith if you'd step out of the light."

Again I nodded without saying a word. Creaking boards warned me of Vala's approach. She paused as she passed, laying the battle wands on the ground in front of my feet without ever looking at me. Then she went to take a seat on Stel's barrel with her back turned to both of us, thus preserving what I had already come to think of as the quintessential Dyad posture—looking both ways.

"My turn," I said. "Though there's no need to actually physically move out of the light. Triss?"

My shadow slid to the left and up onto the ceiling, uncovering Stel. Then it shifted shape, assuming the familiar outline of a small dragon and his normally concealed identity.

"Aren't you going to introduce me?" he asked, his voice strangely diffident.

"If you like." I wondered at the formality, but now wasn't the time to ask him about it. "Triss, this is Stel, her bondmate, Vala, and their Meld, Valor of Steel . . . At least I believe that's how the Meld should be addressed—please correct me if I'm wrong."

The Meld interjected, "VoS will do, actually. Valor of Steel is a formal thing worn only for formal moments. It is also, more rightly, the name of our Dyad, a sort of formalized rendition of the names my motes assumed when they bonded. I also answer to 'hey you.'"

"My pardon. Triss, meet Vala, Stel, and VoS, collectively the Dyad Valor of Steel."

Stel nodded, which was as much of a bow as could be managed in her present position and condition. Vala waved. The Meld repeated both gestures, somehow making them distinct from the originals.

"VoS, Vala, Stel, this is Triss, my familiar, and one of the finest Shades ever to grace our world of Gram."

Triss tipped his wings back and bowed from the waist. "I'm very pleased to finally meet you all. I'm sure that Aral and I will be able to help you recover the Kothmerk."

"What!" Vala spun half around, her hands reaching for the empty wand sheaths at her hips.

"How did you know about that?" demanded Stel, half drawing her fighting rods.

"Very clever." VoS turned Vala back around and resheathed Stel's rods. "You're going to have to tell me how you know about that."

"I'll trade you," I said. "You tell me how you realized who and what I was, and the story of how you ended up here, and I'll tell you what I know about the Kothmerk and how I learned it."

"Deal." The Meld nodded both of her heads. "Oh, and in case you hadn't guessed. You're hired."

"Aren't you going to ask me how much I cost?"

"No. This is a matter that touches on the honor of the Archon. If we recover the Kothmerk, my government will pay whatever is necessary. If we don't, it will be because we're all dead. In which case, money is *really* no object."

I chuckled. "I'm glad you've got such confidence in my dedication to your cause, though I'm not sure how you arrived there."

"Start with the Shade, then," said the Meld. "And with my half of our exchange of notes. A few moments ago, when Vala mentioned that we'd come to the Gryphon specifically to find Aral the jack, your shadow moved of its own accord. I didn't register it at that moment, since I was too busy watching your expression and posture. But later, when you showed such confidence in the face of what seemed overwhelming odds, I knew that you had to be much more than you seemed, so I replayed all our memories of you.

"The movement of your shadow then was the clue I needed to make sense of the chaos at the Gryphon when my motes somehow lost track of you. You didn't *seem* to vanish then, you did vanish, and without using magic. Therefore, you had to be a Blade."

"Makes sense." I nodded. "But it still doesn't tell me why that makes you trust me so much."

VoS looked at me like I was speaking a language she didn't understand. "You are the Kingslayer, Blade of Namara, the living hand of Justice. And our cause is just. What else could we possibly need to know?"

She said it so simply and with such conviction that it felt like I'd taken a knife to the heart. My eyes burned with unshed tears as I remembered what it felt like to have that kind of unalloyed faith in the goddess and the cause I served. Not to mention in myself and my fellows.

That was all gone now; my faith in all things godly had been swept away by the Emperor of Heaven's murder of Namara. Its remains were buried in the ruins of her temple by the Emperor's chief priest, the Son of Heaven. My faith in my fellow Blades had gone into the grave when I found out that some few of my companions lived on, having cut a deal with the most abhorrent of new masters, that self-same Son of Heaven.

My first impulse was to tell the Dyad that, to warn her that we who had once been Blades were just as broken and betraying as anyone else, but somehow I couldn't do it. She had a faith in me and my kind that I had long since lost, and I couldn't bear to take that away from her. Not when I knew how much its loss had cost me. Perhaps because of that, I found myself wanting to help them more than anything I had wanted in a very long time, to see myself as I had once been, if only for a little while and through the eyes of another.

And if somewhere in the back of my head there was a cynical voice reminding me that appearances were not always what they seemed and that the Dyad might turn up on the wrong side of justice, and another voice pointing out that I had already promised to help Fei and that the Dyad's goals and Fei's were not necessarily in alignment . . . well, that was probably all to the good.

Vala might remind me of Jax, but she wasn't Jax. She was part of a Dyad; a creature as alien as you could possibly find inside of a human skin. And long after she had returned to Kodamia, I would still be dealing with Fei. My life would never again be as uncomplicated as it had been when I lived to obey my goddess, and there was no point in pretending otherwise.

"You've gone very quiet over there, Aral," said Vala. "And you look so sad. I hope we haven't brought you pain." Her voice was soft and sympathetic and it cut all the deeper for that.

"No, it's all right," I said as Triss slid down from the wall and laid a comforting wing across my shoulders. "I need to remember sometimes."

And that was true. My old, simple faith might have died with my goddess and my fellows, but over the last year I had finally started to build something new atop the ruined foundations of what I had once been. I might not be a Blade of Namara anymore. Too much gray had spilled across the black and white of my old worldview for that, but I could still serve justice in my own way. And maybe even—on the good days—serve Justice as well.

"You were going to tell me a story," I said.

"It's a long one."

"Then I'd better lay out my blanket and get the whiskey." Triss snapped his wings disapprovingly at me, but I ignored him this time. I needed something to take the sting out of the blow VoS had unknowingly dealt me.

"Let Vala get the bottle," said the Meld. "She's going to go crazy if I don't allow her to get up and move around soon anyway."

"That works for me."

Before I'd finished my sentence, Vala had bounced to her feet and said "Oh, thank the Twins!" A reference to Eyn and Eva, the two-faced goddess at the center of the Kodamian branch of the church. "And now I can take off this damn armor, too."

She shimmied out of the heavy leather vest and then practically bounced over to the place where I'd left the Kyle's six beside my blanket. "Here you go." She flipped the bottle to me like a juggler's club, following it a moment later with the balled up blanket.

"Thank you." I uncorked it and took a long swig. Then I started to drag over the half barrel I'd been sitting on earlier, noting, "It'll make it easier to pass the bottle back and forth."

"Don't bother," the Meld said through Stel's mouth. "I won't be drinking until after I've finished my story. It tends to blur the edges between the three of us, and I'd rather not have that interfere with the telling."

"Well then," said Triss, rather acerbically, "why don't we all just drink water for now? It tends to blur Aral's edges as well."

I rolled my eyes and took another sip. The harsh peaty burn of the six felt wonderful, but I could see how much my taking a drink upset Triss. So I recorked the bottle and set it aside, gesturing for him to fetch me my water skin—which he was quick to do.

"Familiars, what can you do?" I said with a shrug, and it was only after I'd spoken that I realized that the age-old mage complaint about our companions might play differently with a Dyad. "Begging your pardon, if that strikes you ladies as offensive."

This sent both—or perhaps all three—of the Dyad's component personalities into gales of laughter. I took the opportunity of them recomposing themselves to fold my blanket into a pad and take a cross-legged seat with my back against the half barrel.

"I take it I said something funny?"

Stel, who was wiping tears from her eyes nodded. "Oh yes. You see, one of the biggest running jokes among the Dyadary has to do with exactly who is the familiar and who is the master, and thus who it is who suffers whom. The mages usually say it's us 'muscle-heads' since that's the way the mage/familiar bond works. We claim it's them, because, after all, we're the ones with the familiar gift. But . . ."

"But what?" I asked.

"But," sighed the Meld, "when really pressed on the topic, both sides will pick on their poor Melds." She crossed all four of their arms in a deliberately prissy manner. "Which is silly since I don't actually exist in any physical way. I maintain that I am simply a figment of their conjoined imaginations."

"The bossiest figment in the history of ever," whispered Vala, and Stel nodded vigorous agreement.

I decided at that moment that everything I'd ever heard about Dyads was probably as wrong as the crazier stories about Blades, and that I had no real clue how their thought processes worked. And the only way to find out was to observe them in action.

"Tell me about the Kothmerk." I slapped a couple of pieces of pork on a rice cake and took a bite—I could eat and listen.

"All right," replied the Meld. Then she began, switching back and forth between voices as best suited the moment or allowed one or the other of her halves to eat.

*It started when the Archon called us into the high office. I'd never been up there before. It's a round room on top of the tallest tower in the Citadel with the Archon's desks sitting opposite each other against the outer walls. They seated us back-to-back between them so that we would be able to face them and still feel comfortable.*

*"I hear very good things about you from Master Sword,"* said the Meld we refer to as the Archon. *He spoke through both mouths then, as he did throughout the entire interview—adding authority and weight to his words. "Master Wand is also quite effusive about the combat side of your magical training, if somewhat less so about the rest."*

*I blushed at that. I've always been better with the more, shall we say,* active *magics.*

*"I'll work harder on the rest," I began. "I promise to—"*

*But the Archon was already waving that off. "I am not at all displeased. In fact, your martial skills are why I've called you in today. I intend to assign you to your very first real field mission, beyond the bounds of Kodamia even."*

*"But Master Book says I won't be ready to go out among the singletons for years." And I must admit that I wailed a*

*bit here since I'd never even met a real singleton like you—*
*the solos who live in Kodamia are different.* "Not at the rate
*I'm currently advancing, at least. He says I couldn't fool a*
*drunken mercenary in search of a tumble into believing that*
*there were actually two of me."*

*The Archon laughed a good natured sort of laugh.* "Well,
*since this mission doesn't require you to tumble any single-*
*ton mercenaries, or even to pretend to be anything other*
*than a Dyad, that shouldn't be a problem. I have to send*
*something very valuable to the Durkoth of the north and it*
*needs the best protection I can send with it."*

*That's when the half of the Archon that faced Vala pulled*
*out what looked like a small block of gold, maybe two*
*inches on a side and covered in intricate etching too deli-*
*cate for any human hand to have made. The designs*
*reminded me of the patterns frost will make on steel high*
*in the mountains, only more deliberate, as if some thinking*
*hand had stolen winter's brush to paint with.*

*"What is that?" I asked through Vala's lips.*

*The Archon pulled lightly at the top and bottom of the*
*little block. It opened like a jeweler's box, though I could*
*see neither latch nor hinge, nor even a seam twixt the two*
*halves. I've held it several times since then and I still have*
*no idea how it can open. Inside was a lining of some black*
*stone like richest velvet. It held the Kothmerk as a mother*
*holds her babe, firm yet soft, with care against any slip or*
*mishap.*

*The Archon had to tip the box upside down to get it to*
*release the ring. Then he raised the Kothmerk so that the*
*sunlight streaming in through the window at his back shone*
*through the stone.*

"What did the ring look like?" asked Triss.

He'd slipped down from his perch on the wall and laid
his head in my lap and now I was idly running a finger up
and down the ridge of his scaly neck, letting my fingers find
nuance where eyes saw only undifferentiated shadow.

VoS answered Triss as she continued their story.

*It was a king's signet in general shape, though no king*

*of men ever wore so fine a seal on his finger. Nor one carved whole from a single ruby. The band is etched inside and out with more of that thinking winter's frost, deeper than that on the box, though no less delicate. It rises spiral-like to the crown of the ring, then leaves off at the edge of the seal proper.*

*That, you will know from seeing it here and there on Durkoth work, is the circle that eats itself set round the Durkoth character for the evernight. It seems a simple signet, and too easy to counterfeit by far, until you look close and see that both circle and symbol are themselves etched with a fine pattern like the veining of leaves. It was the most beautiful thing I'd ever seen, and as I leaned forward I stilled my lungs so as not to fog it with any touch of my breath.*

*"This is the Kothmerk," said the Archon, "living heart of the Durkoth and a necessary piece in the recrowning of the King of the North that happens at Winter-Round this year."*

*"I don't understand," I said. "Neither the recrowning, nor why we hold the ring." I knew little of our relationship with the Durkoth and less about the people themselves.*

*"Many years ago there was a war fought between the Durkoth of the northern mountains and their southern cousins. Mostly they fought in the deep ways of the earth, far below Gram's surface. But one great battle was fought here aboveground in the gap that splits the mountains and holds Kodamia at its heart. For reasons lost in history the then Archon came to the aid of the King of the North and helped him and his people drive the southern armies from the field. She even personally saved the king's life and with it his throne.*

*"In token of the debt he owed her, the king gave the Kothmerk into the keeping of the Archon and her heirs. It was to be held against the time of our greatest need, when the Durkoth of the North kingdom will redeem it by fighting at our side. We have held it unused for seven centuries, bringing it out of the vaults only for the recrowning*

*ceremony once every two hundred years when we send it*
*back to its rightful master."*

That's when I realized why the Archon had called me
into his tower. "You want me to take the ring to the
Durkoth?" I asked, and my voice squeaked when I spoke.

The Archon laughed. "Yes, though not alone by any
means. There will be a round dozen of the Dyadary in atten-
dance upon the ring and all of them, but you and Edge of
Persistence, are the hoariest of veterans. But I'm a little
short on fully trained death-spinners at the moment, what
with the trouble in the Kvanas."

I interrupted VoS then. "Death-spinner? What's that?"

Vala spoke, indicating herself and her bond-mate. "We
are. Different Dyads have different specialties. We're given
extensive testing soon after the pairing to determine where
our first-order aptitudes lie. My birth sister and her bond-
mate went to study under the research sorcerers. Ours was
close-in combat, so we went to the spinners."

Having seen the Dyad take on a pair of Elite I couldn't
say I was surprised. "And you stay with that for the rest of
your lives?"

"No," said Vala. "When we're older, they'll assign us to
learn a second specialty and then maybe a third."

"That's assuming we get any older," grumbled Stel. "And
that we get the Kothmerk back. If we don't manage that,
we'll probably end up as the only Dyad ever permanently
assigned to mucking out the stables."

"We'll get it back," said Vala. "We have to."

"And we'll help you," said Triss. "But please continue
the story."

VoS nodded.

The Archon put the ring back in the box and closed it.
"Based on the recommendations of Sword and Wand I'm
going to brevet you to field status for the duration of this
mission. If you do well, the promotion will become permanent and you can move out of the cadet quarters, though
I'll want you to continue your training with a new master
in hopes of expanding your range beyond death-spinner*

*and the mere cracking of skulls. An important and neces-
sary skill, but only a first step into becoming a full Dyad."*

The next several days passed in briefings and logistics.
Maps, packs, and orders, none of which is all that important. So I'll skip over all of it except for one tiny detail, the
secondary staff. On any major expedition with multiple
Dyads involved, there are bound to be a number of solos
needed as well. Drivers for the wagons, cooks, porters, and
grooms to name a few.

Among the crowd on this particular trip was a little slip
of a girl who worked in the stables, fourteen, maybe fifteen
years old. Her name was Reyna and she was a refugee from
some disaster south and west, though no one could ever get
her to talk about the details. She'd arrived a year or two
before and went to work mucking out the stalls in exchange
for meals and a spot in the loft. She was so good with the
horses that she was quickly given a job as a groom with
actual pay and a tiny room that she shared with the other
girl grooms. For all that, she was very easy to forget. Stay
with me, she'll be very important later.

We departed the Citadel on foot and in the middle of the
night and met up with the wagons and animals a full two
days later on the Zhani side of the border. They'd been sent
out a few at a time and gathered at an isolated spot in the
hills to wait for us. There had been problems moving the
Kothmerk before, and the Archon didn't want to give any
signal that something so important was on the road. That's
why it didn't go straight into the Durkoth tunnels that come
out near the Citadel either. The trouble's been much on
their end of things.

You see, whatever great noble holds the Kothmerk on
the morning of the recrowning has the right to ascend the
throne, till the next time around. So we were going to haul
it up through western Zhan and Kadesh and hand it over
to the Durkoth at Hurn's Gate pass. Since the Durkoth don't
like it up on the surface, the Archon and the King of the
North figured it'd be safer to send it with us by wagon.

They were wrong.

# 7

---

*It happened while we were in deep forest. I was riding
lookout about a half mile ahead of the wagons. That's
the only reason I'm alive to tell you this story, Aral, that I
drew the straw for forward scout that morning. It's almost
funny. The first couple of days had gone smoothly enough,
well-kept road all the way, and no cause for alarm. It looked
like we'd slipped out of the Citadel clean.*

*There was nothing at all to mark the day out as special,
though you'd think there would have been. So many Dyads
lost, and not just mere cadets, but high lords at the peak of
their power and fame. A couple of them were practically
legends in the Dyadary. And the numbers . . . more Dyads
lost at one time than have fallen anywhere else short of the
great battles.*

VoS's voice burned with pain and loss as she spoke now.

*There really ought to have been a red sun rising, or a
falling star, or a flight of black eagles. Something more to
mark their passing than a bright morning that ended in
blood and the smoke of a mass pyre.*

*I couldn't have been more than a mile ahead at the*

*utmost when the attack happened—and that far only if I'd
badly misjudged the little caravan's speed—but I heard
nothing. Nothing. I didn't even* suspect *anything had gone
wrong till the sun hit noon and my relief didn't show. I
reined in my horses and waited then, nearly an hour, figur-
ing that things had just gotten a bit distracted. But time
passed and no one came and I began to worry. I didn't want
to send up the alarm signal—a red smoke spell kept always
to hand and set to trigger in the event of my sudden death.
There was nothing wrong on my end and I didn't want to
give away our presence.*

*Finally, Vala convinced me and I let her send up a col-
umn of bright blue smoke—a standard signal requesting
orders—though not one that had been authorized for this
mission. I expected a royal chewing-out to come along with
my response. None came, nor any answering smoke, nor
any signal at all. Finally, I turned my horses around and
rode back to meet the wagons. I was worried by then, but
not yet afraid. What could possibly happen to a dozen well-
trained Dyads and forty support staff? I was about to
find out.*

*My fears started to rise after I'd covered a second mile
without encountering any of the wagons. It was possible
they'd fallen farther back than that due to some delay, but
I'd have expected a signal if so, and none had come. Three
miles, and I started to panic. I drove my horses hard after
that, pushing them to a very fast trot for the last couple of
miles. The attack had come early in the day, not long after
I'd ridden out judging by the distance I had to cover to get
back to the site of the attack.*

*They were all dead, Dyad and solo alike, or that's what
I thought then. All those bodies . . .*

VoS closed both of her sets of eyes then and shuddered.
I could see she was fighting tears, so I didn't say anything,
just scratched Triss behind the ears and waited for her to
recover. After a time, her breathing smoothed and she
nodded.

*I couldn't believe it for the longest time. Not even with*

*their corpses there in front of me like so many discarded dolls. They were strewn randomly along the road and off into the forest for a few yards on either side. Nothing could have done this. Nothing. I think the multiply repeated dichotomy of bloody ruin and apparent peace was the worst.*

She canted her Stel head to one side and looked a question at me.

*I don't know if you've ever seen a fallen Dyad, but it can happen like that if death comes fast enough. One half shot in the back of the neck and the other dead without a mark on her. . . .*

*Dagger in Waiting had been the leader of our expedition, the best eavesman and nightcutter Kodamia has produced for at least three generations. Or spy and assassin if you want it spelled out plainer. Impossible to surprise and a deadlier close-in fighter than many a spinner. His Watt half looked like it had been crushed between great stones, covered in blood and with all the bones broken. Dag, his other half, was lying peacefully on his back not five feet away, as though he'd just lain down for a quick nap. If not for Watt's shattered corpse, I might even have tried to wake him to ask what had happened.*

*Seven of the ten Dyads that had ridden out with the Kothmerk that morning had died that way, killed too quick to respond to whatever slaughtered them. Three more had gone down fighting, leaving both halves badly injured. Several of the fallen had been crushed like Dagger in Waiting. Others had been torn asunder or sliced up. Malice in Mysticism had been run through by something the size of a fence post. Clash of Remorse, who was the trailing rider, had come late to the battle and almost certainly better prepared. He had all four weapons drawn. But it hadn't helped. He suffered a double beheading before he'd made it forward of the last wagon.*

*There was even something of that weird mix of destruction and peace to the battlefield itself. Perhaps for the same reason of a quick end. Kodamian bodies lay everywhere, along with tipped over wagons and their wildly strewn contents. All the horses were dead as well. But the road itself, where most of the action had taken place, looked remarkably clean and unmarred. It had none of the rucking and ridging I'd come to associate with a battlefield. But that observation was driven out by another and even stranger one.*

*What about the enemy fallen? That was the question that really got my mind going again. Curiosity is a powerful force and acted now like spurs on a reluctant horse, forcing me to move.*

*There wasn't an enemy body to be seen. Not one. Yet I was sure there must have been casualties, because Malice in Mysticism's blades were covered with dried blood, so dark it looked black—you don't lose that much and walk away. Not even with a good combat healer ready to hand. And his weren't the only weapons that had spilled blood; it spattered the grass in places where none of my people lay.*

*So, where were the enemy bodies? And, since I was asking questions, what about the Kothmerk? Had any of our solos survived? Their bodies were scattered amongst the fallen Dyadary, but I hadn't yet taken their number. What right did I have to stand around like an idiot when there was a mission to finish?*

*That last I heard in my head in Master Sword's voice, and it galvanized me as only your first drill instructor can. I had work to do, and a damned lot of it. I had to figure out what had happened, see to the bodies in an honorable fashion, and recover the Kothmerk if possible. Gawping wasn't an option and mourning would have to wait for later.*

*I looked for the Kothmerk first, as that was the whole point of my mission. Dagger in Waiting had been carrying it in a small, locked, chainmail bag fixed around his Dag waist and hidden under his shirt. The bag was still there but it had been neatly opened and the Kothmerk was gone. Not a surprise, but it got through the numb I'd been feeling and made me angry enough to gut someone.*

*A quick check of Dagger in Waiting's person revealed*

*that was the only thing taken, and the same was true of every other body I checked. If anything, that made me angrier, all this death for one damned little trinket. I mean, there must have been a couple of thousand gold riels' worth of jewelry and equipment there, plus the mission purse and personal coin.*

*I think that's when I realized that it must have been the Durkoth who killed them. That, and how very inhuman the Others really are. No human, solo or Dyad, would have left all that money just lying around for the next person who came along to pick up. We're simply not made that way. Even I couldn't do it, and they were my friends and companions, though I only took the mission purse and that for emergencies. The rest, the durable personal items and individual purses, went into a spell-dug hole for later recovery and return to the heirs.*

*I went back and took a closer look at Malice in Mysticism's swords then and the blood on them. I hadn't noticed before because it was dried and I was in a hurry, seeing what I expected to see, but it was more purple than red, the color of royalty, not humanity. Then I started gathering bodies and piling them up for a mass burning, not having the leisure for proper individual pyres. I worked fast and hard and I burned through my nima like a maniac, but night had long since eaten the sun by the time I dropped the last of the fallen onto the heap.*

*I had numbered the fallen several times by then. Each time, I'd come up one short, Reyna, the girl groom. I hoped that she'd escaped, of course, and that I could find and question her. But if she had gotten away, she was almost certainly long gone into the hills. If she were still alive and around, she would certainly have come out by now. But I hadn't the energy left to do anything about that, much less the more urgent task of going after the Durkoth.*

*So I called fire down upon the dead and collapsed there beside the burning bodies of my companions. Exhausted beyond bearing, I slept only a little less deeply than those I'd just bid on their way to the wheel of judgment.*

*It turned out to be a good thing I'd waited to leave, for the morning brought me fresh eyes. When I looked over the battlefield one last time, hoping for some sign of the missing girl or the departing Durkoth, I found the dead spots I had missed the night before. They were about seven feet long and three wide, loosely diamond shaped, board flat, and completely devoid of any plant life.*

*They lay perhaps twenty feet off the road, in a small clearing in the wood, well beyond the main area of the battle. The four of them formed the radiating points of a star. When I touched the bare earth of the nearest, it felt wrong somehow, as though the dirt had been fused into something approaching the consistency of stone. I couldn't break it with my fingers, and jabbing at it with a dagger left by one of the fallen, barely made any mark at all.*

*I went and got a shovel, and dug down several feet along the end of one of those diamonds, but I couldn't find a bottom to the fused area. I had no other evidence for it, but they felt like tombs to me, and I believe that they were Durkoth burial sites. Somehow that made me feel better. Knowing that they'd paid a price for what they had done to my people.*

*There was a very clear, if very strange, trail leading away from the graves and on up into the mountains, as though a dozen or more of the raiders had gone that way. So I hobbled my horses and I headed up the path on foot— they'd have made noise I didn't think I could afford, the trail was that fresh. I don't know how they do in their element, deep under the mountains, but out in the woods the Durkoth are apparently shit at covering their traces.*

*They'd followed a deer path up into the hills. And, while they'd left no actual footprints, the trail of bent and broken branches along the way would have led the blindest hunter to their camp. But that wasn't the odd part. No, that was the way the trail itself looked as though someone had come along with a fine-tipped calligraphy brush and removed every trace of irregularity from its surface.*

*A deer path is generally a rough thing. It widens and*

*narrows and bumps up and down, even grows the odd bit of foliage. But this had none of that. This trail looked as though it were maintained by a team of deer engineers with a fetish for precision.*

*It reminded me of the state of the main road, which I now realized had shown some of the same signs of smoothing and evening out. Normally, at the site of a battle the road gets churned up by the action. You get scars and clods and horrible red mud from the spilled blood. It's awful and ugly and you can tell something terrible has happened there just by looking at it. But not this one. I still don't know why, but the Durkoth seem to abhor the sight of torn earth. Knowing that's saved my life a couple of times since then.*

*The trail they'd left was my first luck. The second was finding several of the Durkoth still at home. They had shaped a cavern out of the living rock of a cliff face maybe two miles from the place of the ambush. I don't know whether they'd waited for the caravan there for a couple of days, or if they just casually move rock around like that for a single night's camp. Whatever the case, they'd scooped out a space the size of a small manor house, with what looked like multiple rooms, many of them with windows.*

*They were arguing when I arrived, and loudly, or they might have spied me before I spotted them. Like an idiot, I'd walked practically up to the cliff face before I realized what I was hearing. I'm only middling fair at woodcraft on my best day, and I don't speak much Durkoth. Though I'd been studying my heart out since I'd gotten my orders for the mission, I just didn't recognize it at first.*

*Spoken fast and angry, as they were speaking it, Durkoth sounds more like the weirdest cat fight you ever heard than anything a person might say. Eventually though, I did realize what I was listening to. I threw myself down under some brush then, about three feet from what turned out to be the nearest window.*

"What were they fighting about?" Triss asked VoS.

*The Kothmerk, but you'd probably guessed that part already. More importantly, they were arguing about whose fault it was that the thing had gone missing. One of 'em swore up and down that he'd felt a little human girl running off into the woods right before he discovered the thing missing—and maybe one of those ishka-ki Kodamians had survived.*

*The others thought that was ridiculous and just an excuse for his failure on guard duty. How could any human, much less a young one, have possibly gotten into their krith without someone seeing her? And why would a human thief leave the ring box behind when she took the Kothmerk? But even with that, a bunch of them had gone off along the durathian road—whatever that was—to try to get ahead of the possibly mythical girl, and they'd only just left a short while before. I felt a nasty little chill at that, thinking how lucky I was that they'd taken some other route than the deer path.*

*Now, I was only getting maybe one word in three, if that. So, it took me quite a while to make sense of it all. But when I finally did, and heard the bit about the girl, I immediately thought of the missing young Reyna. So I slipped away from there right quick. Then I turned around and hurried back down the path the way I'd come.*

VoS clenched four fists and briefly shut as many eyes, and it was easy to see that the memory hurt her.

*It wasn't what I wanted to do. No, not by a long haul. What I wanted to do was rush in and kill the lot of them. I probably would have tried, too, if I'd thought I had any real hope of managing it, but these Others had brought down eleven Dyads already and with only a loss of four of their own number. I knew that any attempt I made then might as well come with a suicide note.*

*Even that might not have been enough to stop me if it weren't for the girl. What if it was Reyna? What if she had the Kothmerk now? Maybe I could still finish out the mission. Maybe I could make all those deaths matter.*

*When I got close to where I'd left my horses, I slowed down and started moving extra quietlike. I still didn't know what a durathian road might be, but if they were trying to get ahead of the girl and they thought she was one of ours, they might well have come back to the battlefield looking for her. It was a good thing I did, too, because I found three of them standing around one of my horses looking angry and jibbering their jabber.*

*I listened long enough to determine that the rest had gone off, a-hunting after my second horse and the girl who'd taken it. Following the tracks or something, it sounded like, though I can't say for sure. There were a lot more strange words involved and a good deal of pointing and what sounded like swearing. I figured that was all I needed to know, so I got my angles lined up and I used my battle wands to punch nice big holes in all three of them at once.*

*They're the toughest bastards I've ever seen, I'll give them that. The two I got through the heart made it halfway to me before they went down for good. And the one I'd only drilled through the lungs was practically on top of my Vala when Stel beheaded her. Thumb-sized hole running from armpit to armpit and she was still going strong right up till the second she lost her head. I wanted to ride then, but figured I couldn't afford the noise, so I took the mission purse and as much food as I could carry, unsaddled my horse, loosed the hobbles and headed out very quietly.*

*The dead Durkoth had all been pointing back along the road, so that's the way I went. I'm not sure how the Others were traveling, but they left an obvious enough trail, a series of parallel lines running lengthwise along the road where the grade was smoother and straighter than any human would ever have made it. I also don't know how fast they were moving, or Reyna on my stolen horse either, but I kept along at a nice steady march from a couple hours after sunup till near nightfall without catching anyone up.*

*I was just dropping off to sleep when it occurred to me that with the timing and all, the girl would pretty much have had to pass me on that trail I'd followed to the Durkoth krith. That meant there was a good chance she'd seen me coming up, and had decided not to flag me down. That, plus the fact that I hadn't seen her, even though I was looking out for anyone coming my way, left me feeling more than a little hollow.*

*Add in that she'd gotten past the Durkoth guards to steal the Kothmerk from them, and the way she'd somehow managed to avoid getting killed during the battle, and you had to start asking questions. How did she get past the guards? How did she avoid getting killed in an ambush that had taken the lives of nearly a dozen of the finest Dyads I knew? And, further back: Where had she really come from? What exactly was the disaster she'd fled in the southwest? How the hell had she gotten this far without either the Durkoth or me catching her? Etc.*

*I didn't sleep very well that night, and the next day only added more questions. I found my missing horse after about an hour's walk. She was lying dead in a little clearing off to one side of the road with her saddle and bags in a heap not too far off. There were smooth neat lines running along the ground all over the place, and two of those weird burial diamonds. My first thought was that the Durkoth had caught up with Reyna, and by some miracle she'd managed to take two of them with her.*

*But a quick look around changed my mind. First off, there was no crumpled little body, and if the earlier battlefield had shown me anything, it was that the Durkoth didn't much care what happened to human corpses. Second, I followed flies to a couple of huge purple blood patches about forty feet apart. Both had the look of ambush killings, like someone had gotten their throat slit or the big artery in the groin opened up without ever getting a chance to fight back.*

*Once I was finished with looking around the clearing, I went back to the road. There was another set of lines leading onward. Since I was pretty sure I'd fallen behind, I resaddled my horse and mounted up, with Vala riding pillion. About midafternoon I hit a crossroads where all the trails turned and headed toward Tien. As you've probably guessed, I never did catch up to the girl, though I did run into two wounded Durkoth on the way to Tien—too hurt to travel I think—and one of those nearly did for me before I gutted her.*

"You really believe one young girl managed to kill two Durkoth and do all those other things?" asked Triss. "How?"

VoS shrugged Vala's shoulders. "I have no idea. Nor how she survived that first battle, or any of the other fantastic things I've ascribed to her. But I'm pretty sure that's what happened, and what evidence I've found has tended to support the idea. I may not have found Reyna, but I did turn up ten more Durkoth graves scattered along the roadside between there and here, along with the corpses of a score or so of what looked to be innocent bystanders."

"Maybe it wasn't Reyna that did all that," I said as I wrapped up what was left of my dinner. "It could have been a third party as yet unknown." I couldn't help but think of the dead girl that Fei's sergeant Zishin had found—the one with a couple of Elite standing over her corpse—and wonder if that wasn't the missing Reyna.

"A third party who just happened along at that exact moment?" asked VoS. "One who sounded to the Durkoth like a little girl running away? Who also removed Reyna's body from the battlefield, or did something else to get rid of it? And all without leaving any other clues to point to his or her existence?"

"There is that," I said. "Maybe she was a mage of some sort, or had help."

I didn't say it, but killing from ambush like that would be right up the alley of one of my kind. And now that I'd encountered Devin, I knew a number of my brethren had turned their coats at the fall of the temple and might well be willing to take on that kind of job. But I didn't want to share any thoughts on that just yet, not till I had more information. Not about that and not about the dead girl. Not till I was absolutely sure about who was on the side of justice here.

"A mage I'd be more willing to believe," said VoS.

"We've discussed it amongst ourselves," said Vala. "Stel likes the unknown allies theory, but I don't see it. There's never been any evidence for her being anything other than alone. I think she might have been a much older mage just pretending to be a girl."

"How would she manage that?" asked Triss. "Illusion's all right if you're dealing with the mageblind, but I've never heard of a Dyad having that problem."

"We don't," said Stel. "If Reyna was wrapped in an active spell Vala would have seen it, or if not Vala, one of the other mage-halves."

"But there is a way . . ." Vala started, but trailed off when Stel gave her a hard look.

"We are *not* going to talk about that," said Stel.

# 8

———◆———

"Talk about what?" I leaned forward on my half barrel curiously, but Stel just gave me a stony look and stayed clammed up.

"Might as well just tell him," said VoS, after a dozen or so heartbeats. "It's not like he doesn't know more than enough to get us court-martialed and hanged if he wanted to already."

"But no one outside the Dyadary is supposed to even know the spell exists," protested Stel. "It's a state secret."

Vala shrugged. "And one we're almost certainly going to have to use after the disaster at the tavern. Even if we waited till Aral left to do something and then worked the change, it's not something we'd be able to hide from him. Not if we're going to keep working together."

"All right," said Stel, "but for the record, I'm really not happy about this."

Vala winked at her bond-mate. "So write me up when we get home. Maybe they'll let you roam free while they've got me locked in the stockade."

Stel rolled her eyes in a way that suggested this was a

common tease between the two of them. Then she shrugged and gestured for Vala to continue.

"There's a spell we use in the Dyadary that will permanently alter your appearance." Vala grimaced. "We call it the bonewright, because that's what it does. Within certain limits that is."

"By which she means to complain to the unjust gods that there's no way to make her significantly taller," Stel said with a little smirk.

"I've never heard of anything like that," I said. "But that's probably not a huge surprise. While the goddess lived, she clouded the minds of those who saw her Blades, so that we could neither be drawn nor accurately described. There was never any need for us to significantly alter our appearance, or even to think about it."

"I don't think *anyone* knows about this outside of Kodamia," said Vala. "It's extraordinarily painful for the one experiencing the change, and losing control of the process is usually fatal, and always disfiguring. Most mages simply couldn't manage it. The only reason it's come into regular practice amongst the Dyadary is that we sorcerers can cede control of our bodies over to our lovely and charming familiars."

Stel raised her eyebrows. "I think you misspoke there. Don't you mean, oh familiar-mine, that your masters can control your puny little bodies, while you do the petty conjuring?"

"My bond-mate might be right," said Vala. "About my making a mistake, I mean. I'm afraid I have to retract the *charming* part of the description of our familiars, at least in Stel's case. Though she is still lovely." Vala blew Stel a kiss.

"You're not trying to say that Reyna is one half of a renegade Dyad, are you?" Triss lifted his head from my lap and looked more closely at the pair. "Because that makes no sense whatsoever."

"No, of course not," replied VoS. "But it's possible, however unlikely, that some other sorcerer got hold of the bonewright and had a familiar that could handle half of the process. One of the greater dragons or a vampire perhaps. Something with a lot of power and a good mind at any rate. Or, maybe there's some sort of familiar that has some way of mitigating the agony."

"Or," interjected Vala, "—and this is my theory—it's possible that a sufficiently disciplined mage could simply handle the pain. That they wouldn't need help from their familiar to manage the thing."

Stel put a hand up and pretended to whisper to me behind its cover, "She has delusions of mage-grandeur sometimes. Just pretend to agree with her."

Triss flipped a wing up in a perfect mirror of Stel's gesture. "Mine does that, too. Do you think it's a flaw inherent to those born with the mage gift? Or is it learned somehow?"

"I don't know about Aral, but poor Vala's *always* been a little off, if you know what I mean."

"That's too bad," said Triss. "If they'd learned it, there might be some way to train them out of it. Snacks for better behavior, or a sharp swat on the nose whenever it happens, or something. . . ."

Vala marched over to me, slipped her hand through my elbow, and tucked herself in tight against my side. "I've never been so insulted in all my life." She was short enough that she hardly had to stoop to make the connection, though I was sitting. "Take me away from all this, won't you please?"

My sense of humor might be a bit rusty, but it wasn't yet dead, so I grinned and nodded. "Of course, my lady. Where should we go?"

"Be careful there, Aral," said Stel. "She's a dangerous one once she gets her hooks into you. Deadly cute, and too smart by half. I should know."

"Oh, I would never do anything to hurt Aral," said Vala, laying her head on my shoulder and blinking up at me faux-adoringly. "For he is a fellow mage and, like me, he clearly suffers under the crushing burden of a too-insolent familiar."

With Vala pressed so close, I couldn't help but notice the smell of her hair and the warmth of her body. It was the first time that I'd really thought of her as a human woman rather than half of a Dyad, which was the next thing to some sort of exotic creature from another dimension in my book. It was a rather alarming realization, and I felt my face flushing.

I decided to brazen it out and pretend nothing had happened, but the rather smug look that suddenly appeared on Vala's face suggested that I was perhaps pulling it off less well than I'd hoped.

"But I promised to tell you how I came to know about the Kothmerk," I said.

"You did at that." Vala didn't relinquish her hold on my arm, choosing to sit on the edge of the barrel with me instead. "Let's hear it."

I was somewhat distracted as I rattled off my encounter with Qethar, and I wondered if that wasn't exactly the Dyad's intent. But I still managed to tell the bulk of my tale in a reasonably lucid manner. Lucid enough that VoS and company didn't seem to notice the gaps where I omitted things like the pebble Qethar had given me, or the appearance of Captain Fei, both of which incidents I thought better to keep to myself for the moment. Oh, the joys of trying to serve two masters, and justice besides.

When I finished speaking, Vala hopped to her feet and began to pace—the only one of us short enough to manage it in the confined space of the attic. "I don't like the sound of this Qethar even a little bit. Do you think he's one of the group that we followed to the city? Judging by the marks in the road, there were at least a half dozen left by the time they got here."

"I doubt it." Mostly because of things Fei had said about Qethar being well-known in certain circles in Tien, but I couldn't very well tell the Dyad that. "He seemed to know the city like someone who lived here, and that Elite major treated him more like a well-known pain in the ass than a visiting VIP."

"That reminds me of a thought I wanted to mention about the major," said Stel. "You say his dog was practically on top of you when it suddenly turned away?"

I nodded, which stretched sore muscles and reminded me of how very long the day had been already. "Yes. I thought sure it had us there, and then nothing. It was strange and Qethar later implied it was his doing, but I don't see how."

"Maybe he can persuade the stone dogs in the same way he persuades the stuff of the earth itself. They are elementals, after all."

Triss reared back. "Oh, I don't like that thought, not one bit."

"But do you think it's possible?" I asked him through a sudden yawn.

Triss was our resident expert on elementals—being one himself.

"I don't think you could do it to one of us," he replied, his voice low and worried, "but then there are no Others who have a history of alliance with the shadows. And, well, how can I put this kindly? The stone dogs aren't the smartest of the elementals. Much smarter than a dog, certainly, but not even as smart as most men."

I gave him my best raised eyebrow. "Thanks for that vote of confidence, partner."

"Oh, you're significantly smarter than most of your breed . . . about some things at least. And that makes you nearly as smart as the average Shade. But neither you nor I have anything like the mind of one of the great water dragons. A shinsan or a kuan-lun, say."

"He's got a point," said VoS. "You humans are smart enough in your own way, but you're a long way from the brightest lights around."

Vala sighed. "Is she going to go into her thing about how much smarter she is than we are again?"

"It sure sounds like it," said Stel.

"It's not that I'm smarter per se, it's just that I have twice the thinking power, so I can do things both faster and better than either of you could alone."

"Not if I knock back this bottle of whiskey." Vala picked up the Kyle's. "And I've got to tell you that's what this whole line makes me want to do. What do you say, Stel?"

"I'm in . . . if this whole superiority spiel goes on much longer."

VoS snorted through both of their noses. Then she sighed and shook her heads. "Fine. I'll stop. Now, what's next on our agenda?"

I got up and hunched my way over to the chimney, sticking my head through the curtain and looking up. A clear patch of pale rosy gray sky showed at the top.

I closed the curtain again. "I don't know about you, but sleeping is getting pretty high on my list. I've been awake for something like twenty hours straight and on the run for more than half of that. I'll be a lot more useful for planning in the morning."

"That sounds like a damned fine idea to me," said Stel, and for the first time since we'd gotten her settled, I remembered how badly injured she was. "I'm all in."

"Fair enough," said Vala. "I'm pretty knocked down as well." She looked at the bottle a bit wistfully. "Though I wouldn't mind a nightcap if any of you wanted to join me."

I was quite tempted, and because I was tempted, I shook my head. "Maybe tomorrow."

Stel had already slid down the barrel to lie fully prone and closed her eyes.

VoS said, "Save it. You were right about the spell earlier. We're going to have to make some alterations to our appearance before we can show our faces out on the street again, and that means the bonewright. You don't want a hangover for that, and after, we'll all three need a drink or five."

Vala grimaced and set the bottle aside. "We will at that. Aral, this is your aerie. Do we need to set a guard?"

"No, the main risk is a fire started by our downstairs neighbors and sitting up worrying about it won't make one jot of difference as to whether that's going to happen. Beyond that, there's Triss."

My little dragon nodded and spread his wings. "Even with the sun coming up it'll stay pretty dark in here. Once the magelight's out, I'll be completely free to roam around the attic and even to slip down through the cracks once in a while to check on the caras-heads."

"Don't you sleep?" asked Vala. Stel had already started to snore faintly.

"Mostly I nap, and much of that in the day, while I'm dragging along in Aral's shadow, going bump-bump-bump down the street and pretending I don't exist. I'm wide awake now and will be for hours yet."

"I guess that covers everything." Vala looked at me. "Do you want me to do something about the light since I'm up?"

"I was just going to toss it in an amphora and tamp the lid down. You're welcome to the duty if you want it."

She nodded and took down the light. The shadows, all but Triss, danced wildly around as she followed my suggestion. Then it got very dark and I had to follow her progress by ear. First, grabbing up her blanket. Then, laying it out and settling herself.

I'd expected her to put it down beside Stel's, but she actually chose a place on my farther side, bracketing me between her and her bond-mate in a way that I found a bit discomfiting. Especially as she took a spot rather significantly closer to me than Stel was—just the other side of the little half barrel where I'd been sitting.

"Aral?" she said after several minutes had passed.

"Yes."

"I wanted to wait till Stel went to sleep and took VoS with her before I said this. I'm glad we found you. I don't think we could do this on our own. Thank you."

I heard a faint noise from her direction, but couldn't figure out what it was until Triss whispered in my ear. "She's reached her hand out along the left side of the barrel. I think she wants you to squeeze it."

So I did. "You're welcome."

She squeezed me back, then withdrew her hand. "See you in the morning, Aral. Sleep well."

"You, too, Vala."


I woke to the sound of chalk scratching across rough boards, and rolled up onto my side to find Vala busily scribbling diagrams on the floor at the far end of the room. The attic felt breathless and baking, like the inside of a huge and dusty oven, and I guessed it must be getting near sundown. I wiped sweat off my face and took a second look at the huge splash of multicolored chalk Vala was creating.

"That kind of spell, is it?" I mumbled. I've never been much for high magic, especially not the intricate stuff with all the fuss and bother.

"Hush." Triss shushed me from above.

He had climbed high up on the angled ceiling to get the best view of the process. This put him in a very strange position relative to me and the glow of the magelight. Vala had pulled it out and fixed it on the back of the chimney so that it lit her end of the room and left me mostly in shadow. Which meant Triss was just about 180 degrees from where a natural shadow would have been.

I ignored his admonition and kept talking. "I don't suppose anyone's made porridge and toast, or even some of that awful fish soup the locals favor for breakfast?"

"Nope," said Stel from somewhere behind me. "You've got your salted pork, your rice cakes, your salted pork between two rice cakes, or, if you're feeling all bold and experimental, your rice cake between two slices of pork. That one's kind of messy."

I looked over my shoulder. Stel was sitting up against the half barrel with her head leaned back and her eyes closed.

"Ribs bad?" I asked.

She nodded very slightly without moving otherwise. "I took a look under the bandages this morning. It looks like I've been rolling around in raw indigo."

"You want me to get you the whiskey?" I knew how much cracked ribs can hurt.

"No, I can't afford to dull my wits now. Not right before we attempt this damned bonewright trick."

"Maybe you should wait till you're feeling better," I said.

She opened her eyes and met mine, shaking her head slightly. "Without a real healer that could take weeks, and we can't go see a healer until we do something to lower our profile."

"I know a couple of backstreet wound-tailors who will forget they ever saw you if the fee is high enough."

"And how do we get there without running the risk of being seen?"

Stel's face shifted as VoS came to the fore. Even after listening to her tell the long story last night, it was still jarring to watch the shifts in expression and manner when the Meld inhabited one or the other of them. It made the person I'd just been talking to feel like nothing more than a mask to be put on or taken off at the convenience of the creature that ruled them both.

"More importantly," said VoS, "what happens if the Durkoth offer a reward for anyone with information? Will your friends stay bought if they can make ten times as much by turning us in?"

It was my turn to shake my head. "They aren't really friends, and even the most honest of them would probably sell his mother for parts given the right incentive. That doesn't change the fact that Stel's injuries are going to keep her from operating at anything like her best. If this bonewright is that dangerous . . ."

"It is," VoS said flatly. "But we still have to try it."

"Partially *because* of Stel's injuries," Vala tossed over her shoulder, entering the conversation for the first time. "I think that if I work her transformation right I can mend her ribs myself as part of the process."

"Really?" asked Triss. "It's not all cosmetic?"

"No." Vala rose from where she'd just finished a line and turned to face Triss. "Or, at least, it doesn't have to be. If you want to really change the way someone looks, you need to restructure the bones of the face, at least a little bit. That's why it hurts so much. VoS and I don't see any reason why we shouldn't be able to extend that to knitting Stel's ribs back together."

"I'm still not entirely sold on that part," said Stel. "The spell is complex enough without trying something that's not a standard part of the routine. Even the best eavesmen usually don't do much more than surface work below the neck, and you've only ever drilled with this spell."

"It'll be fine," said Vala, but I could see she was worried.

"Wait." I held up a hand. "Are you saying you've never actually performed this bonewright thing before?"

Vala's chin came up. "Not to completion, no. But I can handle it. The structure of the spell isn't that difficult to manage. It's just the pain factor that makes it dangerous, and Stel and I have had a lot of practice dealing with pain. I'd expect spinners like Stel and I to be much better at this than those wimpy old eavesmen."

"But you don't *know* that," said Stel. "And it's dangerous to mess with the big bones. That's what Pride at Valerian said when you asked about making yourself taller."

"That was only because you can't actually add or subtract anything, just move it around. Unlike fat and muscle, there's no good way to make extra bone. If I made myself significantly taller I'd have to thin out my bones so much they'd be as brittle as old porcelain."

"You know, I'm beginning to think I should have taken you up on the offer of a drink," said Stel. "If I passed out we couldn't try this hob-brained scheme."

"You know VoS wouldn't let you do that," said Vala.

"Some days I just want to whack her one," replied Stel. "Unfortunately, the one who'd get hurt would be you."

"And you, through the echo," said Vala.

"That, too." Stel sighed. "Do you have all the chicken-scratching done, Vala?"

"I do."

"Then let's get this over with one way or the other."

Vala crossed to her bond-mate and helped her up. "It'll be fine. I promise I'll take good care of you."

"I'm not worried about that so much as whether I'll be able to do the same for you. I'm not at my best right now."

"That's why we've got to do it, and you're first."

The pair crossed to the chalked up area of the long low room, with Stel leaning heavily on her smaller companion. I got up as well. I wanted to take a closer look at the diagram. I don't *do* ritual magic if I can avoid it, but I was taught the basics, and it was always good to learn new things. Triss flitted along the ceiling above my head, moving in to get a better look as well.

The main figure was a pair of large hexagons that shared one side in common. Sketched in and around the points were great bunches of the usual glyphs and sigils. I'd just started trying to work out the general gist of the structure, when Vala completely snarled my line of thought by the simple expedient of slipping off her shirt, about three feet in front of me.

Her breasts were small and perfectly formed, with nipples like dark coins. She was thin, but not so much so that I could count ribs, and very muscular—an athlete. Before I could even think about turning away or otherwise offering her greater privacy, she skinned out of her pants and underwear as well, exposing a lovely pair of legs and the patch of raven hair at their juncture.

"Uh . . ." I began, but couldn't for the life of me think of anything to say next.

Vala grinned. "I take it you like what you see, then?" She showed not the slightest sign of body modesty and I was reminded that at the Kodamian games, the athletes mostly compete in the nude.

"I think he's actually drooling," Stel said, rather dryly.

I turned toward her, initially delighted at being offered a distraction from staring at the naked Vala. But apparently the spell required nudity for both partners, because Stel was also stripping. Because of her injuries, she'd only just managed to get her shirt off, exposing large full breasts. Beneath were loops and loops of bandages that acted rather like a corset, lifting them up and forward. At that point, I closed my eyes and turned around while I tried to reclaim my composure. Behind me, Vala chuckled low and wicked while Stel snorted amusedly.

"Ah, he's blushing," said Stel. "That's kind of sweet. The legends never mentioned that the Kingslayer was shy."

I wanted to growl at her. For a number of reasons. First off, I'm neither shy, nor am I normally thrown off my stride by the naked female form. Not if I'm somewhere I'd be expecting it, say in a Tienese bathhouse, or on a Kodamian field of sport. But I originally come from a culture where nudity is strongly associated with sex, and if I don't have time to think ahead, that's where my mind goes. Especially with Vala reminding me of the first great love of my life. Though Jax would probably have been more shocked right then than I was. She came to the temple from Dalridia, an even more modest culture than Varya.

Second, there's the whole Kingslayer thing. That guy isn't me. Not anymore, at least. I was him once, but that was before my goddess died and took the Blade part of me with her, the better part of me, really. These days I'm just a jack living in a world of shadow.

I shrugged and turned back around to face the pair of naked women. They were still both attractive, and a part of me couldn't help but react to that, but this time I had it under control.

"I tell you," I said, "you kill one lousy king, and pretty soon people are buying you hats that are three sizes too large with the word 'Kingslayer' writ large across the brim. Don't listen to the stories. I'm no legend, I'm just Aral. What you see is what you get."

Triss had visibly started at my initial comment and now his mouth was half hanging open. "Wait, was that a joke up there at the front?"

"Might have been," I said defensively. "Why?"

"Because it's been an awfully long time since you made one for real, and I'm kind of hopeful right now."

"Didn't have much to laugh at," I replied. "Or, no, that's not it. Say rather that I didn't have much to laugh with, and it'll be closer to the truth."

"And that's changed?" Triss asked, and his voice made it sound like he was trying to keep a particularly tricky spell from exploding in his face.

"Some. Maybe. I don't know for sure, but maybe."

"I'll take that," said Triss.

I turned my attention back to Vala. "Sorry about my silence there a minute ago. The answer is 'Yes.' I do indeed like what I see. You're a very attractive woman." Now Vala blushed, and I turned to Stel who was just peeling off the last of her bandages to expose a huge patch of bruises. "So are you, I might add. Though I think you'd look better without all that black and blue."

Stel didn't blush, she smiled. "It's really not my color scheme. The yellow and green that will come later, on the other hand . . ." She put her fingers to her lips and made a smooching sound.

"Tell me more about this bonewright," I said.

"It'll be easier to just show you and answer any questions you have left after," said Vala.

Vala turned and headed over to help Stel down into a cross-legged position in the nearer of the two hexagons, before settling herself in the farther. The two faced each other, with Stel's back to me.

Vala looked at me over her bond-mate's shoulder with a wicked glint in her eye. "Which do you prefer, Aral, brunette or redhead?"

"Raven, why do you ask?"

"Sweet of you to say," said Vala, whose hair was already black. "But that wasn't one of the options. Brown or red?"

"Then red." Jax was a brunette, and I really didn't need Vala hitting my weak spots any harder than she already was. Not if I was to have any hope of honestly finding the justice in this situation.

"Done." She lowered her hands to rest on her knees with the palms turned up, then began the bonewright.

# 9

---·×·---

The bonewright was a subtle spell, with no overt gestures or chanting to start things off, just a lot of concentration on the proper sequence of the glyphs and their naming. I could follow along with my magesight, as long multicolored threads of light slid from the tips of Vala's fingers outward to connect to first one ideogram, and then another as she named them. Soon she sat in the middle of a cat's cradle of light: green and gold and scarlet and violet and azure and peach.

Techniques learned long ago helped me make sense of the process, and to store enough cues away that I could probably even hope to remember how it was done later, if someone wanted to know. At that thought I felt a little lead ball form in my heart, because for me there was no one left to tell. The art of mapping a spell was something I'd only ever really used when making reports to the masters and priests at the temple, and now they were all gone into the grave. Triss and I were alone in the world.

I was so distracted then that I almost missed the start of the next stage, when Vala raised her hands to touch her face. More threads of light rose from the glyphs then, connecting

themselves to Stel's head and chest, mirroring the structure
that centered on Vala. Making tiny, subtle motions, Vala ran
her fingertips along her own cheekbones.

In response, the lights touching Stel dug into her face,
stretching and twisting, reshaping bones and flesh. Stel
grunted like she'd taken an arrow to the chest, and tears
began to stream down her cheeks. Though she was clearly
in agony she neither screamed nor tried to move away from
the threads. Drops of blood broke out here and there on her
face, prickling up in the wake of the moving threads.

Her cheeks broadened and thickened at the same time
that her lips narrowed. Deeper chin, teeth that shifted to
give her the faint hint of an overbite, higher thicker eyebrows, a stronger nose, eyes that went from deep brown to
shimmering green, hair lightening from black to a chestnut
brown. When Vala finished, Stel was still a pretty woman,
but a very different one.

Now Vala's hand moved down, cupping her breasts and
squeezing and shaping, shifting from there to her sides and
ribs. A tiny high-pitched noise escaped from Stel's lips, like
the dying squeak of a mouse, as her breasts grew higher and
smaller, their nipples lightening and shrinking. The changes
left more blood in their wake, mixing with the sweat that
sheeted Stel's skin. She whimpered a little as the color began
to fade from her bruises, and I could see her ribs shifting
and knitting from ten feet away.

Finally, mercifully, Vala finished. Stel sagged forward
as the light left her. But now it was Vala's turn. The threads
that had fallen away from Stel snapped back to connect with
their counterparts on Vala, collapsing into themselves and
doubling in size. For a couple of heartbeats nothing more
happened.

Then, Stel's face took on a look of intense concentration
as Vala's hand began to move again. The motion was different this time, no less smooth or clean, just much less *Vala*.
Though I couldn't have proved it, I could see that Stel had
taken control of Vala's body. The fingers that slid along
Vala's jaw drawing lines of blood, moved in a firmer, more

matter-of-fact way than they had earlier. Still graceful, but
a warrior's grace now instead of a dancer's.

It was simultaneously fascinating and repulsive, this
obvious invasion, and I wondered briefly if that was how
another Shade might see things when I took control of Triss
to perform a spell or sail-jump. I wanted to turn away, and
yet, I found that I couldn't. It was too fascinating. The process flowed along in just the same sort of way it had for Stel,
though Vala made no noise at all.

Features shifted first: jaw lengthened, lips fattened as if
by bee sting, cheeks hollowed out under freshly razor-edged
cheek bones, eye sockets deepened. Blue eyes became an
exotic amber, streaming tears. Short straight black hair
shifted to a thick curly auburn, and dropped to hang below
her shoulders. A faint scar appeared at the corner of her
right eye like the echo of a tear. When her hands moved
down, her breasts became fuller and farther apart, though
no less firm. A stroke across her pubic hair changed it to
match her hair, and that was it below the neck. They made
no deeper changes to Vala's body, just shifted the areas that
attracted the most attention.

When they had finished, Stel released Vala, or so it
appeared, as Vala suddenly sagged forward like a string-cut
puppet. For several heartbeats she sort of hung there, looking empty. Then, slowly, she put her hands on her knees and
forced herself back upright. Sweat and blood and tears
stained her face and chest. She looked like she'd just run an
endurance race as she sat there gasping for breath.

"Fuck," she whispered as she began to loose the threads
of her magic, letting them fall away one by one. "I hate it
when that happens."

"What?" asked Triss.

"I prove Stel right."

Stel, who didn't look like she felt any better than Vala,
blinked several times, and said, "Could you repeat that?"

"I said you were right. Are you happy now?"

"I'd be happier if I knew what I was right about."

Vala laughed, or tried to—it sounded harsh and forced.

"That bit earlier where I said that a sufficiently disciplined mage might be able to handle this spell on their own. There's no fucking way. If you hadn't been moving my hands I could never have managed to keep hold of the magic. I could *feel* my bones being reshaped—like someone chopping off bits and gluing them on again in less comfortable positions." She suddenly hugged herself, covering her breasts with her crossed arms. "And what it did to my tits . . . never again."

"I'd think a lone mage would need more tools, too," I said. "Like a mirror for starters."

"I don't think so," said Stel. "I wasn't really looking at Vala while I was working with her hands. It's much more about imagining the result you want than it is making conscious visual choices in the moment."

By then Vala'd dropped the last of the glowing threads, and now she simply fell over onto her side without otherwise changing position. Stel was apparently made of tougher stuff. That or she was just more bullheaded. In either case, she forced herself up onto hands and knees and started crawling toward her clothes. Triss, quicker of wit than I was, slid down the wall and picked them up to carry over to her.

"Thanks." Stel crawled into her shirt, then flopped over onto her back to drag her pants over her hips. She tossed her underwear in the general direction of her bandages, then closed her eyes and let her head fall back against the boards with a gentle thud. "*Now* we drink."

Somewhere along about then it occurred to me that I should probably be helping, so I picked up Vala's clothes and brought them to her.

"No way," she said when I set them down in front of her. "I know where those have been." She sighed. "But I suppose I don't have much choice at the moment." Still, she didn't move.

"You could borrow one of my shirts," I said. "I've got a complete change of clothes or two stored here. They're pretty threadbare, but they're clean, and with the size difference it'd just about make a dress for you."

"Yes please."

Stel opened one eye and glared at me balefully as I passed her on the way to the appropriate amphora. "And where were you with your offers of clean clothes a minute ago when *I* was in need?"

"Sorry," I said. "It hadn't occurred to me yet. You're welcome to the other set." I tossed a pair of aging pants and an old threadbare shirt her way. "It'd just about fit you."

She poked at them with a finger. "Ah, you just want to see me naked again. I'd even indulge you if I didn't think changing would hurt more than it was worth. Maybe after I've had a couple of drinks it'll sound like a better idea."

I had no good answer to that, so I just hauled the better of my two spare shirts over to Vala. It fit her more like a tent than a dress, with the too-wide collar continually falling off her shoulder to expose a distracting amount of pale flesh, including the top of a much fuller breast than the old Vala's. And it only covered her to the tops of her knees, a scandalous length in any court in the eleven kingdoms of the east.

That, however, was far less distracting than the changes to her face and hair. I'd only just started to get to know the old Vala, and here she was looking like a whole new person. She didn't even look Kodamian now, more like an Aveni or Osian, though the only place I'd ever seen amber eyes like that was in the mage lands.

"And it's permanent, you say?" I asked as we all moved back over to where we'd created a rough sort of sitting room with the barrels.

Vala nodded and her new red curls tumbled down around her shoulders. "That's going to get really old, really fast." She swept her hair up back off her face, twisting it into a knot on the back of her head for about the fifth time. "I may have to find a pair of scissors before the day gets too much older."

"What if you want to go back to looking like the old you later?" I asked. Triss kept sliding back and forth along the ceiling to get a better look at both Stel and Vala. He'd just slipped around behind them when I asked my question.

Vala took a careful sip of the Kyle's, holding it in her mouth for a couple of beats before swallowing, then passed the bottle over to me. I imagined what it would be like to kiss her then, with the whiskey fresh and sweet on her tongue.

"The bonewright's really not that precise," said Vala. "Between the vagaries of memory and the lack of fine control on the spell, about the best you can hope for is to get to a place where you look like a sister to the old you."

"Some of the older eavesmen probably don't even *remember* what they originally looked like anymore," said Stel. "They've changed their face so many times. Names, too. It's a strange sort of life. Why didn't you change your name, Aral? I'd think here of all places that would have been the easy thing to do."

I took a long pull on the bottle while I thought about how to answer that. It wasn't my first drink, and the bottle was already looking a lot emptier than it had when we opened it. It had been a while since I'd had this much alcohol this fast, and it was hitting me hard. I brought the bottle away from my lips and started to roll it between my palms, just under my nose, letting the rough peaty smell waft over me. It wasn't an easy question, and all the answers I had were hard ones. Triss had frozen when Stel asked it, and now he was peering worriedly my way from behind Vala's back.

It was him I addressed when I spoke next. "I'd like to say it was stupid or habit or some other mistake on my part, but that'd be a lie. I guess the honest answer is that I *wanted* to die. I was away on a mission when the other gods decided to destroy Namara. When I came home, I found my goddess murdered, my friends dead or taken, the temple that was my home pulled down, the grounds sown with salt. . . ." I could feel tears burning down my cheeks and my will breaking, so I took another drink—this had needed saying for a long time, though I hadn't realized it until then.

Triss slid down from the ceiling, and came to curl around my ankles.

"At that moment I thought that everything I'd cared about or believed in had failed, that there was no point in going on. I wanted more than anything to have died in defense of my goddess. At least then I would have been with my friends . . . no, my family. It was almost worse that I'd been successful in my assignment, because it seemed like such a pointless victory. There I'd been, in Gat, satisfied at having performed my duty to my goddess, happy even, when I should have been in Varya fighting to save her. If not for Triss I'd have probably opened my veins beside the sacred pool, a last offering to a dead goddess."

Vala leaned forward and touched my knee. "I'm sorry we asked, Aral. I'm sure Stel had no idea. . . ."

Stel turned around so that both of them were facing me, a very rare occurrence. "I'm sorry, too." Her voice was small and quiet, contrite. "I guess if I thought about it at all, it seemed kind of romantic. Aral Kingslayer, last Blade of Namara, still fighting for justice and the right, refusing to hide his identity even in the heart of enemy territory. What I should have been thinking about was what I'd feel like if I came home to find the Citadel a smoking ruin and all my friends and family dead. I'm a fucking idiot."

I shook my head. "It's all right. It wouldn't have been even a year ago, but it's all right now." And it was, a fact that surprised me. The wound was still there, but it was no longer actively bleeding. "It's a reasonable question. It's not your fault that it doesn't have a reasonable answer. I did it because I wanted to die but couldn't just kill myself because of what that would mean to Triss. I couldn't even admit to myself that was what I wanted without betraying our bond."

I shrugged. "Maybe lying to myself like that is part of why it took me so long to crawl out of the bottle. Speaking of which—" I handed the Kyle's to Vala and dusted my hands together. "You can have the rest. I want it too much to dare drink any more."

I did, too. I could feel the ache in my chest at letting the bottle go. It cost me. The only thing I wanted more was a nice hot cup of efik, but I knew if I started down *that* road again, I'd never get off.

Vala sighed. "It's not very nice of you to go all responsible like that. It sets a terrible example. Fortunately, I'm immune." She lifted the bottle to her lips then froze.

"How much have you two had to drink?" a very muzzy sounding VoS said through Stel's lips.

Vala, or more likely, VoS corked the bottle and put it on the floor. "I take one little nap and I wake up to find my heads packed full of cobwebs spun by tipsy spiders."

"We didn't drink *that* much!" Stel sounded rather like a teenager caught behind the shed with a bottle of cheap sake. "We were going to wake you up soon, weren't we, Vala?"

VoS turned her Vala head my way and rolled her eyes. "You'd think they'd learn how very silly it is to try to lie to the voice in their heads, but somehow they never do."

Triss lifted his head off my lap and looked the Dyad over quizzically. "I don't understand."

"You're wondering how I can be asleep when they're awake?" said VoS. "It's the bonewright. Nasty, nasty spell."

"I can feel Stel's pain," said Vala.

Stel nodded. "And vice versa. In theory, I could also feel Vala's pain at feeling my pain, and so on in an infinite recursive loop that would incapacitate both of us. Part of the reason the Meld exists is to act as a coping mechanism to shut those loops down."

"Now I'm a coping mechanism," muttered VoS. "I like that."

Stel gave VoS in Vala a hard look.

"Oh, all right." VoS shrugged Vala's shoulders. "It's true enough as far as it goes, which isn't even halfway to encompassing all that I am."

"What that means," said Stel, as if VoS hadn't interrupted, "is that VoS sometimes gets a double or even triple dose of what Vala and I are feeling. Because of the level of magical and mental commitment that the bonewright takes, Melds can really get hammered as a side effect."

"When the spell was finished, so was I," agreed VoS. "At least for a little while."

Vala winked at me. "Which is how we came to enjoy a half hour of uninterrupted peace, and a couple of drinks with a handsome Blade."

Then she snorted, or rather VoS did, and shook her head.

"Motes, can't live with 'em, can't Meld without 'em. But downtime is over now. We need to get back to work." She looked at me. "You're the expert on Tien, Blade. Where do we go to find the girl, Reyna."

"It's 'Jack' these days," I replied, "not Blade. And this is where the legwork starts. If your Reyna really does have the Kothmerk, as seems likely, and she doesn't want to keep it for her very own, she's going to need to find a buyer." Again, I thought of Fei's corpse, and wondered if she hadn't already tried—there was only one way to find out. Footwork. "I'll start by talking to a few of my night market contacts in case I get lucky." I had my doubts about how much I'd get from them, but I figured I'd give it a go before I brought that up.

VoS nodded both of her heads. "Then, let's go." She started putting on her leather vests.

"You're not going anywhere. Also, I'm going to need some cash to buy drinks and grease palms."

"You're wrong you know," said VoS.

"About what?"

"We are coming with you."

"One, it's too risky. You've only just changed your appearances and now you want to be seen with me again? Two, I'll get better information if I'm alone."

"I'm going with you," said VoS. "We can always do the bonewright again if we have to." She sounded absolutely firm and calm, though both Vala and Stel winced at that suggestion. "We can have a huge time-consuming argument about this, but the results are going to be the same either way. I'm coming with you."

"Give me one good reason."

"You just told us how much trouble you had giving up this bottle." She held it up. "Now you want me to hand you a large sum of money to go fishing through the bars of Tien. Don't you think that would be better done with a little bit of extra backup?"

I thought about her earlier protestations of absolute faith in who and what I was and how this new argument showed a distinct loss of some of that faith. Then I looked at the bottle, and thought about how much I wanted another drink.

"You might have a point," I said.

So, the Dyad no longer trusted me completely. That was only fair. I didn't fully trust her either.

Stel reached under the tail of her shirt and pulled out a heavy purse, tossing it over to me. "Then lead the way."


"**Look,** Ashelia, I know this isn't your dodge, but I thought you might be able to tell me who to touch for that kind of thing these days."

The smuggler leaned in close as she patted me on the cheek. "Aral, you know I love you, right? You've been a great runner for me in the past, but right now? You're pure fucking poison. The Howlers have your picture up on every wall from here to godsdamned Kadesh and the price on your head would buy a house in a good neighborhood."

"I need this—" I began.

But Ashelia cut me off. "I don't even want to be seen talking to you, much less give you anything that could be traced back to me. I'm sorry, but it's just not going to happen. In fact, in about two beats I'm going to throw my drink in your face. If you ever want to work with me again, you're going to play along by swearing at me as I walk away."

So I closed my eyes and my mouth and breathed out through my nose when she threw the rice-white in my face— you really don't want that shit in your sinuses—and then I hissed obscenities at her back as she sashayed away. After that, I wiped myself off, picked my drink off the Busted Harp's bar, and crossed the common room to sit down at a small table that backed the one where Vala was fending off her third proposition in as many minutes.

This time she used a well-placed boot and a flashed knife to get the message across. It seemed to deter the rest of the crowd as well, at least for a little while, because a space opened up around her and stayed open. Stel had taken up a

standing position by the bar so she could back me up if I
had any trouble with Ashelia, and there she remained for
now. We were doing everything we could to make it look
like Vala was with me if she was with anybody and that she
and Stel had no relationship to each other.

"That went well," Vala whispered to me as I leaned back
in my chair so that our shoulders were only a few inches
apart. "If I'd known you were so popular, I might have
picked a different jack."

"If you'd picked a different jack, I wouldn't be having
these problems." The Harp was the third tavern we'd hit that
night and Ashelia was the fifth shadowside player who'd
frozen me out. "It's the Howlers that are the sticking point.
If it was just the Stingers that wanted me, I'd be getting
somewhere. Stinger attention's just part of the price of doing
business."

"Stingers? Howlers?"

"Sorry." I chuckled. "When I slip on my shadow-jack
face for the locals I tend to fall into the argot. Howlers are
the Elite, named for their stone dogs and the way they pursue
their prey like a hound. And the city watch wears black and
gold, like wasps or bees. Hence, 'Stingers.'"

"All right. So no one will talk to you right now because
of the Howlers. Is that going to get any better as we go along,
or do we need to try a different approach?"

"Maybe. I thought I might get somewhere with Ashelia,
since she's been a bit sweet on me in the past. But apparently
that's not enough. What I need is to find someone who owes
me big for past favors. Clubfoot Tan or Monkeygirl would
have to talk to me, but I wouldn't bet on them knowing what
I want. Issa Fivegoats would be perfect since he's a sellcinders himself."

Stel gave me a quizzical tilt of her head, so I elaborated.
"A sellcinders is someone who deals in hot merchandise.
Fivegoats is mostly a low merchant, but he knows people
who deal with the serious rarities. He's definitely my best
bet for information."

"Great," said Vala. "Where do we find him?"

"At this point? Probably under a rock somewhere. He'll be hiding from me."

"He will?"

"Yep. People have seen me out and about. With the size of the price on my head, that'll get around." I couldn't see Vala's response, but Stel's head turned my way at that. "Oh, don't worry, I'm being careful about which dives we visit. Nobody around here's going to run to the Howlers, because none of 'em want the Howlers to have a reason to remember their faces. But that's not going to keep the word from getting spread."

"I thought you said this Fivegoats guy owed you?"

"He does. That's why he's hiding. If I can find him I can call in the note, but if I can't, he's off the hook. Since I'm poison right now, he's not going to want to be seen with me. Hell, if he can stay out of my way until the Howlers pinch me, he's got a good chance of writing off the debt all together. Nobody shadowside owes nothing to the heads hanging above traitors gate."

"That's a pretty ugly way of looking at things. And these people are your friends?"

"Not really. In Tien, shadowsiders don't really have friends, or at least not many. What we have is professional relationships and debts. Even where there's some genuine affection, business trumps emotion. Take Ashelia. She's let me know more than once that she'd like to have me as a long-term bunk-mate, and I've been more than half tempted from time to time. But the main reason she talked to me tonight was to find out what I want. Then she can sell my questions to anyone who'll deal for them."

"So how are we going to get anywhere?" It was VoS speaking this time, and she sounded really disheartened.

"By digging Fivegoats out from under his rock." I grinned and raised my drink in Stel's general direction. "One of the reasons I'm not being a whole lot quieter about my questions is exactly so that word gets out and scares people like Issa enough to make 'em pull a fadeout."

"I don't understand. . . ."

I chuckled. "I know Issa pretty well, and that includes knowing which rocks to look under. By scaring him into hiding, I'm actually cutting down the number of places I have to look. I'd say it's had enough time to take effect. So, let's go turn over some rocks."

# 10

---·◆·---

Because of my newfound notoriety we kept to the chimney forest as we made our way across the city, alternately walking and jumping from rooftop to rooftop. We had to take a slightly different route than I would have alone since VoS had no Shade to sail-jump her across the broad canyons made by the bigger thoroughfares. But there was an easy enough solution to that, as generations of thatchcutters and other shadowtraders had crafted plank or pole bridges that could quickly be laid in place across all but the largest of streets.

We saw quite a few other chimney runners along the way, since it was a cloudy night, and perfect for a quick bit of second-story work or clandestine delivery service. We pretended not to see them, of course, and they extended us the same courtesy. So no one got hurt. The lack of a moon also could have provided hunting opportunities for the odd urban ghoul or nightghast that had crept in from the countryside, but we saw none of the restless dead in our journeys.

We finally caught up to Fivegoats at a warehouse he used to store particularly hot items while he waited for them to cool down enough to resell. It was a big old stone building on the Royal Docks side of the harbor that had been broken up into numerous smaller stalls that were rented out individually. Regular watch patrols went past at least once an hour, and the only two entrances had attendants who wouldn't let you in unless you showed them your key.

"I don't get it," Stel said to me. "What's a two-kip fence doing in a place that's so upmarket?"

I grinned in the darkness. She was picking up the argot. Fivegoats had just passed by below us on his way into the warehouse—he was easily identifiable even at that distance because of the magelights at the entrance. He'd been carrying three skins and a case that probably held a couple of days' worth of cold trail rations. He was clearly planning on bedding down in his tuckaside while he waited for the Howlers to catch up with me.

I leaned in close to Stel's ear—Vala was about twenty feet behind us, crouched in the shadow of one of the building's light wells. "It's much safer storage than anything up by Smuggler's Rest and the free docks. The Stingers pretty much leave it alone investigationwise, because several important nobles have stalls that they don't want anyone official looking in on. That's why a lot of the smarter night marketeers and smugglers keep stalls here if they can afford the rent. Put on a nice set of clothes and pack your coals in a fancy box and the various minions of the king pay you no mind."

"Coals?" asked VoS.

"Stolen goods so hot they'll burn you if you're not careful," interjected Triss.

"Thanks. Why here, though? If this place is really so high pocket he's got to be running some serious risks by camping out here. That can't be something they normally allow."

I smiled again. "It's not, and the bribes are probably murder. But with the Howlers looking to nail my skin to a tree, staying out of my way is going to be worth a touch of silver—I'm sure Fivegoats thought he'd be safe from having me show up here. He keeps this place quiet enough that I'm probably the only one of his regular runners that knows it even exists.

"And honestly, if I were only what I pretend to be, I *wouldn't* know about it. On top of that he probably figures that if I did know to look here, I'm too hot to risk showing my face in a neighborhood this well patrolled. Now, let's go show him just how wrong he is."

With Stel trailing behind, we slipped back toward the light well where we'd left Vala. The warehouse roof was plenty secure enough to fend off your average thatchcutter or ghoul. It was part of a line of buildings that stood a good story and a half above the surroundings, with twenty feet of empty air between them and their nearest neighbors. The low wall that topped the complex had enough jagged-edged potsherds affixed to it to cut any grappled line.

But they hadn't stopped there. The light wells, which provided a cheap source of illumination as well as much needed ventilation, were covered over with a fine metal mesh that had alarm glyphs threaded through it. They were also narrow and topped with low hanging rain guards, making it just about impossible to get down one. It was a really good system, as far as it went. But it hadn't been designed to keep out a Blade, or any of the other high-end mages for that matter.

That kind of security simply wasn't cost effective for anything short of the layered protection that surrounded kings and great nobles. Even that could be circumvented with the right preparation and a little luck, which is why they'd started calling me "Kingslayer."

I asked Triss to stretch himself out along the edge of one of my swords. As he did so, he opened a door in his soul and became a blade-thin gate into the everdark, the dimension from whence his kind had originally come. With Stel leaning hard on the bricks so that it wouldn't sag and bind the back of my sword, cutting the light well free of the roof took scant minutes. Then we were able to lay the whole thing neatly down, leaving us a nice-sized hole through which to make our entrance. If we'd tried it during the day, the added light would have given us away, but here again the dark and clouds worked in our favor.

Looking down through the hole, we could see a narrow aisle four floors in height with walkways running along the sides to allow access to the storage stalls. Dim magelights provided just enough light for the owners and staff to find their way around at night. I knew from an earlier exploration of the facility that the storerooms ranged from closet sized on the top tier up to a space big enough to park a good-sized coach down on the bottom. Fivegoats had a windowless third-level stall maybe four feet by ten on another aisle.

I lowered myself through upside down and hung by my knees while I extended my arms so that Triss could use them to anchor the great shadow wings he now shaped from his own substance. A guard patrol was passing by on the bottom floor, but they didn't look up and wouldn't have seen much of anything if they had, between Triss's shadow and the starless sky above. When I let go, we flipped over and glided neatly down to the top-level walkway.

VoS tossed me the weighted silk line we'd used to get them onto the roof in the first place. I fastened my end to a rail, while the Dyad anchored hers to the roof with a spell. Then she slid down to join me—first Vala, then Stel. A moment later, the magic faded and the rope dropped free of the light well and I stowed it away in my trick bag.

Fivegoats had stuffed a bit of cloth across the bottom of his door to prevent light from leaking out, but he'd missed the vent along the roofline. He'd chosen to rent a bottom-end Durkoth lock from the warehouse owners. It would have served him well enough against the shadow-jack I was sup-posed to be, but with Triss able to flow into the keyhole and shape himself into the perfect skeleton key, it didn't even slow us down. As I unlocked the door and pulled it open, Stel leaped through with fighting rods drawn.

By the time Triss had gone back to playing the shadow and I followed her through a moment later, Stel had Fivegoats pinned to the floor with one iron-tipped rod pressed firmly into the hollow of his throat. Behind me, Vala closed the door and took up a position outside, where she could watch for anyone coming our way.

"Hello, Issa," I said in the sweetest voice I could muster. "Did you know that I've been looking for you all over town?"

Fivegoats was not a pretty man, short and stout, with a distinct penchant for fatty kebabs that left him with a permanent grease stain in his ratty little beard. He looked even worse than usual now with sweat popping up along his hairline in big oily beads.

"Aral, my friend," he said, his voice hoarse from the pressure Stel was exerting on his throat, "it's so good to see you looking so well. And such a surprise to find you here at my little tuckaside."

"Looks more like a fallback to me." I poked at one of the skins with my toe. "And like you were planning on staying here for a while. Perhaps there was someone you didn't want to see?"

Fivegoats was sweating more and more by the second. "Of course not. I was just having a small libation and letting it get a little darker before I hauled a couple of rarer items back to my shop."

"Really?" I lifted the lid on what I had taken for trail rations earlier. It was full of oiled paper packages of salted meats and dried fruit. "You don't say. Because, if someone was to ask me about my good friend Issa Fivegoats—who just happens to owe me his miserable skin—I'd have to say it looked like he was trying to slither out from under one of his debts. That he was hoping to stay out of someone's way until that someone's head went up over the traitor's gate. That's what I'd say."

Fivegoats closed his eyes for a moment. "Please don't hurt me, Aral. It's just that I'm not a brave man and you're not long for this world, and I really, really don't want to leave it with you. You *know* me. I'm a coward. Right now it's dangerous to even be seen near you, much less give you any help. I'm happy to pay my debts. I just don't want to die for them, and it's not only the Howlers after your hide. There are Others looking for you, too, though they're very tippy-toe about it."

"You don't say. . . ." That was news to me.

Fivegoats lowered his voice. "Yeah, I don't know what you did to piss off the Others, but I hear that there's a small fortune available for anyone who drops a whisper on you to any Durkoth in the city before the Howlers can get their teeth in you."

"That wasn't so hard, now was it, Issa? I think we can deal. You want to pay your debts and you don't want to die. I want a little of what you owe me, and I don't want to kill you. I'm no black jack and I'd rather not start building that reputation by killing an old friend. So, talk to me. Where'd you hear about these Others?"

"It's not up on any posters, if that's what you mean. But it's definitely starting to get around the night markets. Some Durkoth that calls himself Chetha or Karath or something like that's been showing that poster around and asking about you real quietlike. Says he wants you alive and unhurt."

"Qethar?" I said, emphasizing the throaty "hch" sound at the beginning of the name.

"Could be, yeah. Rumor says people that piss him off get buried, and he's not real picky about killing 'em first. Fucking scary, them Others."

That was *very* interesting. Especially the bit about wanting to keep me away from the Howlers. I wondered what he had learned since our last encounter that had him so eager to find me again.

"Good stuff, Issa. A real solid start." I waved a finger at Stel and she removed the rod from Fivegoats' throat and the boot from his chest, moving back to lean against the door. "Now tell me something else I want to hear. You're getting real close to walking away with all your bones intact."

Wisely, he chose not to move, remaining on his back. "What else do you want to know, Aral, my old friend?"

I gave him a hard look and he flinched and held up his hands between us. "All right, all right. Maybe I've heard a few things about the questions you've been asking on the street. I don't know where you can find this girl you're looking for. I also don't know anything useful about a"—he paused—" 'very valuable bit of Durkoth sparkle that she might be trying to hawk.' Though I *have* heard she's still trying to find a buyer, or was three days ago."

There went my theory that Reyna was Fei's corpse. At least if Issa's information was good. *"Really?"*

I tried not to let any of what I was thinking show in my face, but Issa flinched at something he saw there anyway. "No, Aral, it's true. That's absolutely all I know. What I might know is who *would* know something. I don't deal with the really big stuff, and Other artifacts are a complete mystery to me. You know that if you know me at all. But I do hear things. If you wanted to move an item like that quietly—and I *would* have heard if someone tried to auction something that hot on the open market—you'd go to Miriyan Zheng in Goldsmith's Lane in the Highside. She's the expert, talk to her."

"I hate to have to do this—" I began, bending down to reach for his collar.

"Wait, wait." Fivegoats held up his hands again. "I told you the truth."

"Maybe. But you know I can't go anywhere near Highside with the Howlers looking for me. I might just as well saunter up the road a piece from there and hand myself in at the palace. Tell me something I can *use*, Issa. I promise it won't get back to anyone who'd take it the wrong way."

"All right, all right. Miriyan does most of her work out of the Highside place—she's a very fancy bit of business. But if you want to move cinders in Tien you've got to have a toe in dockside. I can put you on to her roost in Smuggler's Rest. It's run by a guy named Coalshovel Shen, and *he's* got a little caras problem that you could maybe use to pry a bit of news loose."

I smiled at Fivegoats and offered him a hand. "There, you just bought back a piece of what you owe me with no blood spilled. Not so hard, see."

He took my hand, and I pulled him upright. "Then you're *not* going to hurt me?"

"It's not something I ever *wanted* to do, Issa. And now I don't have to."

Fivegoats edged backward to sit against the wall. "Then toss me that skin, if you will. I really need a drink."

Stel hooked the cord with one of her rods, and flipped it through the air to Fivegoats. He opened it, filling the room with the floral bite that accompanied the better rice wines. It smelled wonderful. After taking a good pull off the skin, he offered it to me.

Regretfully, I shook my head. "No thanks, Issa, I've got business in Smuggler's Rest just as soon as I get an address."

"The place is down in the luff, next to a kip-claim and three doors to the right of the Spliced Rope. It's got the usual sign in the window, and you never heard nothing from me, right?"

"Not a word, Issa, not a word." I touched my finger to my lips.

"You're a good man, Aral, and not so hard a jack as your reputation."

I let my smile fall away. "Don't you believe that last, Fivegoats, not for a minute. If I'm soft with you today it's because you've given good value. I may not play the bone-breaker when I don't have to, but when I have to, I can be a very hard jack indeed. Never doubt that, and you'll get to keep wearing all your bones inside your skin."

Fivegoats looked at me, swallowed hard, and took another long pull at his wine. He didn't say another word as Stel and I departed, and neither did we. We collected Vala and were just heading back for the little trapdoor we'd made of the light well, when a sharp whistle came from that general direction, followed by the ringing of an alarm bell.

"I think they just closed the back door," said Triss.

"Now what?" asked VoS—the Meld had visibly taken complete control the moment the alarm sounded, pushing Vala and Stel down beneath the surface.

As a matter of reflex, I'd started cataloguing escape

routes while we were on our way in. Assassins, even godly ones like Blades, spend an awful lot of time running away. Keeping one eye on the exits is nearly as deeply ingrained as breathing.

"How well do you swim?" I asked.

"Good enough to compete at the Kodamian games, but nowhere near good enough to medal." VoS sounded as though that latter disappointed her.

"That's better than me." I reversed our course, heading for the nearest set of stairs up to the top level. The bay was a long way from the building and the Dyad would need more altitude to make the jump. "I don't suppose you happen to know a good fast charm for breathing underwater that doesn't need a bunch of diagrams and suchlike?"

"Actually, yes."

I gestured for VoS to precede me up the stairs. "Excellent! Turn right at the top of the stairs and start running."

Somewhere below and behind us another whistle sounded. A moment later, a quarrel thunked into the bottom of the stairs.

"Triss, cover me."

My familiar pooled briefly around my ankles, then slithered his way upward, surrounding me in a cool, silken skin of shadow. When we got to the upper walkway, I turned and knelt with my hands on the stair supports. Taking full control of Triss through the bond we shared, I focused my nima and released a blast of magelightning into the wooden stringers. With a deep tearing noise and a shower of splinters, the stairs fell away beneath me. The smells of dust and freshly sawn wood filled the air.

VoS anticipated me, and by the time I caught up to her, she'd destroyed the stairs at the other end of the fourth floor walkway and moved on to the end wall. Several more quarrels thumped into the wooden planks beneath us as we ran, but the guards hadn't yet thought to climb the opposite stairs to get a decent shooting angle. I was just about to tell VoS we needed to make a door when she raised Vala's battle wands and let loose an enormous burst of magical force.

Masonry exploded outward from the point of the blast, sending a huge chunk of the wall crashing out into the dock-side street below. The walkway sagged alarmingly as it lost its end supports, but the cantilevered beams that stapled it to the stalls kept it from collapsing. I spared a moment to hope that VoS had planned ahead for that and not just blown the wall apart without thinking about it. I stuck my head through the cloud of powdered mortar and shattered sand-stone that marked the demise of the wall, and looked down. There was maybe forty feet of street and dock between us and the bay. Way too far for a normal jump.

"Can you make that?" I asked, but VoS was already moving, tossing one of her battle wands to Stel as she quickly backed up.

Before I could so much as hazard a guess as to VoS's plan, Vala had already taken a running jump through the hole in the wall. Turning in midair, she aimed her battle wand at the building below me and let fly with another burst of energy. The backlash of the blast pushed her out and away to splash down in the bay. Stel followed her a moment later, using the borrowed wand and leaving me to summon up wings of shadow and bring up the rear.

Mine was a gentler descent. I glided out and down, cross-ing over the docks perhaps thirty feet above the water's surface. I was trying to spot the Dyad, when a pillar of ochre light like a giant's staff drove up from a spot maybe a hun-dred yards away along the bayside street and swung around to meet me. Firespike! The spell caster led my course per-fectly, Elite work if I was any judge. He would have batted me neatly out of the sky, if not for Triss wrenching free of my control and collapsing his shadow wings to send us plunging toward the dark water below.

Even so, the swinging pillar of orange light slid along my chest, and clipped the side of my head as I turned away from the burning pain of that contact. It felt like I'd been grazed by the fiery tongue of a gigantic hunting salamander. I was already dazed from the sudden severing of my deep-channel connection with Triss when he'd broken himself free of my command. Now the added pain and shock sent me to dance along the edge of unconsciousness as I tumbled through the air.

The surface of the bay slapped the right side of my body like the cold dead hand of a drowned titan but I barely registered the impact. Polluted water rushed into my nose and mouth as the weight of my equipment dragged me under, but somehow I couldn't bring myself to care. Fortunately, Triss was on the job and before I'd sucked down too much of the dreadful stuff, shadow hands pinched my nose shut and clamped down over my mouth.

Somewhere a million miles away, I thought I could hear Triss shouting at me. But for some reason I couldn't make out the words. My chest hurt both inside and out, and I lost all track of direction as I kept feebly trying to turn my face away from the burns on my cheek. I couldn't breathe and I couldn't think, and more than anything I wanted to sleep. Just a little nap, a few minutes of blessed darkness to put me right again, but Triss wouldn't let me sleep. I could feel him yanking at the connection that bound our spirits, like he was shaking my soul. Or maybe that was just the tug of the currents.

Then things changed, though it took what felt like several thousand years to register the difference. I'd stopped moving, or maybe the world had. It was hard to tell, because it was all fading farther and farther into the distance. Triss was still trying to keep me with him, but it mattered less and less.

# 11

---

I had just about surrendered to the sea and the night when the lightning fell on my lips. It jolted through my face and ran down my throat to ignite my lungs. I screamed and tried to turn away from the pain, but it was already inside me. In the wake of the scream, foul water rushed in, freezing the fire and filling my lungs. I was drowning. Only, I didn't die. Instead, the awful stuff that now gurgled inside my chest brought cool relief and the first flush of returning awareness.

As my thoughts began to flow again, the strangeness of the situation slowly wrote itself into the pages of my mind. I was lying in the dark with thick cold slime pressing against my back and sides. It provided a marked contrast to the warmth that lay along my chest and thighs. I was blind, too, or nearly so, seeing only a few dim and scattered lights through my magesight. The nearest were slender lines like paired worms, with a pair of dots above them. Breathing felt *wrong*, as though the air had gone thick and gelid, but at least I *was* breathing. In and out, in and out, the rhythm of life.

I concentrated on that, focusing first on breathing, then on its implications. I was alive. Alive and underwater. On the bottom of the bay by the feel of the ooze that held me tighter than any lover. And I was breathing. But how? I blinked and blinked again trying to make sense of the lights I saw with mage's eyes. Worms became lips and nostrils. Vala's, a few inches from my own and Stel's farther away, up and back, behind Vala. The spell that allowed them to breathe had lighted the portals of the lungs.

In turn, that meant the warmth that lay its length upon me was Vala's body, and the spell that had saved me was hers as well. I pulled my arms up and out of the clutching muck and slid one hand up along her side and neck to touch those glowing lips—a question, though not voiced. She smiled and leaned in to give me a quick kiss, and I felt the faintest echo of the lightning that had touched me there before. Then she put her hands on my chest, pushing herself up and back, freeing me to rise.

I wanted to follow her, but I was weak and weary and couldn't at first break myself loose of the grip of the mud. Fear shocked through me then, as returning coherence brought with it memories of our situation and a renewed sense of urgency. I began to thrash. I hadn't been without air for long, or I wouldn't have been able to come back from the land that borders death, but every second counted right now.

The Elite who had tried to burn me out of the sky would not willingly follow us into the bay—water was no friend to the stone dogs. But he could send that hound down and under the bay's floor. Even now it might be rising up through the layers of sodden earth beneath me, jaws agape.

Before I could panic, I felt Triss's reassuring presence as he slipped around underneath me. Pressing himself against my spine, he pushed, forcing me up and out of the muck. Long habit made me check my swords and trick bag then, making sure I hadn't lost my most important tools to the horrid stuff. But now what? We had to get up away from the bottom without rising so high as to become visible to the inevitable Elite presence on the shore and docks above.

"What now?" It was Vala, echoing my own question, though it took me a moment to recognize the distorted words for what they were in that medium—still, it was clearer than I would have expected. An effect of the magic, perhaps.

"Up a few yards and out where it's deeper." Tien's bay was a deep one and dredged regularly to keep it open to the largest ships, but this close to shore the water couldn't be much over twenty feet, not enough depth to hide in if they managed to light us up. "We need sea room. Beyond that, I don't know."

"Follow me." Triss tugged at my hand to let me know where he wanted me to go. "We'll cross the bay in deep water."

As I started swimming in the indicated direction, I called up a tiny bit of magic, the precursor to a spell, and let it play about my hand to provide a guiding light for VoS. Swimming a level course with all my gear was hard work. I don't think I could have managed it without the occasional push or pull from Triss. It didn't help that I was still more than a little dazed, and that the side of my face where the spell had touched felt like someone had taken a hot vegetable grater to my skin.

We had gone perhaps a dozen yards when I thought I felt something big moving from right to left down below us, a presence almost more imagined than sensed. At first I hoped that it wasn't a stone dog. But then, after thinking about what else might be moving around in the dark waters, I decided that maybe I hoped that it was.

A few moments later, a brilliant and now familiar pillar of ochre light stabbed down through the waters off to my left—the direction I thought the stone dog, or whatever it was, had taken. The spell briefly lit up the waters around it, but then the bubbles from the steam it created blotted out everything. In the instant of clear sight I got a hazy impression of something big and dark and sinuous getting hammered by the firespike. Something that had been looking our way with an open mouth and lots and lots of shiny white teeth.

My first thought was a shark, or maybe one of the smaller sea serpents that had been spied in the bay from time to time. For an instant I was almost glad to have the Elite up there trying to kill us if it meant he'd saved us from whatever that was. That's when the pressure wave hit, sending me tumbling back and away from the thing the spell had touched, and slamming me into Vala.

I got the confused sense of something vast and pissed off rising up from the floor of the bay.

Then Triss yelled, "Water dragon!" and started tugging me frantically back the way we'd just come.

I realized then that what I'd seen in that flash of light was just the head of a *much* bigger creature. The upside of that was that the Elite on the docks above was about to get a lesson in how bad an idea could be. The downside was that after the dragon was done with them it might decide to blame us for the incident, and that was a very big downside indeed. Because angry dragons are about the worst news there is. Especially if the dragon in question was *the* Dragon, Tien Lun, ancient guardian of the city's bay.

But even if it were merely the least member of the mighty Lun's court, it would be more than sufficient to make an end of us, there in its element, if it wanted to. So I swam like mad, and hoped that the dragon chose not to see us as a part of the problem. Hoping that it hadn't noticed us, or that it couldn't eat the Elite and still catch us before we got out of the water seemed a bit too much like hoping that the Emperor of Heaven would descend from the Celestial City to personally pick us out of the water and set us ashore.

We had gotten about back to where we started from when an enormous banner of golden light rolled through the water in front of us, cutting us off. It came from our right and lit up a good acre of the bay. Turning toward the source of the light, I found myself facing a dragon that compared to the one we'd seen a moment earlier as a gryphon does to a gryphinx. All I could see of it was the head, but that must have been thirty or forty feet long, and eight feet from top to bottom with whiskers like harpoons.

Its massive jaws were spread wide and golden light poured forth, like flames from the mouth of one of its winged cousins. As I hung there slowly treading water, I couldn't for the life of me think of anything to do or say. Vala and Stel, who paced me on either side, seemed just as incapable of any useful response as I. Only Triss was not frozen. My shadow slid forward between me and the great dragon, his wings spread wide in my defense.

He looked like a toy. Fear filled me as I imagined the great dragon turning that blast of liquid light upon my best friend, and I had to stop my hands from sliding back to draw my swords. Any attack I could make would act as little more than a provocation. But instead of destroying us as it so easily could have, the water dragon closed its mouth and cocked its head to one side, as though trying to get a better look at Triss.

The great banner of light that it had spewed forth did not disperse. Rather, its near end hung in front of the giant face, as though it were anchored there somehow, while the long tail of it curled around to encircle us with light, like some sort of huge fishing net being drawn tight around an interesting catch. The increase in light was painful for Triss—I could feel the echoes of it through our link—but he neither flinched nor backed away from the great dragon.

The creature fixed me with one enormous green eye and I felt a terrible pressure in my head. Intense but brief, it ended with a tearing sensation as something seemed to break suddenly free, and a voice spoke into my mind, *Whither go you, oh Blade? And why come you into my domain?*

I found myself answering in like style. *I come out of necessity, fleeing the forces of Tien's master.* It didn't even occur to me to try to lie. *I would not have intruded if I could have avoided your realm. I wish only to pass from here to the far side of the bay where I have business with a trader in stolen goods who knows things I need to.*

*Is your cause just?*

I paused at that. Was it? What would my goddess think of what I was doing now if she could see me? Would she be proud? Disappointed? Appalled? That I didn't know the answer to that hurt me. That I could never know the answer . . . there were no words.

*I hope so.* It was the best I could do. No, it was the best I would ever be able to do.

The eye blinked, then shifted to fall on Triss as the great mind voice spoke again. *What say you, my little cousin of the shadows? Is the cause just?*

I couldn't hear Triss's answer, but whatever it was, the great dragon nodded his head. *Then, so let it be.*

Its nostrils flared and the banner of light flowed backward into them, leaving us once again in darkness save only for the dull green glow of that gigantic eye. For a few heartbeats more it hung there, then an eyelid the size of an Aveni war shield blinked slowly closed.

Before I could think of what to do next, a mighty current sprang up and seized us, dragging us willy-nilly across the bay. If I'd had any doubts about the source or shape of that current, they would have been dispelled in the moment before the current let us go. Just for an instant, I saw that great green eye again, one of a pair hanging unsupported in the water on either side of us as though the dragon carried us in its mouth. Then they wavered and dissipated as the dragon let go of its mortal shape to become one with the waters once again.

The last vestige of the current rolled us into a calm spot at the base of one of the many little piers that dotted the bay and was gone. I didn't have to swim so much as a stroke to put my hand on the bottom rung of the slimy wooden ladder fastened to one of the pilings. I started to pull myself upward, and everything was going fine until my head broke the surface of the water.

The wind across my spell-burned cheek and ear felt like fingers of fire sliding along my skin. When I gasped at the pain, I drew more fire down my throat and into my lungs, and lost my grip on the ladder. The cool water instantly put out the fire in my throat and chest and soothed but didn't completely erase the pain in my face. Vala swam in close then and touched my lips.

"Fool," she said into my ear, though her tone sounded more affectionate than exasperated. "Let me unspell your breath before you try that again."

I nodded and she moved in even closer, pressing her lips against my own. The kiss shocked through me, sending

tendrils of what felt like gentle magelightning down my
throat and into my chest. There was no denying that it hurt,
but in no bad way—more like a lover's teeth nipping at a
tender spot. The electric feeling lasted for a few bittersweet
seconds then faded away.

Vala's lips left mine. As she drew away, I felt as though
someone had seized my lungs and started squeezing from the
bottom up, like a parched man trying to get the last few drops
out of his water skin. The pressure rolled up through my chest
and throat, forcing me to open my mouth as all the water I'd
breathed in burst forth like a drunkard's one too many.

Suddenly, I ached for real air again. Putting my hand
once more on the ladder, I pulled myself up and out. This
time, when the air burned across my injured face, I was
ready for it and kept my grip. By the time I reached the top
of the pier and dragged myself out onto the wooden planks,
I'd grown used to the pain. There were no lights on the
smugglers' docks, and it was as dark as the inside of a troll
up there. Ostensibly that was because the docks were closed
at night, though the real reason was that every time the city
tried to put lights up, they mysteriously went missing.

I cleared the way for the Dyad to follow me, then flopped
down on my back for a moment. I felt like I'd swum the
width of the bay rather than being carried, and I badly
needed to catch my breath. Triss must have felt much the
same, as he sank down into the shape of my shadow without
a word. Even then, hours after the brutal summer sun had
gone away, the boards felt warm against my wet back, and
the night breeze had no bite to it.

Stel followed me out and lay down a few feet away as
well, panting lightly. "I don't suppose we can call it a night
now and skip visiting this Coalshovel fellow?"

VoS shook Stel's head. "No, of course we can't."

"Yeah, didn't think so," said Stel.

It was odd how natural that exchange seemed already,
where under normal circumstance hearing someone arguing
with themselves in two different voices like that would have
had me moving quietly away. Somehow, without my really

noticing it the Dyad had become a part of my world, a friend even.

I wanted to be happy about that, to take pleasure in the simple comfort of companionship, but the great dragon's question about justice kept echoing and reechoing in my mind. Was my cause just? I looked at Stel and hoped that it was, and that someday I might even be sure of it. But until and unless that day came I had nothing but my own badly flawed vision of the world to guide me. For now it would have to do. Just as I would have to hope that my promise to help the Dyad wasn't going to come into conflict with my promises to Fei.

Vala climbed up to collapse on the edge of the pier then, hanging her head over the water and vomiting noisily. "Eyn and Eva but I hate the way that spell ends." She rolled onto her back and up against my side, giving my thigh a squeeze.

"It didn't seem so awful to me," I said. "I never knew a kiss could pack that much punch."

"Honey," said Vala with a touch of her usual fire, "that part wasn't the spell. That's just me."

I squeezed her back. "Then we'll have to try it again sometime."

"You're on. But it'll have to wait till after I get something to clean out my mouth. The spell might not be so bad for you and Stel, but I get both ends of the chain and it doesn't open or close with a kiss."

"I could use a palate cleanser myself." My mouth tasted of bay. And since the bay was the ultimate end of Tien's sewer system . . . and well, I didn't like to think about that. "Now, I just need someone to carry me somewhere so I can get it."

"Not going to be me," said Triss from his spot in my shadow. "I'm done for the night. First that river dragon scared me halfway back to the everdark. And then Tien Lun her own self shows up." I felt him shudder beneath me. "You can get your heavy butt up on your own this time."

"*River* dragon?" I asked.

"Yes," replied Triss. "You can tell by the feel of them,

though what a freshwater dragon was doing out in the bay and wearing its physical form I have no idea."

"Whatever the reason," said VoS, "it turned out to be a good thing for us. We might have done all right on our own, but you never know, and the dragons ultimately saved us a lot of swimming."

Vala rolled up onto her shoulders and then flipped herself from there to her feet. "We've wasted too much time here already and I *really* need to get this taste out of my mouth."

I turned my head to look at Stel, though it made my cheek hurt. "Is she always like this?"

"You have no idea. In school the other Dyads threatened to sleepspell her every other night. Perky is *not* a standard operating mode for our kind. Not even VoS can keep her under control all the time. Ouch!"

"What?" I asked.

"She pinched herself when I wasn't expecting it. That's just mean, Vala."

"And telling tales on me out of school isn't? Here, let me give you a hand up." There was a scuffling noise as the Dyad got her other half upright, then she approached me. "It's your turn now, Aral."

She extended her small hand to take mine and then pulled me upright with a great deal more ease than I'd have expected, even knowing what good shape she was in. She was so tiny it was almost impossible to believe she could be that strong. I suppose I shouldn't have been surprised given my experiences with Jax back in the day. *She'd* saved my life once, too.

I remembered long distant kisses then and almost against my will found myself comparing them against the way Vala's lips had felt against mine—the magic of a spell vs. the magic of first love. . . . I blushed and shook my head. It was an unfair comparison, to both women.

Together, the four of us headed up the pier toward land. By mutual consent we decided to find a tavern and get a drink to wash away as much of the . . . stuff we'd all been breathing as could be managed. Likewise by mutual consent—with one abstention from Triss—we'd decided it should be a sterilization-strength drink. We passed quite a number of people in the immediate area of the docks, mostly carrying darkened magelanterns and pretending that they couldn't see us.

We extended them the same courtesy, of course, it being Smuggler's Rest. That's how you kept out of the sort of conversations that substituted the club and the dagger for hellos and good-byes. Farther in, we started to pass more legitimate traffic that carried its lights with the shutters open.

Mostly yellow and white depending on whether they could afford magelight or needed to rely on fire and oil, though there were a number of lanterns whose gaudy green glass announced the bearer as open to negotiations where virtue came into play. Some of those were quite elaborate, with filigree on the lens casting intricate shadow patterns that told the streetwise that the bearer was into more . . . exotic sorts of play. Several of those swung their lanterns wide, to play across our feet and legs by way of invitation when we passed.

There were just enough of the poor and reckless out to prevent our lack of lights from marking us as anything too out of the ordinary. I had a tiny thieveslamp in my trick bag, but no one carried those openly. I considered conjuring a temporary light onto a bit of rock, but I'd have had to carry it bare, and that *would* have been even more unusual.

The first obvious tavern we came to had a pair of dim torches out front lighting up the sign of a seaweed-encrusted ship's wheel. Vala went in first—crossing quickly to the bar to place an order, then turning back our way—with Stel and I trailing behind. For this one brief appearance we figured it would be all right to be seen together.

As we came through the door, Stel let out a little gasp, and said with Vala's intonation, "Aral, you should have told me how bad you got clipped by that firespike!"

Then she grabbed my arm, spun me around, and shoved me right back through the door before following after. As soon as we were outside she dragged me off the street and into a gap between two buildings.

"What are you doing?" I asked.

"The side of your face looks like a nightmare, blood and mud and blisters everywhere. I couldn't see it till we got into the light there, but Holy Twins, Aral! You must be in some kind of pain. And that doesn't mention the front of your shirt, which is a scorched ruin. I'm half scared to peel it off of you in case your hide comes with it."

I put a hand on my chest. The shirt was a wreck all right and there were definitely some scrapes and blisters underneath, but nothing too awful. My dip in the bay must have helped stave off the worst effects there.

"That's not too bad, but yeah the face definitely feels like I've been to the wars. I suppose the upside of that is that no one's likely to recognize me at the moment."

About then, Vala reappeared carrying a brown bottle. "Tell someone next time!" she growled at me. "I shudder to think what all that shit floating in the bay has already done with the open wounds on your face. I'm going to have to get pretty drastic with both the magic and this—" She raised the bottle to pour some on my cheek and I winced in anticipation.

"Let's go a little deeper into the dark," said Triss. "That'll let me cover you better and muffle any yelps."


**After,** we found a bathhouse that catered to the night trades, and I bought the shirt off a passing workman's back for five times what it was worth. Then we headed for the sign of the Spliced Rope and located Coalshovel's offices next-door to the kip-claim under a tiny plaque that said Dry Goods.

We settled in atop the roof of a small unmarked building across the way while we checked the place out and talked through our strategy. This wasn't going to be like asking questions of old comrades in a bar. Coalshovel didn't know me, though he might have heard of me . . . or seen the wanted posters. He wasn't going to want to talk to me about anything half so hot as the Kothmerk, so this was going to be more like a raid on potentially hostile territory.

We decided I should go in first with Vala, who looked

basically harmless, to say nothing of distractingly sexy. She'd find someplace to perch that put her eyes on the door, while Stel would keep a lookout from up here. That was the initial plan anyway. But that was before we'd spent the better part of an hour up on the roof without seeing any sign of life from the shop front across the way, despite a number of passersby rather furtively trying their luck with the bellpull. I began to get a bad feeling about the thing.

"Does that place look a little *too* quiet to you?" I asked quietly.

"I don't know," responded VoS. "I've never done anything like this before. It's a cloudy night and they're smugglers, aren't they? Maybe somebody's out on a run?"

"It's possible, but if that were the case, I'd expect them to have left some muscle behind to keep an eye on the store. If they do any business at all out of the offices, there's bound to be a strong room for larger valuables plus a chest for cash storage. It's not like a legitimate business. They can't give bank notes to their clients. Triss?"

"Something's wrong. The shadows over there look empty and dead. I can't say for sure without thoroughly tasting them, but that's the impression I get from here. The building's been abandoned."

"So what do we do?" asked Stel.

I shrugged. "To borrow a smuggler's terms, what we *should* do is cut our lines and run for the open sea before the law arrives. But that'd leave us as much in the dark as we are now. It's risky, but I think I'd better go in and have a look around."

"You mean *we'd* better go in and have a look around," said Vala.

I snorted. "Sure, but let's not go in through the front door, shall we?"

"Roof?" asked Stel.

I nodded. "Around back first, I want to check the back door before we try anything. Then up the wall and we can cut our way in."

# 12

———•———

As it turned out, the sellcinders didn't have a visible back door. What they did have was a rabbit run that exited through a trapdoor on the flat lead roof of the office. It was butted up tight against the building's nearest neighbor, a taller structure with a series of bricks removed to make a ladder for the run. So, in event of emergency: out and up, then over and off onto the chimney road.

The trapdoor was sealed from below with a heavy bolt, but after we'd spent a while listening for activity below, Triss was able to slip between the cracks and draw it for us. The door opened down into a narrow space bordered on two sides with rough lath and studs, implying plastered walls. The bricks of the neighboring building made a third wall, while a wooden panel with a latch on our side provided an exit. VoS was sensible enough not to dispute my going first. She couldn't make herself invisible after all.

The wooden panel folded in the middle like a decorative screen, so that it could be slid to one side without taking up much space either in the rabbit run or the large cupboard it backed. Maybe five feet deep by three wide, the space was lined with cedar and full of hanging bundles of expensive cloth. The cloth gave a good illusion of a packed space while still allowing for quick and quiet movement, front to back. Light leaked in from a broad crack at the base of the cedar cupboard's front door, so I spent a few anxious moments waiting while Triss edged his nose under the door.

"Empty," he whispered after a while.

I slipped the latch on the door and eased it open. The room beyond was filled with the sorts of items you would expect to find in the back of a legitimate dry goods dealer, if perhaps a little too rich for the neighborhood. It was lit by a single dim and aging magelamp hung from the ceiling. As I slid forward toward the nearer of the storeroom's two doors, I heard a faint scuff from the cedar cupboard and knew that Vala had started down behind me per our agreed upon timeline.

The door I checked first opened into a narrow front room with a counter dividing it. The second door, at right angles to the first led into a small office with a desk and two more doors, one of which had been reinforced with bands of iron and a heavy locking bar that had been chained in place. The other opened on the front room. That was it. No people, no noise, no sign of occupation beyond the piled heaps of goods.

When I checked the front door, I found it not just locked but also barred from within. Like the strong room, it had been reinforced with heavy iron bands. That gave us an empty building with all of its entrances barred from within. The easy answer was magic, which could drop or raise a bar from without, but that felt wrong somehow.

Still, I checked the front door and the rabbit run and found that the building's owner had gone to the not unexpected trouble and expense of having them tamper-warded. A really good mage-thief could still have opened or shut them without tripping the spells, so that wasn't conclusive, but it was more than a little suggestive. VoS joined me as I was making the check, peering over my shoulder with Stel's eyes.

"Interesting. Do you think there's another way out? Maybe through the strong room?"

"Not the strong room, but there's almost certainly another

exit. We need to find it and check, but I'm willing to lay a bet right now that it's all bolted up, too."

"Don't take the bet," said Triss. "The shadows here taste like death, not abandonment. It reminds me of a tomb, except there are no bodies."

A little while later Vala called out low and soft from the storeroom, "Found the back door. It's hidden behind an empty crate and heavily bolted. I agree with Triss. This place feels like death. I'm going to see if I can't crack the strong room without making too much noise. I think I'd better go through the wall from back here. Stel, give me a hand?"

While they worked at that, Triss and I prowled around the building, looking for any further exits. No luck. And the strong room held nothing but coin and bits of expensive flotsam. I leaned one hip against the counter while I tried to find an angle on the thing that I liked. We needed to get out of there, and soon, but I hated to walk away with nothing. Triss slid back and forth across the floor behind the counter in his version of pacing.

"It's way past time we left," said VoS after several long minutes had slipped past without any further discoveries.

"You're right. I just feel like we're missing something obvious and important. It's possible that Coalshovel and his people are all just out for a walk, but that feels wrong. Doubly so since he's a front man for a big sellcinders up in Highside. There's a small fortune in the strong room. You don't just walk away and leave that unguarded when you've got a boss. Not in this business, not unless you're in a mood to watch someone take your skin off an inch at a time."

"You think this is about the Kothmerk?" asked Vala.

"It's got to be. This doesn't fit the way things normally work in Tien. Especially not down here in Smuggler's Rest. No blood. No bodies. Unguarded money left for the first neighbor bold enough to check out the silence . . ."

"So," said Triss, "say it is the Kothmerk. How does that change the equation? What's different?"

Then I had it. "Durkoth. The Durkoth are what's different."

"I missed a step there," said Stel.

I ignored her. "Triss, check the floor. Look for anything strange, any boards that have been moved, anything."

But Triss was ahead of me, shooting across the floor to a spot at the end of the aisle behind the counter. It was on the very edge of the area where he'd been pacing.

"Fire and sun, but I should have seen it earlier. The boards here aren't seated quite the same as the ones around them. I noticed it before, but I thought it was old work because the nail heads are just as rusty as their neighbors, which they wouldn't be if they'd been recently hammered in again."

"But if they weren't hammered down, but rather persuaded from underneath . . ." I said.

"Exactly." Triss slid down through the gap between two boards, only to reemerge a few seconds later. "There's a big patch of dirt under here that looks like it's been smoothed out by a cobblestone layer. No roach tracks, no nipperkin spoor, no fresh fallen dust. It's a subtle thing. A human would need good light and a suspicious mind to see it, but it's there."

"Want to bet the Durkoth ghosted the lot and our missing bodies are down below somewhere?" I wasn't expecting any takers and I didn't get any.

"Sounds like a lot of digging for not much return," said Vala. "Especially since there's no telling how deep the Durkoth would think is deep enough. I wonder if your friend Qethar had anything to do with this. Fivegoats said he was burying people."

I shrugged. "Could be, but I haven't got any answers. This whole mess makes no sense."

"Time to leave?" Vala didn't wait for an answer, just headed for the rabbit run.

I motioned for Stel to follow her and fell in behind.


"**So,** where does that leave us?" Stel was perched on a little dormer with her back to me, looking out over the harbor—she sounded depressed.

"I'm not sure," I replied from my spot up on the widow's walk. The more I learned about this whole thing, the less sure I was of anything. It was a lot like the way I felt about my life.

We'd taken up a roost on one of the larger houses in the nameless little neighborhood between Smuggler's Rest and Dyers Slope. I find that houses with servants are less prone to check out the occasional odd scuffing noise from above. There's always someone else to blame them on and not a lot of communication between the social layers. Given the location, the place probably belonged to a well-off smuggling captain, which meant there was probably also a fair amount of night traffic that no one was supposed to talk about or pay too much attention to.

"What happened to Coalshovel had the look of the Durkoth snipping off loose ends," I continued as the timesman's bells rang one. "Which means that your Reyna probably *did* try to fence the ring through Coalshovel's boss. I wonder if Miriyan Zheng's dead, too, or if she cut a deal."

"Dead." Triss had taken up a perch on the railing—a gargoyle's shadow without the gargoyle. "There's no way she'd have agreed to what happened back there."

I blinked. "You're not suggesting her heart's too pure to betray her own people, are you, Triss?"

"Don't be silly. If she's a typical sellcinders, the question isn't 'Yes or no?' It's 'How much?' I have no doubt she'd sell Coalshovel and whatever muscle might have heard the wrong things. What she wouldn't do is leave the goods in that strong room unguarded for so long. Counting the time we spent on the roof, how long were we there? An hour and a half? Two hours? Plus whatever time it was empty before we showed up."

"Point," I said.

Vala frowned. "Does that mean that the bad Durkoth have the ring now?" She leaned on the railing beside Triss, keeping an eye up the Kanathean Hill behind the house.

"No," I said. "Well, probably not. For that matter, we don't know which Durkoth are the bad Durkoth. Not beyond the ones that attacked your caravan. Nor if there are any *good* Durkoth for that matter. Take Qethar. I have no idea whose side he's on, beyond his own. He *could* be working with the ones who killed your friends. Or he could be an agent of the rightful king trying to recover it for his master."

"I hadn't thought of that," said VoS. "When did it occur to you?"

"It's been kicking around the back of my head for a while, but it wasn't until you said 'bad Durkoth' that it really gelled. Basically, I know shit about Tienese Durkoth politics. They don't have an official embassy or anything but there are as many as a couple of dozen in the city involved in various businesses. But I couldn't tell you if they're all affiliated somehow, or if they're divided into factions, or hate each other's guts, each and every one. I know even less about how they might interact with the broader Durkoth world, about which, in turn, I know practically nothing at all."

"*That's* reassuring," grumbled Stel. "Do you have any other happy thoughts to share?"

"Well, I think it's a sage bet that your little Reyna's still got the ring, at least if she ever had it to begin with . . . and if she's still alive, of course." That was a tough call. I no longer believed that she might have been Fei's corpse, but a lot of people had a lot of reasons to ghost her. "If she's not, it's probably lost. Maybe for a good many years."

"What makes you think that?" Both Dyad heads swiveled to give me a pointed look. "Or that the Durkoth don't have it for that matter? It seems to me the cleanup operation we just stumbled on is the sort of thing the Durkoth would do once they found the ring."

The rare dual scrutiny gave me an uncomfortable feeling in the pit of my stomach. "Because of what she's got. The Kothmerk's pretty much impossible to fence properly, and the scene we just left illustrates that. Touching it can seriously get you dead. If Reyna hopes to get even a tiny fraction of what it's really worth, she needs a buyer who knows what it is. But anyone who knows what it is will also know it's hot death on a platter to handle the thing."

"I'm with you so far," said VoS.

"Assuming she's not a sort of master mage-thief who had everything planned out, that poses a major problem for her."

"But how can you make that assumption?"

I frowned at them. "Isn't it obvious? The only sane way to steal something like the Kothmerk is to do it on commission for a specific buyer who already has a plan for what they're going to do with it. Make the lift, deliver the goods, get the hell out of town. Maybe change your name and learn a new language. What happened to Coalshovel suggests rather strongly that he was involved, which means it wasn't that kind of deal. But there's another piece as well, and that's the Elite."

"Now I'm lost."

Triss said, "The Kothmerk is too big a headache for anyone in Tien to hold onto short of King Thauvik wanting it for something political. Thauvik would be a great choice for a villain in this piece except for one thing. If *he* was the buyer, the Elite wouldn't be running around making a lot of noise and drawing attention to the fact that the ring's in Tien like they did with that raid on the Gryphon." Which was further evidence against the dead girl being Reyna—more likely someone hired to deliver information and then ghosted for her troubles. "They'd be quieter than the neighbors of your average graveyard on the night of the hungry dead."

"What about someone other than Thauvik?" asked Stel. "Surely there are a few rich collectors around who'd want the thing."

"Not if they have even a shred of sanity." Triss turned to face her. "If you fail, is the Archon of Kodamia going to let it go? Or the King of the North?"

"Of course not," replied VoS. "The King of the North might well send an army after it."

"Exactly." I nodded. "Whoever gets a hold of this thing has to know that they're going to spend the rest of their lives looking over their shoulder. No collector with even a shred of sanity is going to sign up for that. For that matter, no sane thief would take such a commission for pretty much the same reasons. The payback's going to be eight kinds of hell on this one."

"Now," I continued, "you can never completely rule out an insane motive on someone's part, but it's such a wild card that you pretty much have to throw it out when you're placing your bets. No, what I think is much more likely is that Reyna is mostly what she looks like, a kid in the wrong place at the wrong time who saw an opportunity and didn't think about the consequences."

"But how could an ordinary kid have done what she's done?" demanded Stel. "I just can't buy that."

"I didn't say anything about ordinary," I replied. "At a guess, she's a mage of some sort, and a powerful one, but not properly trained. She couldn't be, not as young as she is. Probably she's a Natural."

"Or a Founder," added Triss. "If she's summoned up a brand new type of familiar, she could have resources no one else has even imagined yet."

That was an ugly thought, but it might fit the circumstances. Mostly the mage and familiar-gifted get nosed out early and routed into one or another of the existing mage-schools, but every so often one slipped through the cracks. At that point what you have is a magical accident waiting to happen. Talent is going to come out eventually, and if it's a big talent, it's going to come out in a big way, especially under stress.

If it's a big mage gift, what you end up with is a Natural—powerful magic bonded to whatever familiar-receptive creature is closest to hand. A cat, say, or a lesser air spirit. Some creature from a line that's got established ties to some school of magery, in any case. But if it's a big familiar-gift you might get a Founder. Someone who cries out for help and is answered where no one has ever been answered before.

That's how the Blade association with Shades began, before the school was co-opted by Namara, back in the days of Dain. Really, it's how most of the mage-schools started, with one previously unbound familiar forming a bond with a budding mage in a moment of need.

"All right," conceded Stel. "Maybe she's a wild talent who did just get lucky. That doesn't explain why you think she's still got the ring."

"Or that it's lost," I said. "Don't forget that possibility. She may not know exactly what she's got, though I wouldn't bet against her knowing a lot more than she was supposed to. Anyone who can sneak into a Durkoth krith and lift the ring in the first place is more than capable of listening in on any discussions your Dagger in Waiting had with his under-officers. And she certainly has to know that it's incredibly dangerous to touch; look at the trail of dead Durkoth she left behind."

"True enough," said Stel.

"So, she's talented, smart, and knows a bit about what she's got. If she's not on commission, and we've got good reasons to think she wasn't—in the shape of those dead sellcinders—then she needs to find a buyer and not get dead in the process. We know from Fivegoats that she didn't just offer it up on the open market. We can infer from the raid on Coalshovel that she found out who she should talk to and went to them. That means she does her homework."

"Still with you." Vala was looking more interested and less angry, which I took as a win.

"Given all that, there's no way she just waltzed into Zheng's place and offered up the ring. That'd be the same thing as handing herself over on a platter. So, she sets up a meet somewhere she can control and shows the goods. Zheng's not stupid either, so she's not carrying anything like enough cash to make the deal. Neither one of them wants to be there long, so they set another meet where they can talk things over. Someplace public with neither of them carrying the goods."

I got up and started to pace. "Zheng either recognizes the item, or looks it up after the first meet. In either case, she runs straight to her Durkoth connections and they have collective conniptions. At that point, if they were thinking straight they'd have quietly bought the thing from Reyna.

But I don't think that's what happened. I think they tried to grab the girl at the meet and it went bad." Which would be another way to explain the dead girl—a decoy hired by Reyna. "Either she got away—good chance, given what we know about her—or they killed her and found out she'd stashed the ring in whereabouts unknown. That's when they started leaning on the Elite and all hell broke loose."

"But why kill Zheng's people? Isn't she on their side?"

"She might be," said Triss. "But they know there are other players interested in the Kothmerk, the Elite for example, and they know she can be bought. If they want to make absolutely sure that no one else can find out what they do or don't know, they need to cut down on the number of potential leaks."

"That's why I think the ring's still out there on the loose somewhere," I said. "If they had it, they'd be halfway to the mountains with it by now and they wouldn't need to get rid of past allies who might come in handy in the future. That kind of thing'll cost you on the street later when you're trying to find fresh partners."

"Alternatively," said Triss, "Coalshovel was ghosted by a different faction among the Durkoth to cut off Zheng's friends from potential allies."

"That's possible, too. The main thing is that there's still too much happening aboveground for me to believe the ring's in Durkoth hands yet. That means Reyna, or her tuckaside."

Stel turned and climbed up to join us on the widow's walk. "I'm still not entirely sure that makes sense, but the whole reason we went looking for local help in the first place was because we were out of our depth here. I'm going to vote that we trust you on this one and move on to the next important question on the agenda."

"Where do we look next?" asked Triss.

"That's an important one, too, but I'm more focused on an even shorter term goal, getting something to eat. We've had nothing but aging trail rations and rotgut this side of the day before yesterday and it's really starting to catch up with me. I want to get some real food into my stomach. Is there anywhere around here we can get a good meal?"

I smiled; the client wants dinner, the client pays for dinner. "I know just the place. It's a tavern called the Spinnerfish and it's only a couple of blocks from here. Dinner's on you."

Stel frowned. Then VoS nodded her head for her.


**The** Spinnerfish was one of the city's better restaurants in one of its worse neighborhoods. Smuggler's Rest brought a lot of money into Tien through the night market. That ready cash explained part of the success of the Spinnerfish. The rest belonged to the cook, Manny Three Fingers—who could turn fresh fish into heaven on a platter—and to his boss.

Erk Endfast used to make his living as a shadow captain in Oen in the magelands. Before that he was a black jack, or an underworld assassin, if you prefer bluntness. He'd ended up in Tien after the Magearch of Oen ordered his execution. When he arrived, he'd bought up a burned-out lot lying at the intersection of three of the city's shadowside territories and built the Spinnerfish. Now he ran it as the ultimate in neutral ground and enforced that by the threat of sudden death. He'd been a very very good black jack in his day.

Anyone, shadowside or sunside, could come in and have a great meal knowing that no one sane would try to cause them any trouble. Even the Elite would be reluctant to take a shot at us there. Great food and neutral ground made the Spinnerfish *the* place for meets of all kinds. It also meant Erk could charge an arm and a leg for the fancier dishes and no one so much as blinked. I normally had the special, but with the government of Kodamia picking up the tab I figured I'd splurge this time.

We approached the front door carefully, picking a roost in the chimney forest and surveying the entrance before descending to street level. Enforced neutrality inside did not equal enforced neutrality on the street out front, though Erk had been known to make exceptions. It had been years since the last time anyone got ghosted within sight of the front door, though I'd come pretty close to breaking that rule on a previous job. Fortunately, it was a dark night and raining at the time, so visibility sucked.

Tonight there was a fair pile of muscle hanging around outside dicing and drinking while they waited for their various bosses, liege lords, and owners, but no watch and no Elite. I was reminded again that summer was the hunting Blade's ally as it meant all the windows and doors were propped open, showing the tavern to be equally devoid of the forces of Tienese officialdom.

I took a moment to refresh my memories of sight lines, with an eye for sitting someplace where a bounty hunter with a crossbow and a copy of my wanted poster would have more trouble making his shot. I didn't think they'd survive Erk's response to that kind of violation, but it'd be hard to appreciate the payback from the bottom of the lime pits where Tien dropped the corpses of its criminals and paupers.

Once we hit the street I took Vala in on my arm with Stel loitering along nearly a block behind and playing the loner. Normally I like to get to the Spinnerfish early because that's the only way to get a good table, or, in this case, any table. A lot of heads turned when we came in the door. They always do at the Spinnerfish. What was instructive was how many of them turned back around just as fast. Especially among the faces I knew. Nobody likes to play with poison.

Erk himself appeared from the back within a minute of my placing an order for our drinks, a bottle of expensive white wine for Vala, and a tucker of Kyle's twenty year for me. I wasn't about to drink out of anything but a sealed container anytime soon. Not even at the Spinnerfish.

"Aral," Erk whispered when he got close, "what the hell are you doing here?"

# 13

---•‑◆‑•---

"**I'm** just looking for a fish dinner," I told Erk, "and yours are the best in town."

The owner of the Spinnerfish looked less than happy to see me, which came as no surprise. If the price on my jack's face was high enough to buy a house for the bounty hunter that brought me in, the price on my Blade's face would cover a grand old country estate with all the trimmings. And Erk was one of the half dozen people in the city who knew what I really was. Though he'd made it very clear that he valued his neutrality much higher than the price of my head, having me around always made him a little nervous. Present circumstances would compound the hell out of that sentiment.

"I should throw you out on your ear," he said. "You're a very expensive grade of poison at the moment. Especially with your face all beat up like that and drawing extra attention." Then he sighed. "But that'd violate my neutrality. I don't suppose you're enough in funds to afford a private booth?" he asked none too hopefully. He also knows what I make as a jack.

"Actually," said Vala, who had started to look a bit nervous herself, "I think we can manage that."

Erk raised his eyebrows. "New dance partner?"

I shook my head. "Client."

Vala grinned wickedly. "Why not both?"

Before I could think of anything clever, Erk said, "Why don't you follow me."

As we headed for the back and the private booths, Stel came in the door behind us and wedged herself at one end of the bar. Erk led us into a maze of twisty little passages lined with shimmery green gold curtains. The unintelligible buzz of dozens of conversations filled the air. Somewhere near the back of the building he pulled one of the curtains aside to expose a shallow alcove with a table just big enough for two and a pair of chairs.

Vala shook her head. "We want a three seater."

"Costs more," said Erk, but he didn't argue, just led us forward a few yards and opened a different curtain, exposing a tiny U-shaped booth. "Suits?"

Vala nodded. "Suits."

"Should I be looking to direct a third back here?" Erk asked as we slid into the booth.

"Just don't stop the big brunette when she heads back from the bar," I said. "She'll be able to find her own way."

Erk didn't say anything, just nodded and let the curtain drop, but I caught his eyes flicking to Vala as he did it. He was a damned shrewd man and I had no doubt that he'd just made the right guess. Still, him knowing was safer than leaving Stel out in the main room with no backup.

"Am I really just a client to you?" Vala asked with a sexy little pout. "There's no chance for a . . . *dance*." Her voice dropped low and husky on the last word.

I blinked several times. "I . . . uh . . . well—" Then Triss flicked me playfully on the ear, and my mouth snapped shut as I realized I was being teased.

"Not nice," Triss whispered to her over my shoulder. He hung against the back of the booth in my shape, just as the light would have placed him. "But well played."

"Oh, it's not *all* play," said Vala, dropping her voice into a husk again. "All this cloak-and-dagger stuff does set a spark to the kindling, if you know what I mean." She started to reach across the table toward me, then froze as her posture shifted subtly.

"Can we talk so openly here?" asked VoS. "That curtain seems awfully thin and I could hear a lot of people talking on the way here."

"Did you actually hear any words?"

"No, but Vala wasn't listening that closely."

"Wouldn't have made any difference. Erk protects his clients' privacy. This whole area is protected by anti-eavesdropping magic. Though it has no effect on other sounds." Footsteps could be heard coming toward us from beyond the curtains as if to illustrate my point—distinct but not obtrusive. "Take a really close look at the curtains."

She did. "The shimmer's actually a bit of spell light."

I nodded. "Yep, if you've no magesight, they look like dull cut-rate velvet, which is what they're made of. That's why the booths back here are so expensive."

The footsteps stopped and Stel pulled the curtain aside. "How expensive are they?" Her voice was sour as she slipped into the booth, pushing Vala around the curve of the table so that her knee pressed tightly into the side of my thigh.

I laughed. "Expensive enough that there's no point in economizing on the fish."

A frown touched both faces. "Stel was being extra careful to be quiet on her way here. I tried to make her even more so when I heard her coming through Vala's ears, but it seemed to have no effect. Another part of the magic?"

"Yes," Triss said from behind me. "The chances of someone trying a raid in the Spinnerfish are very low. Erk knows where too many bodies are buried. But the clientele here tends to the paranoid and violent, so Erk made sure they'd have plenty of warning if anything untoward started out in the halls. The curtains block sound going one way and amplify it going the other."

"I think we're going to be very glad we took the mission

purse with us when we came south after the Kothmerk," said Stel.

Just then another set of footsteps announced the approach of our waiter, who tapped on the wall beside the curtain before pulling it aside. He had my Kyle's and Vala's wine as well as a small chalkboard listing the day's fare. After he took Stel's request for a second wine glass, he vanished.

"What do you recommend?" Stel asked rather resignedly. "We don't get a lot of sea fish in Kodamia, and none that isn't packed in salt."

"If you're all right with spicy, you'll want the grilled spinnerfish with salamanda sauce. It's the house specialty."

"I adore hot, Aral," Vala said while giving me a look that smoldered more than a little itself.

Stel rolled her eyes at her bond-mate. "Don't you think you're laying it on a little thick?"

"We're on a compressed schedule for everything else while we're here. Why not the flirting?"

Stel ignored her and turned to me. "What's in the sauce?"

"No idea, it's one of Manny's secret recipes, though I feel confident in saying that no actual salamanders were harmed in the production of the stuff."

"Oh, just get it, Stel," said Vala. "I'm sure you'll love it." She turned my way again. "Don't let that gruff exterior fool you. She's at least as adventurous as I am. She just feels she has to play things serious now that we're in the field."

"Well, you're certainly never going to do it," countered Stel.

"I figure it's VoS's job. That's what Melds are for, right?"

VoS sighed but let it pass. When the waiter came back we ordered up three plates of the spinnerfish for dinner and a small bucket of unicorn scallops for an appetizer. We had just started to dig into the main course—a lovely flaky white fish lightly kissed with a spicy-sweet green sauce—when a distinctly bootlike tromp sounded in the hall outside. In response I drew a dagger from my own boot, an action that instantly drew Vala's attention since the proximity of her leg to mine meant the back of my hand slid along her calf in the process.

"What's happening?" she whispered as she pulled out her battle wands and laid them in her lap.

"Not sure," I responded. "But the only people who wear those sorts of boots in this weather all work for the Crown."

The clomping stopped right outside our booth and a knock sounded on the wall. If there was going to be an assault it was certainly shaping up to be a polite one. I held up a hand to signal the Dyad to wait. The knock sounded again and a hand pushed the edge of the curtain aside.

"Aral, you in there?" The voice was low, barely above a whisper, but it sounded familiar.

I reached out and tugged the curtain fully out of the way. A man in the yellow and gold of the city watch stood in the hall. He had a sergeant's triple sword insignia on his shoulder patches.

"Hello, Zishin." I nodded the faintest of bows. "What does Captain Fei want?"

"A meet." He set a folded slip of paper on the table, then turned and walked away without another word.

I reclosed the curtain, then picked up the slip. It had two words on it, a place and a time.

Stel raised an eyebrow at me and I handed it across. "Nonesuch?"

"It's an alley-knocker." The eyebrow went up again.

"An illegal tavern," interjected Triss. "It's on the western edge of the neighborhood we call Uln North or the Magelander's Quarter, right where it bumps into Little Varya."

Uln North centered on the wedge where the Channary Canal met the Highside Canal, a mile and a half or so east of the Palace Quarter. I knew the alley-knocker well because they'd started to sell efik there, and even though I had no intention of ever going back to the stuff, I kind of kept an eye on the trade. I wasn't sure whether Fei had discovered that I went there, and was trying to send me some sort of message, or if it was just unfortunate coincidence, though I suspected the former. Not much gets past Fei, and why else would she expect me to know where the place was?

"How far away is it?" asked Stel, tapping the paper.

"If we take the chimney road, something over an hour. We could get there faster by taking a boat and using the canals, but if we ran into a customs cutter we'd have to fight our way out."

"Are we going?" asked VoS.

"I don't know about you, but I'd better. Fei's . . . well, not quite a friend, but more than an ally of convenience. She's important to this city." And I really really hoped my business with her wasn't going to get in the way of my business with the Dyad.

"That matters to you?" The Meld sounded casual, but I noticed Vala had a forkful of fish hanging halfway to her mouth and had for some time.

I paused to ponder the question. I hadn't really thought about it that way before. I'd originally come back to Tien in search of my own death. I could admit that now. After the destruction of the temple, there wasn't any place in the eleven kingdoms that I could have gone where there wasn't a price on my head simply for having been a Blade. But here in Tien there was a second, much larger reward because I was the Kingslayer. The current king hadn't cared for his half-brother any more than anyone else did, but he also didn't much like the *way* I'd opened the throne for him to take the seat.

"Tien does matter to me," I finally said.

"You sound surprised." Vala's fork still hung in the air.

"I am. I hadn't expected to be here half so long as I have. I guess that somewhere along the line it turned into home."

I turned and looked over my shoulder to see what Triss thought of that, but all I saw was my own shadow. If Triss had an opinion, he wasn't in the mood to share it just then.

"So we need to go meet this Fei," said Stel.

"I do, but you're free to meet me at the fallback if you'd prefer. I owe Fei a major favor or two, *and* she's got a ton of leverage on me if she chooses to use it. I can't ignore this meet." I didn't mention that I could get there faster without them, though whether that was because I wanted the company, or just because I didn't feel comfortable with them out of my sight, I couldn't have said.

Vala sighed. "Guess we'd better eat fast then. It's a shame, because this is really delicious."

**The** closer we came to the Nonesuch, the unhappier I got about the whole thing. The Magelander's Quarter was well outside my normal haunting grounds. I'd made a point to learn the streets, and this particular alley-knocker was a place I'd visited before, but that wasn't the same as really knowing the place. For that matter, I didn't think Fei spent much time in the neighborhood either.

Unlike her beat-bound fellows, the captain's assignment covered the whole of Tien. But it focused on the trouble spots, and I'd never heard of the local contingent of Magelanders causing anyone any problems. The rest of the watch was supposed to stop and investigate crimes—that whole protect and serve thing. But Fei and her comparatively tiny force had a different job. She was supposed to keep the peace using whatever means were necessary.

In her case, that meant keeping a piece of every major illegal operation in town. If you worked the shadowside of the street, Fei knew your name. If you worked the wrong play in the wrong place, or made a ruckus in a rich neighborhood, she put your name on her list. Then you'd get a visit from Fei's Mufflers—so called because they kept things quiet. If the play was a minor one, you might only get a couple of broken fingers out of the deal. If it was a big one of the sort that drew noble attention or killed the more upright type of citizen in any numbers, you could end up floating out to sea in a nailed-shut barrel.

The Magelander's Quarter wasn't Fei's kind of place any more than it was mine, and it was a damned sight closer to Highside and the palace beyond than I wanted to be while

I had the Elite out looking for me. It was nearly five bells when we finally set eyes on the Nonesuch, and the coming sun had painted the scattered clouds over the ocean a pale shade of coral. It was certainly not cool out, but not yet hot either—the best you could hope for at this season. We'd made our way to the top of a tower on a temple to Shan about two blocks down the street from the Nonesuch. I wanted to give the whole area a look over before heading in and Shan's timekeepers built high towers.

Down in the narrow streets, the last of the night people were wending their way home, marked out by the lights they still carried slowly along like ten thousand exhausted will-o'-wisps. But the first of the morning people had come out as well. Carters and deliverymen brought in the country milk and a bewildering variety of fresh produce for the city's breakfast. Laborers and craftspeople hurried to get to work. The day watch were in the process of replacing the freaks and ne'er-do-wells who populated the night shift. Most of the newcomers hadn't bothered with lights, relying on the early sunrise of summer to see them on their way.

I watched for patterns in the moving crowds around the Nonesuch, voids that could mark out hidden Elite or other frightening individuals, places where the human current moved faster to get away from something that spooked them, or slowed down too much because of a choke point. Like most of Tien's neighborhoods, the Quarter got steadily more residential as you moved deeper into its heart. Traffic reflected that, with more big oxcarts circulating around the edges on the large thoroughfares while the in and out mostly happened on foot.

The Nonesuch lay in the borderland between the Quarter and Little Varya, about a block from the main road that ran between them, where the two types of traffic mixed most heavily. There were plenty of little voids and eddies in the turbulence that created, but no more so than anywhere else in sight of our position and I had to conclude that my misgivings had no evidence to support them.

"Looks like we go in," I said.

"You don't sound very happy about it," replied Triss from within my shadow.

"I'm not, but I can't put my finger on why. I just feel uneasy." I looked at the Dyad. "Maybe you should stay back here while I go in with Triss."

"I don't think so," said VoS. "This has to be about the Kothmerk, and I'm not getting shut out."

I shrugged. "You're the client."

As VoS slipped back into the depths behind the faces of Vala and Stel I couldn't help but wonder how much of their reactions and emotions reflected on their Meld. VoS was clearly more cautious of me than Vala, who looked somewhat embarrassed by VoS's comments. Stel was harder for me to read, but I think she now trusted me more than VoS did as well, though she'd started out leaning the other way.

Who was my client, really? Vala? Stel? The pair of them? The Meld? All three? I couldn't sort that out in a way that satisfied me, but the better I got to know the Dyad the more I knew that I didn't think of them all as one unit. Which was maybe craziness on my part, but true nonetheless. They had different wants and needs and possibly even slightly different agendas.

Triss nudged me then. "Let's get this done before the sun finishes coming up. It's going to be a bitter-bright day and that will limit what I can do for you. Besides, we're almost past Fei's meeting time and she's going to be pissed if we're late."

In seeming response to Triss's words, the great bells in the tower below us began to toll the hour. I made a "follow me" gesture to the Dyad, and headed for the back of the tower where we'd climbed up.

As had become our habit, Vala accompanied me to the door of the Nonesuch, her hand tucked into my elbow, while Stel trailed behind pretending she wasn't with us. It put a distance between the bond-mates that they found uncomfortable, but Stel was actually the one who'd originally suggested it. The Elite were looking for Aral the jack, and/or the female Dyad he'd last been seen with. The fact that

Dyads virtually never came in mixed sex pairs meant that
the simple act of having Vala and I play the couple, with
Stel substantially out of the picture made us all much less
visible.

The sign over the narrow door showed a chimera-like
creature made up of impossibly mismatched parts. Six legs,
each from a different animal and each a different length—
horse, lion, spider, monkey, rabbit, and a seal's flipper. Four
heads on four contrasting necks—hippo, salamander, raven,
and mole. Two tails, one a snake, one an elephant's trunk.
The body of an enormous aardvark. The Nonesuch. I opened
the alley-knocker's door and exposed a rickety set of steps
leading down into the dark—more ladder than stairs.

Vala eyed them dubiously. "There's really a tavern down
there somewhere?"

"A pretty big one actually. There's another door at the
bottom and it opens into a series of galleries that were a part
of the old sewer system before they hired in Durkoth to dig
the whole thing deeper down into the bedrock."

"And they serve food there? In the sewers?"

I laughed. "It's been high and dry for five centuries,
plenty of time to clean things up. This is one of the few parts
of the city where basements make any sense because we're
above the water table but not yet so high that they have to
be cut out of stone."

"All right." She started down the ladder. "But I'm glad
we ate before we came, and I'm not drinking anything that
doesn't come in a sealed bottle with a familiar label."

"That's always a good idea at an alley-knocker," I called
down, having decided it was better not to test the steps with
two people at the same time. "You never know when a shadowside distiller might decide to cut the product with a little
wood alcohol or add in some of the more interesting sorts
of mushroom."

She looked back up at me. "Well, *that's* reassuring. Why
don't—" Vala's expression went suddenly far away.

Her voice shifted and it was VoS looking through her
eyes. "Aral, it's a trap. Durkoth. They've grabbed Stel." She

whipped out one of her battle wands and pointed it straight at my face.

Before I could move, she'd blown the ceiling out of the little staircase. "Run!" she cried and then the earth opened beneath her.

I leaped straight up and caught the jagged lip of the floor above, hauling myself up into someone's parlor. I didn't want to leave her behind, but the familiar link meant that if they had Stel, they had Vala, too. All that my staying would do was add another name to the list of prisoners. Triss slid upward, sheathing me in shadows as I looked around for my next step, a door leading to the stairs perhaps.

A chair toppled over as the building began to shake. It felt like a giant was pulling at the foundations. I opened my hands and pointed my palms at the ceiling. Triss handed me the reins of his will, and I let loose a burst of magelightning, shattering plaster and lath and opening another hole. Up I went. And again. Through an attic crawlspace and onto the roof with a red summer sun rising over the bay. Its angry rays turned the water to blood. Flames fell around me as a sorcerer of the Elite ran out into the street in front of the Nonesuch, lashing at me with his magic. Major Aigo!

Triss screamed and my shirt began to smolder where the fires had touched it. I felt the heat like a slap along the injured side of my face and had to fight down the urge to strike back—more for Triss's sake than my own—because we couldn't afford the delay. Instead, I pushed Triss outward to form a cloud of shadow around me and I ran, leaping across a cramped wynd that ran between the Nonesuch and its nearest neighbor to the southwest.

Fire bloomed red and raging in the roof of the building that held the Nonesuch, sending smoke clawing skyward. A fountain of sparks went up somewhere behind me and whistles began to sound, calling the watch and any other forces the Elite might have in the area. A stone dog howled its deep hunting cry.

The shaking that had battered the Nonesuch followed me to the next building over and I stumbled, almost missing my jump across the narrow street that divided the block holding the Nonesuch from the next one that bordered on the main street between the Magelander's Quarter and Little Varya. I turned more south there, knowing I couldn't make the leap across to Little Varya without spinning shadow wings and exposing myself to any eyes that chanced to look up. I wanted more distance between me and my pursuers before I took that kind of risk.

People screamed and ran this way and that in the streets below me as the very surface of the earth heaved and twisted beneath their feet, shaping itself to the will of the Durkoth moving in the deeps. The smoke from the burning building rose ever higher, telling a tale of fire unchecked in the face of panic. My impressions of the world, filtered through Triss's unvision, read even stranger than usual, faded as they were by the hammering of the sun.

I traveled through a war of the elements. Air was my ally, buoying me up as I made one mad leap after another across the rooftops. Earth and fire bayed at my heels, closing off the north and west. Shadow held and hid me from the rising light in the east as it tried to betray me to my enemies. Time blurred away into a series of distinct but somehow unconnected moments, as I moved south. Before I knew it, I was racing toward the edge of a building with an unbridgeable gap beyond. I sped up, throwing out wings of shadow as I leaped into space.

# 14

---◆◇◆---

The war of the elements continued. Out and down I fell, dropping through empty air until water enfolded me when I plunged deep into the Channary Canal. Full morning had come and the stagnant waters of the canal were a madness of boats of every size and description. I swam a long way through foul water before surfacing in the shade of a small pleasure boat—some noble's fancy, fast and fit and heading out to the river proper. I sank a shadow-pointed dagger silently into the hull well below the waterline to provide me a hold.

I pulled a length of my broken-down blowgun from my trick bag then and put it in my mouth with my free hand. Submerging myself in water and shadow, I clung to the boat like a lamprey battened on the side of some fat sea serpent, letting it drag me along beneath the surface. Breathing quietly through my slender length of reinforced bamboo, I left my enemies behind. Earth and fire and light momentarily defeated by darkness and deep water.

I had a lot of time to think there in the warm shadows beneath the little yacht. About what had just happened and

what came next. About the betrayed look on Vala's face as
VoS cut me an escape route—another vision of failure to
add to the many that haunted my nightmares. About Fei and
Sergeant Zishin, and whether I'd been set up by one or the
other, or if they'd been betrayed as well.

The answer to that question was the next thing I had to
find out. I needed to find and free the Dyad as quickly as
possible, but I couldn't do that until I knew who had her and
why. Until then, I would force myself to box up my concerns
for her and lock them away in the back of my mind. I had
to. Whether it was just or not, the Dyad had come to matter
to me, especially Vala, and I'd failed her.

If I didn't put that aside for the moment, the guilt and
distraction might kill me, and that wouldn't do her any good
at all. So, when the canal disgorged itself into the Zien River,
I pried my dagger loose and swam to a barge heading upriver
toward the Palace Quarter and Fei's office, focusing wholly
on what I had to do next instead of why.

Moving out into the main river was a huge relief at first.
Tien had good sewers and horrendous penalties for not
using them, but people still dumped trash and chamber pots
into the waters from time to time. On the river the ordure
was quickly swept out to sea by the currents, but the waters
of the canals were still and stagnant, and the waste lingered
there stinking things up.

In summer, the sun made the canals blood warm, and
that heat had combined with my exhaustion to spin my head
full of cobwebs. The colder waters of the river came as a
relief at first, bringing me back to full alertness. But I'd
already been in the water for quite a while by then and it
didn't take long for the chill to start seeping into my muscles, bringing a deep ache and shivers with it. Ironic to be
so cold with brutal summer lying barely a foot away, just
the other side of the interface between water and air.

Though Triss remained deep down in the dream state
necessitated by the various feats of magic that had allowed
us to escape, I could feel a growing sense of impatience from
him. It was rare for me to keep him under for so long, but

we were still in too much danger of discovery for me to give up my moment-to-moment control quite yet. I tried to think him a message of reassurance, but couldn't be sure it got through. The difference in the minds of Shades and their human companions was such that we'd always had to rely on the spoken word for most of our communication, a fact that had frustrated the sorcerers of my order for centuries.

*Just a little longer, my friend,* I thought, *just a little longer.* But of course, there was no response. I patted myself on the shoulder in the vague hope that he would feel the reassurance somewhere down there in the depths of my dreams, but I didn't have much faith in the effect.

A few hundred yards after my barge passed the palace docks, I slipped free once more and swam to the western shore, maybe half a mile below Westbridge. The river had cut away the base of the Palace Hill here, exposing the underlying bedrock in sheer bluffs that prevented the estates above the palace complex from spilling all the way down to the river's edge. I took a risk then by climbing the dark limestone cliff in broad daylight, trusting to shadow to shield me from all but the most dedicated observer.

It must have worked, because there was no hue and cry raised, nor any greeting party waiting for me when I chinned myself on the low wall that crowned the bluff and peered over the top. That wall marked the practical boundary of the estate of the Duchess of Tien, titular ruler of the city. Even though it looked down on the river from the top of a hundred-foot bluff, someone on the ducal staff had made sure to keep the wall's defenses in beautiful condition.

The stones were all clean and well laid, the joints freshly tuck-pointed and nearly seamless. One of the predecessors of the duchess had even gone to the expense of having the top liberally studded with silver nails, a sovereign protection against both the restless dead and intruders who couldn't glove their hands in an armor of shadow. They'd interspersed them with a smaller number of iron spikes, an unusual precaution in a great city like Tien where the creatures of wild magic rarely ventured.

I wondered if that was down to tradition, or if it was meant to address the proximity of the river, which provided one of the few conduits for the wild ones to enter the metropolis. In either case, I thought them a bit much. There were simple alarm wards as well, but the maintenance sorcerer had done inferior work there. They were so obvious that even a mageblind burglar could have avoided them if he were halfway competent at his craft. I loosed Triss briefly then, signaling for him to withdraw the enshrouding shadow from in front of my face.

The morning sun that now rode high in the sky behind me had more than half blinded Triss's unvision. I needed to take a look with my own eyes before committing myself to the next step in my plan. I also wanted to give him a chance to voice any concerns that he might have. I hung there for perhaps ten minutes without spying any patrols or having Triss collapse himself down to a speaking shape, though I could feel something like a silent grumble coming through our magical link.

Up and over, and down and drop, and I was in. The ducal estate was huge, second only to the palace complex itself in scope, just as the Duchess of Tien was second only to the king in practical authority. At the moment, she was also second or third in the succession, depending on how you counted things.

Among the many outbuildings that dotted the acres of manicured groves and formal gardens of the estate were several dedicated to various functions of the city watch, which held the duchess as its ultimate commander and liege lady. Temporarily reasserting control over Triss, I moved quickly from the wall into the shadows of a large and carefully kept stand of bamboo. As I slipped deeper into the estate, I made sure to stay under the trees as much as possible, avoiding the numerous groundskeepers and the several small groups of household guards that I passed along the way.

At one point, I walked through a stand of flowering pears, and after that I had stolen fruit to munch on. After all the energy and nima I'd expended to escape the ambush at the Nonesuch, I was hungry enough to ignore the fact that the fruit was still well short of ripe. Eventually, I arrived at my destination, a suite of offices and meeting rooms ceded to the watch on a more or less permanent basis.

The duchess rented them the building so that she had a place she could confer with her officers without having to leave the bounds of her estate or allow the cruder functions of the watch to impinge on her residence. Conveniently for me, the goal of reducing the visual presence of the watch on the estate included planting a dense silverthorn hedge around the building to help hide it from delicate noble eyes. Once I slipped into the space between the planting and the wall, I was thoroughly masked from the broader estate, and could almost have let Triss slip back into dragon shape.

All of the city's watch captains kept offices there, as did several of their more important lieutenants. I peered in the window of Fei's first floor office, the largest of the lot, just in case, but was unsurprised to find it dark and empty. That wasn't why I'd come. Assuming a low crouch I moved carefully along the outside wall, peering through basement windows into the closet-sized offices assigned to minor officers until I found what I was looking for. It was child's play to slip the lock and wriggle through the window—no one breaks *into* a watch office. Especially not one that's in the center of a guarded estate and only intermittently in use.

Once we were safely inside, Triss slid down off my skin, puddling briefly on the floor before reassuming his dragon form and taking up a position covering the door. He flicked his wings back and forth angrily. Since it was impossible for him to really communicate with me in shroud form, this was the first chance we'd had to talk since the attack at the Nonesuch. He was obviously upset about it.

"Care to tell me what the plan is?" the little dragon growled quietly. "Or is that too much to ask from my bondmate?"

"I'm sorry, Triss. Truly. I didn't have one at first, not beyond getting away. Then, when I started to look at next steps, the situation was such that I couldn't have talked to you no matter how much I might have wanted to. Being underwater limits one's conversational options, I have to say."

Triss stopped fussing with his wings and cocked his head at me quizzically. "If I didn't know better, I'd swear that was the second attempt at a joke in as many days." Then he shook himself. "But don't think that's going to get you off the hook, my friend. What are we doing on the Duchess of Tien's estate?"

"We need to free Vala and Stel," I said. "That means finding out who took them. There was an Elite presence at the Nonesuch, if only a small one, and they started whistling up the watch the second I slipped the net. That implies official ties for the snatch, and that means that we were set up, though I'm not yet sure whether it was Fei or Zishin. Which, in turn, means I need to have a word with one or both of them. I don't know where Zishin lives, and if it was Fei, she's smart enough not to go home."

"I can see that, but I'm not making the jump to why it's a good idea to break into the estate of the Duchess of Tien."

"If it's Fei, she's going to be holed up in her office and surrounded by a sea of Stingers. Since my face is up on wanted posters all over this city, I figured that I'd do best to gather up some protective camouflage before trying to sneak into watch central."

"Which brings us into this room right here why?"

I pointed at a little silk pillow tucked unobtrusively on a high shelf above the door.

"Still not following you."

"The lieutenant who belongs to this office keeps a real pillow here, and an expensive one by the look of it. The only reason to do that is if he occasionally sleeps here, and not just naps. Which means . . ." I opened the little cabinet behind the desk and reached inside to pull a neatly folded watch uniform off the shelf.

Behind it I saw a small bottle of brandy. My stomach cooed like a mating dove and cool beads of sweat broke out along my hairline as I imagined taking a long sweet drink.

"Are you all right?" asked Triss.

I nodded because I didn't trust a mouth suddenly gone dust dry to get the right words out. My hands shook as I flipped the uniform open to check the fit. A little big, but not so much so as to draw suspicion. I focused on that. One nice thing about being only middling tall for a man and likewise of average build was that most clothes fit me. Add in that Tienese dress tended to the loose and flowing and I could almost always steal an appropriate outfit when needed.

"What do you think?" I asked Triss, when I could speak again.

"That's pretty clever, actually," said Triss. "You chose the offices here because they were not far out of the way and rarely in full use?"

"That and because the guards here are mostly on the outer perimeter, not in the building. You sound surprised."

"I guess I'm still not used to you thinking like the old Aral. Not after spending so much time with the pickled version the last few years." His voice was dry and acerbic.

"I'd like to say I don't deserve that. But the fact that I'm absolutely dying to have a drink from the bottle of brandy that's in there suggests that you might have a point. It's funny, I can ignore it most of the time when I've got something else to keep my attention, but every time I see a bottle . . ."

"You can do this," Triss said quietly but firmly. "I know you can. I shouldn't have made that dig. I'm sorry."

"It's all right, Triss. I'll take a hard truth over a pretty lie any day."

There was a formal dress jacket of polished silk in the cabinet as well. But that would only draw unwanted attention where I was going, so I let it lie. I did take the broad-brimmed hat the watch sometimes wore in the summer, both for sun protection and because the shadows it made would help hide my face. Especially since I intended to have Triss give them a little hand. At other times when stealing clothes I'd left a couple of riels to pay for their replacement, but I didn't bother this time. I didn't owe the Stingers anything.

I quickly stripped out of my still damp clothes, wincing at the sting as I dragged the shirt over the fresh scabs and bruises on my face. The Elite had done a number on me there, though Vala thought it would heal without scarring after her spellwork.

Then I changed into the uniform. It felt wonderful to have fresh clean fabric against my skin. It was raw silk instead of the cotton of a duty uniform, but the rough texture of the fabric meant you'd have to look close to notice. The biggest problem was the badges on the upper arms. The paired fans of a ranking lieutenant would draw more attention than I wanted. But that could be fixed with a sharp knife and a bit of creative magic to replace them with a sergeant's tripled swords. I'd have made myself a corporal or a private if I could have, but neither would ever wear a uniform as nice as mine.

I still had the problem of my double-draw sword rig and trick bag, both of which were profoundly nonstandard equipment, but I figured I could manage that by stealing a long tool sack from the groundskeepers. My wet clothes went into that as well since I didn't want to leave behind anything that could be used by a tracker, magical or otherwise. The sack fell outside the realm of standard watch equipment, but everybody ends up hauling around an extra bag from time to time so I didn't think it'd draw too much attention my way.

And I was right, though not for the reasons I'd expected. The Mufflers offices were normally very quiet, in keeping with their special mission. But today when I arrived at the little building on the Highside/Palace Quarter border, it looked like an overturned hornet's nest. Gold and black watch uniforms buzzed around everywhere and a sort of haze of suppressed fury hung in the air, though I didn't know why. I kept my head down and my hat pulled forward as I slipped through the crowd.

I'd expected to have to do a certain amount of fancy footwork both verbal and literal to get where I wanted to go, but nobody even noticed one more Stinger in the midst of that angry swarm. I was able to go right in the front door

and through to the small latrine off the front room without
being challenged.

Under normal circumstances I'd have pulled up a few
floorboards and slipped into the crawlspace beneath the
offices. Like many of the newer buildings in Tien's wealthy
hillside neighborhoods, it had been designed with plenty of
room for airflow beneath, both for summer cooling and winter heating using one of the hypocaust furnaces imported
from the Sylvani Empire. The under-floor space provided the
perfect route for moving about unseen if you ignored
the potential problem of the Durkoth coming at you through
the bedrock that lay only a few inches below the surface
here. Not something I was willing to do after what had happened to Coalshovel and later at the Nonesuch.

Instead, I climbed up onto the bench and examined the
narrow, bamboo-framed mulberry-paper panels separating
the attic from the rooms below. The rough unbleached paper
of the ceiling was another marker of a newer building, one
expressly designed to be easily switched from one sort of
use to another.

I much preferred older, more solid ceilings as did the
thatchcutters and other shadowtraders who made illegal
entrances via the roof. The mulberry paper was far too easy
to rip, and it amplified any noise like a drumhead, but I had
no other good choice. Sighing, I pushed up the panel closest
to the wall, and poked my head into the space above. It felt
like I'd opened the door on a fresh-filled drying oven, as hot
damp air smacked me in the face.

I lifted my bag through, laying it carefully across a couple of rafters, then followed it up as quickly as I could manage. Pausing only long enough to have Triss reach down and
open the latch on the latrine door, I reset the panel behind
me. I had to hope no one would enter for the few minutes it
took for the heat I'd just let in to dissipate. I didn't want
anyone wondering about that.

Sweat drenched me in seconds, though I hadn't even
started moving yet. If I wanted to get to Fei's office, I was
going to have to crawl on hands and knees along the rafters

with my sack slung awkwardly in front of me because the roof hung so low it nearly scraped my back. Working slowly and carefully despite the stifling heat I got moving. The bustle and buzz below would cover most of the noise of my passing, but too loud a creak or a slip that ripped one of the paper panels and I'd be fucked.

I had to pause repeatedly to mop the sweat off my face and out of my hair just to keep it from dripping and spattering on the paper panels below. It was a public building and not some noble's fancy, so the panels were inferior paper, very rough and often stained, but the Mufflers were a lot sharper than your average watchman. One of them might actually notice a series of fresh wet spots drawing a slow line across the ceiling and decide to check on the problem with a woldo or some other spearlike object.

Normally, Triss would have caught the drops for me, but a dark shadow sliding along the translucent paper would make an even worse tell than the sweat, especially with the light coming up from below. After crawling for what felt like a thousand years and three hundred miles, I ended up over what I hoped was Fei's office.

I'd only been there once before, and that very reluctantly, to collect a payoff for a small courier job I'd done for the captain. Then, she had occupied a big open room in the building's back right corner which was where I was now. The relative quiet and dark of the room below was reassuring, suggesting closed windows and a place where even watchmen treaded lightly.

I lowered my head into the space between two rafters and lifted a ceiling panel a few inches, giving me a narrow view of part of the room. I recognized Fei's desk. It was covered in a light scatter of writing paper, but the seat behind it held nothing. I lifted the panel higher, listening carefully all the while. Nothing. I poked my head down into the room and looked around. Empty.

I moved a couple of yards to my left and lifted out the panel directly above Fei's desk. That allowed me to lower myself onto the raised top and avoid the noise of a drop to the floor. A quick glance through Fei's papers didn't turn up anything useful, though I did notice there was nothing dated from the last two days in the scatter. Looking around, I spotted a small set of filing shelves. All the most recent reports and paperwork were stacked neatly on the top shelf, implying she hadn't had a chance to look at them yet.

I was just deciding what to try next, when a faint courtesy knock sounded at the door. It was the sort of knock an underling makes when they know that no one is home, but don't want to violate protocol in case they turn out to be wrong. The hinges were on this side of the door, so I stepped into the blind spot that would be created by its opening. I drew one of my swords and waited. A second knock followed, this one even fainter than the first. The door opened a heartbeat later.

A tall, slender man in the uniform of a watch corporal stepped into the room carrying an extra-large sheet of paper rolled up like a scroll. Corporal Anjir—I knew all the Mufflers by sight. As he started toward the file shelf, I pushed the door gently closed and raised my sword. The corporal froze as the latch clicked shut, but he didn't turn around.

"Captain Fei?" he said, very quietly.

"Nope."

Anjir's shoulders slumped. "Didn't think so. I presume that I'll get something sharp and fatal between the shoulder blades if I make any loud noises or sudden moves."

"That's very perceptive of you, Corporal. Keep thinking that clearly and there's an excellent chance you'll get out of this room alive."

"Best news I've had in the last thirty seconds," said the corporal. "Should I keep standing as I am, or would you prefer me to move someplace?" He sounded almost calm, but I could see the trickles of sweat starting to run down the back of his neck.

"Just stay there if you please. I've got some questions for you, and I'd rather you didn't see my face."

"You could bind my eyes if you like. I'd really prefer not

to see your face either. Improves the odds of you leaving me alive and all."

It was a good idea, so I signaled Triss to put a hood of shadow over his head.

The corporal twitched a bit when Triss first covered his eyes, but then seemed to relax. "Nice little spell that, thank you."

I leaned back and put my ear against the door behind me. There was a distant clamor from the front of the building, but it didn't sound like anyone was moving around in the hall. That meant I probably had a little time. If anyone had seen the corporal come into Fei's office and close the door, and found that at all suspicious, he'd already been in here long enough to draw more focused attention. Now it was a question of how long it would be before anyone missed him doing whatever he was supposed to do next.

"You're welcome," I said. And then, because I was curious, "You don't seem nearly as alarmed as I would have expected."

"I work for Captain Fei. This isn't the first time I've had my head bagged on the job. It's always come out all right in the past."

"Speaking of the good captain; where is she?"

"No one knows. She's been missing for two days. That's why the office is in such an uproar."

"That's funny. I talked to Sergeant Zishin no more than eight hours ago and he acted like he'd seen the captain recently."

"Maybe he had," said the corporal. "But if so, he hasn't told the rest of us about it."

"Do you know where the sergeant is now?"

"I imagine he's at home."

"And where is home for the sergeant?"

"Somewhere on the Kanathean Hill, though I couldn't tell you closer without looking it up. I don't suppose you'd be willing to let me go out to the front desk and ask, would you?" He didn't sound hopeful and I didn't bother to answer.

I snarled mentally. So far I hadn't gotten anything useful out of a very dangerous game and I was running out of time fast. The sand in the hourglass had started to empty the moment the corporal came through the door.

"I presume the captain's house has been searched?" I asked.

"Several times, and there are men stationed there now waiting for her to come home."

That was something at least. My original plan had called for me to try Fei's place next if I didn't get anything here, and that removed a stop from my list. I decided to allow myself about three more questions before I put the corporal to sleep for a while and got the hell out of there. No Fei, no Zishin, and no hope of finding either one easily. So, what to ask next?

"What do you know about the operation at the None-such?" I was guessing the answer was nothing, but it was the next most important thing on my mental list.

"Only that it happened and that it failed to get its primary target. At least, that's what the gossip is saying. That was an Elite operation, Major Aigo's people with some unofficial help from the local Durkoth. The Howlers don't much like us down here at Silent Branch, so rumor's the best I can do there."

I felt a little slithering spot of cold moving upward along my spine, like someone running an icy feather across my skin.

"If the Dyad wasn't the primary target, who was?"

The corporal half turned and held out the scrolled paper, opening the roll with a flick of his wrist.

There, looking back at me was as nice a likeness of my face as I'd ever seen this side of a mirror.

# 15

---

"The main target was the famous assassin, Aral King-slayer, of course," said the corporal. "Captain Fei found him!"

I took the poster. It had a much better drawing of me than the one the Elite had put on the posters for my jack face. Fei had clearly paid serious money for her sketch artist. Guessing from the level of detail, she'd also arranged for them to spend some time watching me at the Gryphon's Head. The reward was much higher as well, having doubled my old Kingslayer numbers. I was now worth fifty thousand gold riels. Or, my head was anyway. All you had to do was deliver it to the palace with or without the body attached.

That was enough to buy a palace and staff it. A single gold riel would have paid the rent on my little room over the stable for half a year, or bought ten fancy dinners at the Spinnerfish with drinks and dessert. The king was offering *fifty thousand* for my head. It was hard to even conceive of that kind of money, much less imagine it being paid out for my death. And now that the poster was out there with my old name attached, the likeness would spread.

Before you knew it, the Aral Kingslayer reward posters that the Son of Heaven had up all over the eleven kingdoms would have a picture of me on them as well. If a bounty hunter could figure out some way to deliver my head to both secular and religious rulers, they could add another ten thousand to their potential take—the high church of the eleven kingdoms being a bit more parsimonious than Thauvik IV. I had a brief wild moment of wondering how one might go about that, since I didn't think either one of them would want to part with my head. There was too much cachet to be had by putting it up on a spike somewhere. But that way lay madness, so I pushed the thought away.

"How do you know that's really the Kingslayer?" I asked.

"You'd have to ask Captain Fei. Funny thing really. It turns out the Kingslayer's been hiding here in Tien since the true gods put down his crazy goddess. Just pretending to be a plain old shadow jack, if you please."

I'd already overstayed my time, but I couldn't help ask one last question. "So, no one knows how Fei figured it out?"

"No, though it's supposed to have been quite a recent discovery." He dropped his voice. "They think he probably killed Fei when he found out she'd identified him, and that's why we can't find her, though we're acting as if she'll be coming back. That's why I came in here, actually. Leaving the captain a copy of this new wanted poster the Elite have been putting up everywhere since the thing at the Nonesuch went bad."

I needed to get out of there. "I'm going to have to put you to sleep for a little while now, Corporal. Don't struggle, and I promise you'll wake up. If you do struggle, or make any loud noises, I won't have time to do anything but kill you. Now, turn around."

He tensed, but then nodded and did as he was told. Reaching into my trick bag, I opened a small brass case and pulled out a robin's egg. It was filled with a powdered mixture of efik and opium, which made a powerful and fast-acting soporific. I set my sword aside and wrapped my free arm around his neck. Again, he tensed briefly before relaxing.

I squeezed hard, lifting him off the ground and cutting off his air. He instinctively tried to fight me then, but Triss had slipped down to pin his arms, and there wasn't a lot he could do. I could easily have broken his neck. Instead I let off the pressure after only a few seconds. When the corporal took a deep gasping breath, I slapped the little egg against his face, shattering it and sending the powder deep into his lungs. Within seconds he went limp in my arms. Nothing short of magic would wake him for at least several hours.

I draped him artistically across the desk, where anyone looking in from the doorway couldn't possibly miss him. Then I unlatched Fei's window before climbing back up into the ceiling. From there, I gave the window a shove, opening it wide. Next, I made my way across the rafters to a place just in front of the door. Sticking my head back down into the room, I screamed like a man being murdered.

I barely had time to drop the panel back into place before a half dozen officers of the watch crashed into the room below. From their hurried shouts, I could tell they'd made the obvious connection with the open window and sent men leaping out to see what had become of the corporal's attacker. While that was going on, I hurried across the rafters to the office opposite the captain's and flipped up a ceiling panel. As expected, it was empty now, so I dropped down into the space behind the wide open door.

By then, the pandemonium had grown to such a degree—with Stingers running every which way—that it was a trivial matter for a man in a sergeant's uniform to slip out through the front offices and into the street. As I made my way down through the Highside toward the river and the Magelander's Quarter, I found myself losing track of little stretches of time. One moment, I would be looking toward a familiar landmark like the King's Head tavern. The next, I'd find I'd passed it without noticing.

I was operating on nerves and nothing more and I

desperately needed to get off the street before I got myself killed. Death by stupid is a terrible way to go. Somehow, I managed to keep things together long enough to get down off the Palace Hill and into the streets of Little Varya without falling asleep on my feet or getting caught. At that point, my watch uniform started to draw more attention than it deflected. Since I'd already seen more than a dozen copies of the Kingslayer poster, that meant it was time I ditched it. I couldn't afford to have anyone looking at me too closely. So I turned into the first tailor's I passed and walked straight up to the woman behind the counter.

"I need a change of clothes," I said. "Something simple."

Her face went unnaturally pale. "I . . . uh . . . yes, my lord. Anything you say, my lord."

I rubbed my forehead. "Since nobody wearing a sergeant's swords on his sleeve has any right to a 'my lord,' can I assume that you've seen the wanted posters?"

She swallowed and nodded miserably. "Please don't kill me, Lord Kingslayer. I'm only a poor tailor and I promise no one will hear you've been here from me. No one. You did us a great service by putting the sword to old King Ashvik, and that's no mistake. I've said that afore now, and I'll say it again."

"You're as safe with me as you would be in your own bed," I said as gently as possible. "I swear it. If you know who I am, you also know what I am. No Blade kills the innocent. Not if there's any way to avoid it. But I can't have you running off to the watch the second I leave, and I can't trust your word that you won't, so I'll have to tie you up before I go. Hold on a moment."

I crossed back to the shop's entrance and flipped the little sign to closed before shutting and latching the door. When I turned around, the tailor was already pulling out several suits of clothes and laying them out on the counter. I chose a loose sleeveless shirt and pants of a second grade silk, blue bordering on gray, and I paid more than they were worth. I also bought a nicer bag for my swords and other gear, something more appropriate to the clothes I was wearing. It was all on Kodamia's kip anyway, so what the hell.

I left the shop a few minutes later with my fresh change of clothes on my back and the tailor unbound behind me because I couldn't bring myself to do the sensible thing. Not in the face of so much fear. And especially not with Triss whispering in my ear about it.

The streets of Tien had never seemed so crowded nor the people so curious and prone to stare. Every water seller and kebab vendor from the Weavery to Backpast seemed to have wedged themselves into the Magelander's Quarter intent on getting me to stop and buy their wares. And every one of them seemed to have set up under another copy of that damned wanted poster. I moved as fast as exhaustion would let me, fending off the hawkers and gawkers with an occasional thrown up hand and a frequently barked series of "nos."

I also kept my hat low, risking the telltale of having no personal shadow in order to keep an unusually heavy one across my face. Triss stayed wrapped tight around me in case we had to fight. I figured the crowds were so dense that my shadow never would have touched the ground anyway, so the chances of anyone noticing it when I didn't block a share of their sun were pretty slim. At least, that's what I told myself, and in my ragged state I believed me.

Whether it was true or not, I did eventually make it across the Zien on the Low Bridge, which led to the Stumbles and Smuggler's Rest. And I did it without getting bagged by the Stingers, the Howlers, or some freelance bounty hunter. That put me back on my home ground, where I knew every nook and every cranny. There it was much easier for me to fade into the background, even with all the damned posters nailed up every which where. But I was pretty much out on my feet by the time I made it to the best of my fallbacks, a gutted out old tenement that had been ravaged by fire.

The inside of the ruined building was an unstable maze of broken rubble and charred debris. I normally went up the one remaining outside wall that still had any structural integrity, but there was no way I could have climbed it in daylight without being seen. Not even fully shrouded. Instead, I slipped through a trick board the local kids had rigged, and risked life and limb by threading my way across the shifting wreckage inside on my way to the back tower.

Looking up into that chimney-like void, it was impossible to tell that the very top floor of the old tower was still sound and in place eight stories above. In fact, the careful enlargement of a couple of windows on the floor below increased the light in ways that made it seem as if there was nothing but shattered beams and a scrap of old roof between the ground floor and the sky.

I hopped lightly over the ruin of a door that lay on the floor just inside the tower's entrance and crossed to the far wall. The slab of charred wood covered a big hole where the floor had collapsed into the sewers. I'd long ago burned away what little strength the original fire had left the door, so that the weight of anything much bigger than a cat would break it in half.

It took me more than an hour to make my way up the well of the tower, a route I'd only ever been forced to use once before. I had to take frequent rest breaks, perching on rotting window ledges or the stubs of old beams, and I'd never have made it at all without Triss's ability to make me fingerholds no normal human could have used.

Eventually, I climbed up to just beneath the top floor. There, rather than take the risk of being seen slipping out a window and up the last few feet, I got Triss to unlatch the trapdoor I normally used for a privy so that I could crawl through from below. The tiny room above was an oven, so I cracked the shutters as wide as I dared—too much obvious change might draw attention to the tower. Then I stripped off my outer clothes and flopped down on the old straw mattress.

When I woke, the sun had moved the shadows a few feet, making it early afternoon. My rough sheet was soaked with sweat and I had a pounding headache, but no one had

beheaded me in my sleep, so I had to count that as a win.
The two or three hours of shut-eye I'd gotten weren't nearly
enough, but hunger kept me from just rolling over and trying
for a couple more. It'd been ages since the Spinnerfish, and
I'd long since run off all of my dinner. When I blearily sat
up on the narrow mattress, Triss flowed out from under me
and up onto the wall.

"What now?" he asked.

"Breakfast, or lunch. Whatever the hell meal you have
when you wake up groggy at . . . What time is it?"

"A bit past the second afternoon bell," said Triss. "And
don't think I didn't notice the way you dodged the question."

"It wasn't a dodge so much as a delaying tactic while I
wake up and think things through. I don't suppose you want
to fetch me that breakfast?"

Triss sighed, then slid down the wall and across the floor
to the place where my amphorae were racked. For a moment,
the nearest was covered in shadow, then the big ceramic
stopper thudded gently to the floor. Two beats after that Triss
pulled out a small clay pot and brought it to me before going
back to open another amphora.

I broke the seal and pried off the lid, exposing a dense
brick of a cake and filling the air with the smell of orange
liquor. The cake was mostly made up of dried fruit and nuts
baked in just enough rice flour to hold it together, then
steeped in liquor to preserve it. As long as you left them in
the pot they came in, the things would last virtually forever.
Or, for traveling, you could wrap them in oiled paper and
stow them in the bottom of a pack and expect it to still taste
pretty good after a month or three of bouncing around.

I broke off a piece and started chewing. Heavenly stuff,
but expensive. Which is why I hadn't had any at the other
fallback. While I was munching on my orange cake, Triss
brought me a jar of excellent small beer and a tiny ham
wrapped in oiled paper—likewise much better fare than I
had been able to offer Stel and Vala. That thought gave me
a little pang of guilt now. But the only thing I could do about
it at the moment was to get out there and find them, and

eating a good meal would put me in a much better state to achieve that.

Triss didn't open the amphora that held my Kyle's twenty, and I didn't ask him to, though I would very much have liked a sip or two of something stronger than small beer and the liquor in my orange cake. I'd finished about half of the ham and all of the cake when Triss suddenly whipped his head around and looked sharply at the open trap door.

"What is it?" I asked.

"I'm not sure, hang on."

Triss slipped down through the door, leaving only the thinnest thread of darkness to connect him back to me and the place the sun would have put his shadow. I set the ham quietly on the floor and reached for my clothes. My hand had just touched the rough silk of my pants when I felt a thrum of alarm run back along the line of shadow that linked us. It was the most urgent sort of warning, so instead of putting my clothes on, I just hooked them through the carrying strap of my new bag and grabbed my boots.

Triss reappeared through the trapdoor as I pulled the first boot on. He came up slowly and carefully, slithering over the edge rather than popping back up. I opened my mouth to ask what was wrong, but before I could speak he touched my lips with one claw and shook his head. Then he handed me my remaining boot before wrapping my bag in shadow and lifting it silently to my shoulder for me while I slipped on the boot. For the first time I realized how quiet the world outside my tower had gotten. Shit.

As I rose into a crouch, I lifted my head back and mimed a wolf howling. Triss nodded and held up five fingers, making a circling gesture to let me know they were all around us. That meant we couldn't sail-jump, especially not mid-afternoon when Triss would be at his weakest. I pointed down through the trapdoor and he nodded. This was going to get seriously nasty.

A very quiet scuffing sound, as of someone stealthily climbing a stone wall, came in through the window. I leaped and caught hold of one of the cross beams, quickly swinging my feet up so that I could hang by my heels and free my hands. Triss wrapped himself around me as I pointed my palms at the edges of the floor, submerging his will within my own. I drew a deep breath, then closed my eyes and released the lightning as I let it out. The blast chewed through the wooden planks, igniting them at the same time it severed the two main supports for my little aerie.

With a terrible rending noise, the whole floor fell away beneath me—a burning wheel dropping into darkness. The tower shook, and clouds of dirt blossomed everywhere as bits of brick shattered and burst under the stress, but it didn't collapse. Not quite. I counted to three then let go of the beam, following the floor down into the dense pall of smoke and dust. Extending my arms, I shaped the shadow-stuff of my familiar into huge twinned claws, pushing them out to drag along the walls, slowing my fall while simultaneously adding to the general noise and destruction.

Using that touch point to tell me where I was relative to the height of the tower, I was able to let go and draw the shadows back in a few feet from the ground, dropping free for the last few feet. That was my intent anyway, but the fall was longer than I anticipated. This latest abuse had been too much for the floor. The whole thing had caved in, collapsing into the sewers below. I hit hard, and had to ditch my bag as I rolled across the debris to soak up some of the impact. Rough edges jabbed at my bare back and legs, opening ragged cuts and driving splinters deep into my flesh.

If Triss had been free, he might have armored me from the worst of it. But I had chosen to keep control, reaching for his senses in the same moment that I wrapped him around me now. That saved my life, because it meant that I felt the presence of the Durkoth a split second before he spotted me. Two staggering steps, pivot, and a flick of the wrist as I extended my arm. The dagger in my right wrist sheath slid into my hand and I continued the swing, dragging the edge of my steel across the Other's throat.

Blood hotter than any human's fountained across my hand and sprayed my face and chest. Deep purple according

to VoS—the same as their Sylvani cousins if the stories Siri
had told me about them were true, and she ought to know
after the assignment that earned her the name "Mythkiller."
She'd also told me that Others were damned hard to kill and
the Durkoth proved her point by not going down immediately as a human would have.

Instead, he lurched forward, slamming into me and
knocking me over backward. As I fell, I remembered
Qethar's stone cloak and willed my wrapping of shadow-
stuff into a stiff, barrel-like configuration to protect my chest
and ribs from the impact. But instead of landing on hard
debris as I'd anticipated, we plunged into the main flow of
the sewer.

I felt a moment of disorientation as our progress slowed.
Then the crushing pressure of five hundred or more pounds
of dying Other and long stone robe—this one was dressed
in foreign manner—pushed me deep into the muck at the
bottom of the channel. For a few instants I could feel the
stone fabric of his robe writhing against my shadow armor,
trying to catch and crush me.

Then the Durkoth went limp and his clothing froze in
place—the half-open hand of a stone giant gripping my
chest. I hadn't had time to draw an extra breath before we
went in, and now I thought my lungs might burst before I
worked my way free of that great weight. Only the fact that
my shadow armor had kept the grasping stone from getting
a tighter grip saved me. I had just enough room to slither
free of the dead Other, though I lost some skin doing it.

When my head broke the surface, I drew in a huge lung-
ful of air, then swam to the side of the channel. It ran deep
and fast here under the Stumbles, where the many outflows
off the Sovann and Kanathean Hills came together before
making their conjoined way out to the bay. I dragged myself
up onto the narrow access ledge and released my hold on
Triss, letting him go as I collapsed onto my side.

For a good minute I just lay there in the dark, gasping
raggedly and trying to recover. The stench should have been
unbearable, but after my recent time without any air at all,

the simple fact that I could smell *anything* made it seem almost sweet. An occasional dull crash or sudden splash spoke of the continued disintegration of the tenement above. I found that vaguely reassuring since I didn't think the Elite would be in any hurry to enter a building in the midst of collapse.

Triss slipped away up channel, moving back toward where we had fallen in for reasons he didn't bother to share. Just as earlier, he left a thin thread of shadow to connect us, and just as earlier he hadn't been gone long when I felt a thrum of alarm run back along that connection.

"Aral, downstream, now!" Triss's voice rang out shrill and harsh from the darkness up channel, riding over a sudden increase in the noise coming from above.

Reflex rolled me off the ledge, and long years of training designed to keep my body moving well past the point of physical endurance got me paddling, though my arms felt like lead and my soggy boots kept trying to drag me under. But I couldn't have gone more than a dozen strokes before the world fell on me.

It began with a sound like chained thunder, or the hands of a god beating a mad dance on the drum skin of the sky. Then came the dust, a great, blinding, choking wall of it that rolled down the tunnel from behind me like an avalanche filling a high pass. It clogged my nose and rimmed my mouth with mud in an instant, forcing me to close eyes against the grit. I ducked my head under the surface of the sewage-filled water and scrubbed at my face to clear the worst of it, because it was that or suffocate.

That's when the wave hit. Somewhere behind me the old apartment had given its final gasp and fallen in on itself, dropping nine stories of brick and stone down into the sewer all in an instant. Tons of water and the waste it carried were suddenly displaced, a veritable river of sewage thrown out and away from the point of impact all in an instant. It hit me like a liquid hammer, tumbling me over and over until I lost all sense of direction or self.

# 16

---◆---

**T**he hissing registered first, a low dangerous stream of sibilants like the world's largest asp venting its rage. It should probably have frightened me, but it didn't. Instead, I found it comforting, and so I focused my fragmented attention on the sound. Slowly, it shifted from senseless noise to words spoken in some alien vernacular . . . the language of the Shades. Triss! Angry or frightened or perhaps both, and swearing violently in his native tongue.

Something was wrong then, beyond the fact that I had no idea where I was or how I'd gotten there. I knew only that it was dark and chill and that I felt as though someone had stuffed me into a barrel half filled with rocks and rolled me down a long and bumpy slope. I struggled to sit up, realizing only in the moment of action that I had been lying down. Before I could get much more than halfway upright, the top of my head smacked into something hard and I let out a tiny yelp.

As I fell back I threw out both arms, striking curving stonework on either side of me. I was in some sort of stone pipe, probably a side run into the main sewer where my last memories left me. That would explain the smell. . . .

"Don't move," hissed Triss. "You're safe, but only if you hold still until I've dealt with the nightghast."

I froze. The words came from somewhere beyond the ends of my feet and I did as Triss ordered. Nightghasts ate human flesh when they could get it. They weren't the worst of their kind, not by a long road. But even the least of the restless dead could be plenty dangerous and they didn't have to kill you outright to make an end of you. If the nightghast clawed or bit me I might well survive the immediate damage, but succumb a few days or weeks later to the curse that animated it, becoming one of the restless dead myself.

There came a sudden scuttling sound in the dark beyond my feet. Triss answered with a sharp hiss and some large movement that I could feel through our link though I couldn't see anything. That was followed by a thud like a dull blade hitting old meat, and then a long wailing shriek.

"That's done it," said Triss, coming closer. "It won't be bothering us again soon."

"Thanks, Triss. What happened? The last thing I remember is you telling me to swim for it."

"The apartment building came down and collapsed part of the sewer. There was a big wave, and you got knocked around quite a bit but I couldn't find anything broken. How do you feel?"

"Like the shit I've been swimming in, but I'm basically all right. Next question. What happened at the fallback? I didn't get the chance to ask you anything before we had to bolt."

"Elite, a half dozen of them led by Major Aigo, with a company of Crown Guard in support."

"And Durkoth below. I don't like that alliance at all, not even if it's just a sort of truce of convenience." My hand went reflexively to the hilt of a sword I was no longer wearing. "I don't suppose you managed to save the bag with my gear in it?"

"I did," he said, his voice more than a little smug. "I was bringing it back to you when the roof fell in and I hung onto it as our link dragged me along in your wake. I had to drop it when I fished you out and put you in here, but it's on the bottom not far from here. You haven't been out long and the nightghast has been occupying my attention. Should I fetch it now?"

"Please. Any idea where we are?"

"Somewhere under Smuggler's Rest," he called over his shoulder. He was back a short time later with my bag. "If you crawl up the pipe behind you, you'll come to a storm grate pretty quickly."

**I'll** skip over the details of getting clean—relatively, and finding yet another set of new clothes—lifted but paid for, and move straight to the next stop on my tour of undiscovered Tien.

Sergeant Zishin was collecting the Mufflers' share of a little sellcinders operation when I caught up to him just after sunset. I waited for him to finish his business and walk past the mouth of a tiny alley before I let him know I wanted a word with him. The polite thing would have been to give him a call as he went by, but I was fresh out of polite.

What I did instead was shroud up, slide out, grab him by belt and collar, and toss him head first into the darkness of the little snicket. I also kicked his feet out from under him as he went by, just for good measure. A jindu fighter and Fei's longtime sparring partner, he reacted fast, turning the fall into a roll and spinning and drawing his boot dagger as he came to his feet. He dropped his watchman's lamp somewhere in there and it fell at his feet, painting him with bright light while leaving me in darkness.

"Come on, bastard," he said, "step into the light and I'll gut you."

But I didn't have the patience for a dance, so I set Triss on him. Shadow teeth sank deep into a flesh-and-blood wrist, drawing a high sharp scream and forcing Zishin to drop the blade. Before he could even think about recovering it, Triss shifted shape and became a noose around the sergeant's neck, lifting him half off his feet. As Zishin clawed at the shadow wrapped tight around his throat, I kicked the lamp away down the alley. Then I stepped in close and touched the tip of my steel to the spot just below the point of his jaw.

"You've got your choice, Zishin. You can stop making a fuss and maybe get to walk away, or you can piss me off. Which is it going to be?"

He froze. "Aral?" There was real fear in his voice.

"Call me Kingslayer." I still hated that name, but it was out there now, and I had been trained to use all the tools at hand. "You fucked me, Zishin, and that's going to cost you."

"I don't know what you're talking about, Aral."

"That'd sound a lot more convincing if your voice weren't shaking, Sergeant. Let me refresh your memory. Me, you, a message supposedly from your missing boss . . ."

"Swear to Shan, Aral, that wasn't a play. I know Fei's supposed to be belly up in the bay somewhere with your knife in her back, but she isn't. She was alive to give me that message I gave you. She's got some kind of game going, but I don't know what it is. Maybe the big retirement strike, or maybe something for the king. Whatever it is, she didn't cut me in. Swear to Shan, Aral, that's the straight. Swear to Shan."

He was terrified of me, that was plain enough, and he sounded sincere. But I'd been lied to by frightened men before. That's the problem with going hard on someone. If they were scared enough, or hurt enough, they'd say just about anything to make it stop even for a minute. It didn't help that truthsay is all kinds of tricky, like any mind magic. Zishin was no sorcerer, which was the biggest confound, but I figured Fei had probably paid to have him counterspelled. Question was: how much protection had she laid out for, and could I break it in the time I had?

"Triss, I need you. Zishin, move and die. You know what I am, you know it will happen."

Triss let go of Zishin's neck and flowed back into my shadow. Then up and around, wrapping me in the thinnest skin of darkness, like the first skim of ice on the surface of a pond in fall. As his will faded into an extension of my own, I put my free hand on the back of Zishin's neck. He shivered at the cold of my shadow-gloved hand, but didn't move otherwise. He wanted to live, and that held him long enough for my magic to take hold.

I hated to go quick and dirty, but I didn't have a lot of choice. Extending the penumbra of my shadow, I covered Zishin's head with a hood of living night and whispered a word of command. Light flared under the shadow, and I felt a brief but sharp burn across the skin where my palm rested on the sergeant's neck—the charm of conditional silence coiled around the root of his tongue rising to the surface to strike at me. Zishin whimpered and a brief convulsion rippled the length of his body from head to feet, but that was all the movement my hood allowed him.

The charm that sealed his lips against unbidden truths was strong, but not strong enough. Now that I knew how much opposition I faced, I knew the cost of breaking the spell. I spoke the word again, louder. This time, when the burn came, it felt as though someone had wrapped my entire arm in a fiery blanket, and the pain lasted much longer. When Zishin whimpered and convulsed, I whimpered with him. Closing my eyes, I took a series of deep slow breaths, forcing the pain to bend to my will.

As it faded away, I braced myself for what was to come. I was pretty sure that I *could* have unraveled the charm if I'd had a bit more time, and I desperately wished that I'd had the leisure for the less painful option. But even here in Smuggler's Rest, tossing a watchman into a darkened alley would draw comment and, eventually, investigation.

Bracing myself, I repeated the word one last time, yelling it this time. The world dissolved in fire and pain drove me to my knees. Zishin followed me down, bound as he was by my magic. I managed to hold onto consciousness, Zishin, and my knife, though I only barely kept my grip on that last. My point nicked the sergeant's skin just above the big artery in his throat, drawing a tiny trail of blood droplets in its wake like a scarlet inchworm.

"Tell me true," I said. "Did Fei send you to me with that note?"

"Yes." The sergeant's voice sounded weak and thready. "Or, if it wasn't her, it was one like enough to be her twin."

"And why didn't you let any of your fellow watchmen know about that?"

"She made me promise not to tell anyone, not even the rest of the Mufflers, and you don't cross Fei if you want to keep breathing." His face twisted into a frown. "I think she might have been afraid of something. But that's really all I know."

"Thank you," I said, then struck him across the base of the skull with the pommel of my knife.

The blow was gentle, barely enough to stagger a healthy man. But the sergeant had just suffered through the breaking of a spell housed inside his own head, and now his eyes rolled up and he slumped to the ground. He would be out for a good hour if I was any judge of spell backlash.

I held onto my control of Triss, using his shadowy fingers to find extra holds amongst the stones of the nearest building as I ascended once again into the chimney forest. Then I shrouded up and put some distance between me and the unconscious Zishin. The rooftops were crowded, thick with sleepers and creepers both.

I finally found us a nice secluded little perch at the intersection between a corner post and a huge beam nine stories off the ground in a tenement going up in a lot cleared by fire. In this part of town, that probably meant arson and insurance fraud. And, judging by the sloppy work on the joins and the fact that none of the beams looked like they'd been properly cured, neither the owner nor the construction crew was planning on this building lasting beyond the next convenient fire.

It made me wish I had the time and freedom to track down the bastard. I didn't much care about the insurance company getting screwed or the property damage, but I'd never yet seen an apartment fire that didn't kill someone poor. That shit pissed me off royally. Nine times out of ten, the kind of owner that would burn a building like this had been born to money and claimed blood as blue as the sky. Not that they sullied their precious noble hands with the actual details of things. They usually did all their business through agents and cutouts.

That was a good part of the problem, really. They didn't know a thing about the lives their tenants lived, and they didn't really see them as people, just silhouettes, ghosts of the lower classes. That was the true tragedy of Namara. With the death of my goddess, the people who didn't matter to the mighty had lost their divine champion, the one member of the Court of Heaven who was willing to see justice done on the nobles and landholders. I salved my guilt at surviving my goddess's fall with a promise to look into this if I lived through the next couple of weeks.

When I finally released Triss, he stretched himself out into dragon form on the beam at my feet. Then wrapped around it snakelike, curling back to look at me. "Tell me what the sergeant had to say."

So I did.

"What an interesting conversation," he said after I'd finished.

"Wasn't it just," I agreed.

Zishin was no mage, so it was possible he'd been played by someone using an illusion and pretending to be Fei, but that felt like the wrong answer to me. It'd be one thing if Fei's body had turned up, but failing that, I would be very reluctant to count her out of the picture under any circumstances. After hearing what Zishin had to tell me, I was going to assume she was still with us. But what was her play in all this?

"Do you think Fei set us up?" asked Triss.

"I don't know. I'd like to believe she didn't." Triss cocked his head to one side skeptically, and I continued. "Oh, not because I'd put something like that past her. Just because I'm having a hard time seeing her angle. If all she wanted was to bag the reward for turning me in, she could have done it any old time. No, there's something more going on here, and we need to find out what."

"That's not going to be easy, not with the entire city knowing exactly what you look like now. The whole of

Tienese officialdom is going to be yammering after us like they haven't since the week right after you killed Ashvik. Add in that every single one of our shadowside acquaintances will be measuring you for a coffin and counting the various rewards up, and that we've lost our best fallback, and I'm thinking we're real close to having to head for parts elsewhere."

"What about our Dyad friends? And all that talk about duty?"

Triss shrugged his wings. "You've just named the only reasons I haven't been pushing hard to leave town since we first saw that damn poster. But frankly, I'm at a loss as to how we can help the Dyad when we can't even find out who took her. I'd hate to abandon VoS, but I don't see how us dying for her without accomplishing anything advances her cause any. Or our duty for that matter. I'm willing to sleep on it and see what we can come up with, but if nothing occurs between now and tomorrow night, I think we may have to walk away."

I didn't like it, but he had a distinct point. We didn't know who had VoS and Vala and Stel, much less where they might be keeping them. Or, if I was going to be completely honest about the whole thing, even if they were still alive. It had been twenty hours since the ambush at the Nonesuch, plenty of time for the worst to have happened.

I rubbed at my burning eyes and tried to think of a decent counterargument, but I had nothing. Possibly because I'd gotten all of three hours' sleep since the ambush, and little enough in the twenty-four before that. Exhausted, covered in cuts and bruises, still stinking of shit despite my best efforts to get clean . . . I was all out. Once upon a time I could have relied on my faith to carry me forward when wit and will had failed me, but that faith had long since failed me, too. Maybe it *was* time I gave up.

"Maybe you're right, Triss, but I hate the idea."

"So do I, Aral. So do I."

There didn't seem to be anything more to say at that point, so I dragged myself upright. Much as I would have liked to go to sleep right there on the beam, I needed to get under cover before the sun came up, ideally someplace where I could find a drink. With my face glaring out of posters on every wall in the whole damned city, the harsh light of day had become as much my enemy as it was any vampire's.

Unfortunately, I was running mighty thin of good places to lay up and sleep, a fact that was hammered home when I reached the location of my third-tier fallback, a ruptured water tank atop a condemned tenement in Quarryside. The whole building should have been leveled long since, but the owners had gotten tied up in legal battles, and squatters had taken over until things got settled.

It was a shitty spot, both in terms of the state of the tank and the fact that if the owners ever solved their differences the place would be gone in a matter of days. But I no longer had temple funds covering my fallback expenses, and that meant I had to live with squats.

I'd placed a couple of minor aversion spells on the tank when I parked my cache there. That had kept anyone more desperate than I was from moving in. What the magic hadn't done, as I now discovered, was prevent some of the more enterprising squatters living on the floors below from simply knocking the thing off the roof and putting up a new tank on top of the old supports.

"Now what?" I asked Triss. As if to emphasize my question, a single drop of water plinked free of one of the freshly tarred seams on the new tank and splattered itself across my forehead. A momentary kiss of cold soon lost in the muggy summer night.

"I don't know. I don't like any of the one-nights under the circumstances."

I didn't either. A silk hammock hung high in the branches of an ancient oak in the royal preserve might provide a decent place to grab a few hours' sleep on a dark night when Triss could be relied on to keep watch. But full sun and high summer would render Triss mostly blind, and the place would be teeming with petty nobles taking to the park on the Sovann Hill as a refuge against the city's heat. That would seriously increase the chances of someone deciding to climb the wrong tree.

The one-nights in Backpast and down behind Spicemarket weren't much better, and all three were far enough away that we'd be doing most of our traveling under a new-risen sun. There was only one place I could think of that was close which might serve as a refuge.

"What do you think of going back to the brewery?" I asked reluctantly.

"I hate it," he grumbled. "But I hate it less than cracking into someone's attic and hoping they don't notice or laying up in the sewers with the Durkoth hunting us."

I sighed. None of the neighborhoods within dark-time traveling distance were affluent enough for the attic option to have any real chance of success. Only the well-to-do could afford the amount of empty space that play needed to succeed, and Triss was right about the sewers. We simply didn't know enough about Durkoth capabilities to make that a safe choice. I ran through the options in my head again and finally nodded.

"That's pretty much where I'm at." Going back to a fallback that was known to someone who'd been scooped by the enemy was the worst sort of tradecraft, but sometimes you have to go with the least bad option.

In this case, I figured the brewery would be safe for a few days more. It would take at least that long for anyone to crack the Dyad, assuming they could do it short of killing her. Like a Blade or one of the Elite, Dyads were protected from magical questioning and thoroughly trained to resist the more mundane sort of interrogation. She couldn't hold out forever if her interrogator was good enough, but she didn't have to for our purposes. She just had to keep her mouths shut for a day and a night. Then we could abandon her safely if we had to. . . . Yeah, I didn't think much of me just then either.

I turned away from the water tank. "I was really hoping you'd come up with a better alternative, my friend. As far as I can see, it's the brewery or the Ismere, and I'm not willing to involve Harad in my business when I'm this toxic."

The Ismere was an independent library, and Harad, its head librarian, was one of the only people in the whole world who I could still call a friend.

"No," agreed Triss. "I'd rather we chanced a one-night than bring our poison into the house of a friend. Let's go scope out the brewery and see what's what. It's that or give up on the city and our Dyad client right now, and I'm not quite ready for that."

"**It's** getting light," said Triss.

I nodded. It was, and, as far as I could tell, the brewery remained undiscovered and abandoned. Or, at least, I couldn't spy any watchers, and the dustheads who squatted in the lower levels weren't acting any more paranoid than usual. After working our way completely around the building twice, we'd settled in atop a nearby tannery to give things a longer eyeball—businesses that stank tended to cluster in the worst neighborhoods.

"We need to get under cover," Triss said. "Now."

I nodded again, but maintained my perch in the angle where two sections of roof came together. Everything seemed all right. It even *felt* all right, but going back to a snug that might have been burned really rubbed me the wrong way. I ran through the alternatives in my head for perhaps the dozenth time, but none of them looked any better from this angle than they had earlier.

"I really don't want to do this, Triss."

"Neither do I," he said. "But the sun's coming up and the city is against us."

"Aral Kingslayer?"

The voice that whispered in my ear was so gentle and quiet I barely registered it at the conscious level, but that didn't stop my hands from flying to my swords. I drew them in the same motion that spun me out and away from my perch, bringing the blades up into a guard position between me and . . . nothing. There was no one above me on the roof and no obvious opening in the tiles through which the voice could have come.

"What the . . ." I trailed off as I turned slowly around again.

"There's no one here, Aral," hissed Triss. Then, before I could respond, "But I heard it, too. Show yourself!"

"You *are* Aral!" Right in my ear again, and louder, but still little more than a whisper.

This time as I spun I sliced the air with my swords, but air was all I cut.

"My mommy sent me to find Aral! And I did. I found you right where you were supposed to be! She'll be *so* happy with me."

"Your mommy?" I asked.

"Aral, I'm sorry about yesterday morning. I had no choice." This time the voice sounded firmer and stronger, urgent but still little more than a whisper. "They forced me to it." It also sounded *very* familiar.

"Fei?"

"My mommy!" The weaker voice again.

"I think it must be a qamasiin," said Triss. "One of my cousins of the air, sometimes called the whisper on the wind."

Oho! "And Fei's familiar, if I don't miss my guess. Which would explain a great many things about our captain." An unfaced sorcerer with an invisible familiar could learn an awful lot about all sorts of things in a city like Tien, things that would do someone in the captain's business a world of good. "Fei *is* your mommy isn't she, little one?"

"Uh-huh. Scheroc found you for Mommy Fei. She will be so happy with Scheroc."

"Found us for what?" I asked.

The qamasiin squeaked in alarm, then said, "Bad Scheroc! Bad! Forgets to deliver rest of message." The voice shifted to mimic Fei's once more. "The Elite have me and your Dyad friend VoS. They've got some foreign Durkoth helping them."

Another vocal shift. "Aral, Triss, I think you can trust the captain, at least until we're out of this." It was Vala's VoS voice. "She's not been treated well down here."

Back to Fei. "Get me out of this and all debts are paid.

Hell, I might even owe *you* one. Scheroc can carry a message back to me and—shit! Guards are coming back—Scheroc, go!"

Well, well, well, Fei must have been all kinds of desperate to send Scheroc to ask me to bail her ass out. It was pretty much equivalent to putting a noose around her own neck, handing me the other end, and hoping I wouldn't pull it tight. Being an unfaced mage in Crown service was very nearly as dangerous as being a hidden Blade. The Crown didn't like officers who kept secrets.

"That's all Scheroc has." Scheroc sounded sad. "Will you help my mommy?"

"I might," I said, flicking a hand signal to forestall any interruptions from Triss. "But I need to know some things first."

"Anything!" it said.

"How did you find us?"

"Scheroc went right where the two-faced lady told him to and waited. Scheroc waited and waited and waited, but you never came!" The qamasiin sounded quite cross about that. "No one came, and it was boring. But then Scheroc saw you slinking around the edge of the place, and Scheroc came to listen for the voice of the Aral. You spoke in that voice, and Scheroc thought it must be you, but you were not where you were supposed to be, so Scheroc asked. And Scheroc was right!"

"That's good, now—"

"Aral," interrupted Triss. "If we don't get off this roof in the next few minutes, the sun is going to finish coming up and then we're going to have a hell of a time getting into the brewery unnoticed."

"Point. Were you waiting for us over there?" I pointed at the brewery.

"Yes," said Scheroc. "Where the big magic drawing is. It was empty and boring."

"I guess we'll have to count that as verification that it's still uncompromised. Come on, Scheroc, we'd best finish this conversation inside, out of the light."

# 17

I leaned my head back against the half barrel and closed my eyes. "Triss, have I told you recently what an absolute treasure you are?"

"I take it you're getting tired of trying to draw sense out of our little qamasiin friend?" Triss dropped his head into my lap with a sigh.

I idly scratched the divots behind his ears. "You could say that. Or you could say that I'm just getting tired. How many times has it had to go back to Fei to get us an answer now?"

"Believe it or not, this is only the third, but I'm sure there'll be more. Spirits of the air are neither very focused nor interested in the dealings of the fleshed, not even the mightiest of the mystrals. Scheroc is a qamasiin, a minor eddy born of a lesser breeze, barely one step up from the natural winds of the world."

I opened my eyes just to keep from falling asleep. "I understand that, but it would make things so much easier if it could at least . . . I don't know, tell us exactly where Fei and the others are being kept."

"It has, and in some detail. It's just that neither you nor I can make any sense of its referents. If I tried to tell you how to get someplace using only a shadow's view of the world I don't think you'd get much out of that either. For all that Scheroc speaks the tongue of Zhan, I don't think it actually understands much of what it's saying. So it's no surprise that it makes no sense to us."

"Which is a long way of telling me to suck it up and get ready to spend tonight following an invisible spirit who cares nothing for the limits of the fleshed as it makes its weird way across the palace compound, right?"

"That's about the size of it, yes. Don't forget the part where we have to break into what Fei called 'an impregnable fortress buried deep under the roots of the palace' and fight our way past the Elite guarding the place."

"No fight!" came the sudden whisper in my ear.

"Oh, good, you're back." I sat upright again, though I'm sure the qamasiin wouldn't have cared if I'd been hanging by my ankles from the ceiling. "What do you mean, 'no fight'?"

"Mommy says no fight, guards will kill her and the Dyad. Aral must bargain them out."

"Yeah, I'm having trouble seeing how that's going to work. We've got nothing and nobody to bargain with."

"Crush the pebble, summon Qethar." This last was said in Fei's voice. "You can trust Qethar. They hate him here. Offer him the Kothmerk and he can make us a back door. It's the only way to get past the foreign Durkoth I've seen around the place."

"In case your mommy hasn't noticed, I don't *have* the Kothmerk. I've got no leverage, and if I do crush the pebble, I'm pinpointing my location. Not smart when half the city is looking to turn me over to the Howlers and pick up the reward. Doubly so when I'm not sure whose side Qethar's really on, no matter what Fei says."

"Scheroc doesn't understand, what does Aral want?"

"What I want is out of this fucking box that fucking Fei's fucking poster put me in." I started to rise, remembered the height of the ceiling, and settled back to the floor with a growl. "Dammit dammit dammit, I feel like a wolf caught in a trap, with those wanted posters out there everywhere. No. Worse. If I were a wolf at least I could gnaw my leg off and get free. Gnawing your own face off is a much harder . . ."

"What are you thinking?" demanded Triss. "I don't like it when you go all quiet like that."

But I barely heard him. My eyes had fallen on the diagram left behind by Vala and Stel, the remnants of the bonewright spell. "Maybe I *can* gnaw my own face off." I rose to hands and knees and made my way over to the edge of the nearer hexagon.

"That's madness, Aral." Triss put himself squarely between me and the diagram, spreading his wings wide in warning. "You heard what Vala had to say after they finished performing the spell, how painful it was, how no ordinary mage could hope to handle it alone."

"I am no ordinary mage, Triss. I am a Blade. Fallen perhaps, but still a product of the temple of Namara. From my first days in the order I was taught how to master and control my pain through will alone, disciplines of mind and body that no other school of magery ever taught because they simply didn't have to."

Triss didn't move.

"Other mages have always had their magic to fall back on, spells to heal and spells to numb. But we could never be certain that magic would be an option, not when magesight might spy a spell's light. You know I'm right, Triss."

"No. I don't."

I raised an eyebrow at him.

"Yes, you're far better trained to deal with pain than nine and ninety other types of mage, but that still doesn't mean that you can handle this. You're talking about a spell that rearranges your very bones!"

"Several of them have been rearranged before. With less warning and to no good effect. I lived through it when Devin broke my wrist, and when that guard in Öse shattered my shoulder blade, and both times I got the job done despite the pain."

"I don't think this is a good idea. . . ."

"I don't think it's a good idea either. Frankly, it's a terrible idea and I hate it, but I don't have a better one that solves the problem the posters have made for us. Think about it, even if we can get from here to where Fei and Vala and Stel are being held without those posters getting us killed, I'll still be exposed."

"Help Fei?" said Scheroc.

I pushed myself back and up to squat on my heels, ignoring the qamasiin and focusing all my attention on Triss. "Even if we successfully bust them loose and somehow find the Kothmerk, return it to its rightful owner and then leave Tien, I'm going to have to deal with the problem of my face at some point. That likeness is going to spread to every one of the eleven kingdoms. I'll never be able to show this face anywhere again safely."

"I know but . . ."

"But what, Triss? As long as I look like this"—I touched a hand to my cheek—"I'm fucked. The bonewright gives me a way out. And not just once either. The goddess no longer protects my identity. Say we manage to change my face some other way—and we're going to have to, or I'll never be able to go out again—well, the next face I put on is just as vulnerable as this one. If it's exposed somehow, I'll be right back in the same trap. I know it's dangerous, but if I can make the bonewright work for me, I'll always have an out. I think that's worth the risk."

Triss's wings slumped. "It might be at that, but do we have to do it right now?"

"Not this minute, no. We're both too wrung out to try it short of a couple of hours' sleep and a good meal, but I don't think we can wait much longer than that. If we're going to try it, then sooner is much better than later, because it increases our chances of succeeding at what's going to be a damned hard job under the best of circumstances."

Triss hissed grumpily. "All right. We'll do it after

breakfast, but I reserve the right to say 'I told you so' if you end up with your face twisted into a pretzel."

"So noted."

"Save Fei?" Scheroc sounded awfully pathetic.

I nodded. "Soon, little one. Soon." At least, I hoped so.


I was actually a lot more pessimistic about our chances of making any of this work out than I'd let on to either familiar. Especially the bonewright, since I've never been much for high magic. A fact I was reminded of in ways both obvious and subtle as I worked to duplicate Vala's spinning of the spell threads. Sitting in the middle of one of the hexagons that she had drawn and decorated with symbols, I moved through a slow recreation of her spell, while Triss offered up encouragement and corrections from his place in the other figure.

If Triss and I hadn't watched the whole thing with an eye to reporting how to recreate it at a later date, it would have been utterly hopeless—thank you, Master Urayal. As it was, I had to check and recheck each colored thread of light as I set it in place with my will and the naming of the corresponding glyph, hoping that I had managed both the proper intent and intonation. What the Dyad sorceress had done with ease and verve in a matter of minutes took me over an hour to painstakingly set in place. But I did eventually get there, or at least I hoped that I had.

From within, the spell looked even more challenging than it had from the sidelines. The web of magic was all around me, a continually shifting net of color and light that I could only ever see a part of, since it lay as much behind as in front of me. But even more than the appearance, the *feel* of the spell daunted me. I could sense each of the connected glyphs as a presence anchored in my flesh—the ends of the lines were far more than just dots of light dappling my skin.

Each thread created an almost unreadably tiny replica of its master glyph, a replica that went ever so much farther than skin deep. I could feel the glyphs scribing themselves inside me. Most wrote themselves on the muscles and tissue lying just beneath my skin, others anchored themselves in sinew or bone, while some few drove deep, etching their meaning in heart and mind. It felt as though I were being illustrated from within, a living manuscript in three dimensions.

As I worked through the spell, I kept telling myself that the sensation would probably stop when I finished naming the glyphs, or at least that I would get used to it. Wrong on both counts. The threads of magic never quit moving and I never stopped feeling it as they wrote and rewrote their meanings within the medium of my flesh. It didn't hurt, but it was the creepiest sensation that I'd ever experienced. Perhaps this was how the dead might feel could they be made aware of the worms burrowing through their nerveless flesh. Sensation returned somehow beyond pain, but not beyond the ghost of imagination.

"Are you all right?" Triss asked, and I realized that some long but unmeasured slice of time had passed since I set the last of the lines in place.

"I don't know," I replied a few heartbeats after I should have. "It's a question with no simple answer. Say that I am unhurt, and you will strike as close to the mark as matters at the moment. This is a most disturbing sort of spell, my friend."

"It's not too late to call the whole thing off," he said, his voice low and worried.

"No, but I'm not sure I'd be able to make myself assay the thing again if I aborted it now, and all the arguments I made before are still true. Much as I would prefer to take another path, I don't see any way to get from here to where we need to go without passing through the gates of the bonewright."

And so, before Triss could argue further, I began. Raising my hands to my face, I touched fingertips to cheekbones, sliding them back and down . . . into agony!

When I was thirteen, Siri clipped me beside the eye with a spinning backfist. She was wearing a pair of cestuses at the time, and the iron weight over her middle knuckle cracked the orbit of my eye socket. My whole head filled up with the most excruciating sort of pain, and I'd thought that I could almost feel the line of the fracture, like a ribbon of hot wire dragging along the bones of my skull. This was like that, only more so, a red hot chisel carving away at the planes of my face.

I shrieked and jerked my hands away from my cheeks. I couldn't help myself. Triss responded with a hiss like a whole kettle of tea spilling into a roaring fire as he leaped forward to the very edge of the hexagon that held him. The necessities of the spell kept him there on the other side of the line, but I could see how badly he wanted to come to me.

Shifting to the Varyan that was his first human language, Triss barked my name, "Aral! Aral! Get it under control! You can't make that kind of noise here, not with the caras-snuffling maniacs who live below."

He was right, of course, and I forced myself to inhabit the pain, to own it and make it mine. Make pain a part of you instead of an outside enemy and it becomes your own, a possession that you can put aside for a time instead of an invader you have to fight. My face still burned, but I was in control again . . . for the moment. I knew that I had a lot more work to do and I didn't think I'd be able to suppress the screams when I got to it. Which meant I needed to take precautions.

So, while holding the main structure of the bonewright firmly in my mind, I spun a second spell. Simpler, weaker, freestanding, something that I had learned long ago at the feet of Master Kelos—a zone of silence that would contain my anguish. As I finished, Triss nodded his approval, though I could tell from the set of his wings and the twitching of his tail that he was still deeply upset and worried.

So was I.

Not to mention frightened and hurting. It took an enormous effort of will to bring my hands back up to my face. This time I set my fingertips against the still raw-feeling lines of my cheekbones, and then stroked down from there with my thumbs to the hinges of my jaw. It felt like someone was hammering spikes into my jawbone as I swept my thumbs forward—shifting flesh and bone as I went. This time I didn't scream. I didn't dare, not while working on my jawbone. But oh how I whimpered.

It was the corners of my eyes that did me in. I'd wanted to reshape them to make me look less foreign. I'd never make myself look truly Zhani, not without much better sculpting skills than I possessed, but I'd hoped to at least split the difference between my Varyan roots and my Zhani home. But the nerves in my eyelids were simply too sensitive for what I was trying to do and I started to black out.

I could feel my control of the spell slipping away as I went under and I tried to hang on, but I just couldn't keep it together. The glyphs under my skin started to pulse and jump as the spell backlashed and my muscles convulsed in response, driving my fingers deep into the flesh of my face. I felt my bones bend and twist in response to the magic and knew that I was seconds away from tearing my own face in half.

That's when the voice came into my mind. *You are a Blade of Namara. The* last *Blade. You will control yourself as befits a servant of the goddess, and you will overcome this.*

The voice was firm and cold and genderless, but strongly familiar, and my only thought was that somehow, beyond hope or prayer or death Justice herself was speaking to me. The thought was reinforced by the feeling of a second ghostly pair of hands closing over my own, weakly tugging at them, trying to move them back and away from my face. In that moment I believed that my goddess had returned to give me one last command.

And I obeyed.

How could I not? I reached through the agony and the backlash and the convulsions and I took control of my actions and my pain once again. I followed the guidance of the ghostly hands and stopped my own from tearing at my face. I'd never known pain like I felt then as I slowly and carefully smoothed out the damage I had inflicted on myself. It made me want to curl up and die, but every time I thought I had nothing more to give, the voice would speak again into the darkness of my mind.

*You are Aral Kingslayer. You will not fail. You cannot fail. I love you and I will not let you fail. You will do this. You will survive and you will triumph.*

And somewhere in there I realized that it was not the voice of Namara I was hearing. It was Triss. The hands that guided mine were cold and silken, wisps spun from the shadow that connected us even across the uncrossable lines of the diagram. It should have been crushing—a sort of second losing of my goddess—but it wasn't. It was deeply comforting.

Never in all the long centuries of my order had Blade and Shade communicated that way, words spoken clearly mind-to-mind. To have it happen now in this moment of dire need, was, quite simply, a miracle. My goddess might be dead, but there was no other power but Justice that would grant a Blade that beneficence. Not after we had been damned by the Court of Heaven itself. Somewhere, somehow, the ghost of Justice lived on and had given me what I needed when I most needed it.

With that to hold onto and Triss to guide me, I completed the difficult task of redrawing the lines of my face. Again, how could I not? When I finished, I released the threads of the bonewright, then bowed my head briefly and whispered into the void.

*Thank you, Namara, wherever you may have gone.*

Triss flowed up and around me then, enclosing me in his wings and his love. *She is in our hearts, as she has always been. You knew that once, though for a time you may have forgotten how to listen for her voice.*

I looked inward, focusing my mind on the problems I now faced, and listening for the voice of my goddess to tell me what to do about them. But I could hear nothing but silence. I would have expected that to hurt me, like a new hope snatched away before it could fully form, but it didn't.

Namara might not have answered me in the way I would once have expected her to, but somehow that was exactly as it should be.

Because Triss was right, but he was also wrong. Namara did live within us, but not in our hearts. She lived on in the ideal of justice and our duty to see it done. But justice was not the simple thing I had once believed it to be. In my youth I had seen Justice as a sort of divine idol in the shape of Namara. I had worshipped that idol and served her as best I could, and that was right for the boy that I was. But many things had changed in the years since then and not all for the worse.

In my youth I had believed not just in my goddess but in the *idea* of the gods, that they were our rightful overlords and that they always held our best interests in their hearts. I had seen Namara as a part of something greater than the base strivings of those who walked the surface of our world. Because of that, the death of my goddess at the hands of her fellows had very nearly killed my soul.

It had also rewritten my identity far more thoroughly than the bonewright ever could and in ways that I was only beginning to understand. For one, the gods were us. Whether our evils and petty cruelties were a reflection of those who created us, or whether in some way we had created the gods we deserved through the power of our belief didn't matter. What mattered was that the Court of Heaven held no more claim to true justice than did the courts of men.

While I might still agree with Namara's ideal of justice, I was starting to understand that in simply handing my conscience over to the goddess of justice, I might not have made the justest of choices. It wasn't merely that I no longer saw the world in the stark black and white that I had as Namara's Blade. It was more that by falling into the place where the grays dominated the scale, I had finally started to understand the importance of all that lay between the extremes.

The world was no simple place, and in becoming more complex myself I had begun to see the complexity of that world. It was not a comfortable feeling, nor one that lent itself to the simple act of listening for the echo of the goddess in my heart. I had to *think* my way to the right answers now, an entirely more daunting proposition. Where *was* the justice in my present plight? And with it, my duty?

*Aral?*

Triss's voice in my mind startled me out of the world of ideas and back into the one where my problems wore uniforms and carried death warrants with my name on them.

*Yes?*

Triss had shifted, leaning back so that he could look into my eyes. *When are you going to drop the silence spell? This thinking words at you is much more work than speaking them would be.*

*Is it?* And in asking the question I realized that it was. Mind speech must have something of magic to it, because using it felt a bit like spell casting and drew energy from the well of my soul.

With a thought and a gesture I dismissed my dome of silence. "Better?"

"Much." Triss visibly relaxed, lowering his head back to rest on my shoulder. "How are you?" The words came out low and urgent, yet soft, as though he were afraid I might shatter.

How was I? I ran my palms over my face, feeling for deformities or other surprises. It felt good, smooth skin and stubble. Though I wouldn't know what I looked like until I found myself some time and a mirror, it felt pretty much like my old face. Even the scabs and raw patches from my burns were gone. Externally I was doing fine. Of course, internally I felt like I'd been dragged behind a delivery cart for eight hours. It was a strange mix of wrung out and renewed.

"I'll live," I finally said.

"Good. I had my doubts there for a while."

"How did you do it?" I asked.

"I don't know really. It was like breaking down a barrier within my own head, a barrier made from my own substance—pain and blood, and nightmare giving way suddenly to wakefulness. I wanted so badly to reach you. I was beating at the invisible wall of the spell with my wings and claws, trying to cross into your half of the diagram with everything I had."

Triss squeezed me with his wings again, hard enough to take my breath away. "But I just couldn't get through, not even by following the line of shadow that always connects us. I was watching you die and I couldn't bear it, and suddenly I thought of the way Tien Lun had spoken into my head. How she had torn something in my mind. I looked for the place she had opened and though I didn't find it, I did find a new place to push. I can't really describe it further than that except to say that it lay at the heart of what makes you and I an us. Somewhere in the interweaving of familiar bond, shadow link, and love there was a barrier that is no more."

*I'm glad,* I thought at him.

*So am I.*

"Now can we help my mommy?" asked Scheroc.

"I don't know," I said.

Where *was* the justice in this situation? I didn't know that either. Nor who really deserved to get their hands on the Kothmerk. All I knew for certain was that justice wasn't on the side of the people who'd imprisoned Fei and used her to set a trap for me and my Dyad friend. That, and that I wanted to get the damned ring out of my city.

"I don't know," I said again. Then I pulled Qethar's pebble from my pocket. "But there's one way to find out."

"But not here," said Triss.

"No, of course not. For a number of reasons. I was thinking of someplace high up and close to water. I want the Durkoth out of his element and off balance for this conversation, and I think I know just the place."

# 18

---

"How do I look?" I asked.

Harad leaned in close. "Different enough that I'd not have let you in if you knocked on the front door of my library."

I grinned. "Then it's a good thing I broke in like usual."

"Yes, my wards knew you where I would not. This is, I presume, your response to those rather distressing wanted posters that have gone up all over the city. It seems a little drastic. . . ."

I nodded grimly, and felt a faint cool stirring across the back of my neck at the motion—Scheroc had insisted on coming along and I couldn't think of any way short of a binding to keep the little elemental spirit from doing whatever it wanted. Since bindings range from uncomfortable to excruciating for the bound, depending on their natures, that'd be pretty much tantamount to declaring war on Fei. Not really an option I wanted to pursue even if she was locked up in a royal dungeon somewhere.

I was just trying to decide whether I should mention the

creature to Harad, and if so, how much I should tell the old librarian, when he preempted me. "Did you know that you have Kaelin Fei's familiar trailing along at your back?"

"Uh, yes?" Good answer there, Aral.

"That's a story I'll want to hear more of at some point. But I suppose that if you're all right with having it following you around, it's not a problem for me. Just keep it away from the stacks and any loose paper. The things make a dreadful mess."

I suppose I shouldn't have been surprised that Harad would be aware of the qamasiin. He was, after all, one of the most powerful sorcerers I'd ever met, and the Ismere Library was both his passion and his home. I did wonder how he knew about its relationship to Fei—that was a story *I* would have loved to hear more about.

Founded nearly four hundred years ago by a Kadeshi merchant-adventurer who had headquartered his operations in Tien, the Ismere had grown to house one of the finest collections of books and scrolls anywhere north of the Sylvani Empire. We stood now in the third-floor reading room, my usual point of entry into the private lending facility—via the roof of the neighboring Ismere Club and a little pick work on the balcony door locks.

The Ismere was much better stocked than the Royal Library of Tien, in large part because it had never fallen foul of the sorts of censorship and purges the latter facility had faced over the years. More than one Zhani king or queen had tried to censor the Ismere as well, but they'd never managed to get far, mostly destroying inferior or badly damaged copies the library had intended to get rid of anyway. It's hard to force one of the great mages to do anything they don't want to do, and being a great mage was one of the minimum—if secret—qualifications for becoming chief librarian of the Ismere.

"While we're on the topic of interesting stories, Aral," said Harad, "what *have* you done to yourself? And how? I don't think I've ever seen anyone manage that sort of bone-deep facial reshaping before, short of a full-on shape change, though I can see several ways that one might attempt it."

"Actually, I'm not entirely sure about the what. It's dark out there and I haven't exactly had access to a good mirror. The how's a longer tale than I have time for if I go into the level of detail I know you're going to want. So, if you don't mind, I'll save that part for a later date. In the meantime"—I pointed at my face and smiled—"I don't suppose . . ."

Harad nodded. "I think I can manage that."

With a sweep of his hand and a mumbled word, Harad conjured a full-length mirror clearer than the finest silver. The librarian was an old friend, my oldest in one way, at a shade over six hundred years. His span had been greatly extended by his bond with whatever slow-aging familiar companioned him—the life of a mage and his familiar always tend toward the longer of the two. I didn't know the nature of Harad's familiar because he'd never volunteered that information, and I knew better than to push, but I had no doubt it was something at least as rare and exalted as one of the great dragons.

"Thank you." I stepped up to the magic mirror and gave myself a careful looking over.

We hadn't done too bad a job, Triss and I. The face wasn't the one I'd been born with, of course, but it did all the things my old one had, if that makes any sense. I've always been a bit boring where it comes to looks, medium brown hair, medium brown eyes, skin somewhere between the dark side of light and the light side of dark, features neither ugly nor particularly handsome, medium build. . . . I *am* a touch on the tall side, and certainly my training has put a lot of muscle on that frame, but really, barring the wanted posters, I'm not the type who draws a lot of second looks.

The temple masters had often noted that very lack of distinction was one of my greatest assets as a Blade. The face looking back out of the mirror at me now fit that same old bill in a new and equally boring sort of way, which is exactly what I'd hoped to achieve. The exact details aren't terribly important, but I was pleased with the way we'd managed to tone down the Varyanness of my appearance without really making me look too much like I came from anywhere else either.

If I'd had to make a guess at my apparent ethnicity, I'd have said my new face belonged in the Magelands where there was a lot more blending of bloodlines than almost anywhere else in the eleven kingdoms. Anyone from anywhere could claim Mageland citizenship if they tested positive for either of the mage's gifts. An awful lot of refugees from conflicts and purges in the other ten kingdoms had ended up there because of that.

It made for the densest population of sorcerers anywhere in the east, though there were plenty of citizens who had no magical gifts at all, both native and immigrant, as there were other paths to citizenship. It also meant that mostly the rest of the world left the Magelands the hell alone. It wasn't smart to piss off a population that could throw a thousand and one kinds of spells at you on a moment's notice.

"Well?" Triss asked after a while. He sounded nervous. "What do you think?"

"That we did a good job, my friend."

He let out a sigh of obvious relief. "I'm so glad. I was worried about the parts that I did. I don't see you like your fellow humans see you, and I didn't know if that was going to make for some horrible mistake that you would never forgive me for."

I laughed. "Triss, there's nothing you could do to me that I couldn't forgive after all we've been through, though I am glad you didn't put my nose back on upside down."

Harad smiled. "I don't know. It would lend you some of the character that you've always lacked."

"In my business, character is a dirty word, and you know that, old man."

"And yet, your Master Kelos with his eye patch and tattoos was quite the visible one in his day. And that beard . . ."

Harad had, once upon a time, been brought in as a teacher of the art of deception for my order. That was nearly three hundred years ago, when he'd been involved with an acting company in Varya, one in a long line of careers that he'd taken on over his more than half a millennium of life. It was that association with the Blades which had prevented him from frying me like a bug the first time I broke into his library some eleven years in the past. Well, his wards really, as they'd been keyed to allow the entrance of anyone companioned by a Shade, a condition since narrowed to be specific to me.

"Don't go waving Kelos around as an example at me," I said. "You know very well that he always put in a glass eye, covered his tattoos with makeup, and shaved off the beard when he went out on a mission. The more flamboyant aspects of his appearance were something he used to draw attention to what he wanted people to look for when they thought he might be stalking them. It was a stage magician's trick, one I imagine that was originally drawn from the tool bag you created for the order."

"There is that. But come, you've said you're short on time and I think you've done sufficient homage to the niceties. What is it that you want from me in such a hurry. Questions answered? A banned book to read, like the one you needed when you got sucked into the Marchon affair? Is it something that we can work out over a drink? I've picked up a bottle of that whiskey you favor since you won't drink my tea."

"I'm afraid I'll have to pass on the drink." Though I felt a distinct pang of regret at the thought. "And it's neither answers nor a book that I'm hoping you can provide."

"Well, if it's not information you want, I have to say a library is a strange choice of venue. What *are* you here for?"

"I am looking to have a little talk and learn a few things. Just not from you. I need to speak with a Durkoth and I wanted to borrow your riverside grand balcony for a bit."

Harad blinked several times, the only real exhibition of surprise I'd ever seen him make. "It seems an odd place at an odd time, but I think it can be arranged. Do you mind if I ask, why here?"

"Aral thinks we might have to jump in the river and swim for our lives," Triss said in a dry tone. "Which would be the third time in as many days we've done something of the kind. It's getting to be almost as much a habit as the whiskey, and about as good for him."

Harad nodded. "Ah, you want to oppose earth with water and air. A sensible precaution, and one that answers half my question . . ."

"Yours is about the only balcony around that both over-hangs the river from such a height and doesn't require us to focus at least half of our attention on keeping an eye out for the rightful landlords. I've only just shed the face on the wanted posters and I'd rather not have a new set drawn up because I've been spotted on some baron's private balcony. I know it's an imposition and not without some risk. . . ."

"Tell me a bit more about this Durkoth," said Harad.

I was impatient, but if I wanted Harad's help, I knew I had to give him what he wanted. I quickly filled him in on my earlier encounter with Qethar and as many of the surrounding events as I could manage in a few minutes. More than once during that time an impatient Scheroc tugged at my hair or the folds of my shirt. At the end of my explanation, Harad asked to see Qethar's pebble, so I handed it over. He examined the small stone closely, going so far as tasting it before finally giving it back to me.

"No magic there, but then I didn't expect any. Do you really think this Qethar won't figure out who you are?"

I shrugged. "I honestly have no idea. He's got to know I don't trust him. That means my cover story of being a go-between from the real Aral should be plausible enough, as long as Triss stays out of sight. I guess if I'd thought it through I might have waited to use the bonewright spell till after we'd had our conversation. But then again, I might not. There's some real advantage to be had in convincing him I'm someone else."

"Hmm." Harad stroked his beard. "All right, I haven't had much to do with the Durkoth, though I know their Syl-vani and Vesh'An cousins well enough. Whatever happens, it should be quite interesting. I'll set the grand balcony up for you if you don't complain about my keeping a scrying eye on the whole thing from a safe distance."

Triss snorted. "Does anything happen in this library that you don't keep an eye on?"

"No."

**Setting** the pebble on the limestone floor of the Ismere's grand balcony, I put the heel of my boot on it and . . . paused. Now that the moment had come, I found myself very reluctant to take the next step. In my mind's eye I pictured Qethar's pale inhuman perfection and shivered. I really didn't want to face him and his glamour again. But then, I didn't have a whole lot of choice, not if I wanted to break my associates out of durance vile and solve the problem of the Kothmerk.

Fucking magic rings.

I pushed down hard, expecting resistance, but the heavy little stone broke as easily as if it were a blown-glass bubble. While I waited for Qethar to appear, I hopped up to stand on the sweeping stone rail of the huge half-moon balcony. I wanted nothing between me and the river but air. I didn't have to wait long either.

Within ten minutes, Triss gave me a gentle tap on the heel of my right foot. *The corner of the building. Something's happening there. I can feel movement in the shadows.*

The library's foundations had been built right at the river's edge so that it seemed as though the stone wall grew straight out of the flowing water below. For a brief instant, the corner of the building seemed to ripple in sympathy with the water. Then Qethar was there in all his white marble glory, having simply slid around the corner on a narrow stone projection that grew out of what had been a smooth stone wall only moments before. He stood perfectly still, looking for all the world like the statue of some important past library patron. Though he faced me, the blank white orbs of his eyes could have been looking anywhere.

Like a low wave sliding in to break on a sandy beach, the Durkoth's little ledge rolled up the wall, leaving unmarked stone in its wake. When it reached the level of the balcony, the wave changed direction, sliding across the wall to a place just beyond the balcony's rail. Qethar inclined his head in my direction and stepped forward onto the balcony, passing through the railing as though it were merely the ghost of a barrier. Behind him, the ledge sank back into the wall around it, vanishing as if it had never been.

Though I'm sure he could have persuaded the stone of the balcony to bring him to me, he chose to walk instead. I suspected it was because he knew just how much it unnerved humans to watch his kind moving, and he wanted to throw me off balance. It was a ploy that I was quite sure he'd employed to excellent effect any number of times in the past, and not one iota less effective for the realization.

I couldn't take my eyes off him, or forget how his too-hot skin had felt against the palm of my hand. The smile he threw me when he finally came to a stop a few feet away was almost terminally self-satisfied—call it *Portrait of the God of Hauteur in Marble* by Sebastian Vainglorious and you could have sold it to any art collector in the eleven kingdoms.

I wanted to slap myself for the gut-level reactions I felt for him, both the unease and the desire. If I was going to have to work with Qethar to get Fei and the others free, I needed to break the . . . not a spell exactly, since the Others had no magic. Glamour or geas or simply the human fascination with perfection. Whatever you called it, I needed to figure out a way to neutralize my fascination with its object. As had so often happened at times of trouble in the past, the words of one of my teachers at the temple spoke to me out of memory.

In this case, I heard Mistress Alinthide saying, *"The key to solving any problem is understanding it. Observe, identify, analyze. Think!"*

Start with observation. Qethar looked like a statue, or really, the realized ideal of a statue; gorgeous, permanent, eternal. It was, I suspected, that illusion of eternality that lay at the heart of the Durkoth's weird mixture of allure and repulsion. The senses revolted against the idea of that which should not move moving.

That thought touched a chord in my memory. I'd felt something like it before. When?

Neither of us had spoken yet and now Qethar raised a sardonic eyebrow at me, but I ignored him. I had to if I wanted to regain and retain my equilibrium in the face of his glamour.

Find the memory . . . there. I had it. Walking through one of the Emperor of Heaven's temples as a very young boy—maybe even before I was given to Namara. It was a midnight service for Winter-Round. In honor of the solstice the temple was lit with torches rather than the brighter and steadier magelights used for most worship.

The gallery that led to the inner sanctum was lined with statues of Heaven's Court, gods and goddesses looking nearly as beautiful and haughty as the Durkoth glaring at me now. In the flickering torchlight the carven deities had seemed to shift position between eye blinks. I never actually caught a statue moving, but every time I looked, I felt as though something had changed from the last time.

It was one of my earliest memories. One that had lived on in the nightmares of childhood, and one that Qethar echoed simply by existing. Statues shouldn't change position. So, instead of seeing Qethar move, my mind registered a series of discrete and apparently unrelated poses, each of them feeling as though the Durkoth had *always* been in that position. That was profoundly creepy all on its own, but there was more to my response than that if I could only ferret it out.

Before I could pin it down, Qethar spoke. "I presume you summoned me for something other than a staring contest, Blade. What do you want of me?"

I was still badly off my game, but I couldn't let that pass. "I think you've got the wrong man. I'm no Blade." I turned so that the light from the windows fell more fully on my face. "Though I've come at the word of one."

Qethar's face didn't move but somehow I got the impression of a frown. "Are you daft, Blade? I told the pebble to only break for you. There's no way I could have been summoned by anyone else. Even if such were possible, your shekat does not lie. I can see that you're the same human I contended with in the street the other night. The one since identified as the Kingslayer."

"My what?" I'd never heard the word "shekat" before.

"Your soul-fire, human, your nima."

"You can see nima?" I'd never heard that about the Durkoth.

Qethar seemed genuinely surprised. "Of course, far more clearly than I can see the evanescent housing of flesh in which it resides. In the deep dark under the mountains, the essence of a thing is infinitely more important than how it might look under the light of sun and sky. Yours is an especially strong shekat for an ephemeral, perhaps because the shadow that lives within your shadow has strengthened your lifeline by tying it to his own."

And with that I had the final piece to understanding my response to Qethar. It was in his soul or apparent lack of one. Among my strongest and dearest memories is the day my goddess made me a Blade.

Namara is . . . or rather, *was* the Soul of Justice. *Was.* It's such a simple word and so sad—it stabs my heart every time I have to remember that she is gone. *Lock it away, Aral, focus on the Durkoth and what you need to do about him.*

Namara had manifested herself on this plane as a great granite idol sunk deep within the temple's sacred pool. When she made new Blades, she would come to the surface to test the initiates and to give them their swords if she found them worthy. Like the Durkoth, she never seemed to move, though her position changed. But with my goddess, there had been one incredibly vital difference.

The goddess didn't *feel* like a statue. The statue that was my goddess had a soul. No, the mightiest of souls. When you were in her presence you could feel that with every fiber of your being. You couldn't *not* feel it, whereas the Durkoth felt dead to me. If he had any soul at all, it was hidden deep under stone, reinforcing the illusion of untouchable statue.

But he wasn't a statue and he wasn't untouchable, a fact demonstrated by his obvious and growing irritation. "I have very little patience left for your kind, Blade. I gave you the pebble so that you could call me when you decided you needed my help to find the Kothmerk, and that is the most important thing in your entire stinking human city. If you've summoned me just so you can play games, it will go very hard with you."

"Don't threaten me, stone face. I've been threatened by the best. Push me and you'll just be one more name on the very long list of the dead I have to answer for when I face the lords of judgment. You won't get very far in the quest for the Kothmerk if I kill you, Qethar."

Triss spoke into my mind, *Let me handle this please.* Before I could answer, he reversed his position, moving against the light so that my shadow briefly stretched toward the bright windows behind Qethar.

Then he shifted, becoming the dragon. "Qethar, you want to find the Kothmerk. So do we. At the moment, your best chance and ours is to work together. Once we have it, then we can argue about what to do with it."

"I knew you'd see it my way," he said rather smugly. "Where do we start?"

"With Captain Fei and the Dyad," replied Triss, which was a hell of a lot more diplomatic than what I'd have said. "The Elite and some of your out-of-town cousins have them locked away in the deeps beneath the palace. We need your help to get them out."

Qethar went perfectly still. For perhaps forty heartbeats there was absolutely nothing to distinguish him from the statue he so resembled.

"The Elite have the Dyad?" he asked when he finally spoke again, and the only thing that moved were his lips. "How did you discover this?"

"I have my ways," I said. I sure as hell wasn't going to tell him that Fei was an unfaced mage.

"And you say that the creature is being kept in the hidden vaults beneath the palace?"

I nodded. "You know of them?"

"I do."

"That's good because my source is a bit hazy on the exact location. And it's not just the Dyad, but Captain Fei of the watch, too. I need your help if I'm going to get them out in one piece, and that's the first step toward finding the ring. What do you say?"

"If I help you with this, you will help me to recover the Kothmerk?"

"I'll work with you to find it." Which wasn't quite the same thing, but I felt pretty sure Qethar wasn't being completely straight with me either.

"Then, let us go and see what we can find out."

# 19

---◆◆◆---

"**Aren't** you worried they'll be able to sense us here, so close, Qethar?" Triss breathed the question as he slid off my skin to peer through the narrow slit of the air shaft.

We stood in a sort of bubble in the rock with only a thin curtain of stone between us and the cavelike kitchen where several Crown Guards sat quietly drinking tea and chatting under the eye of the Elite officer commanding them. His stone dog lay against the far wall, a few feet from the doorway, where a quietly scowling Durkoth stood like a sculpture dedicated to the personification of disapproval. He wore robes rather than local garb, so I assumed he belonged to the raiders who'd attacked VoS's people. Another Elite could be seen down the hallway beyond him.

"No," replied Qethar in a voice softer than any whisper. "Several may be near kin of the earth as well, but none are so dear to her as I. She will not betray our presence. Not even to my cousin of the North kingdom."

Meanwhile, I kept my mouth shut and tried to hang onto my breakfast. I am not easily frightened, but our passage through the silent deeps of the earth had left me with the feeling that I had blind and many legged things crawling all over my skin. I almost wished that I had not borrowed Triss's senses for the trip, for my eyes would never have shown me what his unvision had made all too clear.

With silent tugs, wafted scents, and gentle brushes, Scheroc had led us to the place where a narrow and cleverly concealed air shaft emerged from the stone face of the riverside cliffs just north of the palace. Qethar had asked me to take the lead as he wasn't sure where in the complex Fei and the Dyad might be, and it was clear I had sources he did not. I'd worried at first that the simple little spirit might accidentally reveal itself to him in the process, but I needn't have bothered.

Scheroc's years with Fei had long since taught it the subtle art of communicating without betraying its presence. And now I better understood the captain's frequent habit of sniffing the air. Her bond with the qamasiin had probably given her a nose like a bloodhound's—the nature of the familiar always shaped the power of the mage—and the sniffing was a way of communicating with her invisible companion.

That's when things had taken a disturbing turn. Qethar had reached out and touched the rock wall a few yards to the left of the shaft. In response, a narrow tongue of stone had extended itself down to the nearer thwart of the rowboat we'd rented, like a sort of limestone gangplank. Qethar had gestured for me to precede him, so I stepped onto the projection and moved up as close to the cliff as I could get. Or I thought I had, at least.

But then Qethar stepped up behind me, saying something about the durathian road. I felt the stone moving beneath my feet as it slid back to once more become part of the wall and took me with it. Instinctively, I threw up my hands to protect my face when the hard surface came toward my eyes. It's difficult to describe the sensation as my palms touched the stone and moved through and into it. And I don't even like to *think* about the way it felt as the skin of my face sank into the stone.

Imagine a giant vat of rendered pork that's congealed. Thick, viscous, cold, filled with bits and pieces that you'd rather not know any more about. Now dump in some sand to give it grain, as though you wanted to make a scouring soap. Push your hands into the mess, your face, your whole body. Then, just as you realize that you really don't want to have anything to do with the stuff and start to pull away, it comes to life and pulls you under.

Every tiniest particle of this slurry has suddenly developed the power to grab and hold and push, and now it's moving you along through itself wholly against your will. You shouldn't be able to breathe, and yet you can. There is a sort of void around your mouth and nose that gives you a pocket of cold, dank, earth-smelling air to breathe.

In the first instants, Triss wrapped himself around me, providing a sort of silken armor that insulated me from the worst of it. But in my sudden panic at the situation I foolishly reached out and borrowed his senses, giving me something of a view into the matrix that held and moved me. Though mostly what surrounded me was solid rock—or as solid as could be, given the circumstances—here and there were veins of thinner stuff, sheets of aggregate and earth where water worked its way through from higher ground.

And these were filled with life. Worms and slinks and worse. Things of flesh and things of magic, the blind crawling creatures of the deep places. Through Triss I could feel them pass, and though I shall never forget them, I will not speak of them more. Eventually, after what felt like years, we arrived at the far end of the air shaft and Qethar opened a broader space for us to stand in while we watched and listened. Several minutes on and my heart was only just slowing back down to something like its normal rate.

"Come," Qethar breathed into my ear, "we need to find your friends and they're not here. The excavation moves away both to right and left. Let's move on."

I really really wanted to say, "Let's not." Instead, I chewed on my tongue and nodded.

We didn't have nearly so far to go this time, and a few

awful moments later we were peering out through another ventilation slit. Three or four inches tall and a little over a foot wide, it offered a good view into a large domed chamber with two passages and several doorways leading off in various directions. It held a surprisingly opulent sort of miniature throne room, complete with dais, tapestries, and several large and expensive magelight chandeliers. The only current occupants were a pair of Crown Guards standing watch at the largest of the doors with bared woldos.

"Where are the cells?" I asked Qethar.

"There aren't any. This place was built as a refuge for the king and his closest advisors in the event of a major magical attack on the palace or a coup, not as a dungeon. Ashvik ordered it excavated, and hired my people to do all the work at great expense. I supervised the project."

"So where are the prisoners kept?" asked Triss.

"I don't know," replied Qethar. "There are many small chambers that could be hiding them. Guestrooms, storerooms, closets . . . Can't you use the same method that led you here in the first place to find them now?"

I shrugged. We'd lost Scheroc when we entered Qethar's durathian road. The air spirit was either unable or unwilling to ride along with me. I couldn't blame it. If I'd known what I was getting into, I wouldn't have been willing or able to ride with me. I'd hoped that it would follow us down the air shaft, but so far we'd had no such luck.

"I seem to have lost my fix on their location," I said. "Can't you just persuade the earth to tell us where they are?"

"My sister doesn't pay all that much attention to the quicklife that lives upon her surface and burrows into the shallowest layers of her skin. All she can tell me is that there are perhaps a hundred of your kind scattered throughout the complex. If I could point to one and ask her to keep track of that one, then for a time she would hold them in her attention and I might follow in their footsteps. But without me or one of my people to point up the scent in advance, I'm afraid we're out of luck."

Just then, there came a booming knock on the door where

the guards stood. One of them looked through a slit in the thick bronze and then waved at the other while she went to work on the bolts. The second guard pulled out a small silver whistle and gave it a good hard blow. By the time the first guard had the door open, the Durkoth, Elite, and Crown Guards we'd seen in the kitchen earlier had spilled out of one of the open hallways.

As the door slid open, another Durkoth stepped through, this one wearing Tienese garb. She was followed by a lieutenant of the Elite and her stone dog. The latter had a limp human form tied facedown across its back, long dark hair a-drag on the ground. Though I couldn't tell for sure from there, the shape of the unconscious figure's shoulders and hips suggested a young woman.

"Is that her?" asked the Elite from the guardroom, a male captain.

"I certainly hope so," responded the lieutenant. "But we won't know for sure until Roketh here makes an identification." He jerked his chin at the foreign dressed Durkoth who stepped in close to the unconscious girl now.

While the Durkoth was looking the prisoner over, another door opened, this one off to our left. A third Elite peered into the room—another lieutenant, this one male. "Have you got her, finally?" He started across to join the others, his huge stone dog trailing behind.

"That's definitely the girl who killed Merqa and Thelat," said Roketh. "I recognize her shekat. I presume that she didn't have the Kothmerk on her when you took her."

So that was our Reyna. Beside me, Qethar made a low hissing noise, but otherwise remained still and quiet.

"Of course not," said the other Durkoth. "Do you think we'd have bothered to keep her alive if we'd gotten what we needed from her? After all the lives she's cost us?"

A faint breeze cooled the back of my neck and tugged my hair in the direction of the door the male lieutenant had emerged from. Scheroc had returned to point the way to Captain Fei.

"That's it then," said the captain. "We've no need of the

other prisoners anymore." He made a throat cutting gesture toward the male lieutenant. "Time to clean up loose ends."

The lieutenant drew his sword, half turned toward the door he'd entered by and then stabbed Roketh as neatly as could be. At the same time, the two woldo-carrying guards brought the heavy blades of their sword-spears down on the shoulders and neck of the other Durkoth, and kept hacking away as she collapsed to the floor.

Several things happened all at once then: The three stone dogs threw their heads back and howled like demented wolves. Qethar snarled something unintelligible and reached out to open the stone in front of us, parting it like a curtain. Reyna, apparently having returned to consciousness at some point, lifted her head ever so slightly from where it lay against the side of the dog she'd been tied to and looked around. Roketh wrenched himself free of the sword that had skewered him and fell to the ground, crying out something in the Durkoth language.

"Tell Fei we're on our way," I said to Scheroc, and felt the little qamasiin dart away from me.

Triss was swearing at Qethar in Shade as he enclosed me with a skin of shadow once again. I couldn't blame him. This was *not* the way I'd have chosen to go about things if I'd been asked. But I'd been trained to work with what I had and not what I wished I had, and I was drawing my swords as I stepped out into the room on Qethar's heels.

*Leave me a view, Triss.*

*Done.*

As he expanded into a cloud of shadow, he left a thin slit open in front of my eyes. Functionally invisible, I started forward. I identified the Elite lieutenant with his drawn sword as my first target and aimed myself that way, though I tried to keep an eye on everyone in the milling chaos that had exploded in the wake of the murder of the two Durkoth. I would have liked to go straight for Fei and the Dyad, but leaving live Elite at your back was a mistake I would never make again. I'd learned my lesson on the day I killed Zhan's king.

But before I'd gone a dozen feet, the floor underneath my chosen target rose up on either side of him like great stone jaws and smashed him to pulp. And there they froze as Roketh finally died. None of the others had yet noticed us, and I shifted direction slightly to angle toward the captain. Meanwhile, Qethar was riding a moving section of the stone floor toward the remaining lieutenant.

That's when I saw something that sent my heart into my throat. The ropes that bound Reyna's hands to her feet under the belly of the still howling stone dog fell away as if they'd been neatly cut. Then she slid forward, touching down with her palms and cartwheeling to her feet, before vanishing as a cloud of shadow exploded outward from her skin. A moment later, a lacuna of darkness flowed briefly between me and the captain. Then the Elite was clutching at his freshly opened throat as the life gushed down his chest.

It was beautifully done, a perfect realization of one of Master Kelos's favorite moves, and I froze as everything I'd heard about Reyna the thief suddenly rearranged itself in my head. Suddenly everything she'd done made perfect sense. She wasn't working with a Blade as I'd once thought was a possibility. She was one of our lost apprentices, the last children of the house of Namara. That made her my responsibility as surely as if she were my own daughter. I started to move forward again, only then noticing that I'd stopped.

*Triss!*

*I know, I saw. Blade trained and Shade companioned. We've got to catch her, find out who she is, where she's been. . . .*

I reached the remaining group of Crown Guards just as Qethar dropped a foot-thick pillar of stone from the ceiling and crushed the last of the Elite. Within seconds, the fight was over and all of the enemy lay dead.

"Reyna!" I yelled, though I didn't think that was her real name. "Where are you? We need to talk."

Faint and far up the hall I thought I heard, "I'll find you, Kingslayer, someday. I promise."

Closer, Qethar said, "The little witch has vanished, and she knows to mask her feet from the earth, so I can't tell exactly where she went. I'm going to try to cut her off!" A low stone wave rose from the floor and Qethar surfed it toward the door.

"Qethar!" I yelled after him. "That girl's important to me. If you harm her, I'll cut your heart out and feed it to you."

I didn't know what her name really was, or had been, but I damn sure intended to find out. I just hoped she wasn't one of Devin's traitors. More than anything I wanted to follow Qethar and find those answers right now. But I didn't know who or what else might be left down here with me—Qethar had said there were a hundred or so humans in the area, and if I abandoned Fei and the Dyad now, they'd probably die.

Duty before desire.

Swearing bitterly, I put aside thoughts of the girl and turned to run for the door the qamasiin had indicated earlier. As I went, I forced myself to let go of my awareness of the girl, to put those worries and concerns in a box and lock it away deep in my mind. I was on a mission now. Letting myself get distracted could easily kill me. That wouldn't do her any good at all.

As I passed through the doorway, I heard shouts behind me and glanced over my shoulder to see more Crown Guards rushing into the room from the other passage. I kept going. Hopefully, Qethar's presence in the entrance passage would prevent them getting a message to the surface and the palace any time soon, but I wasn't going to bet on it. Time was about to get very short and unless Qethar came back, my exit strategy was well and truly fucked. In light of which, yelling a death threat after him might not have been the best of tactics, but too late to worry about that now.

The throne room door opened into a broad open hallway with heavy wooden doors facing each other every twenty feet or so, all of them closed—quarters for personages of importance not directly related to the king at a guess. The Elite who'd come out of here couldn't have been too far away or he wouldn't have heard the whistle, which meant what I was looking for had to be close. I scanned for signs of occupation and noticed that the corridor got a lot cleaner about three doors down, which suggested not much traffic beyond that point.

*Triss, check under those two doors.* I pointed as I passed them.

*Done.*

While Triss collapsed back down into dragon state, I turned and put my back against the wall just beyond the doors. I wanted to keep watch both ways while simultaneously remaining as inconspicuous as possible. It wouldn't be long before the Crown Guard and their inevitable Elite officers got around to looking in on the prisoners. Triss slid his dragon's nose under the door now on my right, then vanished completely, leaving only a slender thread of shadow back to me.

*Nothing here and no signs of occupation. I'll try the other side.*

The thread contracted, and my familiar returned briefly before sticking his nose under the other door.

*This is it. Noble's suite. Audience chamber. Table with scattered cards and a few kips on it where someone's been gambling. Two inner doors. One for the master, one for the servants. Two guards in front of the latter. It's close enough that if I stretch myself thin I can slip past them to take a look.*

*That sounds pretty risky. I'm not sure it's such a good idea.*

*No, it's all right. As long as I stay behind and under the furniture and keep myself on the pale side, I should be—ooh nasty.*

*What have you got, Triss?*

*Tiny anteroom, basically a large closet with doors on all four walls. Crude peepholes mounted on three of the doors. Destruction wards on two of them and the guards literally a half step away. We'll have to do this fast and clean.*

*Not to mention soon.*

I'd been lucky so far, with no one coming to look down my hallway, but that wouldn't last. Now I had even more reason to hurry. Destruction wards were ugly business and I didn't know what orders the Elite lieutenant had given before heading out to the throne room. Not that I was particularly surprised to find them under the circumstances. I wished I could get a look at the wards through Triss's eyes, but I can only borrow his senses when he surrounds me. Still, I didn't dare move till I knew a bit more.

*Tell me about the wards, Triss.*

*Drawn in blood. Fire, multiple triggers. Magic, breach, door, pull patches for the guards, maybe more.*

I nodded though he couldn't see the gesture. That much I'd expected. There weren't a lot of ways to imprison a mage. If you had plenty of time and skill you could build a special cell with all kinds of passive wards that would cause the mage's own magic to rebound on them. But that kind of thing took constant maintenance from specialists, and really worked best on the lesser sorts of mage.

For quick and dirty yet effective you'd do something like the destruction ward, where any breach of the cell, magical activity—keyed to the blood—or even an unauthorized opening of the door would rain major league destruction down on the inside. Some seriously overpowered version of magefire was the overwhelming favorite for stone rooms, the sort of thing that leaves a fine coating of glass on all the surfaces because the heat is so intense. Really, the only surprise was that they'd warded Fei's room that way, too. It seemed like overkill if no one knew she was a mage, and if they did know, they'd have done something about binding her familiar. Someone was being awfully cautious.

*Death-key? Or anything like it?*

*Hang on,* sent Triss. *I'll look.*

A lot depended on exactly how they'd drawn the things and what, if anything, would happen when we took out the guards. Worst case was a death-key or some other trick that would trigger the wards if the guards died. But that sort of thing usually only happened in serious, cover of darkness, deny all knowledge, espionage kinds of situations. And, if they'd been going to use one, I'd have expected it to be keyed to the Elite lieutenant.

*I'm not seeing anything too drastic, Aral. I think if we can just keep the guards away from the wards until we drop them, everything will be fine. Plan?*

*Can you keep that door closed? All I need is a few seconds.*

*Sure, but I'll have to stay here and hold it.*

*Do it.*

Sometimes subtle and complex is the answer, with all kinds of distractions and reconnaissance and careful efforts to not harm the innocent. Sometimes you just pop the damn door open and cut some heads off, because that's the only choice you have. This was one of those latter times.

Though I generally preferred not to kill guards if I didn't have to, it actually felt pretty good. Maybe because this pair was keeping people who mattered to me locked up. By the time I was opening the inner door to the improvised prison, Triss was sliding across my back trail to close the one that led into the hall.

*Still no interest from the direction of the throne room,* he sent as he used a shadow claw to click the lock into place. *But that won't last.*

*I'm working as fast as I can.*

A double check of the wards reassured me that I wasn't going to kill anyone by opening the doors. Scheroc blew out of the peephole on the right as I was making my check, and started tugging frantically at my clothes. So I opened that door first.

Fei was waiting on the other side, her face bruised and bloody, with a long slice across her right cheek mirroring the old scar on the left. "It's about time you got here, Bl— Wait, who the hell are you?" The look of surprise on her face reminded me of the look of somebody else on mine.

"Aral." I was already turning to the other door. "The new look is your fucking fault, and it nearly killed me, so I don't want to hear any shit from you on the subject. There are two dead Crown Guards out there." I jerked a thumb over my shoulder as she came out. "Grab one of their swords and go keep an eye on the front door. We're a long way from out of this. Oh, and you're welcome."

"Thanks, Aral." She squeezed my shoulder. "I owe you big." Then she went to do as I'd asked.

Stel and Vala were also waiting when I opened their cell—handy little messenger, the qamasiin. They both looked the worse for wear, though not nearly so much so as Fei had.

This time I spoke first, tapping my cheek. "Bonewright. We can talk about it later."

Vala grinned and rose onto tippy-toes to give me a kiss on the cheek. "You look delicious."

Stel kissed the other one. "Don't know if I'd go that far, but I have to say that circumstances do make you look pretty damn fine. Thanks for the rescue, Aral."

I followed them out into the audience chamber. "Don't thank me too much just yet. We're still way down deep under the palace, and the Durkoth who was supposed to be our ride out of here has gone missing."

# 20

---

"**W**hat do you mean, Qethar's gone missing?" Fei growled the question from the position she'd taken up just to one side of the door.

"Come on, Fei, it's not that hard a concept. Last I saw of Qethar he was vanishing up the exit passage on a stone wave. He spotted something he was more interested in and left us in the lurch."

"Like what?" she demanded. "I thought I told you to offer him the Kothmerk. What's more important to him than that?" The look she shot me lay somewhere on the edge between defeated and outraged.

"You offered him the Kothmerk!" said VoS, turning both Vala and Stel's heads to glare at me. "Aral, how could you?"

*I know you told them not to thank you, but I didn't expect the turnaround to be quite this fast,* sent Triss.

*Me either.* Then, aloud, "I didn't promise Qethar anything other than mutual cooperation in locating the Kothmerk, and I'm pretty sure he understood that to mean that we'd probably end up at odds over what happened to it afterward."

"That was stupid," said Fei. "Why not just lie to him?"

"That's not how I work, Fei, and you know it. So does every other shadow captain in Tien. My word is good. But even if I'd lied to him, I think going after the thief who stole the ring might have ranked higher on his list than getting our asses out of trouble. As far as I can tell, he doesn't much like humans."

"Wait, Reyna is here?" This from Vala.

"She was," said Triss. "Very briefly before killing an Elite and bolting."

"Little Reyna killed an Elite, and you saw it happen?" Stel sounded incredulous. "How'd she manage it?"

"Pretty much the same way she killed all those Durkoth, I imagine." Then I held up both hands because I didn't dare let myself think about the girl yet—I had to hold it in a little longer. "But I'm done answering Kothmerk questions for the moment. We have more important things to worry about, like how we're going to get out of this hole."

"And what to do about the soldiers I hear out in the passage right now?" asked Fei.

"Yeah that'd be right up there. Triss, take a peek, would you?" He snapped his shadow wings down, launching himself across the floor and slipping under the door. "Stel, Vala, why don't you check the other chamber back beyond the anteroom there, see if maybe they were dumb enough to keep your gear close by."

"They weren't," said Stel. "That's where they conducted their interrogations. We got to see a lot of it in the last couple days." Her expression didn't invite further inquiries or discussion on the subject, so I just nodded.

"I guess we'll have to do without your battle wands then."

Vala scowled. "They broke them in front of me."

Triss reappeared from the hallway. "They're not coming down this way yet, but they've put two guards on the passage and there's at least a score of Crown Guard milling around the throne room."

"Elite?" I asked.

Triss shrugged his wings. "Probably, given where we are,

but there was too much light in the hallway. I didn't dare try to slip past the guards to look."

"So, basically, we're screwed," I said.

"Then it's a good thing I came back for you when Fei's familiar begged me to, isn't it?" Qethar stood at the door to the inner suite. "Quite a surprise actually, since I hadn't even known the good captain was a mage." He directed a smile at Fei that made me want to smack him.

"The girl got away then?" I asked in my sweetest tone— I couldn't help myself. Though I was using every trick I'd ever learned to keep my concerns for Reyna down below the level of conscious thought, she kept bubbling up to the surface of my mind, and Qethar was really starting to piss me off.

For just an instant, the Durkoth's mask of perfection slipped, and his expression shifted from smilingly predatory to something twisted and ugly and utterly inhuman with startling swiftness. But then he got himself back under control and directed a too-serene look my way—the sculpture once more.

"Why yes, she did. Does that mean you *don't* want me to make you a back door, Blade?"

*Aral* . . . Triss sounded worried.

*I'm fine, Triss.* "Not at all. I think we both saw what happened back there, and I wanted to establish just how much you need us before I let you carry me through any more walls. Lead the way."

Fei shot me a "What the hell did I miss there?" look after Qethar had the floor turn his back to us. But I ignored her and followed the Durkoth. I would have loved to turn him down, if for no other reason than because I desperately wanted to have a go at following Reyna's shadow trail. But there was no way I could get out past an even halfway serious opposition when I'd have to pass through a bottleneck like the long narrow passage to the surface.

The trip back through the stone to the place where we'd left our boat was every bit as unpleasant as the trip down had been, and the less I have to think about it the better.

Even the wet heat of summer slapping me in the face like a bucket of soup didn't improve my memories of the trip, however cool and dark it might have been.

The boat was gone, of course. Tying it up would have risked drawing unwanted attention to the place of our entry. Not that I thought your average guardsman would have been able to make much of the newly aligned granular structure of the rock wall, if they even noticed the slight change in the dark. All of which meant that someone had to go and fetch us a new boat before the sun came up. One look at the various injuries of the women and the attitude of the Durkoth told me which someone got swimming duty.

As we were looking around the nearby palace docks for a boat to steal, Triss alerted me that we'd crossed Reyna's shadow trail. Unfortunately, it led straight into the water, where it vanished. Given infinite time before sunrise and equally infinite stamina, I might have been able to pick it up again wherever she returned to shore, but with my comrades counting on my return and dozens of miles of shoreline to search just within the city, I had to let her go for now.

*We'll find her later, Aral.*

*I know. We have to.*


*So, Reyna,* I sent Triss as I ducked into Fei's privy.

This was the first chance I'd had to talk to him alone since we'd arrived at the captain's fallback, a town house in the Spicemarket. Even now, we couldn't talk out loud. Not with Fei's qamasiin flitting about.

Scheroc had been very quiet since we got the wind spirit's bond-mate free of the complex under the palace. But even without the odd little breezes that caught at my hair from time to time, I wouldn't have forgotten it was around and no doubt monitoring everything we said and did. Because of that and because I had business to do I dropped my pants and took a seat.

Triss slid up the wall to face me. *Reyna's not her real name.*

*Of course not. I don't suppose you got enough of a fix on her Shade in the midst of the fight to identify her.*

*Afraid not. We did pass across her shadow trail long enough for me to get a good sense of her*—he mentally hissed an unfamiliar Shade word—*but I didn't recognize the one it belonged to.*

I raised an eyebrow. *The girl does have to be one of ours, doesn't she?*

*Almost certainly. But she's young, somewhere between thirteen and sixteen at a guess, which makes her somewhere between six and nine at the fall of the temple. We would have been on active field duty for much of her initial training and I just didn't pay that much attention to the little ones back then.*

*Do you think she's with Devin?* I absolutely loathed the idea but I felt I had to broach it.

My one-time best friend among the Blades had turned traitor when the temple fell, along with some unknown number of the others. They'd set themselves up as the new order of the "Assassin Mage," or some such pretentious garbage, and now when they weren't doing favors for the Son of Heaven, they rented their skills out to the highest bidder.

At least, that's what Devin had told me. That and that they were going to become the power behind every throne. But I had no way of knowing what he'd told me was truth and what was lies, and I trusted Devin about as much as I trusted Qethar at this point. Maybe less. The idea of our lost and found apprentice falling into his hands made me want to vomit.

*I doubt it,* Triss said after a long pause. *If she had that kind of organization backing her up, I think there'd be a lot less chaos in the picture and a lot fewer bodies left where people could find them. That's sloppy craftwork under the circumstances.*

*She moves like someone who studied under Kelos and Kaman,* I added, *which suggests she's not a wild card who just happened to hit on a Shade when she summoned up a familiar.*

*No chance.*

*Just exploring all of the possibilities, partner. That would put her name on the wanted posters along with the rest of the Blades that escaped the fall of the temple but didn't go over to the Son of Heaven.*

Though they'd become fewer and farther between over the years since then, all I had to do to pull up the image of that poster was close my eyes—the thing was burned into my soul.

*Let's see. Remove me, Loris, Jax, Siri, and Kaman. That leaves five masters, all almost certainly dead, and all too old for our girl.*

*So are the journeymen.*

That left a dozen or so names. Remove the boys, and you had five of the right age. One of those was Aveni, a pale blonde—rare and hard to forget. That brought us down to four. Omira, Jaeris, Faran, Altia. I named them to Triss.

*Not Altia. Her companion was Olthiss and I'd have recognized that one, very sweet . . . nor Jaeris.* He slid back and forth across the floor in front of me, pacing. *Ssithra, it could have been Ssithra, very easily.*

*Which girl?* I sent my question with a force far greater than I'd intended—this *mattered* to me at some level down below the conscious.

Triss pulled his head back in startlement. *Faran. It's got to be Ssithra, and that makes it Faran.*

I tried to picture her. The name was Kadeshi, but that didn't necessarily mean anything. There were Farans aplenty in northern Zhan, southern Aven, the Magelands, even a few in the Kvanas. But none of those sounded right for some reason. Radewald maybe?

Yes, that was it. She was from up north, by Dan Eyre, right on the edge of the wastelands where things went strange. I got a brief flash of the girl's face, laughing at something, a fall maybe. Laughing, but with a hard determined edge underneath.

Yes . . . on the obstacle course. She'd missed a tricky jump trying to take a shortcut and nearly broken her neck.

But she'd laughed about the incident instead of crying. A smart girl and determined. I didn't know her at all really, but it was easy to imagine the girl who laughed like that surviving where so many others had died.

*We have to find her and take care of her,* I sent. *She's one of ours and we owe it to Namara's memory to do what we can for her. But how do we do it?*

*I don't know. It's damned hard to find any Blade who doesn't want to be found. It took the Elite weeks to catch her and they had the entire weight of the Crown behind them. She's got to be very very good to have survived the fall of the temple and to go on to do what she's done. Whatever mistake delivered her to the Elite last time, you can bet she won't let it happen again.*

"You all right in there, Aral?" It was Fei's voice coming from the other side of the privy door.

"Yeah, just finishing up, sorry." *We'll talk more about this later.* I stood and cleaned up, then closed the lid that covered the hole in the marble bench with an audible bang. It was a nice privy, voiding directly into one of the faster running sewers, and with a good tight seal on the lid.

"We thought you might have fallen in," she said when I opened the door.

She gave me a suspicious look as I stepped into the hall, but didn't say any more, just went in and closed the door behind her. I had no doubt she'd sent Scheroc in to check on me, and was wondering what else I'd been doing in there besides the obvious.

"**Not** bad, Fei," I said as I looked around the sitting room maybe half an hour later. "Not bad at all. And you're sure no one can connect this place to Captain Kaelin Fei?"

She frowned at me over the lip of her ale pot—the expression pulled at the stitches in the big slice on her cheek. "Do I *look* dumb to you, Aral? Or have you just developed a need to spew pointless insults?"

I threw up my hands. "Sorry, it's just awfully fancy for

a fallback by my standards. I can't afford to keep a house as my *main* snug and you've got one you can just throw away on us? The corrupt cop gig must pay better than I'd imagined." It sounded snippy, even to me—this Faran thing was really throwing me off my game.

Fei's expression turned sour. "Oh, I'm not real happy about having to burn the place this way, but having the Elite turn on me like that means I need to stay officially dead, at least for the duration of this Kothmerk thing."

What she didn't say was that with the Elite involved she might need to stay officially dead forever. In which case, she'd have to abandon her Tienese real estate along with her job, any assets she couldn't carry away easily, and probably her name. The king's pet killers can really hold a grudge.

While an individual Elite might fail in his loyalty to a given king, if never the idea of the Crown, there was no fucking way that setup under the palace had been anything other than a Crown operation. Oh, given the politics involved with the Kothmerk, Thauvik would certainly deny his involvement to a degree that would include denouncing and executing the participants if they fucked up badly enough to embarrass him. But if he didn't know *exactly* what they were doing down under the palace, I'd eat one of Qethar's marble shirts.

The Durkoth himself was sitting in the corner on a stone chair he'd shaped from the flagstones he'd drawn from under the rugs. It looked rather like a throne, and probably irritated Fei no end. He hadn't moved or spoken since we'd arrived a good hour earlier. I couldn't say whether that was because he just needed some time to think after the raid on the underground fortress, or if he simply had no interest in the very human tasks that had occupied us since we got to Fei's place.

Food and drink had topped my list after my talk with Triss, while the ex-prisoners had all been in a rush to make use of the house's remarkably expensive and extensive bathing facilities after they took care of things like Fei's stitches. Stel and Vala had yet to return from an extended date with the biggest tub I'd seen this side of a palace. I'd never have guessed Fei for a secret sybarite, but her bathing room belonged in one of the more modern great houses.

I took another sip of my whiskey. It wasn't Kyle's, or even Aveni, but it wasn't bad and it was definitely soothing my raw nerves. It came from a Magelands distillery I'd heard good things about but never had the chance to try before. Sharper and sweeter than an Aveni, but with a really nice layer of smoke left on the tongue after the drink was gone. Fei kept a good liquor cabinet.

Despite a couple of very pointed looks from Triss, I was just starting on my third round. It'd been a while since I'd let myself take a third drink, but I didn't regret it this time. Traveling Qethar's durathian road had left me with a bad case of the creepy crawlies. Between that and my worries about Faran, I really needed something to take the edge off the impulse to try to beat some answers out of our Durkoth friend. I had no doubt he knew more than he was sharing.

"Why don't you just walk away now?" I asked Fei. "We both know what that place down there meant. Say you do solve the Kothmerk problem in a way that doesn't put you permanently on the wrong side of your king. Would you honestly be willing to go back to serving a man who'd use you the way Thauvik just did?"

Fei's expression went from sour to angry and she set aside her beer as she put both hands on the table and leaned toward me. "Don't go all sanctimonious on me, Blade. I'm not the one who walked away from the fall of the house of Justice to become a two-kip jack of shadows."

That hit me harder than any slap in the face, and much harder than it would have if I didn't have Faran on my mind. I'd walked away from her and the other apprentices as surely as I'd walked away from the temple, though I hadn't realized it till now. I set my drink aside as well, instinctively clearing my hands for a fight.

But Fei kept right on going. "My job's never been about the bastard who wears the crown, and I've never had the luxury you temple-raised hothouse flowers did of sitting in judgment over the ass that sits on the throne. Nor do I get to stick to the pretty bits of the city like the shining knights who run the regular watch. My blood's never been Zhani enough to get me that kind of job. Hell, I was barely able to talk my way onto the night watch in the Stumbles back when I started out. These days I'm the one stuck with keeping the fucking peace amongst the monsters and the mobsters any way I can.

"I know a lot of people look down on me because my hands are dirty from all the shadowside shit I have to touch in the course of my job. I want to save lives and keep the shadow wars from eating this city alive, and that means I've had to play kissy face with every kind of leech and law-breaker imaginable. I understand what that makes me. But I will not take condescension from Aral fucking Kingslayer on the subject of crossing moral lines. I may be a crook in the service of keeping the worse crooks from doing too much harm, but I don't see how there's a whole hell of a lot of difference between that and black jacking for the gods."

I expected to feel outrage when she finished yelling at me, and I could sense Triss worrying about my response—his emotions were coming through stronger and stronger since we'd developed the ability to speak mind-to-mind. In some ways I would have welcomed outrage. It would have been easier, less painful. But it just wasn't there. Not after my experience with the bonewright and the thinking I'd had to do afterward.

What I felt was sympathy and shame. Though I'd never realized it before, Fei and I had a hell of a lot in common. We were both the end result of the corrosion of an idealist. So, instead of getting in Fei's face the way she'd gotten in mine, I just nodded.

"Point."

"What?" Fei collapsed back into her seat, deflating like a gaffed puffer fish. "Aren't you going to go all self-righteous on me and talk about how much better your goddess is than my king?"

"Nope. My goddess is dead, Fei. I can't serve her any-more. I realized that recently." I took another sip of whiskey and noticed the glass was empty. "I can still do my best to serve justice, and I've been working to get there again, though it's shit for paying the bills. But that's not really the same thing. Because, no matter how sure I am of my interpretation of justice, I don't have a mandate from Heaven anymore and I can't *know* I'm right. Quite the contrary. The Heavenly Court hates my guts."

I shrugged. "Maybe they always did. Maybe we Blades never had that mandate we believed we did. Maybe Namara's idea of justice was just as subjective as mine."

Triss slid up against my back, wrapping his wings around me protectively. *Are you all right?*

*No. But I think I may finally be heading there. Thanks for hanging in there all these years.*

"You're a strange one," said Fei. "Are you saying you don't believe in Namara anymore?"

"Say I don't believe in authority anymore and you'll be closer to the truth. Not temporal, not religious. Maybe not even moral. It's funny. I loved my goddess and I obeyed her without question. Her followers were and are my family. I killed who she said I should kill and spared those she wanted spared. I'm not at all sure that was right, but if you managed to bring her back from the grave somehow, I'd probably do the same again. Though I'm starting to hope that I'd have the strength not to."

Triss leaned forward so that his head came into view on my right. He looked worried. "Where are you going with this, Aral?"

"I'm not entirely sure, but I think I'm giving up on the idea that having a goddess—or anyone else—define right and wrong for me is a good idea. I—we, have to find our own way to justice now, Triss, and duty, and that's actually a good thing." I turned my gaze back to Fei. "That's pretty much what you do every day, isn't it?"

She snorted. "Hardly anything so high flung as all that, Blade. Justice would probably throw my ass in a cell. I'm just trying to keep my city from drowning in its own shit." She tossed back the rest of her beer and went to the liquor cabinet. "Think of me more as one of those poor bastards whose job is to unblock the sewers, and you're much closer to the truth."

*Yeah, right,* I thought at Triss. It seemed kinder than keeping Fei on the spot. *She can tell herself that all she wants, but she gave herself away earlier. She's as bad as I ever was in her own way.*

*Bad? Not at all. At the moment I think you're both rather wonderful.*

Whether Fei wondered about my sudden blush, I would never know, as Qethar chose that moment to reinsert himself into the conversation. "Will you two stop blithering about pointless philosophical piffle and get back to thinking about how we can recover the Kothmerk. Every hour that it remains in human hands is another hour one of our most sacred relics is profaned."

Since Qethar had pretty much blended into the background for me by then, I just about rolled backward out of my chair when he spoke. Maybe that's what the still and silent treatment was all about, another little way of dicking with the humans.

We're just not very good at paying attention to stuff that doesn't move at all over periods measured in hours. Didn't matter that he was strikingly beautiful. Didn't matter that no ordinary house would have an expensive statue of the sort he now resembled more than ever. Didn't even matter that I'd trusted snakes more than I trusted Qethar. After a while, I simply lost track of him.

I hadn't yet decided how I was going to respond to Qethar's comment, when I heard Fei say, "Well, and fuck you, too, Durkoth. As much as I appreciate the rescue, I don't work for you, and I don't think Aral does either." She stepped over and poured another couple of fingers of whiskey into my glass before I could protest.

She pointed the bottle at Qethar now. "So, if you want my help, stone man, you can damn well be polite about it. You can also wait till I've had a little bit of time to recover and think. I haven't had two hours' solid sleep in the last three days, and I had the shit beat out of me a couple of times in there, too." She touched the tip of the bottle to the long slice on her cheek and winced. "You want something from me, ask me nicely when I wake up, and then we'll see. I'm going to bed." She headed for the stairs.

That's when I realized just how tired I was, too, not to mention how much satisfaction watching Fei jerking Qethar's chain had given me. "You know, that's got a lot to be said for it." I raised my glass. "Here's to sleep."

Fei turned and looked back at me. "Blankets in the closet at the top of the stairs. Couch is next to the stone asshole." She jerked a thumb at Qethar. "There's a second bedroom upstairs. You and the Dyad can wrestle to see who gets that if neither of you wants to bed down next to his marble haughtiness."

"Or we could just wrestle for the fun of it and then all bed down together," Vala said as she came out of the bathing room. She was toweling off her hair, and now she threw me a suggestive grin.

But I wasn't in a mood for banter. "No, it's all right. I can just sleep on the floor in the upstairs hall. It'll be more comfortable than my brewery fallback ever was." I turned to the Durkoth and lifted my drink in a mock salute before draining it. "See you in the morning, Qethar."

The ugly inhuman thing I'd seen earlier looked back at me out of his face for a few brief heartbeats and I found myself wondering how that inner ugliness could coexist with the outer beauty. Then his face slid back to a neutral expression and I found it hard to believe I was looking at anything living.

At the top of the stairs Vala waited for Stel to go into the bedroom, than gave me a kiss. It made the world spin. Well, spin more.

"When this is all over, if we're still alive, I want to . . ." She trailed off and looked suddenly thoughtful and serious. "I'm actually not sure what I want to do. I like you, Aral, maybe more than I ought to considering what you are, and what I am. I'd like to try something more than a quick tumble with you, but I don't know if that can work."

I didn't know how to answer that. I liked her a lot, too, but I had other responsibilities, and the one to a girl named Faran seemed all too likely to come between us, to say nothing of what I owed Fei. Before I could do or say anything though, Vala's normal mischievous smile came back, and she gave me a wink.

She squeezed my arm. "So, I guess we'll just have to start with the tumble and see what develops from there." Then she gave me another kiss, this one rather more serious than the previous one, and followed Stel.

That left me alone on the landing except for Triss. So I sat myself down with my back against the wall in a position that allowed me to keep Qethar's feet in sight and my head from spinning. I really *wanted* to bed down, but I wanted to have another quiet word with Triss even more.

*What do you think?* I sent, before he could take me to task for my drinking.

He snorted grumpily but let it pass without a lecture. *About what? Vala? What you talked about with Fei? Faran and Ssithra?*

*All that, I guess. I don't know what our next move should be. I'm having trouble seeing how we can make this all work out without betraying someone, or several someones.*

*I know. So what's most important?*

*My heart says Faran and Ssithra.*

*We don't even know them, Aral. What if they've gone as bad as Devin?*

*Why do you always ask the hard questions, Triss? I don't know. They're just kids really, and the closest thing we've got to family. I don't want to believe they're anything like Devin, but then, I didn't want to believe it about Devin either.*

*What does your head say?*

*The Kothmerk. If it doesn't get back to its rightful owner soon, there's liable to be a war. No matter how much I want to make the girls my first priority I can't put them over that.*

*Good, then we're on the same page.*

I closed my eyes and leaned my head back for a moment. The world lurched underneath me. I *needed* sleep.

*I'm done for now, Triss. Keep an eye on Qethar, won't you? I have to let go for a while, but I don't trust him and I want to know if he moves from that chair.*

*Sleep. I've got it.*

I think I managed to actually stretch out before I was gone, but I wouldn't bet money on it.

"**Aral,** you surprise me again." Stel set her napkin aside and belched. "I had no idea a person could do so much with a bit of rice, some fresh fish, and a few dried beans and pulses. That was a damn fine meal. I'm impressed. Doubly so, given what you had to work with."

"Fei's spice cabinet is almost as well stocked as her liquor cabinet, and that's a good part of the battle."

"I would never have imagined they'd teach you to cook like this at assassin school," said Fei.

I smiled sweetly. "If you don't know a lot about how to make food taste exactly like you want it to, it's very hard to slip poison into someone's dinner. Or their breakfast, for that matter."

Fei's eyes went very wide for a moment, then narrowed. "That's not funny, Kingslayer."

"That's because I'm not joking."

*It's been so long since you joked regularly that I'd forgotten how evil your sense of humor could be.* Triss sounded more amused than scolding.

*Unlike* this morning when he'd been very unkind about my hangover. An overreaction, I thought, since it was the first time I'd been really hungover since the mess with Marchon had made me take a firm look at my drinking. It was just the once, and now I'd been reminded not to do it again. I was in control of this thing.

I waited a few beats and then threw a broad wink at the table. "But, more seriously, I wish I could have taken the risk to go farther afield and find some fresh vegetables. Unlike my luck with the fish cart there haven't been any to be had in sight of your front door, Captain." I started scooping up plates, then paused before taking them into the kitchen. "Vegetables always make for a better meal. To say nothing of the way adding more color improves the palette of toxins you can use."

Fei growled. "You're a bastard, Aral. You know that, right?"

"It's all in the spicing," I called over my shoulder. "I don't normally bother to cook . . . like that, but you're special, Fei."

I heard Vala laugh behind me and felt that I'd been fully rewarded. The interchange made a nice break from the frustrations of the moment. We'd been back and forth all morning—afternoon really, but who's counting—trying to figure out how to find "Reyna" and the Kothmerk. It wasn't going very well, and it didn't help that I hadn't yet told the rest of them what she was, or that I knew her real name. Which was something I needed to do soon if I was going to do it at all.

*How the hell do we find Faran, Triss?*

My shadow shrugged his wings. *I don't know that we can. It's too bad we can't make her fulfill that promise and find us.*

I froze. *Now there's a thought. . . .*

# 21

———◆———

"That's insane, Aral!" Triss had placed himself on the wall behind the empty chair at the foot of Fei's table so he could more fully participate in the discussion. "You nearly killed yourself with the Dyad's face-changing spell not two days ago, and now you want to risk exposing your new identity to the Elite?"

"Not at all, my friend. I'm talking about spreading a rumor, not putting up fresh wanted posters with my new face on them."

Triss lashed his tail but didn't say anything further.

"I think I missed a step in there somewhere," said Vala. "Why would telling people that Aral Kingslayer had been tracked down to what's left of the Old Mews neighborhood bring Reyna there? Wouldn't she want to stay as far away from the manhunt as possible?"

"There's something Aral hasn't told us, Vala," said VoS, choosing, rather disconcertingly, to speak through Vala's own mouth. "He's got a secret he's reluctant to share, though I haven't figured out what it is yet."

"Is that true?" Vala asked.

"Yeah, I guess that it is." There was no good way to do this, so I figured I might as well go for bald and bold. "Her name isn't Reyna. It's Faran and she's . . . well, not a Blade—as Namara died before she was old enough to confirm—but she is Blade trained and raised. Up to the age of eight or nine."

Vala jerked in her seat, almost as if she'd been slapped.

"That would explain a lot," said Stel after a long pause, though she didn't sound happy about it.

Fei nodded. "That *does* change things. You think that if we can get shadowside buzzing loud enough about where to find the Kingslayer, that'll make her come running to you for protection and help. Clever."

"But you *aren't* going to take her under your protection, are you?" This from VoS, via Stel. "She stole the Kothmerk and it clearly wasn't to return it to the Archon. She was going to sell it, forever staining the honor of Kodamia."

"It's not that simple," I said and Triss nodded his agreement.

"How is it not?" demanded VoS, this time speaking through Vala. "We took her in and sheltered her, gave her a home, responsibilities. Then, as soon as she got the chance, she betrayed us all."

For the first time since I'd known her, Vala looked genuinely uncomfortable about what VoS was saying through her mouth. Interesting.

*It's probably* not *the first time Faran did something like this,* Triss sent my way.

*Just the first time she got caught.* That thought had occurred to me, too. A girl with Faran's skills and talents had no need to play at being a groom to earn her keep. If nothing else, she could simply steal everything she needed. *Let's just hope none of* them *think of that.*

*They will. In fact, Fei probably already has. Look at the way she's pretending to be part of the wall.*

That made me glance at Qethar as well. He'd moved his stone chair in close at the beginning of the conversation but had played statue thereafter. Whatever his thoughts were on the matter, I couldn't read them from his face. And I was growing increasingly inclined to believe that any illusions I'd had earlier about doing so were pure fantasy, that all resemblances between human expressions and his own were deliberate manipulations on his part.

"Do you have any idea what this girl's been through?" I asked, as much to keep VoS too busy to think about what I was thinking about as for anything. "I do. When the other gods murdered Namara and had their followers tear down the temple, they tore down my life, too. I lost everything and it broke me. Completely. I crawled into a whiskey bottle and damn near drowned there, and I was a full Blade, an adult with five years of field duty. The Kingslayer. It nearly killed me. Faran was eight."

*Nine I think, but close enough.*

"Eight years old, VoS, and every single adult in her life was murdered. All of her teachers, her priests, even the servants who cleaned the halls. Most of her friends died, too. Everyone she knew and counted on was murdered along with her goddess. Everyone she cared about. Her family." I slammed the table with both fists, pushing myself to my feet and realizing as I did so that I was actually shaking with anger. "There were six hundred people living at the temple of Namara at the time of the fall. Over five hundred of them died, probably while Faran watched.

"An eight-year-old. And that's only what we know about. She showed up on your doorstep, what a year and a half ago? The temple fell more than six years ago. Who knows what happened to her in the interim? A little girl, with no one to protect her, her name on wanted posters in every town and city in the eleven kingdoms. Don't you dare judge her till you've been through half of what she has!" I was bellowing by the time I came to the end of my speech.

Neither Vala nor Stel would meet my eyes, though I saw Vala glancing uncomfortably at Triss.

*I think you might have made a mistake there,* he sent. *With the Meld if not the motes. They're embarrassed, but she's going to be thinking very hard about what you just said, and it's not going to take her long to start wondering about how little Faran was keeping body and soul together during the missing years.*

*You think she was spying in Kodamia?* I crossed to the liquor cabinet and poured myself a large glass of Fei's Magelander whiskey. My throat felt like I'd eaten a bottle instead of drinking from one.

*I do. Though whether she was freelance or someone's Crown agent I couldn't say. It's the perfect job for someone like her. That or thieving, and she wouldn't have stayed so long if all she wanted to do was make off with a few choice items from the Citadel. Oh, and just so you know how I feel, it's far too early for whiskey.*

I agreed with him, but that didn't stop me. I needed the help in calming down.

"You realize that none of that matters, don't you?" Once again Qethar's entry into the conversation startled the piss out of me—this time I slopped whiskey all over my hand.

"The only important question is whether the idea will work or not," continued Qethar. "Whether the girl lives or dies and who ends up with her if she does is immaterial. Only the Kothmerk matters. It's the most important thing in your whole world." He turned his hard blank eyes on the Dyad. "Your Archon would surely say the same thing if he were here now, Valor of Steel."

Vala and Stel went very still at that. "How do you know our name?" she asked through both mouths. It was a deceptively quiet question.

"I know the names and specialties of all the Dyads that set out with the Kothmerk as well as the pass codes for your mission. I would have thought the reason was obvious. My king sent me that information when the delivery went bad. It went out to all of his chief agents in every city that lay within a couple of week's travel of the ambush. You didn't really think your failures would go undiscovered by the rightful King of the North or that he'd trust humans to get the Kothmerk back for him, did you?"

"Why should I believe you?" asked VoS, again through both of her mouths.

Qethar pulled a thin plate of rock loose from the arm of his little throne and placed it on the table in front of him. Seemingly of its own accord it slid across to Stel.

"Flip it over," said Qethar. "Look at the other side, but show it to no one else if you don't want your Archon's precious secrets leaking out to the rest of the world. No offense, Captain Fei, Blade Aral, but you're both known shadowside operators and Valor of Steel never should have trusted either of you."

"None taken," said Fei as Stel lifted the stone. "We all know what I am, and I'm sure Aral feels the same way."

"Those are the mission pass codes, all right," said Stel. "I guess you are what you say you are." She set the stone back on the table and slid it back to Qethar. "We really are all on the same side."

"Of course we are, and if you'd been more than just muscle for your delivery mission you'd have known enough to send word to my offices when you got into the city instead of bringing in the broken Blade here. Though, now that you've finally hooked up with me, I might be inclined to overlook your failures in my report. Assuming, of course, that we can recover the Kothmerk and get it back to its rightful owner."

"That's very kind of you," said VoS through Stel. She sounded completely sincere, too, though I couldn't help noticing the way Vala's knuckles had gone white as she clenched her hands together out of sight of the Durkoth. Somehow, I didn't think they trusted him any more than I did. "I look forward to working together more closely to make sure that happens."

"Good," said Qethar. "I'd offer to shake on it, but my recent . . . contact with Aral has reminded me of the way my touch affects you children of the later gods."

Qethar turned a smile on me then, a beautiful smile full of promise that I felt all the way down to my knees. It made me simultaneously want to take him in my arms and punch him in the face.

"I *am* sorry about that and the other awkwardness at our first meeting," he said to me, "but I didn't know what your true place in all this was then. I still don't trust you, of course, but I do see the merits of your current plan and how much we need you. I'm sure that my government will agree with me when I say that once this is all successfully concluded you can expect a very handsome reward from the Durkoth."

*This is an interesting development,* sent Triss. *Do you believe a word of it?*

*I don't know. A good deal of it fits in with the facts that we have available, but somehow I can't help but feel there's one sure sign he's lying.*

*What's that?*

*His mouth is open and words are coming out.*

Triss chuckled knowingly in my mind. *There is that.*

While we were having our little side discussion, Qethar looked at Fei. "There will be a reward for you as well, Captain. Never fear. It's clear to me that Aral's plan will require the extensive use of your contacts in the shadow world if we're going to make it work, as well as my own, since Aral's are denied to us by his . . . loss of face. Shall we get started?"

"There's one little problem," said Fei. "I'm officially dead, and I need to stay that way for a bit."

"That is a problem," I said. "But not an insurmountable one. I figure the easiest way to start the rumors we need is for me to trot over to the Old Mews and let myself be seen, repeatedly."

"Aral!"

"It's all right, Triss. I'll be wearing a hood, and a mask of shadow. No one's going to see my actual face, just a man who can vanish into a cloud of darkness. Though it would be nice if we could use Fei's contacts to amplify the effect on the shadowside and get it to spread faster there. That would allow me to take fewer risks."

"Oh, I think I can manage that," said Fei. "I didn't mean to say I wouldn't help, just that it wouldn't be simple. I'll have to work through an agent. Aral, can you deliver a

message to Sergeant Zishin and then escort him to someplace private for a meeting with me? I can't send Scheroc
without revealing what I am."

I nodded. "Let's get to work."


**My** entire back itched in that way it does when you're
expecting someone to put a big fat arrow between your
shoulder blades, and the sweat trickling down my spine
didn't help. I'd been at this for a week and two bottles of
whiskey, and the neighborhood had filled up with Crown
officers and bounty hunters of both the professional and
amateur variety. To keep the rumors going, I had to keep
sticking my hand in the bear trap.

It didn't help that even a year on, the Old Mews still stank
of smoke and ashes. The faint sickening miasma kept swirling up to my perch atop Tien's newest temple to Shan—why
is it that the temples always come back first? Fresh remind-
ers of the fire that had murdered the entire neighborhood
were kicked up every day, as the long slow work of rebuild-
ing broke open the old scabs of burned-out building after
burned-out building. Somehow the optimistic smells of
fresh-cut lumber and raw plaster just couldn't make up for
the occasional whiff of burnt meat and charred bone. At
least for me.

Even knowing I'd killed the woman responsible for that
fire was cold comfort. It wouldn't bring a single one of the
dead back. Nothing would. I shivered then and wished I
could pull Triss more tightly around me, or at least talk to
him. But once again circumstances required that he sink
himself into the dream state that gave me maximum freedom to use both his powers and my magic.

I was lonely and miserable and it would have been better
on an emotional level if I'd picked any other neighborhood.
But the combination of burned-over rubble fields scattered
amidst all sorts of new construction and temporary struc-
tures created an ever-changing maze that made it much
easier to lose even the most determined pursuit. That had

saved my ass more than once as the number of hunters had gone steadily up over the last couple of days.

I could see at least a dozen different groups and single-tons from my current location, every one of them out for my blood. Most notable was the Elite mission under Major Aigo, who had temporarily evicted a well-off merchant from his new mansion to set up headquarters.

There was nothing official to mark the place out as belonging to the Elite, but the constant stream of Crown Guards running in and out in their civvies at all hours of the day was unmistakable. I'm not sure what it is about the military mind that thinks that dressing career soldiers in civilian drag is going to somehow make the arrow-straight backs, battle scars, and drill field muscles invisible, but I've seen it time and again.

The *official* Crown Guard presence had taken over a three-quarters-finished apartment building a few hundred yards up the road, and it was particularly funny watching the out-of-uniform folks ostentatiously not saluting their officers as they went by. The bounty hunters were more circumspect, mostly taking rooms at nearby inns or squat-ting in burned-over basements. The number of genuine civil-ians had dropped off steadily starting on day two. Most of the lanterns moving about on the streets below belonged to one faction or another of the hunters now.

About the only set of lights down there that didn't belong to someone who wanted to sell my head to the king were the green lamps that marked those selling their asses to the hunters. Given the character of the new neighbors, there was plenty of work down there for the sex trades. Which re-minded me, it was about time for me to dangle my own ass out in the breeze again.

"How's my route look?" I whispered to the wind.

"Give it two minutes from when you hear this, then go," the wind whispered back after a bit.

The ability of the qamasiin to blow words halfway across the city was coming in very handy for our little operation. In this case, the wind sounded an awful lot like Vala, who was down on the streets, carrying an intricately inscribed green lamp. The shadows it cast suggested that what she was offering was very specialized and staggeringly expensive.

That helped keep the number of customers she had to turn away to a minimum, but Stel, who had taken on the character of a bounty hunter, had still had to cover for her bond-mate by getting rid of two bodies. The corpses in question belonged to individuals who'd rather forcefully refused to take a whore's "no," at least until it was delivered with the crude battle wands Vala had created to replace her old ones.

After I'd counted off the requisite number of heartbeats, I dropped down the back of the tower and made my way along the spine of the temple. At the end I jumped across a ten-foot gap and down a story to land on the roof of a partially rebuilt tavern. As I moved on from there, I opened a tiny hole at the top of my shroud to give Scheroc a way to find me, the first of many such instances. Since the tactic exposed only the top of my head and that only to someone looking straight down from the skies above it seemed a small enough risk.

After about a four-block run across the hot rooftops, I reached the outer edge of the neighborhood and released Triss. It would have been safer for me if I could have kept control over him through the whole exercise, but Triss needed to be fully awake for the next bit since he would be the one doing the real work. Working carefully and quietly, we made our way back and forth along the perimeter we'd established for our operations, dancing an intricate and risky snake-step with the many hunters who were also quartering the area.

As we went, Triss kept "tasting" for any traces left by another Shade. We worked both on the rooftops and the streets below since I had no doubt that if Ssithra and Faran came a-visiting they'd do it fully shrouded. That was all part of the plan. When a shadow was strengthened by the presence of a Shade within it, it left behind what Triss called a "flavor" in the shadows it passed over and through. Fire and sunlight quickly destroyed such traces, as did moving water, but at night, one Shade could always tell where another had recently passed.

The more present a Shade was in the shadow, the stronger the flavor and the easier it was to both trace and identify. Full-on shroud mode left the strongest trace short of some sort of shadow-magic work, and that's what we'd been looking for since day one. So far we'd found shit, which was pretty damned disheartening considering how much we'd all risked to try to lure Faran here.

*Dammit,* I thought at Triss, as we came to the end of our run. *This is getting us nowhere, and it's getting more dangerous with each passing hour. I'm starting to think Faran's not coming.*

I was shocked at how much that thought depressed me considering that a mere two weeks ago I hadn't spared so much as a passing thought about her, or any of our lost apprentices for that matter—I imagine I felt a bit like a man who suddenly finds out years after the event that he's a father.

*I think you might be right,* Triss replied glumly. *But I don't have any ideas for what we might try next if we have to give up on this.*

*I don't either, so I guess we'd better get ready to let some idiot bounty hunter get a look at us again. If we don't keep showing our colors, everyone's going to assume we've gone elsewhere.*

"Hide!" The whisper in the wind was in Scheroc's own voice this time. "Elite coming this way!"

As if in punctuation of the qamasiin's warning there came the distinctive howl of a stone dog on the hunt. The labyrinthine nature of the Old Mews construction came to our aid once again, as three long steps took us from the center of a recently cleared and cleaned street to the edge of a large pit. There, charred debris from all over had been mounded up, filling in much of what must once have been a huge and multilevel cellar. A gap between two blackened beam ends was just big enough for me to slip through on my belly, though I tore a long rent in the hip of my pants in my haste.

A few yards farther in I came to a place where I could worm my way down into the deeper levels below the street. I would have preferred to make my escape up and out with the stone dogs involved, but haste had directed a different choice. With Triss to guide me, I made my way down toward the sewers and the bedrock where I could break another of Qethar's pebbles to summon him if I needed a pick-up. At the cost of several more rips in my clothes and a couple in my skin, I finally reached a floor grate that opened into a large pipe, which, in turn, presumably led down into the sewers.

That's when Scheroc whispered in my ear again, "Go quickly-quietly. Stone dogs sniffing above."

Fuck. I really didn't want to have to summon Qethar. I'm not sure whether that was more because I didn't trust him, or because calling him would mean another trip along the durathian road. I'd had to rely on him for a rescue twice since I'd started trailing myself like a lure through the Old Mews, and each time I'd come to loathe the passage through the earth that much more. That didn't keep me from pulling the pebble out of my pouch and slipping it into my mouth, where I tucked it between teeth and my cheek before proceeding. If I needed that pick-up, I'd need it fast.

Just above where it opened into the sewer, I ran into a partial blockage of the old stone pipe. I don't know what it was, but it felt like several hundred pounds of cheese that had gone bad, and it smelled worse. For once, I found myself profoundly glad that Triss's unvision didn't work the same way as my eyes, because I really didn't want to know any more about the stuff than I learned by dragging myself through it. I dropped the last four feet face first and landed hard when my attempt to roll out of the fall ran into another heap of drain cheese.

The winds tugged at my hair. "Stone dog has stuck his head into the ground above."

"Thanks, Scheroc." I spat the stone into my hand. Time to—
*Don't break it, she's here!*

"What?" I said aloud.

"Scheroc doesn't understand your question." The qama-siin sounded both sad and confused. "What does Aral want?"

Before I could answer, Triss spoke into my mind, *Tell it to go up and keep an eye on things. A Shade has been through here recently, and I'd like to investigate before we tell the others anything.*

I didn't ask Triss why he wanted me to do it that way, just tucked the pebble back into my pouch and sent Scheroc away. It wasn't the first time we'd looked for Faran in the sewers, but it was the first time we'd found any trace of her. I didn't trust any of the others where it came to dealing with our young Blade either. Not even the Dyad. Not with so few of my kind left. The stakes were too high to let anyone but Triss and I handle this.

*Is it Ssithra?* I asked once I'd sent the air spirit on its way again.

*I think so. I didn't get a good enough taste of her*—he hissed something in Shade—*at the palace to be absolutely sure, but it tastes much the same. Turn left and hurry. She's moving down and away from the Old Mews.*

The pipe wasn't big enough to stand in, so I kept low and ran, using Triss's senses to look out for any obstructions. At least it was dry—like many of the Old Mews sewers its upstream end was still clogged with debris from the fires.

"Stop," Triss said suddenly as we reached a junction where our pipe met another, larger one. Then, "Ssithra"—before he shifted into a long hissing string of Shade.

A moment later he was answered in kind from off to the left. I looked that way, but if Faran and her companion were there, they remained enshrouded.

*Aral, we've found them. Step out onto the accessway in the main passage. Do it slowly—they're both terrified.*

"Master Aral?" The voice was low and throaty but femi-nine, and there was a strong undertone of fear. "Resshath

Triss? Is that you? Have we really found more survivors after all this time?"

*Unshroud us, Triss.*

"It's me," I said as he did so. "And if we're right in our guesses, you must be Faran?"

"Oh, thank Namara!"

She hit me with something midway between a hug and a tackle, pushing me back into the curved bricks of the wall. I wrapped my arms around her more or less instinctively, and suddenly we were both hugging and crying, and I was making vague reassuring noises. It didn't matter that we'd had practically nothing to do with each other back at the temple, or that we were of different generations. What mattered was that we shared a past now lost to us, a past that so very few people could ever even hope to understand.

Without my asking him to, Triss drew on my nima to conjure up a very faint magelight, setting the temporary spell in one of the bricks of the wall, so that I could look at Faran with my own eyes. For a long time, all I could see was the top of her head and the tangled and dirty brown hair that spilled down her back, and that was enough. Even the smell from the turgid flow in the central channel couldn't dent my joy at finding her alive.

"I'm in so much trouble," she said into my chest after the first storm of tears had passed.

"I know. We'll fix it. We just need to get the damn ring back to its rightful owner and everything will be all right. I'll see to it."

"Really?" She peered up at me and I got my first look at her face. There was hope there. Hope and fear, and lines made by the sort of pain no fifteen-year-old should ever have to bear.

"I promise. First we need to get you out of here, then we can arrange for you to hand over the ring and I'll take care of everything."

Her face fell. "Can't I just give it to you now?"

I was genuinely shocked. "You mean you've got it with you?" Judging her path from the outside, she'd looked so smart for so long, it seemed insane that she'd risk everything now by carrying her only insurance into the heart of enemy territory.

"Of course not. It's in the everdark, but Ssithra can retrieve it anytime."

"What!" Triss and I spoke as one. "How?"

"It's a spell I thought up on my own, based on something Master Siri once said about folding shadows and moving things through the everdark."

That triggered a memory of Siri doing something impossible with moving from one shadow to another and then trying to explain to me why it was both dangerous and too impractical to use. She'd gone into a whole lot of gabble about advanced magical theory and mathimagics, and the conversation had made my head ache. I hadn't asked again.

"Wait," said Faran. "It'll be easier for me to show you than to tell you about it. I don't really have the right words. But I'll need better light. Ssithra?"

For the first time I looked around for Faran's Shade. I found Ssithra on the curve of the far wall, where a shadow phoenix sniffed noses with Triss's dragon shape.

Ssithra shifted now to mirror her human companion's form as Faran stepped away from me, moving a few yards up the accessway. I increased the flow of nima to our temporary light—basically a controlled application of the same sort of low magic used in magefire. The long-lasting kind took a much more elaborate sort of spellwork and a good deal of power to create.

It revealed a badly eroded sewerscape with bricks missing from the walls in many places. The central channel looked more like a dried-up creek bed than a properly kept sewer. Though whether that was because of some blockages upslope in the Old Mews, or due to some failure of the water source they used to keep this part of the system flowing, I didn't know.

Faran stood up straight, then extended her arms out to the sides. In response, Ssithra relaxed into her partner's natural shadow, allowing Faran and the bright light to direct

her movements. With my magesight I could see a glow of
magic building within Faran as she folded her arms and then
squatted down so that her shadow formed a rough ball on
the wall across from her. Her inner spell-light slowly bright-
ened, sending out streamers that tied her to the passive
Ssithra. As she worked the lights changed color, becoming
a rich green gold, like sunlight in the deep forest.

Soon the ball of shadow was threaded all through with
spell-light, a dark package tied up with strings of magic
invisible to the mageblind eye. Faran stood up then and
stepped to one side. I expected to see her shadow mirror her
motions again, but it did not, remaining as a ball bound with
spell-light. More light flew from Faran, wrapping around
the slender tail of shadow that connected her to the dark
ball.

Then a bulge appeared in that tail and quickly grew into
a second shadow, mirroring Faran's shape and movements
once again, as Ssithra somehow disengaged from the binding Faran had laid upon her while simultaneously leaving
something of herself behind. As that happened, the ball
slowly shrank, until it was no bigger than a fist.

Now, Faran knelt to one side, reaching out toward the
ball of shadow so that Ssithra, still mirroring her, did the
same. The shadow of Faran picked up the shadow of a ball
and began unfolding it like a paper artist uncreating an
elaborate piece of origami. When she finished, a thin sheet
of shadow-stuff lay on the shadow-Faran's hand with lines
of spell-light marking the creases where folds of shadow
had come undone. In the middle of the sheet sat a ruby ring,
which the shadow brought to Faran.

In turn, Faran stepped toward me, extending her hand as
she did so. "Here it is, Master Aral, and you have no idea
how happy I am to get rid of the thing. It's nearly killed me
a dozen times."

She lurched leftward suddenly, stumbling toward the
open channel for no reason I could see. I lunged forward
and grabbed her wrist before she could go over the side, but
the Kothmerk fell from her hand in the process, dropping

toward the noisome muck. But Triss was there, diving to catch the ring and close it tight in a fist of shadow.

"I saw that," he hissed. "Move the floor again, Qethar, and I'll send this thing back to the everdark in a way that will make it completely irretrievable."

The wall across the way rippled and flowed aside, forming an alcove where Qethar stood, his arms crossed, a cruelly beautiful smile on his face. He looked calm, but I thought I could sense something almost like panic underlying his expression. He was *really* concerned about the safety of the Kothmerk, if I was any judge. Which, of course, I might not be.

"Don't be a fool, Shade," he said. "And don't think I'm one either. If you destroy the Kothmerk it will mean war between Kodamia and the King of the North. I know you don't want that, so if you'll just pass me the Kothmerk, no one has to get hurt and I can finish with this hideous human dance I've been dragged into while trying to rescue a sacred trust."

Faran let out a quiet little eeking sort of noise as she saw Qethar and I put a protective arm around her. Ssithra moved, too, shifting back into phoenix form and putting herself firmly between the Durkoth and her bond-mate.

"It *is* you," said Faran, and something about her tone prompted me to put my free hand on one of my sword hilts.

"You know Qethar?" asked Triss, his voice low and worried.

"Of course I know him, though this is the first time I've heard his name. He's the Durkoth who led the raiding party that killed all the Dyads back in the forest!" She turned her head to look at me. "You're not working with him, are you Master Aral?"

I drew my sword and leveled it at Qethar. "Not anymore, no."

Qethar held out his left hand and made a clenching motion with his right. In apparent response to the latter gesture, the walls of the sewer flexed briefly inward.

"Give me the Kothmerk now and no one else has to die,

Aral. Defy me and I'll destroy you all. And don't think killing me will save you either. I've asked my sister the earth to collapse this space if I die here."

"What's your play, Qethar?" I didn't have a lot of options, and I needed to buy some time. "There's no reason to do this, not if you are what you say. Or was your claim to be the King of the North's chief agent in Tien a lie?"

"Lying to ephemerals is beneath me," he replied. "I am the right hand of the *true* King of the North in Tien. I just haven't put him on his throne yet."

The ugly inhuman thing that lived within Qethar glared out at me again. "I am a high lord of the Durkoth. I was prince consort to the current occupant of the throne for four hundred years before he used some trumped up treason charges to cast me aside in favor of a prettier and more biddable model some twenty years ago. In exchange for handing over the Kothmerk, my new king has promised to restore me to my rightful place at court, if not to the consort's chair."

For at least the hundredth time in the last two weeks I wished I had a better grasp of Durkothian politics, this time to help me keep Qethar talking. As it was, I had no idea what question I should ask next. So I decided to go with what I did know, the Tien end of things.

"Why didn't you hand me over to the Elite when you first brought me down under the palace?"

"Why would I bother?" asked Qethar. "Your petty human squabbles bore me. I want the ring and a return to my rightful place among my people. Once I have them, I will leave the surface forever. Zhan's king and his creatures were a temporary expedient, just as you were, a means to an end."

"Looks like you and Thauvik are two of a kind then, after the way he had your people murdered." I hoped that a reminder of his fallen fellows would jab his conscience.

"He saved me time and effort," said Qethar. "The local Durkoth are all petty criminals and outcasts, unworthy to share my coming triumph, and the soldiers my rightful king lent me would only have served to dilute the honors that belong to me. But enough of this, your time is up. Give me the Kothmerk now or die."

I dropped a few inches and almost fell as the stones underneath my boots tilted me sharply toward the central channel which now flexed, assuming the aspect of a great mouth ready to bite and rend with the jagged bricks of its teeth.

"Aral!" Faran had slipped with me, and she sounded more than a little panicked. "What should I do?"

"Harm them and I destroy the Kothmerk!" shouted Triss.

An incredibly intense burst of blue light slashed across my vision from left to right, striking Qethar and temporarily filling my eyes with burning stars. Somewhere in the blurry darkness beyond my tears, the Durkoth let out a shriek. In response, the whole world lurched and then began to shake erratically like a caras snuffler entering the first throes of withdrawal. I stumbled and went to one knee as the floor leveled itself again, losing contact with Faran as I did so.

"The next one that moves dies!" snarled a new voice.

*Aigo,* Triss said into my mind as the earth continued to shake. *He's come in through a new opening in the roof of the main pipe along with another Elite. There are more Elite above, along with Crown Guards, but I can't see any stone dogs—maybe hiding in the walls around us.*

*Qethar? Faran?*

*The Durkoth is down for the moment, but he's not dead or he wouldn't be bleeding so much. Faran's shrouded up and no longer close enough for me to touch her and Ssithra, but their trail leads straight toward the Elite.*

My vision was starting to come back and despite the dust shaken loose by the ongoing quivering of the earth, I could now dimly see the haze of preset spells that hung around the two Elites—they were armed for dragon. *Toward?*

*I'm afraid so, though I couldn't say whether she's going for Aigo or just trying to get out past him.*

*We've got to give her some cover either way, make a distraction. . . .*

I looked around, sizing up my options—I didn't have

many. The space was too tight to give me any real room for maneuver. The only real cover was the alcove where Qethar lay in a slowly spreading puddle of dark purple blood.

But as Triss had said, he wasn't dead. He might get back in the game at any moment. Might already be on his way even, as a piece of stone had torn itself free of the floor and was now crawling sluglike up his arm toward the huge bleeding gash where his neck met his shoulder. I really didn't want to be standing over him when he reentered the fray.

*When we move, Aigo's going to rain hell down on this whole tunnel,* sent Triss.

*Of course, but if there's anything at all to this idea of being a Blade without a goddess, it's this moment right now. Faran and Ssithra are family. I won't let any harm come to them.*

*So, what's the plan?*

*There's nowhere to run, and nowhere to hide, so it's going to have to be a frontal assault. Give me the Kothmerk, then shroud me up.*

*I don't think that's such a . . . it's gone! Ssithra must have lifted it off me when the two of them bolted.*

"What?" I said aloud.

Then something small and red and shiny hit the wall next to the Elite and went bouncing off into the darkness behind them before splashing into the muck at the bottom of the channel.

As all eyes turned that way, Faran's voice called out, "Was that what everyone's looking for?"

"I've got it!" Aigo jumped down into the channel and went after the ring. "Keep an eye on the Durkoth and the assassin."

Before Aigo had gone five steps, the second Elite let out a gurgling cry as Ssithra tore her throat out. I could tell it was Ssithra because she had to thin out a lot to manage both the kill and the shroud, and I got a flash of Faran's boots as she leaped up and caught the edge of the hole the Elite had come through. Aigo whipped around then and unleashed one of his preset spells.

In magesight it registered as a wave of sickly yellow light
that rolled down the tunnel, breaking over the collapsing
Elite and quickly beginning to dissolve her. Clearly it was
aimed more by hope than any planning, because it slid past
the hole well below the place where I'd last seen evidence
of Faran. However, it didn't stop there, but came straight on
toward me. Out of the corner of my eye I saw Qethar forcing
himself up onto hands and knees then. The bleeding of his
neck had been mostly staunched by a bandage of stone, and
the increasingly violent shaking of the ground seemed to
have no effect on his equilibrium.

Then the world went dark as Triss enveloped me in a
cloud of shadow. I leaped forward and to my right, landing
neatly in the middle of Qethar's back just as the stone slab
that floored his alcove started moving upward toward a
brand new hole in the roof. Behind me, a spike of violet
energy stabbed through the place I had been standing. A
moment later, I leaped again, launching myself from
Qethar's back up and out onto the street.

I hit rolling just as a stone dog breached the surface of
the street, throwing itself into the air like a leaping dolphin.
It would have smashed Qethar to a pulp if it hadn't twisted
suddenly in the air when it saw him, torquing itself around
in the manner of a dropped cat trying desperately to get its
feet under it. The maneuver worked, but only at the cost of
the dog making a hard landing on its side. The ground
lurched under the impact of the elemental, and several cobbles shattered. Then it reasserted control of its element and
sank into the stones.

The street was in utter chaos. The ongoing and steadily
worsening quaking of the earth had brought several nearby
buildings down, though from what I could see, the effect
extended a few blocks at most. Crown Guards were running
to and fro, shouting madly and brandishing their weapons.
Several Elite exchanged spells with what I guessed to be
Vala and Stel sniping from a couple of nearby buildings—
the incoming blasts looked an awful lot like the discharges
from the former's wand. Thick clouds of dust from the

falling buildings were clumping heavily around the Elite and any remotely organized looking group of the guard in a way that strongly suggested the intervention of a wind spirit.

Faran and Ssithra's presence made itself known by the rather large number of soldiers bleeding out through opened throats. The pair were both very good and completely ruthless, a combination that went a long way toward explaining how they had survived the fall of the temple when so many others had not. I was trying to sort out where the pair might have gone by the simple but gruesome expedient of extrapolating along the line of dead they'd left in their wake when Aigo came up out of the ground a few feet in front of me. He was riding the back of his stone dog Graf, like a horse.

"It was a fake. The bitch assassin's still got the ring!" he yelled, though the only reason I could hear him over the general sounds of mayhem was that he was so close. "She went that way!" He pointed with his sword. "Find her! Kill her!"

Neither he nor Graf even looked my way, just charged off in the direction I'd already decided on myself. As I started after them, I couldn't help but notice Qethar sliding in to follow in their wake as well. He was still atop the stone slab from the sewers, riding it along the surface of the street like a one man raft. I moved in close behind him, but didn't kill him yet. I might need the distraction he could provide.

He remained on hands and knees, nose up like a pointer and utterly focused on Aigo and Graf and whatever lay beyond them. It was easy enough to remain unnoticed even from just a few feet away. Faint threads of purple continued to leak out from under the stone bandage on his neck, and though he remained marble pale he had lost the look of perfection. His flesh seemed to be collapsing in on itself. None of which prevented him from going very nearly as fast as the racing stone dog. It was a pace I was hard-pressed to sustain, and neither of us was making any gains.

As we moved onward, the tremors traveled with us,

bringing down more buildings. A huge stone temple crashed down practically on top of us, filling the street with a wall of rubble and crushing a half dozen Crown Guards who'd rallied behind Aigo. It would have gotten me, too, I think, if I hadn't been so close to Qethar. The falling and bouncing stones seemed to avoid him with uncanny prescience.

We made it another couple of blocks, with me slowly losing ground on Qethar and the gap between him and Aigo also growing steadily wider. I'm not sure what happened then, because Aigo was around a corner somewhere in front of us, but I heard a sudden shriek from up ahead, followed by a terrible angry hissing.

*Ssithra!* sent Triss.

*And Faran.* I pushed harder, finally passing Qethar.

I could have killed him then, but it would have cost me seconds I wasn't sure I had. Instead, I gathered my nima and sent a sheet of magelightning flashing down the street in front of me. I hadn't a chance of hitting Aigo or Graf, but I could hope to draw their attention away from the girl. I heard Qethar snarl something behind me about saving the Kothmerk. Suddenly, the whole street on which I was running started to move with me like a horizontal avalanche. More buildings fell as I accelerated toward the corner and whatever lay beyond.

I drew my swords and readied myself. Just before I reached the corner, I threw one high into the air ahead of me as a decoy. Then I dived forward low and fast, rolling as I hit the moving cobbles. Some sort of really nasty blue-green spellburst briefly converted the flying sword into a burning metal torch before it exploded above me, but better it than me. Tiny drops of molten metal flew everywhere. Some of them struck my back and legs, burning deep holes in my flesh that stung bitterly as I rolled across them and up onto my feet again just beyond the mouth of the street.

Faran lay crumpled at the foot of a statue of some long-dead general, her hair half burned away and blood streaking her face. She wasn't moving, but Ssithra was still there and unfaded, which meant she was alive. Major Aigo and his stone dog stood between me and her, the former facing me, while the latter repeatedly reared up on his hind legs and then drove down with his front paws like twinned sledgehammers, striking again and again at something on the cobbles.

The major whipped his head back and forth, scanning the darkened and dusty street, his hands raised high and strung with ready spells. That's when Qethar came around the corner, riding his little stone slab. Aigo brought his hands down sharply, sending long strands of spell-light snaking toward the Durkoth like dozens of snapping whips. That distraction was the opportunity I'd been waiting for, and I dashed across the short distance separating me from the Elite.

Aigo must have seen something out of the corner of his eye, because he turned midcast and tried to wrench one hand's tail of streamers sideways away from Qethar and toward me. But the spell had a lot of inertia, and he was only able to redirect a few of them with any hint of accuracy. Add in the ongoing shaking of the earth and my lacuna of shadow, and those few arcing trails of spell light that did come my way went wide enough of the mark that I never did find out what they would have done to me.

I heard Qethar's hoarse grunt of pain from somewhere behind me in the same moment that I brought my remaining sword around in a two-handed stroke, separating Aigo's head from his shoulders. I didn't even pause long enough to watch it bounce, but raced straight on past him to the place where Faran had fallen. Dropping to my knees beside her, I checked her breathing and pulse—both ragged but still going. I wanted to sweep her up into my arms and get her the hell out of there. But I knew better than to move someone with unknown injuries, for fear of making things worse.

I was just reaching around to check her neck when she opened her eyes and looked up at me. "Master Aral?"

"I'm here, Faran. Don't move. We don't know how badly you're hurt."

She smiled and shook her head. "I've had worse. Much." Then she laughed that same hard little laugh I had first heard from her so many years ago on the obstacle course, and levered herself up onto her elbows. "What happened to the Kothmerk? Please, I have to know."

"I don't know," I said, "and I don't care." But I did. I had to—even now the cursed thing could still start a war.

She opened her mouth to speak again, but I shook my head. "No, you're right. I have to find out, and quickly. We can't stay here for long. Bide a moment."

But Triss was ahead of me again. "It's here, shattered," he called from somewhere behind me, and his voice sounded like it was coming through six feet of grave dirt. "That's what the stone dog was doing. Destroying the ring so that Thauvik can have his war between Kodamia and the Durkoth."

And then, presumably, he could sweep in and pick up the pieces afterward and own the gap of Kodamia and the gateway to the west. I swore.

Faran's expression went cold and flat. "Show me."

I helped her to her feet, and with Ssithra trailing along behind, we followed my own shadow trail to where Triss was waiting. The stone dog had fallen on his side, leaving behind a deep divot where he had driven one cobble some inches below the level of its fellows with his hammering paws. The Kothmerk had taken a lot of breaking, carving a roughly ring-shaped hole in the hard granite paving stone, a hole that was now filled with shimmering red dust and shards of ruby. Blood stone it was called sometimes and now blood would come of it. We had failed.

I turned away, looking back toward the fallen major and Qethar. The latter lay broken and bleeding atop his shattered raft of stone, as ruined as the ring he'd tried to steal. I thought he was dead at first, but then his hand moved and reached out. Catching the edge of a cobble, he dragged himself a few inches along the shaking ground in our direction, then reached for another cobble.

I raised my sword and pointed it at him. Though it was already far too late to do anything to protect the Kothmerk—Graf's great stone paw had seen to that—I still didn't trust him or his purpose.

"Let me through," he whispered as he dragged himself closer. "Please, I must get to the Kothmerk."

"It's gone, Qethar, utterly destroyed. We all failed. Everyone except Aigo and Graf, and they're dead."

"No." Qethar closed his eyes and hissed in pain, then opened them and dragged himself a few feet farther. "I failed my king. My ambitions. Myself even. But I will *not* fail my honor. The Kothmerk is the soul of the Durkoth and the soul of a Durkoth can restore it. Please, badly injured as I am, I could still save myself if I let the earth take me into her heart and hold me sleeping for but a few years. I would live then, but my honor would die. Let me keep that and spend my life instead. Let me make right the horror you and your kind have wrought upon the Durkoth. Let me through so that I may give my life to the sacred Kothmerk."

*What can it hurt?* Triss whispered into my mind. *The ring is shattered.*

I sheathed my sword and reached to help Qethar, but he ignored the hand I extended him. Faran looked like she wanted to argue at first, but then she shook her head and moved aside. Qethar thanked us with his eyes, though no words passed his lips. It took him a good minute more of agonized crawling to reach the place where the broken ring lay on the scarred cobble.

He reached out his bloody right hand and laid it in the deep hole Graf's blows had driven in the street. With an effort that must have cost him a lifetime's worth of pain, Qethar pushed himself up onto hands and knees, keeping his right hand firmly in place in the hollow that held the shattered ring.

The stone bandage fell away from his shoulder and he began to shake in rhythm with the ground as the rich purple blood rolled down his arm from the great wound in his neck and shoulder. Somehow he held himself there as it slowly filled the indentation, rising to cover his hand and the destroyed ring.

When it began to overflow the print, Qethar closed his eyes, drew a deep breath, and rattled off a long string of the

Durkoth language, rich in *Q*'s, *Ch*'s, and *Th*'s. The only words I recognized were the two that began and ended the phrase; Kothmerk and Durkoth. As Qethar finished speaking, something seemed to go out of him and he collapsed, falling onto his side and then slumping to lie on his back within the curve of Graf's great paws. Dead, or at least that's what I thought.

The hand that had covered the shattered Kothmerk had fisted up as he fell, coming free of the blood-filled paw print. Before I could decide what I should do next, Qethar's eyes fluttered open.

"It is done. Now I can die." Qethar's hand relaxed as life left him and there on his bloody palm lay the restored Kothmerk.

I knelt and closed the dead Durkoth's eyes. "May the lords of judgment show you mercy." Then I took the Kothmerk from his hand and held it up in the moonlight.

It was the first time I'd really gotten a look at the ring that had brought us so much fear and doubt, and I couldn't help but feel that VoS's description was a pale shadow of the reality. The moon shining through the great ruby transformed the ring into a shining eye that burned with a deep cold flame, and it no longer seemed a strange fate that such a small thing could bring so much harm to so many. Here lay a spark that could light whole kingdoms afire were it given the chance.

"But not this time," I said aloud. Then I closed the ring tight in my fist and turned to Triss. "Now what?"

"Now you hand over the ring and the girl," said two voices speaking in perfect unison. "Then we pay you your fee, and you're done."

I turned around to find VoS standing behind us, wands and rods at the ready.

*Triss, tell Ssithra to get ready to shroud up. Oh, and not to hurt the Dyad.*

"The ring is yours, VoS, but you'll take the girl over my dead body." I looked straight into Vala's eyes. "You don't want to do this."

"No, I don't," she replied.

"But it's not her decision," continued VoS through her mouth. "We can't let the girl just walk away after what she's done."

*On my count, Triss.* I shifted the Kothmerk within my hand. *Three. Two.* Without any warning I threw the ring underhand, fast and about three feet to the left of Vala—just out of the reach of those short arms. *One.* She had to lunge forward to catch the ring, and for a brief instant both wands and eyes left me.

That was all the leeway I needed, as both Faran and I vanished into shadow. VoS was very good, turning Vala's lunge into a cartwheel that allowed her to both catch the ring and send a blast of magic my way. It clipped the edge of my shroud as I dove forward, and Triss let out a low grunt as the magic punched a hole in his substance. Not a bad injury, but it pissed me off royally and increased my resolve for the next step.

Before Vala could get off another blast, I'd drawn my sword and bounced to my feet with my blade's edge against Stel's throat.

"Don't make me kill you," I growled. "Drop 'em."

Stel let her rods fall to the ground and Vala her wands.

"You win this round, Blade," said Vala.

"But only because one of my motes betrayed me," continued VoS, through both mouths, and she sounded wholly disgusted. "Don't think I didn't notice you resisting me like that, Vala. You could have had him, but you let your feelings get in the way."

"I did," said Vala. "Because it was the right thing to do. We've got the ring back. That's all that matters. That's all that ever mattered, and it wouldn't have happened without Aral's help. Without the *Kingslayer's* help. You know what relations were like between Kodamia and Zhan back when Ashvik was king. Without Aral Kingslayer acting as he did then, there'd have been a war with Zhan." She held up the ring. "And without Aral Kingslayer acting as he did now, there would have been a war with the Durkoth."

"Not to mention that you would have died." Faran faded

back into view behind Vala, a long slender dagger in her hand. "Aral asked me not to harm you, but if you'd killed him I'd have sliced your throats and thrown the damn Kothmerk in the ocean." There was no threat in her tone, but no mercy either, just a statement of fact.

"Maybe you're right." VoS looked at Vala through Stel's eyes and spoke through her lips. "Maybe he did save us a war. But this girl committed a crime against Kodamia. Probably more than one, and that I can't forget or forgive. It's not in my nature."

She turned both her heads toward me. "Good-bye, Aral. Here's your fee." She threw a heavy pouch at my feet. "Take the girl and go to hell."

"I'm sorry," said Vala. "I so wanted to make at least a try of it."

"I'm sorry, too," I said.

Then they turned and walked away.

Faran looked at me and the cold killer that had spoken a moment before seemed to fade away, replaced by the scared teenager I had briefly glimpsed earlier. "Were you and Vala really . . ."

I shrugged. "I don't know. Maybe, given time. I don't think it would have worked, but it probably would have been good for me to try."

Her eyes slid to the ground. "I always liked VoS and her motes. They seemed a lot more human than some of the older Dyads. I'm sorry you had to fight over me."

"That's funny. I can't think of anything I'd rather fight over."

She looked up, startled. Hopeful. "I don't understand."

I wanted to tell her that it was because just this once, I *knew* where justice lay, but I didn't think it would make any sense to her.

Instead I said, "Nothing's more important than the future." Because that was true, too, and because I could see the future, a future where Aral Kingslayer was no longer the last Blade of Namara. "And that's what this fight was about."

# Epilogue

---

Captain Fei's private table at the Spinnerfish had space to seat ten, though it only held two at the moment. Two people anyway, and neither Triss nor Scheroc took up any space.

Fei reached out and almost touched my cheek. "I can't get used to the new you."

"It's your own damn fault," I growled.

She dropped her hand and looked down at the table. "Yeah, I know. I didn't mean it to work out that way. The guy who was supposed to hand the poster over to the watch and make all my other arrangements was also supposed to make damn sure I was dead first."

"Other arrangements?" I asked.

"Let's just say you're not the only one who's pissed off at me. I'm going to be catching shit from his fuck up for a long time to come."

"I hope you explained to him how much trouble he's caused."

"I did. I used short words and a long knife. He got the point." She drew a thumb across her throat.

"So, what happens next time you turn up dead?"

"I haven't worked that out yet, but I can promise it doesn't include a wanted poster for Aral Kingslayer."

"Good."

"Look, Aral, I'm sorry. I fucked up big time and now I owe you double." When I didn't say anything, she awkwardly changed the subject. "Where's Faran now?"

I decided to let her off the hook for now. "Damned if I know, but she's supposed to meet us here."

Fei raised an eyebrow.

"Don't give me that look. You think it's easy to suddenly inherit a teenage daughter?"

"Oh, come on. How hard can it be for the great Aral Kingslayer to keep an eye on one young girl?"

"I guess it depends on whether the girl is a Blade-trained thief and spy who survived six years on her own with a five thousand riel price on her head."

"So she really was spying in Kodamia? For who?"

"Whoever happened to be the highest bidder of the day," said Faran as she suddenly appeared in one of the empty seats—Fei just about jumped out of her skin, but I barely twitched. I was starting to get used to her comings and goings. "Mostly that was Thauvik, which is why I trusted him further than I should have."

"How the hell did you get in here without either of us noticing?" demanded Fei.

"By arriving ahead of you and hiding under the table," replied Faran, sounding more than a little disgusted. "You shouldn't always insist that Erk give you the same table, Captain Fei. It makes things too easy."

*Triss, did you know she was here?*

*No, there was no Shade trail at the entrance. She must have come in quite early and unshrouded, though I've no idea how she could have gotten past Erk like that.*

*Damn but the kid is good.*

"What did you mean about trusting Thauvik when you shouldn't have?" asked Fei.

I knew the answer to that one already, but I wanted to see what Faran would tell the captain.

"After I sold Thauvik the information about the movements of the Kothmerk, he sent me a message promising a hundred thousand gold riels if I got the chance to steal the ring and bring it to him."

Fei whistled. "That kind of money is enough to cloud anyone's thinking. What happened?"

"I was supposed to deliver the ring to a pair of Elite on Sanjin Island in exchange for an anonymous draft from a Magelands bank."

"The dead girl," said Fei. "The one Zishin found those two Elite searching. You sent her in as a decoy. But I thought you said you'd trusted Thauvik too much. Am I missing something?"

"Qethar and the rest of the Durkoth," I replied. "Thauvik had cut a separate deal with them. He figured he could have it both ways. If Faran stole the Kothmerk and brought it back here, he could destroy it and start a war between the Durkoth and Kodamia, which latter is the biggest obstacle to his ambitions. But if Qethar succeeded, the new King of the North would owe his throne to Thauvik."

"And," said Faran, "as a side benefit, if Qethar succeeded, the only one who knew about the other plan, namely, me, would die in the attack on the Dyad caravan. He won either way."

"Right up until he got greedy and tried to get the ring from your decoy without having to pay the fee." Fei looked very unhappy, and who could blame her? Thauvik was her boss again now that she'd returned to the Mufflers. "Stupid bastard."

"More a panicked one, I think," said Triss.

"I think I missed a step," said Fei. "Why would Thauvik panic?"

"Because Faran, good as she is, wasn't able to shake the Durkoth off her trail. That meant that everyone knew the Kothmerk had come south and that the loss might get wrapped around his neck instead of the Archon of Kodamia's."

Fei nodded. "And that could have started the wrong war."

"Exactly."

"So, why did Aigo destroy the ring?"

"Trying to salvage the original plan maybe," I said. "I imagine Aigo knew he didn't have much chance of getting away from me and Qethar both under the circumstances. With Qethar firmly in opposition to Thauvik now, he went with the surest choice. If he'd managed to kill Qethar as well, it would have worked."

There was a long pause, then Fei spoke again. "I heard that the King of the North has been recrowned, and that a Dyad by the name of Valor of Steel was awarded Kodamia's highest honors for service to the realm."

I nodded. "I heard that, too."

Another pause. "I'm sorry, Aral. I know you and Vala were . . ."

Fei looked into my eyes for a long moment and then stammered to a halt, while Faran did everything she could short of shrouding up to fade into the background.

*A little intense there, Kingslayer. You might want to back it down a notch.*

*What do you mean?*

*The face you're wearing now could blister paint.*

*Oh.*

I took a deep breath and forced a smile. "It's all right. I made the only choice I could and so did she. Sometimes that's just the way things work. Besides"—and now I looked at Faran and my smile turned into something real—"as I've told Faran several times, it was the right choice, the just choice."

Out of the corner of my eye I saw Triss nod his approval. I might have lost whatever I had with Vala, but I'd found a piece of myself, and that seemed a fair trade. More than fair.

No story ever ends, but we all have to leave it sometime. I left this one as I had entered it, sitting in a bar, with a glass of good Aveni whiskey in my hand. Though now I raised it in a toast.

"To things lost and things found."

# Terms and Characters

*Aigo, Major*—An officer of the Elite.

*Alinthide Poisonhand*—A master Blade, the third to die making an attempt on Ashvik VI.

*Alley-Knocker*—An illegal bar or cafe.

*Altia*—A onetime apprentice Blade.

*Anyang*—Zhani city on the southern coast. Home of the winter palace.

*Aral Kingslayer*—Ex-Blade turned jack of the shadow trades.

*Ashelia*—A smuggler.

*Ashvik VI, or Ashvik Dan Pridu*—Late King of Zhan, executed by Aral. Also known as the Butcher of Kadesh.

*Athera Trinity*—The three-faced goddess of fate.

*Balor Lifending*—God of the dead and the next Emperor of Heaven.

*Black Jack*—A professional killer or assassin.

*Blade*—Temple assassin of the goddess Namara.

*Bontrang*—A miniature gryphon.

*Calren the Taleteller*—God of beginnings and first Emperor of Heaven.

*Caras Dust*—Powerful magically bred stimulant.

*Caras Seed-Grinder*—Producer of caras dust.

*Caras Snuffler*—A caras addict.

*Channary Canal*—Canal running from the base of the Channary Hill to the Zien River in Tien.

*Channary Hill*—One of the four great hills of Tien.

*Chimney Forest*—The city above, rooftops, etc.

*Chimney Road*—A path across the rooftops of a city. "Running the chimney road."

*Coals*—Particularly hot stolen goods.

*Cobble-Runners*—A gang in the Stumbles.

*Dalridia*—Kingdom in the southern Hurnic Mountains.

*Devin (Nightblade) Urslan*—A former Blade.

*Downunders*—A bad neighborhood in Tien.

*Dragon Crown*—The royal crown of Zhan, often replicated in insignia of Zhani crown agents.

*Drum-Ringer*—A bell enchanted to prevent eavesdropping.

*Durkoth*—Others that live under the Hurnic Mountains.

*Dustmen*—Dealers in caras dust.

*Eavesman*—A spy or eavesdropper.

*Elite, the*—Zhani mages. They fulfill the roles of secret police and spy corps among other functions.

*Emberman*—A professional arsonist.

*Erk Endfast*—Owner of the Spinnerfish, ex–black jack, ex–shadow captain.

*Eva*—With Eyn the dual goddess worshipped by the Dyads.

*Everdark, the*—The home dimension of the Shades.

*Eyespy*—A type of eavesdropping spell.

*Eyn*—With Eva the dual goddess worshipped by the Dyads.

*Face, Facing*—Identity. "I'd faced myself as an Aveni bravo."

*Fallback*—A safe house.

*Familiar Gift*—The ability to soul-bond with another being, providing the focus half of the power/focus dichotomy necessary to become a mage.

*Fire and Sun!*—A Shade curse.

*Ghost, Ghosting*—To kill.

*Graf*—A stone dog, familiar of Major Aigo.

*Gryphon's Head*—A tavern in Tien, the capital city of Zhan. Informal office for Aral.

*Guttersiders*—Slang for the professional beggars and their allies.

*Hand of Heaven*—The Son of Heaven's office of the inquisition.

*Harad*—Head librarian at the Ismere Library.

*Hearsay*—A type of eavesdropping spell.

*Highside*—Neighborhood on the bay side.

*Howler*—Slang name for the Elite.

*Ishka-ki*—Durkoth oath.

*Ismere Club*—A private club for merchants.

*Ismere Library*—A private lending library in Tien, founded by a wealthy merchant from Kadesh.

*Issa Fivegoats*—A sellcinders or fence.

*Jack*—A slang term for an unofficial or extragovernmental problem solver; see also, shadow jack, black jack, sunside jack.

*Jax*—A former Blade and onetime fiancée of Aral's.

*Jerik*—The bartender/owner of the Gryphon's Head tavern.

*Jindu*—Tienese martial art heavily weighted toward punches and kicks.

*Kaelin Fei, Captain*—Watch officer in charge of Tien's Silent Branch—also known as the Mufflers.

*Kaman*—A former Blade, crucified by the Elite, then killed by Aral at his own request.

*Kanathean Hill*—One of the four great hills of Tien.

*Kelos Deathwalker*—A master Blade who taught Aral.

*Kip-Claim*—Pawn shop.

*Kodamia*—City-state to the west of Tien, controlling the only good pass through the Hurnic Mountains.

*Kothmerk*—The original signet ring of the first king of the Durkoth.

*Krith*—A Durkoth word for a cave dwelling.

*Kuan-Lun*—A water elemental, one of the great dragons.

*Kvanas, the Four*—Group of interrelated kingdoms just north of Varya. Sometimes referred to as the Khanates.

*Kyle's*—An expensive Aveni whiskey.

*Little Varya*—An immigrant neighborhood in Tien.

*Loris*—A former Blade.

*Magearch*—Title for the mage governor of the cities in the Magelands.

*Mage Gift*—The ability to perform magic, providing the power half of the power/focus dichotomy necessary to become a mage.

*Magelands*—A loose confederation of city-states governed by the faculty of the mage colleges that center them.

*Magelights*—Relatively expensive permanent light globes made with magic.

*Magesight*—The ability to see magic, part of the mage gift.

*Mage Wastes*—Huge area of magically created wasteland on the western edge of the civilized lands.

*Malthiss*—A Shade, familiar of Kelos Deathwalker.

*Manny Three Fingers*—The cook at the Spinnerfish.

*Maylien Dan Marchon Tal Pridu*—A former client of Aral's.

*Miriyan Zheng*—High-end sellcinders specializing in Durkoth art.

*Mote*—Dyadic term for their constituent halves, mote and Meld.

*Mufflers*—Captain Fei's organization, so known because they keep things quiet.

*Namara*—The now-deceased goddess of justice and the down-trodden, patroness of the Blades. Her symbol is an unblinking eye.

*Nightcutter*—Assassin.

*Nightghast*—One of the restless dead, known to eat humans.

*Night Market*—The black market.

*Nima*—Mana, the stuff of magic.

*Nipperkins*—Magical vermin.

*Noble Dragons*—Elemental beings that usually take the form of giant lizardlike creatures.

*Old Mews*—An upscale neighborhood in Tien that burned to the ground.

*Olen*—A master Blade who taught Aral.

*Oris Plant*—A common weed that can be used to produce a cheap gray dye or an expensive black one.

*Others*—the various nonhuman races.

*Palace Hill*—One of the four great hills of Tien.

*Petty Dragons*—Giant acid-spitting lizards, not to be confused with noble dragons.

*Qamasiin*—A spirit of air.

*Qethar*—A Durkoth outcast living in Tien.

*Rabbit Run*—An emergency escape route.

*Restless Dead*—Catchall term for the undead.

*Riel*—Currency of Zhan, issued in both silver and gold.

*Risen, the*—A type of restless dead, similar to a zombie.

*Sanjin Island*—Large island in the river below the palace in Tien.

*Scheroc*—A qamasiin, or air spirit.

*Sellcinders*—A fence or dealer in hot merchandise.

*Shade*—Familiar of the Blades, a living shadow.

*Shadow Captain*—A mob boss.

*Shadow Jack*—A jack who earns his living as a problem solver in the shadow trades.

*Shadowside*—The underworld or demimonde.

*Shadow Trades*—The various flavors of illegal activity.

*Shadow World*—The demimonde or underworld.

*Shan Starshoulders*—The god who holds up the sky, current Emperor of Heaven.

*Shekat*—Durkoth word for the soul, which they see far more clearly than they do faces.

*Shrouding*—When a Shade encloses his Blade in shadow.

*Silent Branch*—The official name of the Mufflers.

*Siri Mythkiller*—A former Blade.

*Skip*—A con game or other illegal job, also a "play."

*Sleepwalker*—An efik addict.

*Slink*—Magical vermin.

*Smuggler's Rest*—The unofficial name of the docks near the Spinnerfish.

*Snicket*—Alley.

*Snug*—A resting place or residence.

*Son or Daughter of Heaven*—The title of the chief priest or priestess who leads the combined religions of the eleven kingdoms.

*Sovann Hill*—One of the four great hills of Tien.

*Spinnerfish, the*—A shadowside tavern by the docks.

*Ssithra*—A Shade.

*Stingers*—Slang term for Tienese city watch.

*Stone Dog*—A living statue, roughly the size of a small horse. The familiar of the Elite.

*Straight-Back Jack*—A shadow jack who gets the job done and keeps his promises.

*Stumbles, the*—Neighborhood of Tien that houses the Gryphon's Head tavern.

*Sunside*—The shadowside term for more legitimate operations.

*Sunside Jack*—A jack who works aboveboard, similar to a modern detective.

*Sylvani Empire*—Sometimes called the Sylvain, a huge empire covering much of the southern half of the continent. Ruled by a nonhuman race, it is ancient, and hostile to the human lands of the north.

*Tailor's Wynd*—An upscale neighborhood in Tien.

*Tangara*—God of glyphs and runes and other magical writing.

*Thauvik IV, or Thauvik Tal Pridu, the Bastard King*—King of Zhan and bastard half brother of the late Ashvik.

*Thieveslamp/Thieveslight*—A dim red magelight in a tiny bull's-eye lantern.

*Tien*—A coastal city, the thousand-year-old capital of Zhan.

*Timesman*—The keeper of the hours at the temple of Shan, Emperor of Heaven.

*Triss*—Aral's familiar. A Shade that inhabits Aral's shadow.

*Tuckaside*—A place to stash goods, usually stolen.

*Tucker*—Tucker bottle, a quarter-sized liquor bottle, suitable for two or for one heavy drinker.

*Twins, the*—Eyn and Eva, the patron goddess or goddesses of the Dyads. Sometimes represented as one goddess with two faces, sometimes as a pair of twins, either identical or conjoined.

*Uln North*—The Magelander's Quarter of Tien.

*Underhills*—An upscale neighborhood in Tien.

*Vangzien*—Zhani city at the confluence where the Vang River flows into the Zien River in the foothills of the Hurnic Mountains. Home of the summer palace.

*Warboard*—Chesslike game.

*Wardblack*—A custom-built magical rug that blocks the function of a specific ward.

*Westbridge*—A bridge over the Zien, upriver from the palace and the neighborhood around it.

*Worrymoth*—An herb believed to drive away moths.

*Wound-Tailor*—Shadowside slang for a healer for hire.

*Zass*—A Shade, familiar of Devin.

*Zhan*—One of the eleven human kingdoms of the east. Home to the city of Tien.

*Zishin*—A sergeant of the watch answering to Captain Fei.

# Currency

------◆-◆------

*Bronze Sixth Kip (sixer)*
*Bronze Kip*
*Bronze Shen*
*Silver Half Riel*
*Silver Riel*
*Gold Half Riel*
*Gold Riel*
*Gold Oriel*

## Value in Bronze Kips

*~0.15 = Bronze Sixth Kip*
*1 = Bronze Kip*
*10 = Bronze Shen*
*60 = Silver Half Riel*
*120 = Silver Riel*

## Value in Silver Riels

*0.5 = Silver Half Riel*
*1 = Silver Riel*
*5 = Gold Half Riel*
*10 = Gold Riel*
*50 = Gold Oriel*

# Calendar

———————

(370 days in 11 months of 32 days each, plus two extra 9-day holiday weeks: Summer-Round in the middle of Midsummer, and Winter-Round between Darktide and Coldfast)

1  *Coldfast*
2  *Meltentide*
3  *Greening*
4  *Seedsdown*
5  *Opening*
6  *Midsummer*
7  *Sunshammer*
8  *Firstgrain*
9  *Harvestide*
10 *Talewynd*
11 *Darktide*

# Days of the Week

---◆◆◆---

1 *Calrensday*—In the beginning.
2 *Atherasday*—Hearth and home.
3 *Durkothsday*—Holdover from the prehuman tale of days.
4 *Shansday*—The middle time.
5 *Namarsday*—Traditional day for nobles to sit in judgment.
6 *Sylvasday*—Holdover from the prehuman tale of days.
7 *Balorsday*—Day of the dead.
8 *Madensday*—The day of madness when no work is done.

Read on for an exciting excerpt from
the next Fallen Blade novel

# CROSSED BLADES

by Kelly McCullough
Now available from Ace Books!

**T**oday I saw a ghost in an old lover's eyes. I hadn't realized how much I would miss my face until the moment Jax looked at me and saw a stranger.

I was sitting in the Gryphon's Head, as I have so often in the past, and drinking too much whiskey—likewise. Only it wasn't my usual whiskey, and I wasn't my usual self. The bells of Shan had just sounded the sixth hour. The sun slanting in through the open windows of the tavern was still hot, but the first touch of evening had started to steal the fire from its bite. I'd taken a seat far from my usual table and ordered the Magelands whiskey instead of my favored Aveni to reinforce my recent loss of face.

I recognized Jax the instant she stepped into the Gryphon, though she had the sun behind her and shadow hid face. First love is like that. It writes itself into your heart and your memory in letters that can never be erased.

Or can they?

The look Jax gave me when our eyes first met cut as deep as any. Not for what it said, but for what it didn't. There was no recognition there, no hint of what had once been between

Jax Seldansbane and Aral Kingslayer. No love and no loss, just the cold assessment of a professional killer sizing up a room for threats. She gave me a single measured glance, alert for any trouble, then moved on when she didn't see it, just as I would have in her place. I should have expected that, should have remembered what I had become, but I didn't, and that indifference from one I had once loved tore at me. I was invisible to her, the ghost in her eyes.

*It's all right, Aral.* Triss's familiar voice spoke directly into my mind, sweet and clear and wholly reassuring. *It's you that have forgotten your face, not Jax.*

As usual, my familiar was right. I felt a pressure on my shoulder like a friend's hand, squeezing briefly and then gone. I glanced at the shadow that stretched out behind me and gave it a wry smile. Him really. Triss is a Shade, a creature of living night. He lives in my shadow, quite literally.

*Thanks, my friend,* I sent back. *Even a month on it's hard to remember what the bonewright did to my face.*

I reached up, rubbing a rueful hand down my cheek and across my chin. Not that different from my old face, really, not from the inside anyway, and not to my fingers. But I knew that no mirror would show me the face of Aral Kingslayer ever again, nor even the somewhat more haggard and haunted version that I'd worn for my years as Aral the jack. That was for the best, considering all the wanted posters. I kept telling myself that, and until the instant Jax's eyes had passed me over unrecognized, I had mostly even believed me.

I've never had a particularly distinguished sort of face. Medium brown everything, from eyes to hair to skin. Not too pretty, not too ugly, the kind of face that's easy to ignore or forget. The masters and priests who raised me to be an assassin in the service of a goddess now dead had always told me it was one of my strongest assets.

My new face shared all the best of my old face, improved on it even. I had deliberately reshaped skin and bone in a way that removed most of the markers of my native land, worked at making myself look like the product of a mixed heritage. It was the sort of face you might see in any of the eleven kingdoms of the east—never a native, but not a clear foreigner either. In so many ways it was the perfect face for what I had once been. Aral Kingslayer, Blade of Namara, the goddess of justice. How ironic then that I put it on only after the murder of my goddess, her temple's destruction, and the death of all but a handful of my friends and fellows.

*Easy.* Triss squeezed my shoulder again—a shadow's touch—this time in warning. *Remember where we are and control yourself. They are hunting us still.*

Again, he was right. The Gryphon was a public place, and one where I was known to have spent a good deal of time before my second life as a shadow jack was exposed. Looking around the room I could spy several tables' worth of potential trouble. The place in the corner that I used to consider my regular spot, for example. A man and a woman sat there, both with their backs to the wall, both exhibiting the alert calm of the waiting hunter.

She was slender, tall and long limbed yet muscular and far from fragile. Ice blond hair and white skin marked her out as foreign as did her hard blue eyes, and her quick precise movement made me think of some sort of giant praying mantis. The man was also tall, but broad where she was slender, with heavy muscles showing through the thin silk of his long-sleeved tunic. He was as dark as any of the locals, but the angles of his face and his thick black beard suggested a Kadeshi background, as did the short broad-bladed axes he had tucked into his sash.

He caught me looking at him and raised an eyebrow ever so slightly, touching one of his axes in a way that told me he thought I was a thief. I pretended to be intimidated, swallowing heavily before looking down into my drink, and he snorted and went back to talking to the woman. Trouble averted easily enough, but dammit, I shouldn't even be here. I should have walked away and found a different bar to haunt, a new place to start building myself a new identity to go with my new face.

But somehow I just couldn't walk away from the old me that easily. Not even the drunken wreck of a version that had earned his bread as a shadowside jack, the underworld's all-purpose freelancer. Packages delivered, bodies guarded, the occasional contract theft. All in a day's work for Aral the jack and, oh, what a very long fall from the days when the world had called me Kingslayer and the unjust had shivered when they thought of me.

Which brought me back to Jax. We had grown up together at the great temple of Namara. She had entered the service of Justice a year after I did, barely four. A tiny girl with long dark hair, pale skin, and a winsome smile that had grown into a wicked one as the years transformed the girl into a beautiful young woman. Though she had never grown all that much in physical stature, she had more than made up for it with her skills as a sorceress and assassin in the service of Justice, coming third in our generation for the quality of her kills, after Siri and I.

Why had she chosen this moment to walk back into my life? I didn't make the foolish mistake of thinking her presence in the one place in all of Tien I was known to have frequented was any kind of coincidence. I also wondered where she had been hiding during the six years since the temple fell. Not in Zhan, I guessed by the lack of color to her skin. Nor anywhere else with brutal sun, unless she had become a creature wholly of the night.

Aven perhaps, or back home in Dalridia, or the mountains of the Magelands. One of those almost certainly. She would have had to hide someplace she could blend in, and someplace close enough that she could have reached Tien in four weeks or less. That ruled out Öse, Varya, and Radewald.

The news that the Kingslayer had been unmasked would have flown fast and far on wings of magic. Everyone in the eleven kingdoms with any sort of governmental or shadowside connections would have heard the message within a week, two at most. But unless she wanted to spend a lot of money and draw the sorts of attention that one of our kind couldn't easily afford, Jax would have had to travel by more mundane means. No ship or horse could have brought her here from any farther afield so fast.

I knew that right after the fall Jax had spent time in the grip of the Hand of Heaven, the human instrument the gods had used to destroy the temple and Namara's worshippers. As the personal enforcement arm of Shan's highest priest, the Hand was known for its willingness to employ torture and the stake to achieve its aims. That no doubt explained the dozens of thin scars that threaded Jax's face and arms, white on white like fine lace on a marble table.

But where had she been since her escape? And what had she been doing? Her clothes told me nothing. Like anyone both sane and in-purse who found themselves facing Tien in summer, Jax had opted for a vest and loose pants in the thinnest of silks—gray in this case. She had eschewed the more common sandals for light boots of the same sort that I wore for roof-running. The short, curved swords she wore in a double sheath on her right hip looked Dalridian in design, but they could have come from anywhere. No clues there. No clues anywhere really.

I wanted to go to her, to take her in my arms and tell her who I was and how very happy it made me to see her alive. But six years as a fugitive had taken its toll. I would wait and I would watch, and only when I was sure there was no trap would I make a move. Even then, caution must come before trust.

For several long minutes she chatted quietly with Jerik at the bar, obviously asking questions, though I couldn't make out specifics. He kept shaking his head no and shrugging despite the fact that she flashed several heavy gold coins at him. Finally she seemed to give up, flipping her hair back with an angry snap of her neck that I'd seen too many times to count in the short, tumultuous year we had shared a bed. Without another word she stalked straight out the front door of the Gryphon.

It should have been funny watching hardened shadowside bonebreakers twice Jax's size getting quickly and prudently out of her way as she gave them *the look*. But she'd caught me so off guard with the suddenness of her departure that I barely had the leisure to notice. I was far too busy trying not to *appear* as though I was following her when I knocked back my drink and then rose to do just that.

*What's the plan?* Triss asked silently. *I thought we were going to take this slow.*

*That was before she left so quickly. We have no way of knowing if she'll ever come back, and I want to know why she's here.*

*Point. How shall we play it?*

*Cross her shadow. Tell Sshayar to let Jax know to meet us somewhere private at midnight. Walk away.*

It was an old Blade trick for passing secret messages one to another. Shades had a means of silent communication that would allow Triss and Sshayar to exchange basic information, but with the exception of my newfound ability to communicate with Triss, no Shade could bespeak their Blade companion mind-to-mind. So, when we had a need to share secrets we passed them Shade to Shade for later verbal relay.

Great plan in theory. In practice . . .

*I hate it when we do that,* I thought at Triss. *Where the hell did she go?*

*That way,* replied Triss, unobtrusively nudging my right foot. *I can taste Sshayar's essence on the street, but only very faintly. She's hiding deep in Jax's shadow and the sun is strong today, burning away the traces of her passing. We'll have to move quickly if we want to keep track of her.*

Jax had been barely forty feet ahead of me leaving the bar, but by the time I got out the door, she'd vanished into the crowd. Some of that was simply height. At a hair under five feet, Jax stood almost a head shorter than the average citizen of Tien. Thousands of whom were out wandering the streets in search of dinner. The Stumbles, where the Gryphon is located, is one of Tien's worst neighborhoods. The streets are narrow and poorly kept—there are cobbles down there somewhere, but you have to dig through a lot of filth to find them. At the moment it was hard even to see the filth beneath the swirling mass of people that filled the street.

As was so often the case with slums, the Stumbles was also one of the city's most heavily populated neighborhoods. The accommodations mostly varied from miserable to inadequate, but rooms and parts of rooms could be had for a few kips a day, and that meant that people who'd have been sleeping on the street in other parts of the city could put a door between themselves and the night while they slept. That meant a lot, especially in a place like the Stumbles.

As I threaded my way through the crowds guided silently by Triss, I kept an eye out for Jax. But between her height and the fact that almost everyone in that poor neighborhood wore light browns and middling grays, I never caught sight of her. I did spy a half dozen pickpockets and cutpurses, and had to warn off two of them with a look when they got too close to me. That last was a shock. Another painful reminder of my lost face—people knew Aral the jack in the Stumbles and would have known better than to even consider picking his pocket—but they didn't know me.

No one knew me. Not the petty criminals, not Machim the beggar, nor Asleth the noodle vendor. No one. That should have made it easier for me to pass through the crowds, as people who would normally have wanted a piece of my time ignored me. It didn't. Aral the jack was a dangerous man, a drunk maybe, and down on his luck, but people knew to get out of his way. Nobody knew to get of the way of . . . who?

I stopped in the middle of the street as the weight of that question hit me. Who was I, really?

Aral Kingslayer had died with his goddess. The man who wore that name had crawled into a bottle and not come out again. In his place a new Aral had emerged, Aral the drunk who had paid his bar bills by playing the shadowside jack. Doing things for money the older Aral would never have contemplated. Petty little illegalities, and all freelance so that there was never a chance he'd owe any loyalty to anyone ever again. Never anyone he'd have to care about.

That had all changed a bit over a year ago when a woman

named Maylien had found an echo of the old Kingslayer hiding under the skin of the jack.

For a little while I thought I'd found a new purpose in life, a new Aral who might have a chance at doing some good in the world again. That was the plan anyway. I'd even thought it was working right up till the moment I realized how much of me I'd lost with my face. I didn't even have a name anymore. Not really. Not one I could wear in public. If your only name was a secret, was it even a name anymore?

*Aral! Come on, we're losing Jax.* Triss gave me a sharp slap on the side of my foot and I got moving again.

But I'd lost my hunger for the chase and I hardly even blinked when we lost the trail as it left the narrow streets of the Stumbles and plunged into the human river of Market Street.

*Fire and sun!* Triss growled into my mind. *It's gone, and I can't tell whether that's an effect of the sun or if Jax did something clever to break her trail.*

I found it very hard to care about the answer when what I really wanted was to go back to the Gryphon and drink until the world went away. I couldn't tell Triss that though, not with the way he felt about my drinking. Instead I just stood and stared at the passing parade, full as it was of walkers and riders, carters and rickshaws, even the odd palanquin. Sandals and boots and hooves and wheels, all of them grinding away at the dust and dirt and . . .

Wait. Back up. Think, man!

And there it was. So simple and elegant I had no idea why it hadn't occurred to me before.

*My guess would be she got into one of those.* I pointed at a passing oxcart. *If she made sure that her shadow didn't spill over the edge of the bed, a cart would make a very good getaway vehicle. That or one of those closed palanquins. Hell, she could even have had a covered rickshaw waiting for her here.*

*I'm an idiot.* Triss sounded shocked. *The idea of a shadow trail is new enough to you that I can understand why you wouldn't have thought of that before now. But, why didn't it ever occur to me?*

*For the same reason it didn't occur to me probably. Blinkered thinking. We both knew fire and sun and running water can break a shadow's trail, so it didn't occur to either of us to think beyond the big and flashy to simpler means. That and the fact that Blades almost never travel by cart. Not fast enough, not versatile enough, not enough control. We prefer to run or walk when we can, or ride if we must trade control for speed. Is it any surprise that our Shades never get a sense of those other means of travel either?*

I could count on the fingers of one hand the total number of cart rides I'd taken since I was big enough to straddle a horse.

*So now what?* Triss asked me.

*The Gryphon, I think. Maybe Jax will come back.* Triss didn't say anything, but I could feel his disapproval as he thought about me having another drink. *I could also use some dinner, and it's Jerik's cooking or go home where we'll have to deal with Faran and Ssithra. . . .*

*I guess one more whiskey won't kill you.*

*I thought you might see it my way.*

Faran was almost sixteen and a problem and a half. She'd been eight when the temple fell. A combination of talent, smarts, luck, and utter ruthlessness had allowed her to escape an attack that killed most of her peers and teachers. For six years she and her familiar, Ssithra, had lived completely on their own, spying and thieving their way across the eleven kingdoms to stay alive. Her last assignment had gotten away from her in a way that would probably have killed her if it hadn't also brought her to my doorstep. I'd had to abandon my old face as part of fixing that mess.

Now she'd become my . . . apprentice? Ward? Surrogate daughter? Faran and I were still working out the details of what we were to each other. So far, the process involved a lot of snarling and baring of teeth and I desperately wanted another drink before I faced the next round. Though Triss's relationship with Ssithra was harder to parse, the level of hissing in Shade that went on between the two of them suggested to me it wasn't any less fraught. In any case, the Gryphon sounded a hell of a lot more like home to me right at the moment than the rented house we shared with Faran and her familiar.

The Gryphon had started to fill up by the time I got back. Jerik just grunted and pointed me toward an empty seat at the end of the bar when I called out my order for whiskey and a bowl of fried noodles topped with shredded whatever happened to fall off the back of the cart today. His indifference stung a bit since I was used to being treated like a regular. A few minutes later, he dropped my bowl and a small loaf of black bread that I hadn't ordered in front of me along with my glass, then turned away before I could say anything about getting my order wrong.

I was tempted to throw the bread at his retreating back, but just sighed and took a sip of my whiskey instead. It tasted smooth and silky, like liquid magic. Kyle's eighteen, the special cask reserve, if I knew my whiskeys, and nothing like what I'd ordered. As I paused before taking another drink, Jerik spun around to drop a beer in front of the smuggler sitting three stools to my right. I raised my glass ever so slightly in Jerik's direction as well as an eyebrow. Jerik responded with something that could have been the faintest ghost of a wink or perhaps nothing at all.

I took another sip. It was top-shelf Kyle's all right, the spirit old Aral the jack had drunk whenever he felt deep enough in the pockets. Since I'd ordered nothing but Magelands whiskeys at the Gryphon since I changed my face, and the Kyle's wasn't sitting somewhere you'd get them confused, I had to figure the switch was intentional. But why? To cover my confusion I took another sip of my excellent whiskey and then followed that with a mouthful of noodles. The hot pepper sauce almost covered the aging vintage of the fried bits of meat and vegetables. Almost.

I considered my bread then. Jerik makes a hard black loaf that will keep you alive for a long while if the effort of chewing it doesn't kill you first. It's cheap and awful, and over the years I've spent almost as much time living on it as I have avoiding it. This loaf looked more battered than most of its fellows, with several dents and dings and a wide crack splitting it nearly in half along one edge. Hmm. I jammed a thumb into the crack, then broke off a tiny corner of the loaf when I felt a bit of paper shoved deep into the bread.

As I was twisting the scrap of bread in my pepper sauce, Jerik slid back past. "Tab?"

I nodded and he left. Jerik only runs a tab for serious regulars, and the face I was wearing now simply hadn't been around long enough. He knew who I was, he had to. I suppose I shouldn't have been as surprised as I was.

Jerik's a damned clever man. He used to hunt monsters for a living, and mostly on Crown lands, which adds dodging royal patrols to the long list of dangers involved in the trade. The dumb don't last long, and the smart can get rich if they live long enough. There's a good deal of money to be made by selling the bits off to various magical supply houses, and he was at it long enough that he really didn't need to work for a living anymore.

He retired from the business after the gryphon he ultimately named his bar after ate about half of his scalp and one of his eyes. The scars are terrible and a good part of the reason he keeps the lights low I think, but I think he missed the thrill of it all. It wasn't too many years after he got mauled that he first opened the Gryphon's Head and nailed the damn thing's skull up behind the bar. I've always figured he bought an inn down here in the Stumbles among the shadowside players when he could have afforded a better location because he missed spending time around dangerous predators.

Despite a burning desire to read my little note right then and there, I just nibbled another corner off my bread. Then I finished my noodles and sipped my Kyle's down nice and slow before scooping up the loaf and heading out into the Gryphon's yard. I used to rent a room over the stables back there and now I took advantage of long familiarity to slip into the lower level and find an empty stall before I cracked open my bread envelope.

By the time I'd got it split in half, Triss had defied the conventions that light normally enforced on shadows by sliding up the wall to a place where he could read over my shoulder and changing his shape. Most of the time he pretends to be nothing more than light would make him, a darkened copy of my form, but when we're alone he will often reshape his silhouette to assume the outline of a small dragon complete with wings and a tail. When he does that he assumes some of the other aspects as well, and now I reached out to give him a light scruff behind the ears where his scales always seem to itch.

He made a happy little noise at that, but then shrugged me off and jerked his chin at the tightly rolled piece of paper I now held. *What's it say?*

Unrolling it revealed a folded sheet with a small blob of black wax sealing it. There was no imprint in the wax and no name on the outside of the letter, but magesight revealed the faintest glow of magic on the seal. I held it up to Triss and he reached out with one clawed finger and touched the seal. There was a hiss and the wax dissolved. I raised an eyebrow at Triss and he nodded. As I had expected, it responded only to the touch of a Shade. Any other attempt to open the thing would have resulted in the whole thing burning instantly away to ash.

I opened the letter. Inside it said: *Ashvik's tomb. Two hours past midnight. The anniversary of the day you broke my heart.* And that was all. No names. No signatures.

Clever, just a location, the time, and a date no one but I would know. The day I told Jax I wasn't going to marry her. The fifth of Firstgrain, one week in the future. The whole thing was smart. There had been six kings of Tien with that name, and their tombs were scattered widely through the royal cemetery. Anyone who intercepted the message and didn't know it was intended for me would have to guess not only the date but which one was the intended meeting place. The tomb of Ashvik VI, the man who had died to give me the name Kingslayer.